DUTY AND DISHONOR

Dale Dye

═══════════

Praise for Dale Dye's previous novels:

Outrage: "Firsthand knowledge . . . an inside view."
—*Kirkus Reviews*

Conduct Unbecoming: "The tragic ordeal of a Marine on trial."
—W. E. B. GRIFFIN

═══════════

"Dale Dye has a flair for telling stories and evoking images. His details about Marine life are accurate . . . Dye has the ability to draw the reader far enough into the story that the reader sees with the author's eyes and feels with his emotions . . . Dye's ability to tell a story the way it really happens is rare, and one sincerely hopes this book will not be his last. *Conduct Unbecoming* is a book for our time."

—*Orlando Sentinel*

Also by Dale Dye
From The Berkley Publishing Group

CONDUCT UNBECOMING
OUTRAGE
PLATOON
RUN BETWEEN THE RAINDROPS

DUTY AND DISHONOR

DALE DYE

JOVE BOOKS, NEW YORK

DUTY AND DISHONOR

A Jove Book / published by arrangement with
the author

PRINTING HISTORY
Jove edition / December 1992

ISBN: 0-515-11010-8

Jove Books are published by The Berkley Publishing Group,
200 Madison Avenue, New York, New York 10016.
The name "JOVE" and the "J" logo
are trademarks belonging to Jove Publications, Inc.

PRINTED IN THE UNITED STATES OF AMERICA

10 9 8 7 6 5 4 3 2 1

For

Dale A. Dye and Della K. Dye
who launched me downrange...

Colonel Charles R. Stribling III,
who called the shot and adjusted my
fire, and for...

Adrienne Kate Dye,
who brought me home at last

"Life is a tour of guard duty;
you must mount guard properly
and be relieved without reproach."

Charlet, 1650–1720

CONTENTS

PART ONE

HOOK

SA MOI, LAOS—1970

At first blush, being dead seemed better than being alive. In fact, death had a lot going for it. Alive he'd been hurting: exhausted, tense, scared, cold, wet, miserable. Now he was none of those uncomfortable things. Maybe a little scared still, but that was fading.

There was no pain from the mine explosion or the long spill down the jungle mountainside through razor-sharp vines and tangled foliage. The old guy with the beard and the big logbook hadn't showed up to make him account for his earthly sins. Maybe he could slide right through from life to death without all the normal hassle of checking into a new unit.

Staff Sergeant Wilhelm Johannes Pudarski, KIA, lay prone—at a modified position of attention—along a muddy loop of the Ho Chi Minh Trail somewhere in Laos—and awaited further orders from a heavenly honcho.

That's when Salt and Pepper showed up and threw shit in the game.

DANANG

"Gentlemen, this debriefing is classified. Please clear the tent."

He rubbed watery eyes and wished the staff colonel from MACV would stop pacing. Shifting his eyes caused his brain to slosh around inside his skull. Concussion—and three straight days of Dexedrine insomnia—made it hard to concentrate on death and resurrection. He rubbed the bridge of his nose and tried to squelch the stereo white noise lancing into his eardrums.

"Colonel, he's really in no shape for this . . ." The Navy doctor, summoned hastily to the Command Post of the 1st Recon Battalion near Hill 327, looked up from packing his instruments.

"He needs at least twenty-four hours under full sedation."

The colonel put a fatherly hand on Pudarski's lacerated shoulder and rolled some steel into his gravelly voice. "He'll get that and more, Doctor, as soon as we've concluded this preliminary debriefing."

"Sir, you must be aware that Staff Sergeant Pudarski is lucky to be alive . . . and he's due in Washington at the end of the week." Different voice. Pudarski opened his eyes and tried to smile as his commanding officer stepped out of the tent's dark shadows. A loopy grin was all his trembling jaw muscles would allow.

The Old Man's kickin' his own ass for lettin' me outside the wire so close to the Big Event . . . He shifted on the cot to take pressure off a shrapnel-riddled buttock and waved a hand at the conscience-stricken officer. "No sweat, Skipper. Let's do this thing . . . until the colonel gets what he needs . . . or I pass out, whichever comes first."

The colonel gave Pudarski's shoulder a painful pat and moved to where he could speak privately with the Recon Company commander. "I know what's bothering you, Captain, but believe me, I'd have made the same decision under the circumstances. We can't shut down the war effort just because one of our men is scheduled to receive the Medal of Honor."

Pudarski's CO shook his head and tugged thoughtfully at an earlobe. "Christ, Colonel, he's the best we've got. That's why I let him go. If he'd got blown away chasing spooks . . . and the week before the President's supposed to hang that Medal around his neck . . ."

"But he *didn't* get killed. I'm not here to harass your people. General Westmoreland sent me up from Saigon personally. That's how concerned he is with this situation. Now take the good doctor and get some coffee. I'll make it as quick and painless as possible for Pudarski."

When the tent was clear, the MACV colonel uncoiled the microphone of a battery-operated tape recorder and perched on a camp stool near Pudarski's cot. He smiled as he examined the man's chiseled, deeply tanned features.

Handsome guy despite his beat-up condition. He'd look great on recruiting posters. And that's right where he'll be after he gets that Medal next week. Why did the Marines always get the ones who looked like they were carved out of ancient granite?

"Pudarski's quite a mouthful. They call you something else, don't they?"

He watched as the colonel clinically examined the fistfight

nicks on his face and the emaciated body parts that showed through his torn, bloody camouflage utility uniform.

Scope it out good, Colonel. Can't have been many Chi Town Polacks at West Point.

"Willy Pud, sir. Everybody's got a nickname in the Corps. If they don't hang it on you at Parris Island or Dago, you pick it up soon as the first sergeant sees your name on a duty roster."

"Well, Willy Pud, I regret having to put you through this right now but I'm sure you understand the importance of . . ."

Waving the apology off with an upraised hand, Willy Pud leaned forward and froze the colonel with all the ice he could project through swollen, bloodshot eyes. "Sir, I been in the 'Nam almost three years now. Line grunt before I come to Recon . . . and I seen my share of bad shit. What I ain't never seen—and what I can't even stand to fuckin' think about—is two *goddamn traitors* out there killin' American troops . . ."

The intensity of Willy Pud's words caused the MACV colonel to lean backward on his rickety stool. He fiddled with the tape recorder for a moment and then shrugged.

"When we first heard about Salt and Pepper, no one at MACV gave the stories much credence. But the reports kept coming in and . . . well, we all had this feeling of genuine outrage. I know how you feel . . ."

Willy Pud tuned the rest of it out. *Can the crap, Colonel. You don't know how I feel. This ain't a scuff on your spit shine just before inspection. This ain't some war protestor who just irritates your ass. This is fuckin' treachery down on the gut level; out in the bush where people get killed.*

"Believe me, if I had command of a unit capable of running these two down . . ."

No need to apologize. Your days down in the mud and the blood and the bullshit are over. Some people can't help being REMFs—just like other people can't help being bohunks or splibs or beaners—or gooks for that matter.

"There was some thought at first that Salt and Pepper might be a couple of mercenaries. Maybe a Russian or an East German . . . and an African or Cuban . . ."

"No way, sir. Salt and Pepper are—or were—Americans. I can guaran-goddamn-tee you on that score."

The MACV colonel started the tape recorder and leaned forward with his elbows on his knees. "Let's take it from the top."

Willy Pud picked up a canteen cup of cold C-ration coffee and drank deeply. The Dexedrine buzz began to recede.

"Well, sir, last week sometime . . . I forget the exact date . . . I'm hangin' around the COC bunker keepin' an eye on a unit of the Third Marines in contact up in the northwest corner of the A Shau Valley. Gooks in that area like to break contact as soon as we call arty or air and *di-di* across the border into Laos.

"Sometimes we launch a Recon team to keep tabs on 'em. My team was next up on the rotation, so I passed the word to stand by. About that time we hear from some platoon commander up there that he's takin' fire from two guys that definitely *ain't* gooks. A white guy and a black guy . . ."

The MACV colonel gave Willy Pud a quick hold signal and spoke into the microphone. "Following is background on subject's prior knowledge of Salt and Pepper: Had you heard of such a thing prior to this instance, Sergeant Pudarski?"

Willy Pud didn't seem to notice the break in cadence as he sipped again from the canteen cup. "Yessir. Damn near every grunt in I Corps has heard about Salt and Pepper. Sighting reports been coming in for six months or more. Black guy and a white guy—supposedly American turncoats—fighting with the gooks. I always filed it in the bullshit locker. Figured it was some propaganda crap sent over here by the assholes back in the World and it just got out of hand. Grunts like to gossip . . ."

"But reconnaissance units have checked out these reports in the past . . ."

"Yessir. First thing I was told when I come to Recon was to be on the lookout for 'non-orientals' operatin' with the gooks. We went out to look—lots of times—but nothin' ever come of it."

"Then what made you so anxious to chase the sighting up in the A Shau Valley?"

"This was an ongoin' contact, sir. All the other times, the units that claimed they saw these guys didn't mention it until they got back in from the field. The trail was always a couple days to a week or more old. I figured this was a chance to either prove there's something to the story or put it to rest once and for all."

"OK. We've already covered your request to launch an immediate Recon team insert. Permission was granted—reluctantly—by your commanding officer. What happened then?"

"Well, I know this gungy dude up in Division ISO . . ."

"ISO?"

"Yessir. Informational Services Office. They run with the grunts, take pictures, write stories, shit like that. Anyway, Sergeant Benjamin is good with a camera and he's good in the bush. So I talk him into goin' along with a big telephoto lens. By the time everybody

is set, they got a helicopter bouncin' down on the hot pad and
we launch. It's rainin' like Hogan's horse pissin' on a big, flat
rock . . ."

A SHAU VALLEY

Lying on his belly, hanging halfway out the lowered rear ramp
of the twin-rotor CH-46 Sea Knight helicopter, Willy Pud could
easily follow the snarling firefight on the ground below. Red
and green tracers lanced through the scrubby foothills of the
Annamese Cordillera separating Laos from Vietnam. The NVA
were rubbing their backs up against the verdant green velvet
that covered the misty mountains of the border area. They were
spitting and hissing like a coiled, cornered cobra Willy had seen
on an R&R in Bangkok.

And like the wiry mongoose that killed the deadly snake in
a fifty-baht freak show, the Marines were pressing for a quick,
decisive strike at an exposed flank. From long experience as a
line infantryman, Willy Pud knew the gooks would melt away like
dawn shadows once they managed to break contact and slither into
the high jungle. The grunts in the assault below also knew they
were running out of time and space. Only an hour or two until
sunset and they intended to slam the escape hatch on the NVA.
Frantic calls for artillery fire missions crackled into his borrowed
headset.

Willy Pud felt the rotors change pitch as the pilots put the
helo into a higher, wider orbit over the jungle. He struggled to
his knees as the aircraft commander's laconic drawl buzzed into
his ears. "Uh, Recon, we're gonna have to make your insert or
call it off before long. Grunts have got some heavy arty inbound
and we need to clear the air space." Pulling a plastic-coated map
from the cargo pocket of his trousers, Willy struggled forward to
visually guide the aircrew into the landing zone he had chosen.

He gave a reassuring slap to every shoulder he passed on the
way to the cockpit. Five men—six with the ISO sergeant—all
staring out the portholes of the orbiting helicopter, chewing on
air, trying to keep the spiders from crawling up their spines.
Handpicked people; not a goosey bastard in the bunch. All on

a second or third tour, running with Recon because they wanted to be with other pros out there on the edge of the human endurance envelope.

Willy felt a twinge of sympathy for the platoon sergeants and squad leaders from the DMZ to the Mekong Delta plagued with reluctant draftees who hoped the worst was over, dopers who turned their tours into a quest for the ultimate high, and half-trained zealots who thought they saw a light at the end of an endless tunnel. Good money after bad. The Marine Corps—the entire American military—would never be the same after 'Nam.

Just as the rear landing gear bumped the ground, the helicopter reared like a dump truck to spill Willy Pud and his Recon team into the mountains near the Laotian border. The Marines fanned out automatically and sprinted for a gloomy bamboo thicket. Willy tossed a thumbs-up signal over his shoulder and a gale of rotor-wash pushed him into the green and black void. Blade clatter and turbine whine echoed off the craggy mountains for a few moments and then they were left in relative quiet.

Willy knew the silence was an illusion. The jungle was never really still—especially in the mountains that served as monsoon spa for noisy birds, apes, and big cats. It would be a few minutes before his people could control the deafening roar of adrenaline-charged blood and begin to classify those normal, nonlethal bush sounds. Danger lurked in moving or speaking before that time, so Willy left his people in place and tried to formulate a plan for finding a pair of needles in this monumental haystack.

The helicopter pilots were bang on the mark. Willy oriented his map to the ground with a lensatic compass and stood cautiously to look at the misty mountains. They were on the military crest of a long, craggy finger that crooked into Laos about five klicks to the northwest. Below them was a broad valley that meandered parallel to its mountain walls until it reached the border. There was good cover and concealment in those gloomy depths and Willy knew from aerial photos that they ended in a long tunnel of triple canopy that hid one of the NVA's primary infiltration routes.

With a sibilant hiss that built rapidly to a roar, another wave of winter monsoon rain began to pelt the jungle. Willy shivered and wondered briefly how a place so fucking hot could seem so cold. When the tympany boom of heavy artillery began to echo off the mountainside, he signaled silently for his team to melt more deeply into the bush.

If his instincts were right, the NVA would have broken contact by now. Cannon-cockers at The Rockpile and Vandegrift Combat

Base were stretching high-explosive fingers out into the sunset, trying to slam the back door leading to Laos. Shrapnel would lash the shadows and whip the NVA into the valley below their perch. Willy Pud and his team would run a parallel track—for as long as it took—and when the gooks emerged into daylight near the triple-canopy tunnel for the final dash to safety, the legend of Salt and Pepper would either be proven or put to rest.

DANANG

"How long were you in the harbor site before you spotted the NVA?" The MACV colonel looked up from his notebook as Willy Pud paused to pick at a scab on his right elbow. He was losing track of the story. So many impressions, so many emotions, his mind tended to shut down rather than try to sort them all out in sequence.

Willy silently examined the stained interior of the empty canteen cup and groped for the thread of the narrative. Before he could find his place, the Recon Company commander suddenly stepped through the blackout curtain of the muggy tent ushering in a chilly gale of rain-spattered air.

"Beg pardon, sir. But you said you wanted to see these as soon as they were ready."

The MACV colonel vaulted off his stool and snatched a sheaf of dripping photos from the Marine officer. Willy smelled the pungent developing chemicals when the colonel returned to his seat. There was a tragic, vanquished look on the man's face as he handed over a black-and-white glossy. It was almost as if the colonel's martial armor had been pierced by evidence that the lovable, patriotic GI Joe of his youth could become a treacherous turncoat willing to piss on the flag, rape his mom, and stick his dick in the apple pie. Willy Pud felt genuinely sorry for him.

"Sir . . . these guys . . . you shouldn't . . ."

There was enough heat in the MACV colonel's glare to cauterize Willy's sympathy. He bit his lip and accepted the rest of the dripping prints. A familiar emotion twitched in the officer's eyeballs. Willy Pud had felt the same thing at first glimpse of Salt and Pepper.

"Look closely now, Sarn't Pudarski. For the record, are these the two men you saw traveling with the NVA unit you tracked into Laos?"

As he studied the two figures caught in the grainy embrace of high-speed film and a telephoto lens, Willy Pud understood why people pay good money to see carnival freaks. It's a perverse fascination with the human condition, he realized. It's why people gang up for a glimpse of a mass murderer or a child molester. They're wondering just what the hell is the difference. Why them and not me?

Salt was not so different from some of the kids Willy Pud had inherited in his own infantry outfits. Feather Merchant. Slight and slim with no obvious physical prowess. The kind of kid who joins the Marines to show his buddies or his girlfriend he can hack it with the big boys. Willy would have adjusted the guy's attitude in a big fucking hurry. Kind of a pouty sneer fixed around his mouth . . . but maybe that was the fever blisters.

And Pepper . . . big 'fro topping a face that had the sweaty sheen of polished ebony. Mean motherfucker with a major-league chip on his muscular shoulder. Wide nostrils and red-rimmed eyes that reminded Willy Pud of the black winos his father had steered him around in Chicago's downtown Loop. The hard-drinking Polish stool-owners at his old man's favorite bar told him "there ain't nothin' more dangerous than a buck nigger with a head fulla Thunderbird." Smart men would give a guy like Pepper a wide berth, drunk or sober.

"Sarn't Pudarski . . . ?"

"Yessir. These are the two men we seen runnin' with the NVA."

"Go on with your story."

"We got to the tunnel area about . . . I figger about twelve hours before the NVA. They was movin' only at night to keep from bein' spotted by air and dodgin' H&I artillery all the way, so we had plenty of time to set up and get ready . . ."

LAOS

Hamhock, Willy Pud's trusted radioman and assistant patrol leader, was relieving the ISO photographer near the camera mounted on a low tripod when he spotted the NVA column. They were yawning and bitching as they entered the tunnel of heavy bush, shaking out the cramps and picking up a purposeful stride as they headed into sanctuary, safe from prying eyes in the sky. Hamhock smiled. He always got a weird kick out of looking at the enemy when they couldn't see him. And these dudes looked just like a platoon of overloaded Marine grunts stretching it out on the homeward leg of a long hump.

He quietly shifted to let the ISO sergeant slip back behind the specially rigged Nikon and craned over his shoulder to spot the spoke in the defensive perimeter where his team leader should be sleeping. As usual, there was no need to wake Willy Pud. Hamhock jealously guarded his sleeping shifts in the bush, but Willy Pud . . . well, he had that fine-tuned internal alarm system . . . and those little white pills that wired him directly into the situation.

Hamhock caught Willy Pud's silent query and conveyed the enemy sighting with his hands. Pointing at his eyes: enemy in sight. Two fingers and a fist: about twenty gooks. Three fingers, pointed down and then to the left: approaching below us from the left front, range about three hundred meters. Willy Pud nodded and dug around in his rucksack for a pair of rubber-covered 7×50 binoculars. At his gentle prodding, the rest of the team began to roll over behind their weapons, forming a barrier against any flanker that might stumble into the harbor site.

Butting his shoulder hard against the camera tripod, Willy heard the muted snick of the silenced shutter. The ISO sergeant removed his hand from the focusing ring of the long telephoto tube and showed a thumbs-up. There was a tight grin on the man's filthy face as he kept his eye screwed to the viewfinder. The bush-wise ISO man wasn't about to waste film or risk exposure for NVA family snaps. Even as he focused his binoculars, Willy Pud knew what he would see.

They jumped out of the blur and riveted his attention like a pair of signal flares. Both men stood a head or more taller than the NVA troopers humping along beside them. They wore an admixture of ratty GI and VC gear that contrasted starkly with the muddy green of the gooks' baggy uniforms. There was no longer any doubt. All the stories were true. Salt and Pepper were real.

It looked a little like a prisoner escort situation, but the two tall men were clearly not POWs. They loped along in a relaxed column, holding positions across from each other within the NVA formation. The white man carried an M-16 with two bandoliers full of loaded magazines and a brace of ChiCom stick grenades in a pouch looped over his shoulder. Skinny, leech-bitten calves showed between the shredded hems of his GI trousers and the tops of his well-worn jungle boots. The black man wore a ripped Army-style flak jacket, exposing arms corded with muscle and a pair of muddy black VC-style trousers. He carried an M-79 grenade launcher over his shoulder like a squirrel hunter and humped two RPG rounds for the NVA rocket gunner walking ahead of him.

Despite the weapons, Willy Pud noticed the NVA bush veterans were keeping a wary eye on their two foreign comrades. He felt a flash of professional empathy with the gook grunts. *Figures. Just like we keep an eye on the former-VC Kit Carson Scouts who get assigned to our units. It's a good bet a guy who turns once won't have too many qualms about turning twice.*

The ISO photographer's hands were shaking as he opened the back of his camera and fumbled with a film canister. Willy Pud put a reassuring pressure on his elbow and circled a finger to show the man he wanted to keep rolling as long as Salt and Pepper were in sight. Below them, Salt shifted his M-16 from one shoulder to another and Willy focused on the movement.

Skinny, scarecrow frame. Musculature undeveloped by hard work or hefting weights. Pale, watery eyes behind a set of black GI glasses held together at one temple by a wad of filthy, formerly white tape. Sandy hair sticking out from under a VC bush hat emblazoned with a red star and a peace symbol fashioned from grenade pins. GI load-bearing equipment, but it was the attitude that clinched it for Willy Pud. Dignified carriage, slightly aloof as if grunting through the jungle is beneath him, a temporary burden to be borne for a cause. The burden on his mind, not on his back. American, candy-ass variety.

Pepper was the physical opposite. Broad shoulders tapering into narrow hips. Ripples of cleanly cut muscle showed with every move. Jock or furniture-mover. Maybe both. Shaggy, unkempt hair framing a blocky face. Broad, flat nose with nostrils that flared like an angry bull. Hard ridge of scarred eyebrow beneath a long forehead. Coil of black thread through a lanced earlobe. Bracelet of braided black bootlaces on his left wrist and an ebony carving of a clenched fist around his neck. All the signs and symbols were there but it was the stride that told the tale.

Pepper swung along the trail like a swimmer stroking into a sprint finish: step, swing, reach, and repeat; shoulders rolling, hands cupped somewhere near a fist. Willy had walked behind enough ghetto refugees in uniform to recognize the urban strut.

As he watched Salt and Pepper, Willy Pud felt something burning deep in his guts. He clenched his teeth tightly and let the hot bile that flowed up from his stomach drip unheeded out of a corner of his mouth. All the bullshit back in the States, all the bandwagon political rhetoric from kids who wouldn't know a gook from a gumdrop, all the anger and confusion because Vietnam didn't feature a Pearl Harbor or focus on a world-dominating, barbarian enemy; that was one thing. But this? This was something that couldn't be ignored no matter how hard a guy in the 'Nam locked into survival and disregarded his orphan status. This was the fucking atom bomb that would fuse it all together for the assholes that blamed good warriors for a bad war.

Tapping him on the shoulder, the ISO photographer held up three canisters of exposed film. They had proof of Salt and Pepper's existence. At his other shoulder, Hamhock held up the radio handset and shot Willy Pud a questioning glance. They should send a burst transmission requesting immediate extract, run for the border, and get the evidence into the right hands.

And then what? If America pulled out of Vietnam—and units were already being shipped home under Nixon's Vietnamization Program—the traitors would never be brought to trial. If the ARVN couldn't hold the fort—and Willy Pud had no illusions about their ability to do that—Salt and Pepper would become heroes among the victorious North Vietnamese. Despite the odious stain of treason, Salt and Pepper's treachery might even be justified by the growing crowd of people who viewed the gooks as some sort of pitiful oriental elves being beat up by an American giant.

Willy Pud refocused his binoculars and thought about killing. It wasn't something he did very often in the bush, virtually never when he was deep in enemy territory, but the rage inside him seemed hell-bent on a violent outlet. Like most combat men, Willy Pud viewed killing from a technical perspective. It was something unpleasant made less so by a clinical approach; like making a comfortable load out of a heavy pack or digging a precise slit trench. After a few firefights, Sunday school morality questions ceased being a bother.

There were other times—a few in Willy Pud's memory—when killing was a memorable high; something that seemed to be charged with righteous virtue. Sometimes you got a shot at unsullied vengeance; tit for tat, righting a terrible wrong, and it felt good. You walked away from such bloody encounters . . . proud—there just wasn't any other word for it—proud to have blown away a sonofabitch that deserved it very much. This was one of those times.

The NVA officer commanding the retreating unit ordered a halt and said something that made his men laugh. Willy Pud watched as he kicked at the decayed underbrush and set his troops to gathering firewood. Wordlessly, Salt and Pepper came together on one side of the trail and dropped into a gook-squat. Salt pulled a book out of his pocket and began to read. Pepper reached into his pack and began to munch on a ball of congealed white rice. When a thin column of camphor-wood smoke drifted up from the fire and a battered aluminum teapot appeared from an NVA private's pack, Willy made a decision.

Hamhock's eyebrows lifted when his patrol leader whispered the orders. It wasn't that he had anything against killing gooks. A good, tight ambush run by pros could take out twenty easy . . . and get everybody back to brag about it. But this was something else; something special, and everyone in the team knew that. Hamhock sucked on a thick lower lip and then whispered into Willy Pud's ear.

"Recon, man . . . snoop, poop, and scoot. We got what we come after."

"I want them two motherfuckers *dead* . . . and I want to haul the bodies back to prove it."

"Too deep, Willy Pud. We try to haul a couple of stiffs back with the gooks chasin' our ass and we won't make the extract point."

Hamhock was right, of course. To set up an effective ambush they'd have to run hard and fast ahead of the gooks, pick the perfect site along the trail, kill all or most of them, and then hump two dead bodies five or six klicks back across the border to a preselected pickup zone. If something—anything—went wrong . . .

Willy closed his eyes for a moment and tried to bank the anger. All he could see was two self-righteous bastards leading a parade through long rows of U.S. government grave markers. Not on his watch. Not while he still had a round in his weapon and one good eye to hold a sight picture.

"The photographer stays here with the radio and one other man. If something goes wrong, they split for the border and get that film back to the rear. Leave the packs and move out."

Willy Pud didn't like putting his people on the man-made trail just a hundred meters above the NVA's track but there was no other way to buy time. Hard telling how long the gooks would linger over tea and bulling bush was too slow and noisy. He signaled for a halt and then signed his intentions to Hamhock up on point. L-shaped ambush. Just around the hard curve in the trail about fifty meters ahead. Go.

As Hamhock took off in a running crouch, Willy Pud moved up behind him where he'd be in position to quickly slot his men into the ambush pattern. That's when Hamhock's right boot snagged the tripwire.

There was a blinding flash and the jungle tilted violently. Willy Pud saw Hamhock's body slam into a tree and slump to the ground but it looked as if the man was falling up rather than down. *So death rescinds the rules of gravity . . .*

Willy Pud concentrated hard and felt his facial muscles begin to cooperate. When his left eyelid finally lifted it felt like someone was drawing sandpaper across the eyeball. Still, he couldn't blink. Not while Salt and Pepper stood over him and glared. The bass hum in his ears changed pitch and Willy began to distinguish sounds. His ears and his eyes would have to suffice for what was left of his life. Nothing else seemed to work no matter how hard he tried to move. Somewhere—off in the distance to his left— staccato rattle of a running firefight. His team likely; scrambling for the border.

"They all gonna die, honky mothahfuckah . . . jes' like you gonna do." Pepper reached inside a pocket of his flak jacket. The TT-33 Tokarev pistol looked like a toy in his huge hand. He crouched over Willy Pud and pressed the muzzle of the weapon into a blood-clotted nostril. "You done whipped yer last slave, white boy . . ."

Willy Pud's right eye cracked open as Pepper thumbed the

hammer back and started to squeeze. A white hand crossed into his field of vision and pushed the pistol away from his nose. He could feel fresh blood begin to trickle toward his lips as Salt crouched next to Pepper and peered into his face.

"Recon dude. Real bush-beast. He looks like a survivor, doesn't he?"

Pepper moved the pistol back into view. "Not for long, he don't . . ."

"Think it over, man . . ." There was a pleading note in Salt's voice but he seemed resigned to lose a disagreement with the black man. It was as if he'd played out this scene before and knew the ending. "He ain't no oppressor, man. He's a goddamn slave—a puppet—just like we are."

Pepper's nostrils flared. He seemed to forget about Willy Pud for the moment as he casually turned the pistol toward Salt. "I ain't no mothahfuckin' slave, asshole. Not no more. White man got his last licks in on me. Now it's my turn . . ."

The muzzle of the pistol returned to the original target. Willy Pud wondered briefly if his old man would be sober when he went to the White House to collect a posthumous Medal of Honor. Probably not . . . and that would mean tears.

"Listen, man. Let the dude live. He might make it back. And if he does . . . he can't keep it quiet. Think of the moral victory. Think of the propaganda value. They'll know there are other choices . . . and at least two of us have made them. Heroes of the Revolution, man . . . on both sides of the world."

Pepper blinked once, twice, and then cut a wary glance around the jungle. Willy Pud had visions of the man as a juvenile delinquent on a street corner watching for cops. There was a guilty, furtive tic in his eyes as Pepper leaned over him and poked a finger into his chest.

"Get the slave masters to send you back to the World, mothahfuckah. Crawl up in the bosom of the Beast. Then you find out who the *real* niggers are."

Pepper rocked back on his heels, uncoiled, and repocketed the pistol. Willy Pud tried to watch him depart, but Salt filled the narrowing frame of his vision. "You're lucky, man. Once he gets into that head trip, he doesn't normally come out of it . . . until he kills somebody."

Salt seemed to be pondering something as he glanced up the trail toward his departing partner. He worried his lower lip and twisted a gold ring on the third finger of his right hand. When he pointed that hand at Willy Pud's chest, the ring jumped into focus. A word? Name? Initials? "CHE" or "C.H.E." molded and carved into a heavy gold band.

The ring hand disappeared as Salt picked up his rifle and stood. He smiled to reveal straight white teeth and nudged Willy Pud's rib cage with a muddy jungle boot. "Check out what's happening back in the States, man. Find out why you get used like a simple tool. This revolution is almost over . . . and your side lost."

DANANG

"And they both just disappeared into the jungle? Nothing else was said?"

Willy Pud shook his head at the MACV colonel who had resumed his pacing. "That's all I remember, sir. I passed out again pretty quick after the white guy walked off. Figured I was gonna die. Probably would have, but my team diverted the main body of gooks and then circled back to pick me up. They still wound up humpin' dead weight back across the border . . ."

The colonel scanned his notebook and then snapped it closed. "Let's get back to that ring for a moment . . . you said the letters were C-H-E?"

"Yessir. I figure maybe those are the guy's initials."

"Do you recognize the name Ernesto Guevara?"

"Yessir. One of Castro's boys, ain't he?"

"Yes. Violent communist revolutionary. He's become a sort of folk hero in the Third World. He goes by the name of Che, C-H-E."

"Hard tellin', Colonel. Maybe that's what it meant. Both those guys talked like they were . . . you know, brainwashed or something. Lots of political crapola in everything they said."

"That kind of stuff seems to be popular these days."

"Yessir. Most of the time it don't mean nothin'. Just guys runnin' off at the mouth . . ."

"You think it's different with Salt and Pepper?"

"Yessir. Gotta be. I mean, a guy born in our country . . . he don't say shit and do shit like they done unless he really *believes* it."

"That sounds a lot like an apology, Staff Sergeant Pudarski . . ."

"No way, sir. I don't owe those two assholes nothin', even if they did let me live. I'll be the first sonofabitch to volunteer for the firing squad after the court-martial."

"Hmmm, yes . . . well, that about wraps it up here." The MACV colonel seemed tense, excited as he pocketed his notebook and extended his hand. "Thanks very much, Sergeant Pudarski. I'm damn glad you made it back." If the man had a tail, it would have been wagging furiously.

Willy Pud shook the outstretched hand. "Sir, who are these guys? Somebody must know."

The colonel shoved the tape recorder into a map case and turned to leave the tent. "We're checking the AWOL and deserter lists now, Willy Pud. Given the photos, we should be able to put a name to the faces soon."

"What happens when you know who they are, sir?"

"That depends on lots of things . . . it's hard to say."

"It ain't hard to say what *ought* to happen to the bastards . . ."

The MACV colonel drew himself up near attention and made sure Willy Pud knew he was hearing official orders.

"No, that's not hard to say, Staff Sergeant Pudarski. Meanwhile, you are hereby advised that your mission, all the details thereunto pertaining, and the entire content of this debriefing session are classified *Top Secret*. You are to talk about this incident with no one unless you receive written orders to the contrary from competent authority in the MACV chain of command. Violation of these direct orders can result in your prosecution under the Uniform Code of Military Justice and applicable laws of the United States. Do you understand?"

"Yessir. I understand."

Willy Pud spent his last night in Vietnam wishing he did. He woke up in the morning washed by welcome waves of pain. Understanding might come later, or it might not. It was enough to be hurting, which meant he was alive.

NEW YORK

"God help me . . . it would have been different if his mother had lived. She had such a wonderful sense of values. Never lost that . . . even when I started making enough money to spoil them both rotten."

The MACV colonel ran a finger between his button-down collar and a freshly shaved neck and tried to sense the mood of the man who'd just been told his only son was a traitor.

"It's this rebellious streak that's running through the country, Cleve. Goddammit, kids burning draft cards . . . even flags, for Christ's sake! Some units in Vietnam are refusing to carry out lawful orders. And these are the same little shits who grew up starry-eyed over Kennedy . . ."

Cleveland Herbert Emory, chairman and chief executive officer of Emory Technology, turned away from the skyline view of the city provided by the glass panorama of his office and arched a shaggy eyebrow at his visitor. That look, flashed across the polished surface of boardroom tables, had disemboweled multimillion-dollar deal-makers.

"Ask not what your country can do for you . . . ask what you can do for your country. Let's all join hands and dance around the Maypole. It was bullshit then and it's bullshit now . . ."

"That didn't stop a lot of kids from falling for it." The MACV colonel took a deep breath and tried to ignore a nagging hot spot on his instep. The custom-made wingtips fashioned by his Chinese tailor in Cholon were giving him fits. And the jet lag he'd dragged across the International Date Line from Southeast Asia was making him more irritable than he should be in such delicate negotiations.

He reached over to unplug the cassette tape recorder that had occupied their undivided attention for the past hour, then shuffled a sheaf of eight-by-ten photographs and stuffed them back into a manila envelope.

Cleveland Emory had conducted enough negotiations in his life to recognize the symbolism. There was still a deal to be struck here. He left the window and walked over to sprawl in a leather chair at the elbow of the man whose phone call from Saigon had caused him to clear a very busy calendar. This was not the kind of business that could be conducted from behind his battleship of a desk or in a secluded alcove at The Four Seasons. Conspiracy was always dangerous. It demanded intense personal contact between conspirators; eyeball-to-eyeball where the stakes were on the table and the threat lines clearly drawn.

"I should have taken a hand when he started that radical crap in college, you know. SDS . . . hell, I thought it was some kind of fraternity! And then he volunteered to go to Vietnam . . . infantry, for Christ's sake. I thought sure he'd turned around. Had it placed in all the papers. Gonna fight the war with the tools his old man provided . . ."

The MACV colonel consulted the notebook on his knee. "Records indicate he turned up missing less than sixty days after he arrived in-country and joined his unit, Cleve. Nosed around a few dives that were known VC fronts and then just disappeared. My professional opinion is that he enlisted and got himself sent to Vietnam intending to do just what he did."

Emory arched both eyebrows for full effect and glared into the colonel's florid face. "There's no error here? No chance of mistaken identity?"

"Cleve, I've been on this thing exclusively since you called me about his missing status. As a senior intelligence officer, I'm not without power and influence. You've seen the pictures. You've heard the tape. And the ring clinches it. The one they call Salt *is* Cleveland Herbert Emory, Junior."

The signet ring he'd worn for so long—the one he'd had duplicated for his only son on the boy's eighteenth birthday—felt like an ice cube on his finger. Emory rubbed it distractedly and pondered the stakes. So much to lose; so much that had nothing to do with business or finance or efficiency or who made the better mousetrap. The boy had made a stand. Totally, inconceivably, and irrevocably wrong—but he'd committed to his beliefs. Hardheadedness inherited from his father. Could his father make any kind of different stand?

"Is there a chance that he'll survive?"

"Hard to say, Cleve . . ." Reaching down to unlace the troublesome shoe, the MACV colonel considered favors done and favors returned. His position seemed secure. "Survival in combat sometimes depends on nothing but dumb luck. He's made it so far . . . against the odds. My suspicion is that they'll take him out of the field before too long. He's already helped create an illusion for them among the fighting troops. In future, he'll be of much greater propaganda value doing other things . . . witness the Jane Fonda incident."

Emory winced visibly at the images that brought to mind. No amount of money, no power on earth, would ever erase the shame or restore the value of his good name in the world's powerful business circles where breeding and background were the cornerstones of every transaction. *Frankenstein!* He'd lose everything he'd fought so hard to create and wither in the shadow of a monster of his own creation. No, by God, he would not! Not as long as he had a dime in the bank and breath in his lungs to keep him afloat.

Cleveland Herbert Emory, Senior, shifted mental gears and turned on the juice that had made him one of the most powerful businessmen in the world.

"Who's the colored guy?"

"Uncertain at this stage. Best guess is a draftee from St. Louis. Disappeared at about the same time your son did. Dimwit. Part of McNamara's One Hundred Thousand who couldn't pass the qualifying exam in other circumstances. Black Power advocate. If he's the guy I think he is, he killed a white NCO before he went missing."

"And this Polack who made the sighting?"

"Not a problem. Typical Marine NCO. Does as he's told and he's under orders not to talk. He's due to get the Medal of Honor at the White House at the end of the week. He'll be too choked up to think about anything else."

"How about the rest of the men who were with him?"

"Cleve, look . . . these rumors about two American turncoats have been circulating for months now. Nobody can believe . . . hell, nobody *wants* to believe they might be true. If those Marines try to make an issue of what they saw, they'll be laughed at . . . maybe even held in-country while some sort of investigation is conducted. They'll let it drop and get out while they can. Meanwhile, the Army denies everything. Don't you see? Without proof, they can't do anything else. And I've got the only proof: photos, negatives, and the only copy of the debriefing tape."

"Loose ends, Justin. They can bite you in the ass. Your story includes a Navy doctor and Pudarski's commanding officer."

"The doctor heard nothing, Cleve. He's on his way home with a gong for patching up the hero of the hour. Leave the Marine captain to me."

Emory looked into the colonel's cold eyes and knew instantly he was on solid ground. The man understood the deal . . . and all its ramifications.

"How long have we been doing business with each other, Justin?"

"That might not be a wise way to measure our relationship, Cleve—at least not until I retire. Let's say we've been, uh, kindred spirits for the past three or four years."

"Regardless . . . it's been a profitable relationship. Hasn't it, Justin? For both of us."

"I like to think it's been profitable for the nation too, Cleve. We couldn't have done what needed doing in Vietnam without Emory Technology. And there's no doubt that technology will carry over into benefits for society at large."

"There were a lot of bids on a lot of lucrative contracts. We were lucky to find you when we did . . . a right-thinking man in the right place, Justin. A narrow-minded military bureaucrat would have tossed those bones to the lowest bidder. That would have been a mistake. Lots of American boys would have been killed just to save a penny."

"My sentiments exactly. Witness the debacle with the M-16 rifle when we first fielded it in Vietnam. Horror story. As I told you when we first met, Cleve, I made a promise not to let anything like that happen while I was a procurement officer in the Pentagon."

"I trusted you then . . . why not now?"

The MACV colonel ejected the tape cassette from the recorder and dropped it into the manila envelope with the prints and negatives. "And in the future?"

Cleveland Emory forced himself to sit still and carry out the final round of negotiation. "The future beyond what, Justin?"

"Beyond Vietnam, Cleve . . . beyond my retirement."

"It's your ticket to write. There's no reason why a man of your proven reliability shouldn't start high in this organization and advance even higher."

The MACV colonel retied his shoelace and smiled at his benefactor. "Look for two things to happen in short order. Massive B-52 strikes will obliterate the Ho Chi Minh Trail leading from Laos. At least one bomb will fall in every square meter of the area where Salt and Pepper's unit is camped. You have my personal guarantee on that."

"And?"

"And you'll be officially notified that your son has been killed in action against the enemy in Vietnam."

The MACV colonel shook Emory's hand and then relinquished the only proof that Salt and Pepper ever existed.

WASHINGTON, D.C.

Willy Pud woke with a jolt and pawed desperately at the claws biting into his throat. Someone—something—was trying to choke him to death. Asleep on watch, goddammit! Fire the Claymores! Salt and Pepper . . . inside the wire!

Only Stanislaus Pudarski's hammer-hardened hand and a stern blast of conditioned air kept him from murdering the row of cut-crystal liquor bottles arrayed just beyond arm's length in the spacious backseat of the limousine. He dug at the cloying leather-neck collar of his newly fitted dress-blue uniform, gazed out the window, and tried to unwind. No gooks in Georgetown . . . although there were concertinas of barbed wire left over from demonstrations staged by college students who supported them.

"Relax, Vilhelm. You're home now." Willy Pud smiled at the name. He hadn't heard it said that way since he left Chicago back in '64. *Vil*-helm. The Slavic pronunciation still lingered despite the fact that no one in his family had spoken Polish since his grandmother died almost fifteen years ago. His old man never called him *Vil*-helm unless he'd done something extremely bad or extremely good. On neutral occasions—and that was most of the time around his father—he was called Willy . . . with a W.

"Big day for you, Vilhelm. Have a little snort with me." On the other side of the broad, blue velvet seat, Willy Pud's father poured himself a second double-knuckle of the finest scotch whiskey Marine Corps money could buy. The preened and pressed Marine officer sent to escort them to the White House had asked Stosh Pudarski if there was anything he could do to make the ride more comfortable . . . and Stosh Pudarski had not hesitated to let him know there was.

"Later, Pop . . . I drink anything now and I'll probably puke on the President's shoes." Stosh Pudarski chortled with glee at the image. What memorable highlights there were in his sketchy career as carpenter, framer, and cabinet-maker centered around thumbing his fist-twisted nose at bosses and bureaucrats. Sitting around a rickety kitchen table Willy had heard the tales—and the gales of laughter they always inspired—from the time he was a little boy sketching clown faces into the wet rings left by his father's sweaty beer bottles.

"Like that time we was framin' them duplexes down in Skokie. Remember that story? Jesus! Me and Frank Hovitz got drunk and while the boss was chewin' us out and tryin' to can our ass . . . we unhorsed and pissed all over his shoes. Christ! You remember me tellin' you about that?"

Willy Pud smiled. He remembered the story but it wasn't half as funny as the fiery red flush crawling up the buzz-cut neck of the Marine officer in the front seat. The man's head turned in his dress uniform collar like it was mounted on a spindle. "Might be time for one more quick one, Mr. Pudarski. We'll be at the White House in about fifteen minutes."

Willy Pud shook his head at the bottle his father inclined in his direction. His old man was getting nervous. The warning from the sideline had set him on edge. The final drink went down with a gulp and a grimace. Now Stosh Pudarski sat fussing with the unaccustomed wide lapels and tight trousers of the first new suit he'd worn in twenty years.

"Pop . . . be cool when we get there, OK?"

"I'm fine, Vilhelm. It's this pansy-ass suit that guy at Monkey Ward talked me into buyin'. Like a goddamn cheap hotel . . . no ball-room . . ."

"You know what I mean. These guys are gonna talk . . . friendly and everything . . . but they don't wanna hear stories. You know—don't start tellin' 'em how it was on a tin can in the Pacific or anything like that."

A shadow fell over his father's features. Maybe it was just the gate guard blocking the sun, but Willy Pud thought it made the man look old, lonely, and unloved, the way he'd looked when his wife died eight years back. As the limousine accelerated up the circular drive toward the White House, he reached over and felt for his father's hand. Stosh Pudarski smiled and tapped the back of his only son's hand with the hard ridges of his fingertips. It was the closest thing to an embrace between them since Willy Pud had come home from the war.

"If only your mom could be here to see this . . ."

Willy Pud squeezed his father's hand, then sat quietly, waiting for the limousine door to be opened by a Marine sentry. He tried missing his mom; tried to conjure up enough emotion to match the tears welling in the old man's rheumy eyes. Nothing. There was nothing. Down deep inside where remorse and grief hide until someone dies, Willy Pud was empty. All the other deaths had layered over his emotional core like thick scar tissue. He didn't want to think about dead people anymore . . . not his mom or any other corpse.

And he'd have to find a place in the White House for the old man to piss before he met the President.

Willy Pud stood paralyzed between his father and the President of the United States. While the old man tried to re-create the salty sailor smirk he'd worn in the photos from his Navy days, the President flashed a practiced grin that made his face into a long, beetle-browed wedge. Willy was doing his best to look pleasant but he could feel the grin he'd plastered on at the beginning of the photo session distorting into a snarl. It was the stroboscopic flutter of flash units and the hot glare of the little goose-necked lights mounted atop the TV cameras that did it.

He'd just met the President. Shook the man's hand while the resident White House photographer was applying pancake makeup to the Chief Executive's shadowy jowls. Willy Pud had himself locked firmly into the here and now until they walked out of the Oval Office and smack into a press ambush. The bright strobe flickers reminded him of muzzle flashes. When the TV lights came on, he felt like he'd been caught flat-footed, perpendicular to the deck with no cover at hand, sniper bait in the harsh glow of a mortar illumination round. His instincts urged him to seek cover but the Commander in Chief of the entire United States Armed Forces held him in place with a firm hand on his elbow.

The crush began to subside when two senior Marine officers stepped into the alcove. One of them guided Willy Pud's father gently out of camera range and handed the President a large blue box like jewelers use for expensive necklaces. The other officer stepped up to a podium bearing the presidential seal and flipped open a file folder. He began to read in a firm, dignified voice that carried a hush over the room.

"The President of the United States, in the name of the Congress, takes pride in presenting the Medal of Honor to Staff Sergeant Wilhelm Johannes Pudarski, United States Marine Corps, for service as set forth in the following citation: For conspicuous gallantry and intrepidity at the risk of his life above and beyond the call of duty while serving as a squad leader with Company F, Second Battalion, First Marines, then Sergeant Pudarski was assigned to secure a strategic hilltop against enemy threat to the flank of his unit which was then engaged as part of a battalion-sized sweep of a major North Vietnamese Army stronghold in Quang Tri Province, Republic of Vietnam . . ."

He recognized his name but little else. Willy Pud had no idea who they were talking about as he listened to the saga of heroism unfold.

QUANG TRI PROVINCE—1969

"Hey, I made a mistake . . . alright? What are you gonna do? Shave my head and send me to fuckin' Vietnam?"

Willy Pud smacked his squad radio operator on the helmet with the useless handset and thought about strangling the man with the cord. "I oughtta send your dumb ass back down the hill to *find* that spare battery, Collins. You got any bright ideas about how we send our position down to Six or call for fuckin' support if the gooks decide they want to take the high ground?"

Collins didn't have a clue. And without a functional radio, neither did Willy Pud. Still, it didn't make much sense to start another war. There was plenty to go around the grid square if the roar from the valley below their rocky pinnacle was any indicator. Stuck up on the scabby knob of a jungle-covered peak with only ten men and a pop-gun 60-mm mortar, the situation could get tense in a hurry and Willy Pud didn't need players who constantly dropped the ball.

"Get your ass up and grab an e-tool, Collins. Help Fowler and Martinez dig a hole for the tube. And tell Fowler I said *you* do most of the diggin'."

He should have known better than to give Collins the radio. Should have humped it up the hill himself like the mortar tube . . . and about half of fat-ass Foreman's gear. *Should have, would have, could have . . . if . . . if . . . if. Shit in one hand, wish in the other, and see which one fills up first.* He wished he had some experienced bush-beasts in his understrength squad . . . but the only other man besides Fowler with more than three months in the field was medevac'ed a week ago with malaria. *Shit!*

And here he'd have to sit, right in the middle of it with no contrary orders and no radio to call for them. If the gooks tangling with the grunts below decided to consolidate and make a stand, they'd sure as hell pick this hill to do it. A guy like Collins—who made a big effort to let everyone know he was a draftee and never volunteered to be a Marine—might decide it was not the time or place to prove a point. There were at least three other new guys who made it clear they didn't think there was one square inch of Vietnam worth the sweat off their balls.

The sun was about two fingers above the horizon and sinking. Willy Pud tried not to dwell on the difficulties of defending the hill. They probably wouldn't have to anyway. The skipper sent them up here to guard the company flank. When he had the time to think about it, he'd send a patrol or a helicopter if one was available.

"Somebody find Fowler and get him up here!" The nearest people were Stokey, the boot machine gunner, and Wop Gerardi, his assistant. They were digging a fighting hole for the M-60 near the military crest of the hill. The two men looked at each other over their entrenching tools and grinned, playing the age-old game: first one to follow orders is a candy-ass.

"Pass the word, goddammit! Get Fowler up to me!" Voices began to call for Willy Pud's first fireteam leader as he walked downslope and squatted next to a boulder where he might get some sense of the turmoil in the valley below.

It didn't take a radio to discern that the battalion was in heavy contact. They'd been patrolling for the past four days, poking and prodding in the thick bush to find a rogue NVA battalion that was troubling the ARVN units around the provincial capital of Quang Tri. They hit unwelcome paydirt shortly after Willy Pud's squad reached the crest of the hill on their exposed right flank.

Smoke drifted in an angry grey pall over at least three large areas. Flights of tropical birds were being driven up through the thick canopy, into the darkening sky and away from the barrage of gunfire slicing into their nests. There was the occasional flash of tracer arcing through the green roof of the jungle. Willy heard the metallic thump of 12.7-mm machine guns, the roar and sizzle of rocket-propelled grenades. That kind of firepower went with a battalion or regimental CP. His outfit had stepped directly into a large basket of shit, but there wasn't much he could do about that.

"We maht could dump a coupla sixty rounds down there just for drill . . ." Corporal Fowler, the guitar-picker from Austin,

shucked his flak jacket and sat next to his squad leader. Willy
Pud could tell from the contemplative grin on his face that Fowler
wasn't thinking about tactics or fire support. The Texan was twice
wounded and short . . . just under two weeks left in the 'Nam and
on his last operation. He was delighted to be stuck up on a hill
and out of the fight.

"Drill is all it'd be. Can't see shit. We'd wind up droppin' HE
on our own people."

"Don't mean nothin' anyways, Willy Pud. Word is we ain't
supposed to get in no runnin' fights with the gooks no more.
Ain't you heard? Tricky Dick says it's time for Marvin the Arvin
to start kickin' ass on Luke the Gook."

"That'll be the day . . ." Willy Pud lit a C-ration Lucky Strike
and offered the last one in the four-pack to Fowler, but the
Texan's attention was riveted elsewhere. He stood and pointed
to a spot on the horizon where the orange disk of the sun was
dipping into the jungle.

"Ah reckon that'll be in about the next thirty minutes, Willy
Pud! Unless the NVA done shit theyse'ves an Air Force, them
choppers yonder are gonna pull us outta here."

As Willy Pud stood and squinted into the setting sun, six
helicopters rolled into a tight orbit over the jungle searching for
a landing zone. Almost immediately a stream of green golfballs
shot skyward as the NVA heavy machine gunners sent tracers up
to search for the lucrative targets. Willy Pud quickly checked the
sun, his watch, and the horizon for more helicopters. Less than an
hour to dusk. Only six helos to lift the entire battalion. *Typical.
Somewhere between mighty tight and fucking impossible.*

"Have everybody pack their trash in a hurry. It's gonna be full
dark before they get around to picking us up."

Fowler sprinted up the hill, yelling for the squad to break down
the mortar, saddle up, and fall in on him. Willy Pud turned away
from the first helicopter lift staggering up into the gloom and
wished he could trade Collins's ass for a working radio. Surely
they wouldn't be left up here all alone until daylight. A night
extraction in these hills would be dangerous, but they'd try. Surely
they would.

"OK, here's the deal from what I can figure without a radio."
Willy Pud cut a lethal glance at Collins and then turned his
attention to the heavily loaded grunts standing around the hole
they'd dug for the tiny mortar. "Battalion ran into a shit-pot full of
gooks somewhere down in the valley. Choppers are pullin' them
out right now. They'll send a bird for us sometime tonight . . .

probably after dark, so we gotta mark the LZ somehow."

Willy Pud directed their attention to a clearing about seventy-five meters below the military crest of the hill; a long, oval hollow in a thicket of teak trees and bamboo. "Ain't no level ground up here, so we'll hump down there and set up a perimeter. Soon as we hear the bird, we'll light up a bunch of heat-tabs and bring 'em in on that . . ." Solemn faces, hard to read in the gathering gloom. They may be boots but they can read the scoreboard. "Any questions?"

"What happens if they don't come for us?"

"Shut the fuck up, Collins. You done enough damage for one day. And I'm personally gonna see your ass gets back to the rear for Office Hours." A few snickers escaped from the others who could envision draftee Collins filling sandbags and burning shitters while the *real* Marines sat around and watched.

"Shit. Fuckin' gooks are gonna want this hill. They prob'ly on their way up here right now . . ."

"How long you been in the Marine Corps, Martinez? Ain't nobody gets left hangin'. That's the way it is. They'll come after us and then the fuckin' gooks can *have* this hill. Now, move out."

Fowler fell in beside Willy Pud as they cautiously picked their way through the dark, over a rocky crest, and down through tall grass to the selected landing zone. "It was you told the first sergeant not to give me that job in the laundry before we come out on this op, wasn't it?"

Willy Pud didn't see any sense in lying. Fowler deserved the truth. "Yeah. It ain't nothin' personal, man. You know that. But look at the boot-camp assholes we got in this squad. I need your help to keep 'em in one piece."

"Cain't blame 'em for backin' up, man. Ain't like it was when we first come over here. Nobody wants to fight this fuckin' war no more . . . 'cept maybe the gooks."

"Don't get yer bowels in an uproar, Fowler. I'll turn you loose on the laundry soon as we get back in . . ."

"Maht be too late for that, Willy Pud. If ah get killed on this hill, tell 'em don't bother to bury me. Ah'm just gonna come back and haunt your ass."

Feeling around for the pile of rocks on which he'd placed three trioxane ration heating tablets, Willy Pud shivered and hoped the dense fog drifting in and out of moon shadows would pause in its climb up the mountain for just fifteen more minutes. It was hard to tell with the rotor noise clattering in and out of the echo chambers formed by dips and draws in the hill mass, but he figured the helo crew would sweep over their LZ in about that amount of time. They'd been searching nearby for nearly all of the full hour Willy Pud had promised himself he'd wait before giving up and climbing back up to their defensive positions.

He shouted across the clearing to where Fowler squatted near another pile of heat-tabs. "They're headed this way. Soon as you hear 'em, light off and get your people ready to load." The helicopter sliced across the low winter moon and Willy Pud caught the silhouette. Huey. Probably the battalion commander's bird. It would be a tight fit with ten men, a machine gun, and the mortar. As the helicopter turned in their direction, he lit a match and held it to the heat-tabs. Across the LZ, a second blue-white beacon flared.

Rotor noise pounded at his ears and he saw the helicopter flare nose-up as the pilots slowed to drop into the zone. Willy Pud began to grab in the dark and jostle his anxious people into a line for the quickest possible loading. Suddenly the Huey staggered sideways. Willy heard the throb of a heavy machine gun and saw green tracers spear up through the fog, searching for the vulnerable helicopter. He ran to the center of the zone, waving his arms frantically, and was nearly blown off his feet as the pilots pulled pitch and screwed power onto the turbine engine.

The helicopter dipped and dropped below the horizon, chased out of sight by a cascade of small-arms fire. He heard the solid crack of AK-47s as the machine gunner lost sight of his target and lifted off the trigger switch. Gooks—a sizable number of them from the sound of the firing—were on the hill. Willy Pud had just enough time to scream for Fowler and toss a handful of dirt on the blazing pile of heat-tabs when the first incoming rounds began to crack into the tough bark of the teak trees. There would be no rescue tonight. It would be morning before Willy Pud and his Marines got off the hill . . . most likely wrapped in bloody ponchos with their dog tags in their mouths.

By the time Willy Pud reached the line of fighting holes they'd prepared during the day, there was no telling if Fat Ass Foreman was alive or dead and no time to check. The impact of several slugs had knocked Foreman flat during the mad dash from the LZ back to the base of the hilltop. Since Foreman was hot on Willy Pud's heels as they scrambled for cover, his swan dive took them both to the ground. Willy Pud waited for a second swarm of rounds to drone overhead before he snatched Foreman's body, rolled it onto his shoulders, and staggered after his wildly retreating squad.

Doc Grouse tumbled into the hole without being called and panted out a dismal report. "Collins took one through the gourd . . . dead before he hit the deck. Taggert and the Wop both took rounds, but they're functional."

Willy Pud pointed at Foreman's prostrate form and screamed over the din of gunfire echoing off the rocky escarpment at their backs. "Find a hole . . . pair off and break out all your ammo and frags! Hold your fire 'til you've got a decent target!"

The tinny spang of outgoing M-16 began to taper off and Willy Pud forced himself to think. The wink and flash of muzzles in the copse of trees surrounding the LZ told him there was a good-size gook unit preparing to assault the hilltop. Below his hole, about halfway between the perimeter and the tree line, was a rocky berm. They'd assemble there for the final rush. If only they had a radio! Artillery or an air strike would hold the gooks at bay . . .

But there was no radio, no support, and damn little firepower available in his cut-up squad to make the gooks think once, much less twice, about waltzing up the hill at their leisure and killing them all. Dawn was at least six hours away. Willy Pud knew he would never see it. The realization didn't bother him and *that* was a mental jolt. *There's an insight,* he thought. *I'm gonna die and I don't give a fuck.*

"Foreman's gone, Willy Pud. One of them rounds must have tore him up inside."

Foreman, fat, full of shit about being an All-State tackle, dead. Collins, dead by dumb-ass mistake and decree of his draft board. Sullivan, shot through the right eye in that shitty little hill fight last week. Smitty, gut-shot and bled to death when they sent us up the same fuckin' hill two days later. So many. What? Fifteen or twenty in '67. Triple that in '68 and this shit goes on and on and on . . .

"Willy Pud! You OK? Fowler's yellin' for you . . . back by the mortar hole . . ." Doc shook him sharply by the shoulder and Willy Pud spun to face him. He felt high, tight, springy; the way you feel when you drop a heavy pack after a long hump. The decision was made. It was out of his hands now.

"Police up all the wounded and dead, Doc. Get 'em in one hole and get ready to move." Willy Pud vaulted out of Foreman's grave and sprinted upslope toward the middle of the perimeter where they'd dug the deep emplacement for the mortar. The NVA in the tree line below triggered probing bursts as he dashed through the cloying fog. They'd be moving forward on their bellies, flowing with the mist that crawled up the hill from the jungle below, maneuvering to cut off any possible escape route. There was very little time left.

Fowler snatched at his leg and tripped Willy Pud into cover just as a long burst of AK fire spattered off the rocks behind the hole. Martinez was crouched near a packboard full of mortar rounds, using his web belt to stem the blood flowing from two bullet holes in his thigh. Fowler was wide-eyed and shaking but his voice was under control.

"Ain't no fuckin' question anymore, Willy Pud. We gotta get off this goddamn hill, man."

"There it is. I got Doc in a hole down below roundin' up all the dead and wounded. You're gonna have to hump some dead weight. When I give the word, you pull everybody together and slip down through that cut . . . the one we was gonna cover with the machine gun. Don't stop for shit until you reach the low ground. Hold 'em in place and keep 'em quiet. Choppers'll be back at dawn and you can find a way to signal . . ."

Fowler had been set to crawl out of the hole and begin the muster when the implication of Willy Pud's plan hit him. "What about you, man? You ain't thinkin' about stayin' up here . . ."

Willy Pud snatched him by the collar and screamed into his startled face. "Don't be fuckin' with me, man! This is the way it's gonna be. Everybody takes a rifle and four or five magazines. Leave all the frags, extra ammo, and the machine gun. Don't take anything that's gonna slow you down. Now, move!"

Willy Pud shoved Fowler out of the hole and stared downslope where the drifting fog was glowing in the pale moonlight. Something moving from side to side . . . greenish glow, like a lightning bug. Signals. Gooks moving toward the berm. They'd come over the top soon . . . very soon. Fowler would need more time to assemble his people.

Willy Pud felt around the bottom of the hole and located four fragmentation grenades. There was a loaded magazine in his rifle but he'd have his hands too full to deal with the weapon if he got caught out there on the berm. He stuffed the frags in his trouser pockets, jacked a round into the chamber of his .45 pistol, and thumbed the safety on. There was an entrenching tool embedded in the earth outside the hole and he decided to take it along in case the pistol was not enough to deal with what he might encounter out there.

"You tell Fowler to haul ass as soon as he hears the grenades go. Got that, Martinez?"

Martinez was staring at him in wide-eyed fascination as he coiled to spring out of the hole. Willy Pud shrugged, smiled, and set him to work unpacking mortar rounds from their protective tubes. It was useless make-work but Martinez looked like he might be slipping into shock. Willy Pud wanted no more deaths on this hill. His own didn't count. Not anymore.

He let gravity do most of the work as he half crawled, half slid down the slope toward the berm. He could hear the wheeze of heavy breathing and a few guttural murmurs from the other side of the rise. Two short, two long, and scramble back for the holes. The grenades might just buy enough time.

Willy Pud rolled onto his back and dug the frags out of his pocket. He pulled the pins on two, let the safety levers fly, and popped them over the top of the berm. Rolling over onto his belly, he had the other two grenades ready to fly as the first one cracked and lit the gloom. He was flash-blinded and shrapnel pelted his face, but he heaved the remaining grenades deep into the tree line.

He got a foot under himself and started to run when he saw the two figures loom out of the fog that had filtered between the berm and the perimeter. There was a stab of yellow light as if the two men had snapped on powerful flashlights and Willy Pud's right leg collapsed beneath him. He rolled and dug at his waist for the pistol as dirt from another burst blew into his face. He snapped forward into a sitting position and fired twice before he could blink away the debris in his eyes. When his vision cleared, there was only one gook standing between him and the perimeter.

As the man hauled back on the trigger of his AK-47, Willy Pud snap-rolled to his left and emptied the pistol into the muzzle flash. His right leg felt like some sadistic bastard was reaming the thigh muscle with a white-hot poker. It would have been easier all around if the gook had aimed center mass instead of snap-shooting in the dark. Now he'd have to try to crawl back to the perimeter or die in place. Somehow that didn't seem right, and he needed to know if Fowler had managed to get the squad under way off the hill.

He heard equipment rattle and the swish of wet grass against cloth to his rear. Willy Pud tried to run but his right leg wouldn't bear weight. He crumpled to the ground and stared at the dark figures lunging toward him through the mist. He groped for a weapon, hoping to find an AK from one of the two men he'd shot. His hand banged into the entrenching tool. It would have to do.

As the first two NVA troopers cleared the berm like hurdlers abreast, Willy Pud swung hard and felt the edge of the short shovel bite flesh. The man he hit grunted and lurched sideways into his partner. Jerking the spade free, Willy Pud drove it into the wide eyes showing beneath the second NVA's Soviet-style helmet. Two more gooks cleared the berm, firing long, scything bursts up the hill. They didn't see Willy Pud immediately, which gave him a few seconds to snatch a weapon from one of the dead men and rake rounds into their flank. Both men went down like wet sandbags and Willy Pud began to shove himself back up the hill, gritting his teeth against the throbbing pain in his wounded leg and trying to disappear into the mist.

When he located the M-60 in the second hole he investigated, Willy Pud took stock and figured he might live another hour or two at the outside. He tied a hasty tourniquet above the two oozing holes in his thigh and maneuvered himself behind the gun where he could sweep the slope below him by simply shifting his shoulders. There was very little else to do until the gooks decided to make their rush. Fowler and the rest of his squad were nowhere in sight but they'd snapped together all the available machine-gun ammo, left two loaded M-16s and a fair-sized pile of grenades. The mist was still flowing up toward his hole. Perfect for the NVA to get close before they loomed up at him and finished the job of taking the hill.

Why don't they get on with it? That little fight down on the berm couldn't have been very discouraging. Four down but plenty more where they came from. Come on . . . come on.

Willy Pud saw the arms whip up through the fog and heard the plop as the stick grenades landed just outside his hole. He ducked behind the machine gun but a spray of hot shrapnel lanced into his left arm. He heard the snarl and rattle of AKs and crawled up to shoulder the machine gun. *This should be it,* he thought. *This is all she wrote . . . right here, right now.*

But the firefight was elsewhere. Off to his left rear; downslope in the heavy bush below the hilltop. Willy Pud knew what it was all about, even as he reached for the first grenade and tried to create a diversion. It was too late . . . too late for Fowler and the others. The NVA had caught them trying to escape.

When his barrage of grenades blew away some of the mist, Willy Pud saw them coming. Grim-faced men, snarling out of the mists, trotting forward up the hill in a staggered line, on their way to put an end to it, once and for all. He put his cheek onto the knuckles of his left hand and squeezed on the trigger. Outside

Willy Pud's hole, the NVA began to reel, stagger, and fall like wobbly bowling pins.

As he crawled up the hill toward the mortar pit, Willy Pud wished the gook who kept banging away at him would set his sights and get it right. It was too much . . . had been for too long. It needed to be over. He didn't want to take any more lives but something wouldn't let him surrender his. There was a pool of blood below him when they finally forced him out of the machine-gun position. He couldn't lose that much blood and still live. Impossible. Yet his heart was still pumping and he was still moving slowly toward another weapon.

The machine-gun ammo ran out in less than an hour and he'd fired everything else he could find including all the AK ammo from the two gooks who died inside the hole. His last two grenades had gone down the hill . . . when was it? An hour ago? Maybe two? Now there was only the mortar left . . . and then it would be over. He rolled into the mortar pit and put his bloody hand on the tiny tube. Something dark loomed on the other side of the hole and Willy Pud stared at it as he cradled the mortar and felt for the hand-firing lever near the base. A shadow? How could that be?

He ignored the ricochet of a close round and stuck his head up over the rim of the hole. The jungle below the hill glowed a pale green and the mist was swirling down, away from the high ground. Dawn. It was nearing dawn! They'd come now, in full force, before it got light enough for helicopters to fly in reinforcements. As he fumbled to pull the fuse pins from a mortar round, Willy Pud stared at the carnage on the hillside. Bodies were stacked in grotesque positions like spiky tree limbs in a disorderly woodpile. Could he have done all that killing? Surely not. Every bare spot on the scarred slope had been turned into some kind of bier for dead warriors.

Not all dead. Willy Pud saw movement near the tree line. It was time. He dropped the mortar round into the tube, elevated the muzzle, and pressed the lever. The weapon recoiled sharply and dug into the dirt on the side of the hole. Willy Pud saw the angry black blossom as the round detonated just short of three charging NVA soldiers.

Too late the dawn. It's been too long coming. For me; for everyone in Vietnam. Sunset is all that's left for us. Get out; get it over with. Too much pain and too much death. And it don't mean shit. Not now. Not when the sun comes up tomorrow.

Then he cleared his mind, shifted into boot camp mentality, and continued to load and fire like a robot. He was aiming the second to last high-explosive round when a bullet punched through his bloody shirt and drove him into the ground.

WASHINGTON, D.C.

" . . . despite his painful wounds, Sergeant Pudarski refused to surrender his position and fought on single-handedly through the night, repulsing wave after wave of enemy soldiers. He was personally responsible for killing more than fifty of the enemy and was making a gallant last-ditch stand with the squad's mortar before a final wound rendered him unconscious. His selfless concern for the safety of his men in covering their attempt to escape from the hill demonstrates the highest order of military leadership in the face of overwhelming odds. Sergeant Pudarski's gallant action and courageous fighting spirit reflects great credit on himself and upholds the highest traditions of the Marine Corps and the United States Naval Service."

Willy Pud barely felt the President's fingers at the back of his neck. He was numb and sweating inside the rigid embrace of his uniform. Something thudded into place at the base of his collar and he realized it was the Medal of Honor. He was alive and he was a hero. And Fowler didn't live to get that laundry job in the rear or catch his Freedom Bird back home. Willy Pud understood then that the World was a truly fucked-up place.

The President stepped around and adjusted the Medal to hang squarely between the two Marine Corps emblems at Willy Pud's throat. He had to reach down and snatch at a hand before Willy realized the ceremony was concluded.

"You have my personal congratulations and the gratitude of the entire nation, Sergeant Pudarski. We are all very proud of you."

As the press swarmed forward and the President pumped his hand, Willy Pud heard a whispered command. "After the photographers are through, I'd like to see you for a few minutes in my office." He nodded, standing like a stone and trying to ignore the droning buzz in his ears. It sounded like distant helicopters . . . or the big black flies that gorge themselves on leaky body bags.

THE OVAL OFFICE

"My Navy aide is a destroyer man. I had him take your dad down to his office for a nip. I suspect they'll be a while telling sea stories . . ."

Willy Pud pulled his eyes away from the President of the United States and cut a glance around the Oval Office. It was tastefully and somberly decorated, reeking of power. The pastel walls seemed to mute the hum and throb that vibrated everywhere else in the White House. Ghosts of great men and the lingering air of momentous events seemed to lurk in the shadow of shaded windows.

Despite the plush padding of his chair, Willy squirmed as he'd done as a boy sitting next to his mother on the hard pews of St. Stefan's Catholic Church. He felt the same awe and reverence that held him slack-jawed as he watched the parish priest labor at mass under the looming, agonized presence of Jesus slumping from the cross. All that was missing was the fecund scent of burning incense. And even here, in the climate-controlled atmosphere of the Oval Office, there was some strange smell . . .

"Anyway, I wanted to spend a few minutes with you alone . . . sort of get your impressions about Vietnam."

Willy Pud glanced back at the President, sprawled on a low, overstuffed couch across a polished coffee table from his seat. The Chief Executive had stripped off his right shoe and was vigorously massaging a big toe emblazoned with a bunion that threatened to burst through his thin nylon sock. The President of the United States had vile-smelling feet. There was an odor in the air that reminded Willy Pud of being inside a hooch at that putrid moment when a weary squad of bush-beasts peel off the remnants of their socks to acquaint jungle-rotted feet with fresh air for the first time in weeks. He passed a nicotine-stained finger under his nose and tried to think coherently about the war.

"Tough nut to crack, sir . . . that's really all I know how to say about it. I mean, it was different back in '67 . . . seemed like we all knew which direction to march. All that rice-paddy-daddy shit with the straw hat and black pajamas . . . that was a Saigon problem. Out in the bush, it was a clearer picture. Ain't never no problem tellin' a gook in a green uniform with an AK and a steel helmet from an innocent villager. Seemed like we was kickin' ass and takin' names . . ."

The President was digging around the inside of his shoe, searching for the errant piece of leather that was bothering his bunion. When he spoke, the voice seemed to filter through a bushy ridge of brow that hid his downcast eyes.

"And then came Tet of 1968. The incident that cost President Johnson his seat behind that desk."

Willy Pud glanced over his shoulder in the direction indicated by the President's shoe. Eisenhower, Kennedy, Johnson, and now this man; all sat behind that aircraft carrier of a desk. Willy had hidden from incoming rounds in smaller spaces than that desk occupied. And he was probably in better shape for it, current domestic-problems considered. Each of the presidents had sat right there and wrestled in his own way with the crisis in Southeast Asia. And each of them in turn had failed to get a grip on the situation.

Willy Pud had a sudden vision of a beleaguered Chief Executive crouched behind that desk, ducking incoming rounds and screaming at Congress over a Prick-25 radio for fire support. Combat could erupt anywhere in a war like the one being fought in Vietnam . . . even in the White House. Unless the newspapers and TV programs he'd absorbed since arriving Stateside had it all wrong, the whole fucking country was one big Free Fire Zone. And all a guy had to do to get his ass shot off was talk about Vietnam.

"He didn't get no Purple Heart for it, but you gotta figger President Johnson was KIA, sir . . . just like a lot of other guys durin' Tet."

The President replaced his shoe, put both feet on the plush carpet, and leaned across the coffee table to fix Willy Pud with onyx eyes. "Where were you during the Tet fighting?"

"Hue City, sir . . . Fifth Marines . . ."

"And were you upset when the Vietnamese government refused to let us bomb and shell the Citadel?"

Willy Pud cocked his head and returned the President's questioning stare. At least the guy had done his homework. He knew about the Marines who died trying to penetrate the ancient fortress surrounding the seat of the Imperial Emperors without fire support.

"Look, Mr. President . . . you should understand something about grunts. We don't think about political stuff when the shit's hittin' the fan, sir . . . you know, I mean you got more pressin' problems . . . like too many gooks and not enough ammo. What's happenin' here in Washington, or in Hanoi . . . or on some college campus . . . hell, we don't even hear about it most of the time. When we do . . ."

Willy Pud squinted and strained, searching for some words to make the most powerful man in the world understand the feelings of powerless men living out on the edge of human endurance. "Even when we do hear somethin' . . . it just don't *mean* nothin'. You ain't got time for it when you're tryin' to slam your way out of an ambush and the goddamn rain is keepin' all the TacAir support grounded . . . or you got a dose of clap that won't clear up . . . or the gunny puts you to work fillin' sandbags . . . or you get the last meal in a box of C-rations and it's ham and motherfuckers again or . . ."

The President's cackling laugh cut Willy off in midstride. "Ham and what . . . ?"

Willy Pud felt a flush crawl up onto his cheeks. "Sorry about the language, sir. It's what we call one of the C-ration meals . . . ham and lima beans . . . everybody hates it."

Flustered by his profanity, Willy Pud unconsciously pulled up his trouser leg and reached for the pack of cigarettes stashed in his sock. The President nodded his permission to smoke and moved a huge marble ashtray closer to Willy's elbow.

"You're saying most of the men in Vietnam are apolitical. I'm glad to hear that. Clearly, most of the people here at home are not, particularly over the war in Vietnam."

Willy Pud blew smoke at the ceiling of the Oval Office and decided to go for broke. "What I'm sayin', Mr. President, is that the professionals in Vietnam ain't concerned with the politics of the war. Never were and never will be. But the war ain't bein' fought by strictly professionals like it was back in '65 when we first went in. These days it's bein' fought by whoever gets caught in the draft. And a lot of them guys are comin' over to the 'Nam with political baggage they picked up before they got drafted. I mean, we got guys steppin' off the fuckin' plane—they ain't seen shit yet—and they start runnin' off at the mouth about how they shouldn't be there, how nobody should be there, how the war is all wrong and stuff like that."

The President sighed mournfully and laced his hands behind his neck. "And so it spreads . . . like a disease. Enough talk about how lousy the war is and suddenly it becomes a self-fulfilling prophecy . . ."

"Yessir. There it is. You get enough people sayin' one thing and it takes too damn much courage to say any different. Grunts tend to save their courage so they'll have it to spend on somethin' important."

"Well, after nearly five years of inconclusive war, we can't expect starry-eyed idealists. All we can ask is that the American soldier do his duty."

"They're doin' that, Mr. President . . . with a couple of major exceptions . . ."

The President arched his eyebrows and showed a note of specific interest in Willy's comment. "Are you referring to the recent incident when an Army platoon refused orders to advance? That gave the anti-war types more fuel than they deserve, believe me . . ."

Willy Pud smashed out his smoke and pondered the last orders from the MACV colonel. Surely the prohibition didn't include the Commander in Chief. Surely the President knew all about Salt and Pepper.

"Sir . . . you got to understand. Shit like that happens all the time. It ain't mutiny. It's just experienced grunts stickin' to what they learned the hard way about survivin' in the bush. They don't mean to be disobeyin' direct orders because they think the guy givin' the orders is a prick or anything like that. They just ain't gonna do somethin' stupid and get blown away. Most of the time a good CO or platoon commander listens to his vets and they get the job done the right way. When a guy gets hardheaded or the press is around, it gets blown out of proportion."

"I got that much from the official investigation into the incident, Sergeant Pudarski. You'd never know it from what you read in the papers, but I feel confident every American sent to Vietnam will do his duty until I can arrange some sort of honorable peace settlement."

"Like I said, sir . . . with a couple of major exceptions."

"And what would those exceptions be?"

Willy Pud drew a deep breath and exhaled loudly. His orders were clear but there would never be a better opportunity to make sure Salt and Pepper didn't get off the hook because they were lost in some political fast-shuffle.

"Mr. President, you probably know all about this already but there are at least two American soldiers who have gone over to the enemy side. Black guy and a white guy. I know for a fact that them two are actively fightin' with a North Vietnamese Army unit."

He stared at the President's basset-hound features for some hint of surprise or outrage. There was none. The Chief Executive forced his lower lip into a wet pout and stared at the ceiling. He seemed to be processing information somewhere deep in the recesses of his brain. Finally, he nodded and brought the interview to a close.

"I have a report somewhere on my desk concerning that situation, Sergeant Pudarski. It's of grave concern to me."

Willy Pud stood and extended his hand to meet the President's dismissal handshake. The man's triangular face remained blank but there was something furtive in his eyes. *Lots on his mind . . . maybe he didn't catch what I said. Piss on reports. The fuckin' President of the United States can't ignore a clear case of treason, for Christ's sake.*

"Sir . . . about them two traitors—we call 'em Salt and Pepper . . ."

The President eyed the Marine escort officer who had appeared at the door of the inner sanctum as if in response to some silent summons. A congenial smile slanted across the officer's chiseled face. It seemed to send the President a signal: nothing could be too wrong with an American military that contained such stalwart men.

"What would you have us do with people like that, Sergeant Pudarski?"

"I guess . . . well, I guess just make sure they don't get away with it, sir. If they do, ain't no grunt in God's world ever gonna forgive or forget."

The President craned his head and neck forward until he looked slightly hunchbacked. There was a fervent glint in his eyes and his words came across in a throaty, conspiratorial growl.

"I assure you, Sergeant Pudarski, there will be peace in Vietnam . . . and peace in this country too. A peace with honor. No one who dishonors America will escape just punishment."

Willy Pud felt the Marine escort officer's hand on his elbow. As he walked out the door he felt uneasy, unsure, unfulfilled, un . . . un-what? *Unfucked* came to mind as he joined his father and a couple of White House Navy officers who had recently become old shipmates.

When somethin' is fucked up in the Marine Corps, immediate action is to get it unfucked. That must be what the President was gonna do: get them two traitors unfucked in a hurry. Ain't no President goes around lyin' to people.

• • •

They were four blocks and two drinks away from the White House before Willy Pud spoke to his father. The old man—slightly shell-shocked from the close encounter with power brokers so alien to his world—had simply poured whiskey and waited respectfully for the certified hero who had been his son to break a meditative silence. Wearing that Medal and fresh from a personal interview with the President of the United States, there was an aura of power that clung to Wilhelm Pudarski. His father had been canned from enough jobs in his life, been arrested enough times, and paid enough taxes to have a certain reverence for power.

"Pop, when's the last time we slammed 'em down together?"

"Been a long time, son. The night before you went off to Vietnam . . ."

"Did we have a good time?"

Stosh Pudarski chuckled deep in his throat. He didn't remember exactly . . . except for what his cronies had told him the next day at work.

"Goddamn right we did! Got kicked out of three bars, by God!"

"I been away a long time, Pop. Let's go for four."

Propping his aching feet on the corner of his desk, the President dug around in a stack of manila folders until he found the one he wanted. It was buried among several reports from Vietnam including planned withdrawal statistics, reports on the Vietnamization Program, the latest body counts and estimates of ARVN capabilities. He perched a pair of reading glasses on the bridge of his nose and began to reacquaint himself with the pertinent details of the case.

The report indicated Salt and Pepper were nothing more than apocryphal battlefield myths. All attempts to confirm or disprove the persistent rumors of two American turncoats had proved futile. In his summary, the officer who compiled the report put it all down to communist scare tactics, a typical propaganda ploy. Such rumors fueled the fire of anti-war sentiments among the troops in Vietnam. The myth had apparently taken on a life of its own among gossipy grunts who longed for something—anything—out of the ordinary to talk about. There was a reference to the way rumors became accepted truth and then legend among early sailors exploring the uncharted waters of the world. The first man on watch sees a large dolphin or a whale and mentions it to his shipmate. By the time the story reaches the fantail, everyone on board has spotted a marauding sea serpent.

The President examined the signature block on the report and closed the folder. If a MACV Intelligence colonel in Saigon said Salt and Pepper were a myth, that was good enough for him. There were more pressing problems at hand.

THE HOMEFRONT

During his survey of the lobby bar in their expensive downtown hotel, Stosh Pudarski had seen nothing but ties, tassels, and tits. He'd admired the well-endowed, clear-eyed women with obvious class and expensive taste. At least there were none of the barefoot, hippie snot-noses with untethered tits like the ones they'd seen in Georgetown. What worried Stosh were the male patrons in the bar panting and pawing around the women. Puny little shits with tassels on their shiny shoes and big wide ties with so many colors and patterns it looked like they puked down the front of their shirts. Lots of long hair, droopy mustaches, and fat sideburns. Brainy bastards who sat home and bullshitted about the war while his son went off and fought it. In that company, a man in uniform would be about as welcome as a silver tray full of turds at a tea party.

He heard his son shut off the shower and opened the door to the bathroom. "How about we order us up a jug and a case of beer from room service?"

Willy Pud stood naked in a maze of polished mirrors. A heat lamp in the ceiling of the steamy chamber gave his skin a strange amber glow except where the white pucker of bullet holes and the jagged ridge of shrapnel scars glowed in livid relief. Stosh tried to cut his eyes away from the sight but everywhere he looked another mirror reflected the toll Vietnam had taken on his only son. He caught his own image over Willy's shoulder and realized he was staring slack-jawed like some addled rube at a freak show.

"Seems like there's a lot more scars than there were telegrams, Vilhelm . . ."

Willy Pud grinned and shrugged, reaching for a clean set of skivvies and his shaving kit. "I knew the stakes when I ante'd up, Pop. What's the problem? You plannin' on enterin' me in a beauty contest?"

Stosh Pudarski grinned into the mirror as Willy began to shave. "I remember when you was little . . . that time you ran your bike into old man Cheever's big '47 Olds and cut your eyebrow open? Your ma like to had a fuckin' heart attack. Thought you was gonna be scarred for life and we'd have to send you to a special school. All kinds of crazy shit over them stitches you got. I told her it don't hurt for a man to have a few scars and nicks. Makes people think twice about fuckin' with him . . ."

"So? This shit make you change your mind?"

"I wasn't talkin' about no bullet holes and these here . . ." Stosh gingerly ran a finger along a rigid welt that ran from the back of Willy's deltoid to a shoulder blade.

"Shrapnel, Pop. Gook eighty-deuce mortar. Sometimes it gets inside and tears your guts apart. Sometimes it's little stuff and they pick it out like buckshot. Marine Corps woulda gone broke if I had 'em send you a telegram every time I got some iron in my ass."

Watching Willy splash the remnants of shaving lather from his cheeks and neck, Stosh Pudarski felt the stirrings of a long-dormant emotion. It was the same feeling that washed over him unexpectedly sometimes when he'd watched his wife meticulously iron his work clothes. She knew those old khaki pants and shirts would look like hell after the first hour on the job, but she wanted her husband to start fresh, clean, looking good for his boss and his buddies. No reason for her to do it, except . . . well, you do stuff like that when you love somebody. It's the little things like not wanting her to worry when he lost another job and there wasn't enough money for the rent. He'd borrow from his buddies down at the bar and never let her know. That's how you say it; that's how you let someone know. And Wilhelm hadn't wanted him to worry over the shrapnel wounds.

"How 'bout that room service, Vilhelm? Them people down in the bar, they all look like they got paper assholes. Probably have to teach the bartender to make a fuckin' boilermaker . . ."

Willy Pud tossed his razor into a beat-up green canvas kit and began to brush the thatch of short, thick hair the Marine Corps had allowed him to keep on the top of his head.

"Pop, I spent the last three years duckin' from people tryin' to kill me. I ain't about to let no ignorant bastards in my own country force me into a bunker."

"I should have brought you some civilian clothes from home."

"Wouldn't know how to wear 'em, Pop. Now let's get this show on the fuckin' road."

With a sixth—or maybe seventh—boilermaker churning around inside his stomach Willy Pud finally felt capable of returning some of the frigid stares that swept over his back like Arctic wind. He straightened up and pulled his elbows off the dark, stained bar. The effort made the layers of medals on his chest clink loudly. Stosh Pudarski cocked an eyebrow at his son and grinned.

"Your eyeteeth singin' 'Anchors Aweigh' again?"

Willy Pud ran a finger between chafed flesh and unyielding uniform collar. "I'll piss in one of them potted plants before I pass in review again for this gang of assholes."

They'd been astride adjacent stools for the past two hours but Willy Pud had made only one reluctant trip to the toilet, a trek that required him to shoulder through a throng of well-dressed drinkers clamoring for the attention of two overwhelmed bartenders. The hotel bar was packed; noisy with travelers' tales, Washington gossip, and after-work unwinding that made Willy Pud's sole effort to relieve the pressure on an overburdened and undertrained bladder such an ordeal. Wearing his dress-blue uniform, Willy had parted the crowd like a leper, pushing a wave of stony silence ahead of him.

Now, as his son swept the dark room with slightly glazed eyes, Stosh was delighted to notice most of the patrons refused to return his glare. They mumbled into their drinks or stared into space if there was no other logical place to look. Upending his beer glass, Willy gestured at the gleaming brass fittings that caged the bar's perimeter.

"I ain't seen this much brass since boot camp, Pop. You gotta figger it would take a ten-man workin' party two days and twenty gallons of Brasso to square this place away for inspection."

Stosh Pudarski swiveled to follow his son's comment but Willy was no longer staring at fixtures. His green eyes had locked solidly onto a pair of shapely legs that poked out from under one of the free-form mushrooms that served as cocktail tables in the bar. On one end of those legs was a pair of spiky high-heeled shoes. On the other end—above a lavender miniskirt—was a bosomy brunette who tapped her teeth with a polished fingernail and openly appraised both Willy Pud and his uniform.

Stosh handed his son a shot and beer wondering if there was enough money left to buy him another room for the night. "There's one you wouldn't want to kick out of bed for eatin' crackers."

Willy Pud held the brunette's eyes until she dropped her gaze and then brought it back up to focus on the two men locked in animated conversation at her table.

"Truth be told, Pop, I'd eat a mile of comm wire just to hear that woman fart over a Double-E-8 field phone." Willy was just sliding off the bar stool when he felt a snatch at his elbow. The bartender was jerking a thumb over his shoulder toward a TV set mounted in a corner of the room. It was too noisy to hear the commentary but Willy discovered his trip to the White House was worth thirty seconds on the nightly news.

He stared at himself in abject fascination. There he stood like some rigid scarecrow while the President fussed around behind him and finally got the Medal of Honor hung around his neck. He saw himself grin—grimace was a better description—as various officials crowded around to insure they were within camera view. He even saw himself standing next to the President and his pop, flanked by two smiling bookends, as everyone shook everyone else's hand.

Stosh could not contain an exultant whoop. He smacked the bar with his hand and slid an arm around Willy's shoulder. "Goddamn! Don't you know them guys down at Hogan's and the boys over to the VFW are shittin' themselves right now! You and me on the goddamn TV—all across the fuckin' country, Vilhelm. Ain't that somethin'?"

"Guess it is, Pop . . ." Willy was watching the faces staring up at the television screen. He didn't see much hero worship in them. He didn't even see much interest in the fact that another American had won the nation's highest decoration for heroism in combat. What he mostly saw was disinterest or disgust that turned him back to the bar and an empty glass.

Before he could order a refill, the bartender shoved a brimming glass at him and dumped in a shot of whiskey.

"On me, man. *Semper Fi* . . ." He stuck out a slightly damp hand for Willy to shake. "Should have said something sooner but the crowd was bustin' my ass. Bravo One-Nine. Walkin' Dead . . . '66–'67."

Willy introduced his dad and toasted the bartender. "Thank Christ for small favors, man. I was beginnin' to feel like a fart in a spacesuit."

The bartender ignored the shouts for service on his side of the bar. "Don't see many uniforms in the city anymore, Sarge. Even the people stationed here are wearin' civilian clothes these days.

People talkin' shit, but they ain't seen any of it, right? Don't mean nothin'."

The bartender finally yielded to his other customers and Willy sat drinking in silence. A gas bubble suddenly rippled up from his stomach and he let it escape in a loud, growling belch. His father swallowed air and echoed the sentiment, working his belch so that it came out sounding like some raspy-throated giant saying "fuuuuuuuuuuuck!" Both were delighted to see shocked expressions as heads turned in their direction.

"So, Pop . . . . what do you think I ought to do?"

"Now that you got a Marine buddy behind the bar, maybe we ought to stay parked right here. Probably shouldn't get tossed out on our ass with you in uniform and all."

"I mean later, Pop. You think I ought to stay in the Marine Corps or what?"

Stosh Pudarski tongued the sticky remnants of peppermint schnapps out of a shot glass and stared into his beer. "Hard sayin', Vilhelm. Them guys at the White House told me you wouldn't have to go back to Vietnam no more . . . and you'd be a big wheel in the Marines with that Medal and all but . . ."

Willy Pud saw the frustration on his father's face. He was embarrassed by something unsaid . . . something he couldn't bring himself to say. Like the time when he was fourteen and the old man had tried to have a "man-to-man" talk with him about sex. Embarrassment had led to frustration and ended in anger. Trenchant advice tossed over his shoulder as Stosh Pudarski stormed out of the house headed for the comfortable environs of Hogan's Bar: "Keep your dick in your pants and there won't be no problems!"

"But what, Pop? Spit it out."

"It's all them scars, Vilhelm. Everybody's got odds you know . . . can't beat 'em. I knew this sumbitch on an old tin can . . . gunner's mate. He got torpedoed twice and made it. Got blown clean off the decks one time when one of them fuckin' kamikazes hit, you know? Fucker thought he was ten feet tall and bulletproof after all that. Then just as we was comin' home, he gets hit by a crane that was off-loadin' ammo. Killed him deader'n shit . . ."

Willy ordered another beer and shoved it over at his father. "You think somethin' like that might happen to me?"

"You been awful lucky, Vilhelm. Can't say you ain't. But there's only one reason for havin' a Marine Corps and that's to fight. I seen enough of them poor bastards floatin' facedown out in the South Pacific. You stay in the Marines and you're gonna fight. You keep fightin' and you start pushin' the odds . . ."

"Say what you mean, Pop."

Stosh Pudarski drained his beer glass, knocked back a shot of whiskey, and turned to face his son. "What I mean to say, Vilhelm, is I love you, boy . . . and I don't want to see you hurt no more."

Willy Pud blinked twice and then stared at his beer. His father also dropped his head and looked deeply into a tall pilsner, fidgeting on his bar stool. It was a difficult moment; as if they couldn't bear to face each other with such an unaccustomed sentiment hanging in the air between them.

"OK, Pop . . ."

"OK what?"

"OK, I'll get out of the Marine Corps . . . maybe go to college. They'll pay for it."

"Vilhelm, I don't want you doin' nothin' you don't want to do . . . not for me. Not for nobody."

"Ain't that simple, Pop."

"Why the fuck not?"

"Never thought about it before, but it turns out I love you too."

"So you're gonna get out and go to school?"

"In a little bit. Right now, I'm gonna go over to that woman at the table and see if I can get laid."

SAIGON

"It just seems strange, Colonel. A pretty radical departure from SOP for either Linebacker or Freedom Deal strikes." The Air Force Intelligence officer leaned back and eyed his Army counterpart on General Westmoreland's joint staff. "Overkill . . . you know what I mean?"

The only other man in the airless room beneath the MACV Tactical Operations Center glanced up from his study of a large-scale map and checked his watch. "We're getting pressed for time, Johnny. And we've been through it all before. The target was developed from solid sources . . . Igloo White readings backed up by HumInt DO."

Fishing was lousy. This extraordinary request was prompted by sensor data and human intelligence from agents who directly observed something important on the ground. So what? The Air Force colonel wanted to know what the sensors detected and what the recon units saw.

He glanced again at his mission assets list. It wasn't that the BUF crews from U Tapao in Thailand or Anderson on Guam couldn't handle the saturation strike but why commit such a huge payload to a single grid square? Why concentrate all that bomb tonnage on one location when there was so much of the enemy's resupply and replacement pipeline that needed pounding?

"Look at it from a tactical standpoint, Justin. It's better to do a little damage to a lot of areas than do a lot of damage to one little area. Takes the gook engineers longer to fix it that way."

The MACV colonel leaned into the light hanging over the map of the Ho Chi Minh Trail and mashed his finger down on a grid square outlined in bright red. "You saying your B-52 boys can't flatten this little area into a parking lot, Johnny?"

"I'm not saying anything of the sort, Justin. Ever since the withdrawals started the B-52 crews have been carrying the bulk of offensive combat and you know it. I'm just trying to justify this commitment of assets in my own mind when we're pushing to get out of Vietnam."

Stoking a cold cigar with a kitchen match, the MACV colonel squinted into the smoke and glare of the small room where so many monumental decisions were made. "Johnny, I'm gonna let you in on this one. Strictly need-to-know. Nothing I say can leave this room. You read me on that?"

The Air Force officer leaned forward and rested his weight on his knuckles. He felt the familiar adrenaline rush that coursed through his veins when he was yanking and banking in the cockpit of an F-4 Phantom. Now that he was relegated to straight-and-level behind a G-2 desk, it didn't take much to prime the pump.

"Roger your last, Justin. Now what the hell is down there under those trees worth committing three entire cells of Big Ugly Fuckers to a single target?"

"Johnny, you ever wonder what morale must be like along the Ho Chi Minh Trail?"

"Gotta be lower than white whale shit on the bottom of the deep blue sea. I can't figure out how those little communist shit-heads keep going with the pasting we give 'em."

"Motivation, Johnny. You don't sit down there and let guys rain high explosive all over your ass day after day and then crawl

out of your hole and pick up a shovel unless you're highly motivated. Like most soldiers, gooks get motivated by inspirational
leaders. When morale begins to slip, Hanoi sends somebody with
major-league charisma out into the bush to prop up the sagging
spirits."

"You mean we're dumping all this shit onto the trail to kill
some party hack out on a consciousness-raising tour?"

"I guess that's it, Johnny . . . if you want to call the Commander
in Chief of the PAVN a party hack."

The Air Force colonel felt the sweat begin to seep through his
shirt. With Uncle Ho dead and buried since '69, it could only
be one person. "General Giap? Vo Nguyen Giap is out visiting
troops along the trail?"

The MACV colonel tapped the red-rimmed grid square with
his finger and puffed on his cigar stub. "You said that, Johnny,
not me."

"Holy shit! We nail that cocksucker and the war's over tomorrow!"

"Nothing survives in that grid square, Johnny. Nothing. Not
even a piss-ant."

LAOS

It was two—maybe three—weeks since Fighter Comrade
Cleveland Herbert Emory, Junior, had a chance to bathe. He
lay exhausted in his hammock beneath the sheltering branches of
a large teak tree and smelled the cloying, stale stench of himself.
As he had nearly every day since he and Fighter Comrade Theron
Clay had been detached from their combat unit, he wondered why
the Vietnamese who sweated and strained alongside them on the
trek north didn't seem to stink with the same gagging, malodorous
vengeance.

Earlier, somewhere back along the trail when the debilitating
malaria attacks had swept through the veteran unit of porters and
sappers that formed their escort, Emory decided the lack of body
odor among the Vietnamese must have something to do with a
purity of spirit. Only those who were rotten on the inside smelled
bad when the sweat of honest labor pumped from their glands.

His Vietnamese was insufficient to inquire about such a vague concept. He could only be sure about one thing. Their fellow fighters of the National Liberation Front thought he and Theron smelled terrible. They were forced to sleep outside the communal tunnels. *Thi sao?* Why? The North Vietnamese veterans, men—and especially the women—merely giggled and pinched their flat noses.

At first he was offended. Such blatant ignorance of true communist ideology. Such disregard for the basic principle of one world, one people, one struggle. Such abject prejudice against two volunteers from the western proletariat. But they were simple people, Comrade Emory told himself, banking his anger and rolling over in the hammock. Unversed in theory and philosophy. Otherwise they would never be content with life along the trail, humping huge loads day after excruciating day, pushing rickety, overburdened bicycles through the ruts and mud, back and forth like mindless drones. They sat nodding and slack-jawed during the political lectures. Giggled like schoolgirls during revolutionary theater performances, totally missing the point of even the simplest metaphors.

It was difficult sometimes to bear in mind that the struggle revolved around—really was for the sake of—such people. Fortunately, he was destined to struggle on a higher plane. The orders had reached them through a political officer shortly after their encounter with the Marine who had been watching them along the trail. They were to detach themselves from their combat command and link up with the chain of porters moving north. Destination: the Democratic Republic of Vietnam. Mission: unknown . . . but Comrade Emory felt sure he was about to become a very well-known revolutionary, as famous for his burning zeal to free the oppressed as his capitalist father was for exploiting them.

A slight breeze swept in from the north and slithered through the foliage covering the labyrinth of tunnels and bunkers that marked this wide spot in the trail as a major logistics and administrative terminal. Comrade Emory shoved his glasses up onto his forehead and pinched his own nose as the wind carried a pungent reminder that he was not the only one on this trek who suffered from an obvious impurity of spirit. Fighter Comrade Emory reflected that Fighter Comrade Theron Clay smelled like a ripe rice paddy just after it had been fertilized with human shit.

The stink seemed to pour off the man in tangible waves as he sat silently under a nearby tree, mouthing words he couldn't possibly understand, from the English language version of *Quotations from Chairman Mao Tse-tung.* Even the voracious mosquitoes that swarmed up from the rancid pools in the bottom of bomb craters could not penetrate Clay's feral cloak.

Everyone gave Comrade Clay a wide berth, staying upwind and out of his gaze whenever possible. His eyes, burning from a thick skull that swept from target to target like the turret of a marauding tank, served as a warning beacon. Clay was dangerous, deadly, burning with a livid hate that needed regular rekindling. While others talked about the revolution in terms of social change, Clay thought only about murder. Bloodred revenge was his version of righting social injustice. Others could play at taming The Beast. Comrade Clay wanted only to kill it.

Emory thought surely the worldwide revolutionary council would recognize Comrade Clay for the rogue elephant that he was and ship him off to Africa or some other dark place where people of his own kind were fighting to be free. He'd certainly recommend it. The last thing Comrade Emory needed, after all the artifice and sacrifice he went through to take an active part in the struggle, was to be associated with a murderous neanderthal when he was making a statement about the righteousness of the uprising in America. Still, there was no point in mentioning any of this to Clay.

"Hey, Theron . . . I heard they're gonna pick us up in trucks when we get up to the Mu Gia Pass. Be good to get out of the bush for a while, won't it?"

When he got no response, Emory pulled his glasses back on and turned toward Clay. "Hey . . . Theron . . ."

Clay's head slowly swiveled on his thick neck until his dark eyes were cutting two clean holes through Emory. His voice was deep and threatening like the distant rumble of thunder. "You want to talk to me, white boy, don't be callin' me by no mothahfuckin' slave name. I ain't gonna say it again. My name is Mustafa."

It was a good name. Full of grunts and pants . . . like the sound of Black Panthers in his old neighborhood as they practiced karate. Sometimes—like now with this honkie, whitebread motherfucker running off at the mouth—Mustafa wished he were back on the block near Boyle and Olive in St. Louis. Sometimes—when he let his mind wander away from the task at hand—he wondered how he came to be in this jungle fighting with these little yellow dudes against a white man's army that was mostly black.

At such times, Mustafa had flickering images of his mother, a slave to the white establishment all her life, working for coolie wages with no chance to ever get off the clean-up crew at the General Motors plant out on Kingshighway. She wanted him to get on the janitorial crew when she finally let the white teachers drum him out of high school. She wanted him to labor for the massa like she did and forget all that "jive-ass nonsense from them worthless niggers on the streets." That was what cut it. That's what kept him out of the plant and drove him into the ranks of the Black Muslim army. He believed the only worthless black men were those who refused to fight the white man for their dignity.

He was doing that, helping to organize an urban strike force over across the river in East St. Louis, when he turned eighteen. And then The Beast reached out his claws and snatched at him. They'd had it all worked out. Like Muhammad Ali, he was going to claim religious beliefs kept him from submitting to the draft for a white man's army. But Theron Clay was no kin to Cassius Clay and the cops made it clear that he would wind up doing hard time if he refused to report for induction. That's when the brother from Chicago came along and brought the instructions.

There was a cadre of black men—all revolutionary brothers—doing time in Vietnam under the guise of soldiers. The brother from Chi had called them "undercover agents of the revolution." The mission was to fuck up whitey's war machine from the inside and the movement was growing, but it needed a steady influx of dedicated replacements. So Mustafa cooperated and went along to Vietnam carrying a list of names and units. He'd been trying to make contact when that lifin' white motherfucker of a sergeant started in on him. Working in the motor pool grease pits, filling sandbags, burning shitters . . . slave labor designed to keep him strapped to the yoke of oppression. He'd stood it for a while—waiting for the right moment to strike—and then a brother from battalion supply had handed him a fragmentation grenade.

Whitey's army was minus one cracker sergeant but Mustafa was facing a court-martial. There was no proof but everyone knew who killed the NCO and the Army wasn't about to let it rest. Before they could complete the investigation, Mustafa slipped out of the perimeter and headed for a nearby ville where two AWOL brothers had a secret crib. The brothers hid Mustafa for a while, their Vietnamese girlfriends keeping the MPs off the track at first, but the heat was on and building.

When it got too intense, even the brothers turned their backs on Mustafa. A fugitive—a dude wanted for murder—was a threat to their dope operation. And there were too many smack-junkies; too

much money to be made for them to risk exposure. Confused—
so angry he couldn't think straight—Mustafa headed off into the
jungle with some vague notion of reaching a seacoast and finding
his way to Africa.

That's when he was captured by a patrol from the 24C North
Vietnamese Army Infantry Regiment. Mustafa was stripped of his
boots, fed a handful of rice, and shackled to a patrol with orders
to move him north as a prisoner of war. Fortunately, he was inter-
rogated by an English-speaking political officer near the border
of I and II Corps or the NVA B-5 and B-3 fronts. The way the
dude strutted and crowed reminded Mustafa of the Panther block
organizers he'd listened to back in St. Louis. Same revolutionary
rap, same preacher-in-a-pulpit delivery. Amen, brother. There it
is. Whether you're black or yellow, a yoke is a yoke. Mustafa
was digging it all the way.

When the brother asked him if he'd be willing to kill his
countrymen for the sake of the revolution, there was only one
answer. Right on, right on.

Mustafa was making a name for himself; kicking ass, scaring
the shit out of the honkies and the Oreos who fought for them.
And then one day they threw him in with jive-ass Emory. The
dude talked more revolutionary shit in five minutes than Mustafa
had heard in five months back on the block. Claimed his old man
was a fat cat exploiting the people back in the World. Mustafa
could dig that. What he couldn't dig was no rich, white motherfucker telling him he joined the Army and came to Vietnam to
help destroy the establishment and set up a new world order. You
don't shit in your own nest. Mustafa had seen too much of the old
world order to believe anything like that.

Emory was probably some kind of spy; a bogus ofay motherfucker. The little yellow brothers would spot that soon enough
and lock him away in a cage where The Beast belonged. If they
didn't, Mustafa would kill him.

At the tail end of the afternoon's hottest hours, Salt and Pepper
stood in the lengthening shadows along the edge of the trail. The
wounded and dying were as comfortable as possible in hospital
bunkers far underground. Those able-bodied enough to continue
the trek north stood in quiet clutches waiting for the order to
move..The sector commander, responsible for operations along
this stretch of the Ho Chi Minh Trail, screamed loudly at a unit
of sappers who were having trouble loading their tools securely
in a spindly cart towed by a muddy water buffalo.

Everyone understood they would have to wait for the sappers. Without their engineering skills, no underway repairs could be made to the road following the inevitable American bombing raids. Still, the sector commander was nervous and angry about the delay. It was very dangerous to have all these soldiers, porters, and valuable equipment assembled in the open for too long. Movement, dispersal, and concealment were the keys to survival along the great trail. One never knew when a marauding eagle would dive out of the sun.

The thought made the sector commander glance up through the foliage at the clear sky. Was that a shadow across the sun? Or was the wind stirring the branches? There was a sighing sound somewhere above the branches like the onset of a monsoon rain. But it was too early for the monsoon . . .

The first five-hundred-pound bomb detonated with a jarring blast south of the muster point. The ground rocked beneath his feet and Salt understood immediately what was happening. Arc Light . . . a B-52 raid! The Vietnamese were flooding past him, heading for the area last hit by a bomb. It was SOP along the trail. Bombs fell in long sticks. If no cover was immediately available, safety lay in running out of the impact zone, toward the rear of the marching line of explosions.

But the fighters headed in that direction were being shredded by shrapnel and beaten into the ground by horrendous concussion. Salt ran after Pepper, headed for the bunkers spotted throughout the jungle, but their path was blocked by more explosions. Trees were falling, crushing people like grapes or impaling them on sharp limbs. All around them, the jungle had become a boiling caldron of heat, flame, shrapnel, and broken bodies flung through the air like rag dolls. Pepper stood in the middle of it, his dark skin covered with a pale patina of dust and cordite. He was screaming at the sky but Salt's ears were clogged with thick blood and he could hear nothing. A silent shock wave punched him in the back and he vomited. He tasted blood as he fell to his knees, gagging and gasping for breath.

Pepper was slammed in the chest by the bloody head of the sector commander. The impact knocked him staggering backward and he tripped over Salt's prostrate form. Sizzling shrapnel rattled off the charred tree stumps. Nothing vertical was left standing and still the bombs fell in a tightly woven carpet of death. Bodies lay everywhere, limbs and skeletons contorted into grotesque postures by the battering ram of continuous concussion.

Driven into the decaying floor of the jungle by the incessant pounding, riddled with slivers of steel, swollen and bleeding from shock and blast, Salt and Pepper watched the black bomb blossoms chewing and churning toward them. They tried desperately but could not move so much as a finger. They were doomed, pinned, petrified.

And then the ground below them yawned widely. They fell, tumbling and turning toward the bowels of the earth.

NEW YORK

Cleveland Herbert Emory, Senior, ignored the jackhammer pounding behind his eyeballs and slowly strode to a position behind the podium bearing the Emory Technology corporate seal. He'd drunk an overlarge quantity of whiskey last night and been rewarded this morning with the puffy eyes and haggard look he wanted but the hangover was a killer. He poured a large draft of cold water from the pitcher on the podium and reassured himself—as he'd done during a long night of soul-searching— that the gain was worth the pain.

An untidy clutch of microphones arrayed before him picked up the rustle of the papers he pulled from his pocket and sent a sound like the rattle of dry leaves in a cold wind through the speakers mounted around the room. He closed his bloodshot eyes against the sudden glare as TV cameramen fired up their lights but there was time for a quick scan of the reporters in the front row. As promised by his PR staff, the network and national newspaper heavyweights had been lured onto a beat that was normally covered by their financial or business specialists.

The story would get the major play it deserved and Emory Technology—even in this grotesque period of venomous anti-establishment rhetoric—would be seen as a company with a heart; a company whose chief executive officer, like so many thousands of other parents across the nation, had lost his son in pursuit of an American goal. And when the war was over—when the breakneck impetus of necessity was gone and some semblance of sanity returned to the military-industrial marriage—such goodwill, such sacrifice, would be remembered. He cleared his throat and began.

"Ladies and gentlemen, I've asked you here to share a very personal—and very tragic—time in my life. The telegram I have before me arrived yesterday. It's from the President and it informs me that my only son—Private First Class Cleveland Herbert Emory, Junior, United States Army—has been killed in action in Vietnam . . ."

As a hush fell over the room, Cleve Emory pinched the bridge of his nose as if to get a grip on his emotions, to stem an impending flood of tears. He was rewarded with the stutter and whine of motor-driven cameras. Only agony or ecstasy made headlines. Everything else was wasted.

"As a businessman, I'm unused to public airing of personal problems or tragedies. The business of business is business . . . and nowhere in the world is that more true than in this great nation of ours. Mixing business affairs with personal affairs is a recipe for disaster in most cases.

"Yet I feel compelled—at this moment of intense personal grief—to make my thoughts and feelings known to everyone in America. I feel compelled to let those other fathers and mothers across the land who have lost sons in defense of our nation know that I am one with them. No matter what position, privilege, or power I may have . . . no matter how much money I may have or what material possessions separate my situation from that of the poorest in this land . . . as I stand before you today with this telegram in my hand . . . I am one with them. And I feel their pain as I feel the agony of our President who is trying to bring this tragic war in Vietnam to an end.

"I am taking this unusual step because there is something important demonstrated in my son's death and I want to insure that message is clear. There are those on the streets . . . on college campuses across the land . . . yes, even in the highest levels of government and industry who deplore the war in Vietnam as a travesty of American ideals being fought by the poor, the uneducated, and the underprivileged. I am here to tell you that my beloved son Cleve was none of those things. Yet, he enlisted—as a buck private—ignoring all the privilege and position that could have been his . . . and volunteered to go to Vietnam. He phoned me before he left for Southeast Asia just to insure I understood why he was going.

" 'Dad,' he told me in the very last conversation I had with him, 'I'm going to Vietnam because I think it's my duty. The war might be right or it might be wrong, but that's not the point anymore.' My son told me he believed the real issue was repaying a debt to the country that had given him so much. He said he could no longer stand by and see young Americans his age go to Vietnam—to fight and possibly to die—while he stayed at home. In his mind that was neither fair nor honorable . . . and my son was an honorable man.

"I wanted to share his thoughts with you—now that he's no longer able to voice them—and I wanted to appeal to you to convey a message to the American people: as long as we continue to raise and nurture young men and women like Cleve—like the silent majority of our sons and daughters—this great nation will survive and prosper. No war, no pestilence, no fracturing of our social and moral structures, will ever destroy America."

Cleveland Emory dropped his eyes, took a deep breath, and felt the presence of the uniformed military officer at his shoulder . . . right on cue. A brigadier general flown in from the Military District of Washington stood ready to deliver the ancient symbols of a warrior's destiny.

"Mr. Emory, you have the deepest sympathies and most sincere condolences of the Commander in Chief and of the entire United States Army." There was a muted rumble as still photographers scrambled for position. Cleve Emory kept his eyes downcast until silence returned and then faced the general with grim reluctance. He accepted the Purple Heart in its blue velvet box and then held both arms out for the flag folded into a tight triangle of star-spangled blue. Nodding to acknowledge the officer's rigid salute, he slowly turned, the Purple Heart perched on the folded flag, and faced the blinking barrage of strobe lights. It was a triumphant moment, but Cleve Emory forced his face into a solid mask of grief and remorse.

An aide from his PR staff finally retrieved the articles and placed them on a long, low table for public display. With a silent nod, the aide signaled to the dean of the assembled reporters that his boss was now capable of fielding a few discreet questions.

"Mr. Emory, Pentagon records had your son listed as Missing In Action. Was his death somehow related to that status?"

Cleve took another deep drink of water and cleared his throat. "I was notified about three months ago that Cleve had not returned from a patrol and was listed as missing. Since then, the Army has informed me that the patrol—or what was left of it—has been found. No one survived."

Another reporter stood at the rear of the room. "Did this patrol have anything to do with the recent incursion into Cambodia?"

Cleve shot a glance at the brigadier general and got a discreet but clearly perceptible nod. "I'm told this is no longer classified information, so I guess I can reveal that Cleve volunteered to go with a very dangerous reconnaissance mission across the Cambodian border to spot enemy sanctuaries for the follow-on border crossing operations. All this had to be kept very secret naturally and that is the reason Cleve was officially listed as missing when his patrol was ambushed."

The same reporter remained on his feet and outshouted his competitors. "How do you feel about your son risking and then losing his life in a country that's nominally neutral?"

Setting his jaw and jabbing a finger at the reporter, Cleve put some venom into his voice. "I'll tell you, mister . . . I'll tell all of you . . . that I feel about that just the way Cleve must have felt—the way all of our soldiers must feel when the enemy escapes to safety across a border after attacking and killing Americans . . . I feel damn glad the President had the guts to take their sanctuary away for once. I feel damn proud my boy was the bearer of the kind of message we ought to be sending to all enemies of democracy: you can run but you can't hide!"

There was a smattering of applause from the senior staff members of Emory Technology but the reporters just blinked and scribbled in the face of Cleve's tirade. He took a deep breath and painted on a pained smile for the grey-haired female reporter who rose for the next question.

"Mr. Emory, will there be formal services for your son? And where will he be buried?"

"Ma'am, you're taking part in the only services there will be for my son. You have to understand . . . he was killed in very violent combat . . . and the . . . his . . . body laid out there in the jungle for quite some time before it . . . before what was left of it . . . was recovered. I have seen his remains and . . . well, I don't want him remembered that way. He'll be buried without funeral in our family plot on Long Island . . . next to his mother."

A senior vice president for corporate public relations moved to end the question period. Cleve started away from the podium when a lanky specter in granny glasses unfolded from a chair in a far corner of the room and barked out a final question. "Mr. Emory . . . doesn't it all seem a bit ironic, sir? Here we are in the headquarters of a corporation that makes an enormous profit in war-related industries . . . discussing the death of your son who was killed in the war your company is supporting?"

There was a loud collective groan and a few muttered curses from some of the reporters but Cleve Emory silenced them all with a wave of his hand. He returned to the microphones and chewed on his lip for a moment, holding his head to one side and then the other, as if pondering the fate of his ill-mannered inquisitor.

"It's pretty easy to see which side of the fence you're on so I won't look for an accurate quote, but let me tell you something for the record. Emory Technology does not advocate war or wish to profit from death in any way, shape, or form. Emory Technology advocates only America and its rightful position as the leading democratic industrial power in the world today. Any and all things we can do to insure that, we tackle with vigor. Now, sometimes you have to fight for what you believe in, for what's right, and Emory Technology is not about to back away from that fight. Not Emory Technology, not Cleveland Emory, Senior . . . and not— God bless him—Cleveland Herbert Emory, Junior—who lost his life doing what was right!"

The growing crescendo of applause in the room gave Cleve a second wind and he was about to give the assembled reporters a few more pieces of his mind when an aide approached and whispered in his ear. The press would have to do what they would with what they had. The President was on the phone wanting to express his personal sympathy and gratitude for Cleve Emory's brave stand in backing America.

AN HOA

Pulling his black eyes reluctantly away from the lime-green snake that slithered out of a cut bamboo section near his hide, the Nung warrior glanced down the jungle hillside and into the Marine base camp that sprawled across one end of the An Hoa basin. Heat waves shimmered from the sticky asphalt of the helicopter landing pad making visibility difficult. Even with his razor-sharp vision it was hard to distinguish detail, yet he was sure the bamboo viper was a sign. His target would appear and he could finally strike after three long days of waiting.

He heard the whine of turbines and the flatulence of steel-stiffened helicopter blades as they chopped into the humid air.

A pair of fine American binoculars quickly picked out the one helicopter in five parked below his perch that was coming to life. Three Marines stepped out of a droopy tent nearby and began to walk toward the aircraft. As he'd done so many times during his long vigil, the Nung pulled a laminated picture out of his uniform pocket and dropped his eyes to the smiling face of his target.

Another glance through the binoculars . . . yes, the tall captain at the rear. The snake was a good sign; reliable as were all such signs in the jungle once you learned to read them.

When the Marines boarded the helicopter and the turbine noise grew to a scream, he rolled over on his back and slid a high-explosive warhead into the B-40 rocket launcher. He'd fitted the weapon's sights with a handmade bamboo extension that allowed him to accurately lead moving targets. He would probably not need the special sight but it was his way to be thoroughly prepared. Study of flight patterns at An Hoa over the past three days had led him to this firing position. The helicopter carrying the Marine Reconnaissance Company commander would pass less than fifty feet over his head. And when his rocket pierced the metal skin of it—like an arrow through the heart of a tiger—there would be another sun in the sky. And he would be rich; richer than any man in his tribe had ever been.

Rising to his knees, the Nung warrior steadied the RPG launcher and watched the helicopter fill his sights like a huge dragonfly. When the nose touched the second spike of his sight extension he pressed the trigger and felt the slight jolt as the rocket roared away, burning brightly through the blue sky. Shock waves from a huge fireball forced him to the ground briefly but he was up and running south before all the flaming debris fell into the jungle.

It would be a week—maybe two—before he could reach Saigon but he was very patient. And the MACV colonel was bound to be very generous.

DANANG

Sergeant Spike Benjamin pushed the proffered pack of Stateside Marlboros back across the desk and waved a hand at the clerk who was typing his rotation orders. "I'm too short to be smoking filter tips, man. I'll just look around for someone who's got about half a Camel."

The clerk cracked open a bottle of correction fluid and glanced up at the tall Marine NCO who wore the same lopsided grin whether he was facing a flustered private or a bellicose brigadier general. The guy didn't seem to take anything short of an AK round between the running lights as much to worry about.

"You ISO guys got more shit than a Christmas turkey. The Freedom Bird don't leave for another twenty-four hours and you ain't gonna be on it unless I finish typing these orders."

Benjamin leaned across the rickety field desk and growled. "That's *hours,* man! It ain't days and it ain't weeks and it ain't years. That's twice around the clock and I'm back on the block!"

The clerk lit one of his own smokes and pointed at a crude sign hanging over his desk. DILLIGAF. Do I Look Like I Give A Fuck?

"Is that any way to act, man? Huh? Ain't I the guy who wrote the story about you defending the headquarters perimeter when that rocket blew away the officers' shitter? Ain't I the guy who gave you copies of the flicks to send back to the World?"

Turning back to his typewriter, the clerk began to pound on the keys. Guys like Benjamin kept everyone from going bat-shit. He deserved a huss. "Come back in an hour. I'll have your orders ready and you can start checking out of this shit-hole."

Benjamin pointed his finger and aimed down his thumb. "I'll hold you to that, man. If you need me, I'll be down at the Photo Lab policing up my gear."

Before he could clear the Headquarters Battalion S-1 hooch, Benjamin was halted by a shout from another of the harried clerks. "How short are you *really,* Sergeant Benjamin?"

"I am *so short* . . . when I got up out of the rack this morning, I free-fell for five minutes before I hit the deck!"

At the Division Photo Lab on Hill 327, where the regular Marine photographers loaned a kindred spirit from the Informational Services Office a locker, Benjamin dialed his combination and removed three precious photo albums. Two of them contained examples of his work as a photojournalist at war. Frontline combat stuff. Plenty of action and agony. With luck—and some help from the civilian media vets now working back in the World—they might constitute an acceptable resume and get him a good job.

The third album was thicker than the others. It was private; so personal that Benjamin doubted he could ever bring himself to show it to another human being. The album was a diary of sorts; the sole repository of his pain, anger, frustration, and despair. Between the cheap cardboard covers were happy snaps and action photos taken during two consecutive tours in Vietnam; black-and-white images of Americans and Vietnamese at war. He'd spent long hours poring through thousands of negatives, looking for the ones that could never be released because shortly after Sergeant Benjamin shot those photographs, someone else shot the subjects . . . and killed them.

To keep himself from becoming one of those ghostly images in the third album, Benjamin understood he'd have to cement the facade that carried him through Vietnam. He'd have to live his life in another time, another place. Jerk out all the film and hold it up to the sunlight. Erase Vietnam and get on with it.

Still, if all else failed, he had an ace in the hole. Benjamin slipped a thumbnail beneath the binding of the album cover and removed a single opaque negative jacket. He moved to a dirty window and held the 35mm negative up to the pale yellow light. Salt and Pepper were tiny specks on the emulsion but they could grow to epic proportions in an enlarger.

If he blew it back in the World, if he desperately needed juice, he could always sell the only remaining picture outside the Pentagon's top secret vaults of two American turncoats fighting with the enemy in Vietnam. It would be a dirty trick to play on the people in his third album but combat had taught Sergeant Benjamin that the only real trick is to survive.

MU GIA PASS, SRV

The female doctor with the twisted teeth told Salt he had been unconscious for seven days. She said it would likely be another four or five weeks before he could be moved to a better hospital. That was all he could comprehend before the pain shorted out his circuits and he slipped back into a troubled sleep during which he screamed loudly about being crushed by huge boulders that fell from the sky.

Another time when he passed briefly through a period of consciousness the doctor told him that Fighter Comrade Mustafa Clay was badly injured but expected to recover some—if not all—of his faculties. During this same period, confused and robbed of sleep by a body that was painfully mending, Salt was visited by a senior PAVN officer who pinned a small enamel bust of Uncle Ho to the bloody bandages covering his chest.

The unusual ferocity of the bombing had caved in one of the deep tunnels alongside the trail, he said, and that stroke of fortune had saved Salt's and Pepper's lives. The sapper unit sent into the area two days after the bombing had been digging for precious medical supplies when they ran across the two American volunteers. Within the one-thousand-square-meter area covered by American bombs, the officer indicated with clinical appreciation for such military efficiency, not one other living thing had survived.

When Pepper finally regained consciousness nearly a full week later, the officer returned with word that the American volunteers were to be moved—as soon as they were able to travel—to a rest area near the Chinese border. Facilities existed there to see them through what was expected to be a long and difficult period of recovery and readjustment.

PART TWO

LINE

CHICAGO, ILLINOIS—1972

Not much new and different on the crowded shelves at F. W. Woolworth's. Same back-to-classes bullshit his mother bought when he was gearing up for another elementary school ordeal. Different endorsements. Willy Pud remembered his Red Ryder lunchbox and Lone Ranger pencil case with built-in sharpener in a twinge of unusual nostalgia for those restless days. His dime-store heroes had disappeared like so many other touchstones of his pre-Vietnam life. Chicago's current crop of crumb-snatchers would rather enjoy a leisurely lunch with Fred Flintstone or George Jetson. Color cartoons; cavemen or spacemen. Apparently anything in between was too crude for consideration.

Willy strolled down the teeming aisles, focusing his attention on the more adult brand of school supplies. Spiral notebooks, three-ring binders, sophisticated pen and pencil sets; the sort of stuff that should have been—but never was—stuffed in his gym bag as he caromed through high school with a basketball under one arm and a football under the other. Who gave a fuck about formal education back then? Who was going to know diplomas and degrees would mean doodley-squat in a world of fixed measures and preordained neighborhood destinies? You got money? You go to college and make a living with your head. You don't? You go to work and make a living with your hands. End of message; break transmission.

Funny how things got screwed around; out of familiar shape while you did penance in the Marine Corps monastery. Red Ryder and Little Beaver disappear into the sunset; Ralph and Alice Kramden in grainy black and white become Fred and Wilma Flintstone in living color. And everything seems to glow, to throb with pulsating pastels in distorted shapes.

He'd spent an aimless morning at a westside neighborhood newsstand searching for comic books only to discover that Sergeant Rock and the Combat Happy Joes of Easy Company had been wiped out by the Fabulous Furry Freak Brothers. Unsure of the in-thing among freshman students at Chicago City College, Willy Pud selected a plain grey binder, some ruled paper, and a bargain pack of steno notebooks. He still had a full box of government-issue black ballpoint pens souvenired from the Admin supply locker at his last duty station.

A long line of shuffling, coughing customers waited for a teenage technologist to get the hang of her new electronic cash register. Willy fell quietly, comfortably into the queue. Sometimes this civilian world seemed to have so much in common with the military. So much time spent standing in lines. But it wasn't the same in Chicago as it had been at Camp Pendleton waiting for a discharge date. There were no NCOs at Woolworths or the Kroger Supermarket telling people to put out their smokes, knock off the grab-ass, and get a haircut. This was an undisciplined, route-step world of people who wore strange uniforms and frequently got their stool samples mixed up with their shoe polish.

Somebody is several tent pegs short of a field transport pack, Willy Pud mused as he paid for his purchases with money from his first GI Bill check. *It's either them or me. Either I have learned to tell shit from Shinola, or they have. That's one of the things I'm going to school to find out.*

A meandering path toward his el stop led Willy Pud past the clothing store where half his discharge mileage allowance was invested in what he'd been told was the absolute basic issue for a civilian's seabag. He paused for reassurance that his new uniform of the day matched the display in a polished plate-glass window. Roger that . . . but Willy felt uncomfortable, false, nearly naked in a bright paisley patterned shirt with loose, floppy sleeves and crotch-constricting bell-bottom trousers. No matter how many people passed by wearing variations on the same theme, Willy couldn't help thinking he looked like a sailor bound for a hell-raising rip through Waikiki.

And the haircut—obtained automatically at the PX barbershop the day before his discharge—was a dead giveaway. Long hair, sideburns, and droopy mustaches: right on. Visible scalp or ears: right off the stage with the rest of the service trash and other remnants of the Dark Ages before the dawning of the Age of Aquarius. Willy Pud smiled at the unfamiliar image and made a mental note to stop shaving from the top of one ear to the top of the other. Maybe he could cultivate a mask and wear a hat until his hair grew to regulation length. Whatever it took to ease his injection into the student body.

Low SAT scores left Willy Pud little room for maneuvering through the schedule of classes his first year at CCC. There

was bonehead Math and bonehead English, set at a pace below
the normal freshman level for students who vaulted out of high
school and into college over the low hurdles of diminished aca-
demic standards. His bonehead English class was salted with a
few other obvious veterans—quiet men who either attacked the
course material like an enemy bunker complex or sat staring at
the blackboard with watery eyes, looking at words but seeing
something else. For them, tense had no relation to verbs.

There was an elective Business Administration course that left
Willy adrift in a sea of unfamiliar terms and confused about "management theories for today's increasingly sensitive work force."
He'd drawn a C for the course as well as a firm conviction that
the average Marine three-striper with six months time-in-grade
could solve just about any management problem facing American
industry in a hot second or less.

Even after his hair grew long enough to hide his former occupation from the campus activists who condemned it, Willy Pud
found it hard to relax. He was much older than most students—
older by a couple of years than some of the teachers. There was
a rugged, world-weary stigma in the lines around his mouth
and eyes that made him feel like apologizing as he took up
space in lines waiting to register for classes or pay for a parking
permit.

When sleet appeared in the chilly winds that blew off Lake
Michigan and swept through the city streets, he broke out his
faded and worn Marine field jacket. Everyone else on campus
seemed to be wearing one that year, either dug out of a family
footlocker or purchased for a few bucks at surplus stores bursting
with military gear discarded by waves of returning vets anxious
for total divestment. Only the clique of campus veterans who
staked claim to a corner table in the crowded Student Union
recognized his jacket as the genuine article. Only they recognized
the odd stencil across the shoulders as the designation of his unit
in 'Nam.

That led to coffee and probing conversations that gave way
in a day or two to beer and bullshit with guys who thought
service in the war gave them all a common denominator. Willy drank, smiled, and listened while they found out otherwise.
There was no common thread; no single, sentient experience
that created instant empathy. Some were drafted; others joined
the service. There were guys who served in support outfits and
spent off-duty hours chasing whores in Saigon. There were sailors
from the Brown Water Navy in the Mekong Delta who thought

Vietnam was like Holland or Venice. There were guys from three different artillery outfits who couldn't believe the other storytellers were even in Vietnam because of the differences in terrain and enemy activity between II Corps and III Corps. There were two men who had fought with the same brigade of the same infantry division who couldn't relate because the war had changed radically between 1966 and 1970. There were Air Force guys who whined about "working overtime" to keep jets flying from Tan Son Nhut and constant commodity shortages at the PX. There was a confused Marine who had exactly forty-six days in-country when an NVA sniper sent him home with two new navels. From his limited perspective up in I Corps on the NVA-infested DMZ, the Marine figured anyone who faced only ragtag Viet Cong guerrillas never really fought a war at all. Everybody had the hardest time in Vietnam, and nobody who wasn't there in exactly the same place, at exactly the same time, in exactly the same company, platoon and squad facing the same unit of hard-core motherfuckin' gooks, could really understand how bad it had been.

Yet there was a common passion in these gatherings. Dead, dry eyes came alive with liquid fire. Anger burned; hostility seethed just below the surface. Sometimes the beer gave rise to bursts of fiery frustration and the vets crossed the lunatic fringe like a berserk patrol in a Free Fire Zone. The daily jolt of TV news with pictures of disgruntled troops heading home en masse evoked images of cockroaches scrabbling out of the structure they had invested so heavily in building. How could such a seminal experience in their lives turn to instant shit? Peace with honor simply pissed them off.

Willy Pud drifted out of the circle when one of the guys who had done his twelve months as an MP at Vung Tau demanded he join something called Vietnam Veterans Against the War. "I ain't against the war," Willy Pud told the organizer. "Can't say I'm too pleased about the way we been fighting it and I sure as fuck don't think we ought to be pullin' out after all the effort we put into it . . . but I ain't gonna stand up and call myself a jack-off because I went to Vietnam instead of Canada."

"Look, man . . . guy like you . . . Medal of Honor and all . . ."

"Who told you about that?"

"Word gets around, man . . . you could really do some good for the cause . . ."

"Like them other jerks? Throwin' their medals over the wall at the White House?"

"Whatever, man . . . we got to get it together if the shit's gonna stop. We been there, right? People will listen if we tell 'em it's all bullshit."

"It ain't all bullshit! It was the highest time in my life. I go sayin' anything different and I'm a hypocrite."

"You go sayin' you dug the fuckin' war and people gonna think you're a lunatic!"

"Not the people who know the score won't . . . and it don't sound to me like many of them are gonna throw in with your outfit."

"Pudarski, man . . . you seen some shit. You can't believe what we did over there is right. You can't believe all the dudes who got wasted died for a righteous cause!"

"What I can't believe is somebody died and left me in charge of rights and wrongs. I went where they asked me to go and I did what needed to be done. You want me to be ashamed of that, you can kiss my shrapnel-scarred ass!"

Stosh Pudarski heard about the exchange on BBQ Rib night down at Hogan's Bar. As usual, the old man cut to the nut of the issue before Hogan could pull the first refill. "Good thing you told them jerks to fuck off, Vilhelm. Hang around with assholes and you're bound to get shit on."

Willy tried for a while to make friends with younger students. He met them for coffee or beer at the Student Union or one of the college hangouts, but most forays into idle conversation ended in ambush. For a while, he skirted the issue of his background—even lied once or twice, making up a story about deciding to return to school after spending years in factory work—but that seemed a cowardly thing to do, disloyal, dishonest. Willy Pud found himself suffering from sudden sweats and unexplained bumps on his lying tongue.

He told the truth and the symptoms disappeared. So did most of the young students he sought as companions. Those who stayed had varying reactions when they discovered he'd spent six years in the military and three years fighting in Vietnam. Sometimes he encountered the painful angst of kids who wanted everyone to join hands across the continents and chant a secret mantra for peace. Other times he was sniped at by rear-echelon revolutionaries who empathized with the downtrodden masses struggling to be free. Some students launched sneak attacks, expressing an avid interest in his military experiences, inevitably leading up to that all-consuming question: What's it like to *kill* another human being?

Thoroughly disgusted—full of Rolling Rock beer and peppermint schnapps one maudlin night during Happy Hour at a local
hangout—Willy Pud committed social suicide. Fending off the
Big Question until he had two or three tables full of ardent
listeners, he stood, glaring around at the wisdom-seekers like a
guru burning with inner truth.

"The only thing I feel when I kill," Willy Pud said in a straight,
strong voice, "is recoil . . . and a slight pressure on my trigger
finger."

After that, he took to hanging around with Stosh and his
pals down at Hogan's Bar where the framed picture of him in
dress blues wearing the Medal of Honor obviated most political
discussions within earshot of his bar stool.

The black-and-white world in which he'd established a cold
yet comfortable value system was greying at an alarming rate.
Instincts honed in the bush—*fade left here, hard right there, feel
for the tripwire*—were deserting him. Confronted on all flanks by
unfamiliar terrain, robbed of the signals and standards that kept his
compass on a true bearing, Willy Pud did what most infantrymen
do in similar situations. He slowed to a shuffling route-step, then
dropped his pack, sat down, and waited for word.

At the end of his first year in college he was a straight C
student: anonymous, middle of the road, across the board.

Willy Pud spent the summer of '73 helping his father and Frank
Hovitz make custom cabinets for a renovated brownstone on the
westside. He did rough assembly of the raw wood, leaving the
detail work and installation to Frank and his dad who worked
like two pistons in the same well-oiled engine. Planing the soft
pine; feeling long slivers of wood curl over his fingers like warm,
salty water had a soothing effect on him. He could lose himself in
the emerging grain, focus right down there where the fine brown
lines flowed through the blond surface, and barely hear the two
old carpenters arguing baseball or planning a fishing trip.

Using a fine, rat-tail file to smooth a corner joint, he thought
about the hardback hooch he'd built with his squad during a
stand-down at Camp Evans shortly after Tet '68. Navy Seabees
and Marine Engineers were busy all over I Corps repairing battle
damage and clearing ordnance, trying to get the military machine
back in gear while the moguls at MACV argued with the press
over who won and who lost. There was plenty of available building material, but no time to erect hooches for grunts who probably
wouldn't get to use them much anyway.

Willy was on light-duty, recovering from a wound, when his unit packed up and moved to Camp Evans. He found himself standing in the middle of a dusty compound full of rotting canvas tents and bursting sandbags. The previous residents had been unstuck and sent to Khe Sanh in a big hurry. The situation during Tet didn't allow for caretakers to watch the compound and the ARVN in the area had made off with virtually everything they could carry or disassemble. Willy could have ordered his people to clean out a couple of bunkers, refill sandbags, and let it ride until the next big operation, but that would have given him time—too much time—to think about what he'd seen during Tet. He needed a productive diversion, something to show he could create as well as destroy.

And so, "Pudarski's Palace" began to rise from the flat, sandy earth of Camp Evans, dwarfing the other slap-dash structures inside the compound and drawing sidewalk supervisors from the regimental commander to Marvin the ARVN. They gawked at the sweaty grunts, marveled at the animals taking such pains with building their own pen, and shouted instructions for this or that beautifying touch.

For two delicious, diverting weeks Willy Pud called to mind every carpentry trick or technique his father had ever taught him or even mentioned in passing. Willy's squad worked like demons and loved each other for every clumsy, comical mistake. The war, thoughts of home, discomfort, frustration, petty irritants, were all lost in the ring of hammer on nail and the snarl of saw through plywood. If only they could keep working, everything would be OK; no one would cry or hurt or suffer or die.

When it was finished, everyone agreed "Pudarski's Palace" was a genuine wonder. It featured a fireplace, loft, railed balcony, and a walled-off cubicle for each resident, slash wire for field phones, and a tacked-on shower stall made from a fifty-five gallon fuel drum among the amenities.

It was also much too good for a simple squad of Marine grunts. Willy's company was in the field for two weeks chasing a gook rocket artillery unit that they never found. When they got back to Camp Evans, staff officers had taken over Pudarski's Palace and turned it into the Regimental CP.

Willy Pud was too tired to bitch very loudly or treat the shock into which his men slumped when they saw they'd been evicted. That night, the Regimental Sergeant Major came by the squalid bunker that served as their new home and delivered two cases of iced beer with the colonel's compliments and his apologies. Willy and his men got wobbly drunk and forgot about Pudarski's Palace. It was the construction that counted, not the building. And they could remember those good times no matter how deep the shit got elsewhere.

Through the sweltering days in the dusty kitchen of the brownstone, Willy used the snick of a light finishing hammer on fine nailheads to set a comfortable rhythm for himself. Concentrating on perfect spacing, countersinking the nails, doing a craftsman's job for a workman's wage, made him feel worthy; allowed him to ignore the bombast and rhetoric over the worsening situation in Southeast Asia that swirled through the nation.

On his way to or from work, the radio in his father's old GMC truck told him horror stories. Nixon and Kissinger ate a brace of Le Duc Tho's crow and signed a peace pact that clearly marked the gooks as winners. He didn't need a dictionary to understand "honorable settlement" meant his country had finally got its ass kicked. The President—the very same man who promised peace with honor—had thrown in the towel and ordered a halt of all U.S. offensive action in Vietnam. There was no more MACV, only a few burned-out advisers scattered throughout the country, trying to convince the ARVN to keep a stiff dick while their Ship of State sank like a rock and the Americans went over the side in droves. On TV, Walter Cronkite said there would be no more than fifty American military people left in Vietnam by Christmas. He was gloating when he broke the story but sobered up to announce 46,163 U.S. KIA to date. Willy Pud unplugged the television set and shoved it into a closet. He kept the truck radio tuned to an FM rock station that did not break for news, but none of that kept him from feeling very empty inside.

He spent most of the muggy summer nights getting fried at Hogan's corner bar, which featured a comfortable foot rail, plenty of elbow room, windows frosted against the outside world, and lots of kitschy neon signs that worked on his beer-burdened brain like a lava lamp. Willy found solace here. There was solitude when he wanted it and enough respect when he didn't want it to insure none of the regulars would run off at the mouth about Vietnam.

He usually sat along the short leg of Hogan's L-shaped bar with his father and Frank Hovitz on either side until they commandeered a back booth to play penny-a-point cribbage or went home to bed. Drunk or sober, he stayed late; sometimes competing with himself at barroom shuffleboard, sometimes simply staring at the image in Hogan's stained, faded excuse for a mirror.

Sometimes—when all the other customers had cleared out and Hogan was busy refilling the coolers—he stared so hard at his own eyes that the pupils would gape and dilate and he'd be looking down the muzzle of a double-barreled shotgun. And that's when he'd see the ghostly images playing peekaboo over his hunched shoulders.

Salt and Pepper. Gloating, grinning, haunting, proud, and sassy over abandoning a loser and backing a winner. They got away with it after all. And the well-kept secret of two American turn-coats would damn sure get out if the NVA had the sense to put them in the vanguard of the inevitable victory parade. Willy Pud shivered and swallowed cold beer but the fire in his belly would not bank. So, the President with the stinking feet was a liar . . . and a crook to boot if you bought all that Watergate shit.

"Stosh says you got a future as a wood-butcher." Hogan spun a cold beer bottle down the bar and touched a kitchen match to a fresh cigar. "You gonna work with him from now on or go on back to school?"

Willy shrugged and shook his head. "Who the fuck knows, Hogan? Seems like before I left they said you couldn't do shit without a high school diploma. Now they say you're fucked if you don't go to college."

Hogan poured himself a shot of rye whiskey and set it on the bar next to Willy's bottle. "We done that to you kids, you know? Always pushin' the education bit . . . mostly because we never had much and wound up bustin' our asses to make ends meet. Now I get a chance to think about it . . . who says that ain't the way it's meant to be? Know what I mean, Willy? Where's it say every fuckin' kid grows up in this country has to be a high-paid executive sittin' on his ass in the air-conditioning? Seems like the only ones makin' shit with their hands anymore are the goddamn hippies."

"Ain't it a bitch, Hogan? Everybody wants to be an officer. But you don't need fuckin' officers if you ain't got troops for 'em to lead."

Hogan chuckled and shook his head. "They might have given you a discharge, Willy, but you're still in the fuckin' Marines. So, you goin' back to school or what?"

Late customers on the way home from a Cubs doubleheader distracted Hogan and kept Willy Pud from having to answer. Should he give it another shot? He liked books, or most of what he found in them. There was so much he hadn't realized about the worlds he traversed as a Marine. So many feelings and observations he'd like to understand. In school, in classes he chose, he was constantly running across revelations in human thought, behavior, and motivation. Every few days, he'd look up from something he was reading and the world around him would appear a little clearer, a little more understandable. Things he'd seen and things he'd done or seen others do suddenly began to make sense in a way that superseded the standard yardstick of right and wrong. His frame of reference was expanding rapidly.

That's one hell of a good reason to stay in school, he decided. Another good reason walked in the door just as Hogan was announcing last call for alcohol.

She perched on a corner stool, dropped an armload of books on the bar, and ordered vodka. Willy watched while Hogan checked her ID and then served the drink. Tough to pick out detail in the soft neon light, but her profile glowed over a long, straight nose and high cheekbones. When she winced at the first bite of liquor on her tongue, Willy saw fine lines—like tiny arrows in a quiver—at the corners of black velvet eyes.

Collecting change from the bar, she slid off her stool and headed for the cigarette machine in the corner. The journey there and back gave Willy ample time to admire a pair of long, muscular legs that rippled and flowed beneath the hem of a leather mini-skirt. She stared straight back at him as she returned to her drink. There was the hint of a smile, but Willy dropped his gaze back into the foamy head of his beer. A flash of heat crawled up his neck and onto his cheeks. It was embarrassing to suddenly realize that he didn't have the first clue about how to begin maneuvering on an objective like this one.

She fumbled around in a huge suede saddlebag of a purse looking for a match. Willy saw Hogan start to move and waved him off, reaching for his own battered Zippo. Flipping a hank of long, straight hair over her shoulder to avoid the flame, she accepted the light and squinted up at him.

"Thanks. They used to give you matches in those machines . . ."

Willy craned over the bar and reached around to find the box of advertising book matches Hogan kept back there.

"Owner likes to hand these out to people he wants to come back."

"That probably doesn't include me."

She stared directly into Willy's eyes and he noted the little arrow lines also appeared at the corners of her mouth when she smiled. He stretched for his beer and cigarettes and pulled them closer. It seemed like the right move.

"Yeah? What makes you think that?"

"He didn't seem too happy to pour my drink."

"It's a neighborhood bar, you know? Not many strangers. We don't get the drop-ins from the disco crowd."

A throaty laugh from below her neck ran up the scale and back down again to a chuckle. Willy wasn't sure what made her laugh, but he wanted to see it again. She was lovely with her head tilted, hooting mirth into the smoky air.

"You been out to the Cubs game?"

"What?"

"Cubs and the Cards. They played out at Wrigley."

That did it. She chortled again and chased the laugh with a drink. "That's two strikes. I hate baseball and I hate discos."

Willy opened the cover of one of her books and saw the CCC library stamp. "So what do you do? Study all the time?"

"Summer semester. Some electives I need for my teaching certificate. What's your major?"

Hogan passed by on the way from the cooler and Willy motioned for two more drinks. All the other customers had left, but Hogan wouldn't force them out until he was ready to leave. Willy grinned and lit a smoke.

"We got classes together or what?"

"You're kind of hard to miss on campus."

"Yeah. The old fart who looks confused all the time. How come I haven't seen you?"

"You probably have. Just didn't notice."

Willy laughed, sat down on a stool, and shoved a stack of bills at Hogan for the refills. "Jesus . . . and I'm supposed to be a trained observer."

"Trained by the military?"

Willy paused, swallowed, and stared into her dark eyes. There was challenge in the stare but it didn't seem hostile.

"That shows too, huh?"

"Some friends of mine . . . they said you were in Vietnam."

"I was. And I did what I needed to do. Then I got out. Now I'm in school. OK?"

She accepted another light and sipped at the fresh drink. "OK . . . except it's a shame so many other guys never made it back to school."

"Look . . . what's your name anyhow?"

"Ricky Roberts."

He stuck out a hand and she took it lightly, still holding his gaze with those ebony eyes. "I'm Willy Pudarski."

"Willy Pud. My friends said that's what everyone calls you."

"Those friends wouldn't be the other vets on campus, would they?"

"Some of them. They say you spent a long time in Vietnam."

"Let's not screw this up, OK? How'd you get a name like Ricky?"

"My full name is Jane Frederica. Go figure."

"You from around here?"

"Evanston. My dad's a dentist. He pays the bills. I share an apartment over on Selby Street."

"I live over on West Calumet . . . with my old man."

"So . . . you going back to school or what?"

"Yeah. I think so. I kind of like it. Maybe I'll be a teacher. Got any room in your classes?"

She smiled but there was a sad shadow in her eyes. Willy felt the familiar flash of embarrassment as she swallowed the last of her drink and gathered up the books.

"Goin' home?"

"Classes tomorrow. And I've still got some stuff to read."

Willy Pud stuffed his cigarettes and lighter in a pocket. "You got a car outside?"

"It's just a few blocks. I walk it all the time."

"OK if I walk with you?"

She shrugged and headed for the door.

The night air was cool and bracing after the stuffy atmosphere of the bar. Willy breathed deeply and fell in with her long, steady stride. There was no mince in her step and she kept her eyes locked straight ahead. He glanced at her and chuckled.

"Share the joke?"

"I was just thinkin'. You would have done just fine in the infantry . . ."

She stopped suddenly. Willy was two strides ahead before he could turn.

"What the hell is that supposed to mean?" The anger was real this time and it hit Willy like a hard shot to the solar plexus.

"Jesus . . . sorry. No offense, Ricky. I just meant you walk . . . different than most women. Kind of like we used to walk in the grunts. We call it humping."

She stared, blinked, and then the lines around her eyes and mouth crinkled into view. She laughed and picked up her stride.

"Where I come from, humping means something entirely different."

"Yeah. Shit . . . I'm sorry. Can't get a grip on the vocabulary."

They turned right into Selby Street. Willy began to eye the tightly packed houses, but Ricky kept her eyes riveted on him. She seemed to be thinking, examining him with a critical gaze.

"Did you do a lot of *humping* in Vietnam?"

He returned her smile and felt a warm glow spread up from his belly. She was so beautiful.

"Which kind?"

"Either . . ."

"I walked a hell of a lot, that's for damn sure. There wasn't much time—or opportunity—for women where I was."

"That's not what I heard."

She stopped abruptly and put a foot on the stoop of a brick four-family flat. Willy glanced up and scanned the address.

"Everybody had it different over there. People doin' the fightin' fought. Lots more of 'em screwed around in the rear areas."

She took another step toward her door. "Good night, Willy Pud. I'd invite you up, but my roommate's probably asleep by now."

He was desperate for her company. This had to lead somewhere beyond her front stoop. "How about I call you later? I'd like to see you again."

She glanced over her shoulder, seemed to be considering something beyond her schedule, and then walked back down the stoop. She coiled, sat, and began to dig around in her purse. Willy squatted beside her on the warm concrete.

"Everybody's got a sad tale to tell, right? Well, here's mine. I was going with a guy . . . first couple of years in school. We lived together for a while and then he lost his deferment . . ."

Willy watched her eyes, shining from the glow of a nearby street lamp. There was no sadness he could see. The black liquid hardened into onyx. "And there he went . . . off to the Land of the Lotus Eaters . . .

"He got sent to Vietnam . . . and he got killed. I didn't much give a damn before. Now I hate that fucking war . . . and I hate what it's doing to people."

Ricky pulled a slim joint out of her purse, tweaked the ends, and lit it with a match. She inhaled deeply and Willy watched her eyes soften. He gently pushed her hand away when she offered him a toke.

"I thought all you guys did grass."

"Not all of us. Seemed to me it was hard enough staying alive when you were straight."

"You never did dope over there?"

Willy shrugged and lit a cigarette. "Did some Dex. Too much sometimes. Got it from the corpsman in my outfit."

She dug in her purse again and emerged with a tin pillbox. Inside were five or six familiar white tablets.

"Jesus, you're a walking pharmacy . . ." He cringed at the arch of her eyebrows. If he kept saying stupid things, she'd get up and leave. Who needs lectures outside the classroom? He pinched one of the pills and popped it into his mouth. There would be no sleep tonight but that didn't seem to matter when he looked into her eyes.

She snapped the pillbox lid and turned her attention to the smoldering joint. His indulgence seemed to relax her and she leaned back against the stoop, stretching her long legs onto the sidewalk.

"Whatever gets you through the night . . ."

"That's what they say . . ."

"What do *you* say, Willy Pud? Did Vietnam turn you into a speed freak?"

"Don't think so. This is the first hit I've had since I been back in the World."

"Good to be back?"

"Nice rush . . . you pay the price later . . ."

"I mean is it good to be back home?"

Willy Pud stared at her and felt stirrings in the area of his crotch. The little electric sparks were snapping and popping through his body again. It felt good; strong and vibrant.

"It is . . . and it ain't, you know? I don't know . . . things seem so slow. It's hard to give a shit . . . about grades and checking accounts. It's like . . . there oughtta be more to it."

She pressed a cool palm against his stubbly jaw. Willy could feel the facial muscles twitching against her skin. The speed was working on its own now. He wanted to leave, to run. There was no telling what he might say.

"You need to open up, Willy Pud. You should try acid."

"Maybe . . . look, I gotta go now . . . can I see you again . . . I really want to . . . you know . . ."

She tore a page from one of her notebooks and scrawled a number on it. "No promises, Willy Pud. Call me. We'll see."

Willy watched her all the way inside the flat, fighting to keep his itchy feet still, to look cool, nonchalant, in what he hoped was a handsome, memorable pose at the bottom of the stoop. When a soft light glowed from a window on the second floor, he began to run.

The old man was up and making coffee when he burst through the door and into the kitchen. "Hope you got laid. Ain't much else worth losin' a night's sleep over."

Willy grinned and headed for the kitchen sink. The long run home had blasted the speed out of his system. He gulped a glass of cold water and mopped at his sweaty brow with a coarse dish towel.

His father handed him a cup of steaming coffee and a thick envelope with an embossed seal on the flap. "You ain't gonna be worth a fuck today, Vilhelm. Stay home and read your mail."

He finally got around to the letter after a long, cold shower. He was being installed in something called the Medal of Honor Society. He'd be contacted by a representative in the near future.

Summer school finals kept her from making the dates Willy called for three times over the next couple of weeks. When they finally managed to hook up for pizza at a popular joint down on the Loop, she showed up with her roommate. Lucinda Harris was also an education major but from Willy Pud's point of view that was all she could possibly have in common with Ricky Roberts.

She was short and stocky, almost muscular, with red hair cropped around her small skull and a fine spray of freckles across a flat nose. She had an odd way of shaking hands: clasp, grip, single pump, and then she jerked her stubby, square fingers back as though she wanted to keep contact at an absolute minimum.

Lu seemed pleasant enough over dinner, laughing heartily at Willy's lame comments about his upcoming class schedule and nodding in affirmation when Ricky offered advice about electives, but she was clearly being protective of her roommate. She sat close to Ricky, on the same side of a small table, and there was a hard glint in her green eyes when she stared at Willy.

He kept his attention riveted on Ricky but he caught Lu openly appraising him several times. When their eyes met, he was always the one who broke contact. She had an irritating way of arching an eyebrow at him as if she'd discovered some flaw but was too polite to mention it. By the time they'd polished off a large combination pizza and two bottles of red wine, Willy Pud felt like he'd been through an iron-ass personnel inspection.

Still, it seemed to go well, a pleasant, intimate evening among friends. As he fumbled with cappuccino and the check, Willy found himself desperate for more intimate contact with Ricky. For the first time since a major infatuation during his final year in high school, he felt panicky, nearly violent, with desire for a woman. Ricky had been fairly aloof during dinner but Willy thought he saw a willingness in some of her sidelong glances. He felt certain there was a way through her defensive perimeter. If he finessed the attack—made the right moves at the right times—she'd show him where it was.

Headed west out of the downtown district in his old man's truck, Willy suggested a couple of beers at Hogan's since the bar was close to home for all. Without waiting for a response from Ricky, Lu declined for both of them, indicating they had course work to prepare. Willy soared up out of a depression when Ricky said she'd like a couple of beers and they could swing by to drop Lu at home on the way to Hogan's. When Lu got out of the truck with a minimum of mumbled pleasantries, Willy swung the stiff old truck like he was manhandling a jumpy little sports car. Ricky stayed planted next to him on the seat rather than shifting over toward the passenger door. He was sure the firm pressure of her thigh against his marked the first stirrings of love.

Stosh Pudarski was parked on a bar stool playing liar's poker with Hogan when Willy walked in behind Ricky. The old man waved but made no move to join them at a back booth. Willy went to the bar for drinks and leaned over to look at the serial number on the dollar bill his father had cupped in his hand.

"Go for seven tens . . . he'll never believe you got that many zeros."

Stosh nodded and sipped at his beer. "That the one you been callin' all the time?"

"Yeah. Come on over and meet her."

Stosh helped Willy carry drinks to the booth and slid in next to Ricky. They shook hands and appraised each other for a moment before Ricky lifted her glass and made a toast to newfound friends. Stosh was on his best behavior, asking questions and listening politely while Willy and Ricky discussed school. As a favor, performed only for regulars, Hogan came by with a trayful of drinks on the house. Willy felt elated, warm, and comfortable. His father and Ricky seemed to like each other and he had fuzzy visions of sitting around a kitchen table with

Ricky as his devoted wife and his father's beloved daughter-in-law.

Stosh excused himself to "go pump the scuppers" and Willy was left staring into Ricky's smiling eyes. He lightly laid his hand over hers, wishing with all his heart that the night would never end.

"Your dad seems like a nice guy . . ."

"Yeah, it was hard on him after my mom died . . . with me overseas and all. Since I been home, it's different. He seems—I don't know—happy again."

"Are you happy these days?"

Willy squeezed her hand lightly. "Tell you the truth, Ricky . . . I'm happy as a clam sitting here with you. Wish there was a way to make it go on . . ."

She smiled like a child pondering mischief and glanced around the gloomy interior of the bar. Out of her purse came the little tin pillbox. She snapped it open, pinched a pill, and popped it in her mouth.

"Better living through chemistry . . ."

Ricky shoved the pillbox toward Willy and smiled. "Care to intensify the moment?"

He didn't see how it could be much more intense. Willy Pud felt his heart pounding and heard the rush of blood in his ears. It was like movement to contact and he wanted to get it right; set those familiar instincts free to guide him through Indian country. He palmed the box of meth tabs as Stosh returned to the table and then got up to head for the toilet.

He smiled as Stosh slid in comfortably beside Ricky. It looked just right; the way it should be. "Hold the fort, Pop, I gotta go make room for more beer." Standing in front of the urinal, he popped the speed and wondered idly what effect it might have on a rapidly developing erection.

When his eyes readjusted to the dim bar light, Willy saw that Ricky and Stosh had abandoned the booth. He swept a glance over the shuffleboard table and then caught sight of them staring at the wall near the end of the bar. There was nothing to draw them over there except the framed picture of him wearing the Medal that Hogan had hung in a gaudy gilt frame like some revered icon. She'd be getting all the gory details from Stosh. Goddammit!

He grabbed them both by the elbows and began to back away from the picture. "C'mon. You wanna look at pictures, I'll take you downtown to the museum. Let's drink beer." Back at the booth, Willy glared into his father's watery eyes until the old man began to mumble about bedtime and excused himself.

Ricky lit a cigarette and exhaled with a nervous sigh. "Jesus . . . was that natural nastiness . . . or is the speed turning you into a jerk?"

"He deserved it."

"For what? He was just showing me your picture with your Medal and all."

"He can carry that proud Papa shit too far. It never occurs to him some people don't want to hear it."

"Some people like me . . ."

"He don't know how you feel about Vietnam . . . I do."

"How *do* I feel about the war, Willy Pud?"

"You lost somebody over there. Like you said, you hate the war . . ."

Ricky snaked her knees up onto the booth and leaned in toward Willy. He thought he could see the speed sparkling in her eyes. Or maybe it was the reflection of his own intense gaze. Her eyes were so liquid, so wonderfully warm. It was like watching moonlight glint off rippling water.

"I feel sorry . . . sad . . . like I'm watching a bunch of brain-damaged kids in some state hospital . . . you know . . . it's like the little boys got a chance to play cowboys and Indians . . . so they strapped on their six-guns and rode off on some fucking big adventure . . . you know . . . and the longer they played, the harder it was to call King's X . . . and now all the boys are big grown-up men and they don't like the game because you can get killed playing it . . . so you know how I feel about the war . . . I feel happy that the Viet Cong won . . ."

"Jesus, don't say that, Ricky . . . please don't say shit like that . . . it ain't over . . ."

"It *is* over! You were there . . . you think the South Vietnamese stand a chance without the American Army? It's over, Willy Pud . . . and all that's left is hate and bitterness and people on both sides saying I told you so."

"Not me . . ."

"Why not you, Willy Pud? Because you're one of the ones that survived . . . because you got the Medal of Honor . . . because you don't want anything more out of this country than a piss-ant job and an empty bar stool at Hogan's . . ."

Her voice trailed off. She was riding the speed, waiting for the next wave to crest. Willy felt a sweaty desperation. He wanted her so badly but the war had blown them off a romantic track like a command-detonated mine. He put both hands on her dimpled knees and squeezed.

"Please, Ricky . . . this is what I got right now . . . but it ain't all I need . . . that's why I'm goin' to school . . . that's why I'm tryin' to see more of you . . ."

She shivered slightly and then he felt the tension drain out of her body. Maybe it would be alright. Maybe he could bridge the gap. She put her feet back on the floor and hit her drink hard, draining the glass.

"It's really sad, you know? I know of at least ten girls from my high school class back in Evanston who lost boyfriends over there. So many big plans . . . right in the dumper. Some of them will probably never have another man in their lives."

"That's dumb. Life goes on . . ."

"Yeah? And you fall in love with another man . . . and he goes off to another war . . . or another woman . . . and your whole life becomes one big bummer."

"It don't have to be that way."

"Yeah? Are you so sure?"

The light hit of speed had run its course through both of their systems. Willy wanted to hold her, keep her head out of the trough that followed the waves. He surprised her with a kiss at the nape of her neck and then began to slide out of the booth. She followed him out Hogan's front door and around to the alley where he'd parked the truck.

They rolled down the windows and moved wordlessly into each other's arms. The kisses were tender; the nuzzling quiet and comfortable. She let him fondle her breasts under the loose peasant blouse; even responded more ardently with her tongue as he squeezed gently on her nipples. When he pressed her toward a prone position, she grabbed a handful of hair at the back of his head and gently pulled them apart.

He felt constricted, congested, as though he couldn't suck enough air into his lungs. His voice cracked when he tried to complain. "Christ, Ricky . . . let's not stop now . . . please . . ."

She smiled but began to rearrange her clothes. "Don't beg, Willy. Give it time. There's lots of things to think about besides just fucking each other . . . lots of things."

He was slightly shocked at her language. And then decided he shouldn't be. In a way it was pleasant to hear her speak her mind in honest terms. Parris Island taught him things that come easy don't mean much. Whatever had been started would not be concluded, not tonight, not in his old man's raggedy pickup truck. A special thing like making love with Ricky rated a special moment, a special place. He grinned back at her and cranked on the sloppy old engine.

"School starts Monday for me. How about we meet for lunch?"

"Lu has class with me second period. She'll probably tag along."

"Bring the rest of the student body, Ricky. Long as you're there, it don't matter."

He looked over at her as the truck passed a streetlight. Willy Pud thought he saw a smile for his witty comment. But it might have been a grimace.

Late registration and the first day of classes came along with an early winter storm. Sleet blew across the campus and turned the few grassy spots designed to fend off concrete contamination at an urban college into slushy quagmires. None of that kept campus activists of one stripe or another from setting up their recruiting booths and competing for the attention of students bound for business in overheated buildings.

Wearing his wool Marine Corps horse-blanket overcoat against the icy wind that snapped and snarled through Chicago, Willy made his way via the quickest route from the el stop to a first period political science class. Along the way, he was glad-handed by the Young Republicans, ridiculed by the Students for Democratic Society, hailed as a returning hero by the Army ROTC unit, pitched for membership by the Vietnam Veterans Against the War, handed a business card by a beefy man who claimed to be recruiting for the CIA and the FBI, and asked to actively support the Gay and Lesbian Student Alliance. He automatically waved away the clipboard thrust at him until he noticed Lucinda Harris was holding it.

Her cheeks were ruddy and wind-burned, which made the freckles on her face glow with a bright orange hue. He smiled, trying to be civil in the face of her smirk.

She stared directly at him. The green flecks in her eyes flashed and made Willy Pud uncomfortable. He glanced down and nodded at the petition on the clipboard in her gloved hands.

"What's all this about?"

"It's about freedom of choice. They told you to fight for that in the Marine Corps . . . didn't they?"

Strong, rhetorical tone. Lucinda expected neither response nor argument. He cut a glance at the students huddled under the snapping banner that announced their affiliation. Mixed bag of campus cause-backers huddled around a rickety card table or handing out mimeographed leaflets. A few men and women, pawing at each other through thick winter clothes, letting the activity indicate standard sexual orientation while proximity announced their liberal attitude toward those who chose another direction. Singles in the crowd included mostly men and a few women fighting hard against stereotype.

Willy Pud turned his attention back to Lucinda Harris and felt the warm flood of sudden understanding. Pieces of her attitudinal puzzle began to fall into place. He leaned toward her, barking so she could hear over the wind and the babble of student activity.

"Different strokes for different folks . . . ain't that what they say?"

She spun the clipboard and shoved an attached ballpoint pen under his nose. "That's what they say. What do *you* say?"

"I say let's make a deal."

Lu arched her eyebrows and shot him an inquisitive look. Willy Pud grabbed the petition flapping from the clipboard and scanned the introductory paragraph.

"This just says I support equal treatment and consideration for homosexuals, right? I can live with that . . . but there's a few things I want to know before I sign."

"So . . . ask. We're here to provide information."

He scanned the petition again, searching for hooks or snags involving money or incriminating language. It seemed relatively straightforward; a political screed that boiled down to a you-do-your-thing-and-I'll-do-mine credo.

"So not everybody who signs this thing is a, uh, homosexual, right?"

Lu nailed him with a condescending smile. "Some are, some aren't, Pudarski. Some people are just saying they understand and support alternative life-styles. Now how about you?"

"How about you?"

"Give me a break, willya? You think I'd be standing out here in the cold if I didn't believe in this issue? Now, you gonna sign, or what?"

"That's not what I meant."

There was a challenge in Willy Pud's eyes; a dare in the smirk he spread on his mouth. He wanted Lu to squirm, but she merely glanced away for a moment and then locked back into his gaze. He'd seen the look before, on men determined to survive combat against contrary odds.

"You mean am I a lesbian? Let's just say there are still plenty of available women on campus . . ."

"I'm only interested in one right now."

"Yeah . . . well, I've got a first period class." Lu glanced at her watch and reached for the petition. Willy Pud held it against his chest.

"I ain't decided whether to sign it or not . . ."

"Look, man . . . let's cut through the bullshit here, OK? I'm Ricky's roommate and you're not. That pisses you off? That's your problem. Ricky does what she wants to do. She goes out with you . . . she signed the petition. Let's stop fucking around out here. You're not my type."

The heat in her words startled Willy. He couldn't remember getting off to that bad a start with her. Far as he could tell from a quick scan of his feelings, he had nothing in particular against Lucinda Harris. He scrawled his name on the petition and handed it back.

"Sorry if I got out of line. Guess I'll see you around."

She grabbed the clipboard and headed toward the administration building. "Guess you will. Guys like you don't give up easy."

Willy had no idea what she meant by the parting shot. He headed for class trying to fit the encounter with Ricky's roommate into context. Jogging up the steps of the Social Studies building, he decided she was a bull-dyke or at least headed in that direction. If Lucinda Harris wanted to fuck other women, it was no skin off his ass. He felt elated as he slipped into the classroom. At least there wouldn't be a lot of other guys sniffing around Ricky's apartment. By the end of a boring lecture on contemporary American foreign policy he'd slotted Lucinda Harris into a quasi-comfortable niche. Lesbians were like gooks. In the flesh, they scared the shit out of you, so the safest bet was to avoid contact.

The subject of Lucinda's sex life spilled over the dinner table while she was away for a weekend visiting family in Springfield. Throbbing with unrequited passion—fanned and banked in his truck, on Ricky's doorstep, or in some dark booth at the back of a bar—Willy pressed for a quiet dinner at her apartment. He arrived early with wine, two steaks, and a large bowl of the tangy Polish potato salad that was Stosh Pudarski's specialty. They were lingering over wine, passing a joint back and forth over guttering candles.

"Why didn't you ever tell me about the Medal of Honor? That's some pretty heavy shit."

"I don't know . . . guess it don't mean much . . . the way things are goin' over there and all . . ."

"My father had his good conduct medal from World War II framed. He's got it hanging in his office."

"Yeah, well . . . stuff like that means a lot more when you're on the winnin' side. It ain't too popular a subject these days."

"Was it a hard thing to win?"

"Ricky . . . combat ain't like a track meet. You don't set out to win a gold medal. Shit just happens . . . and you do whatever you have to do to survive."

"Did you have to kill a lot of people?"

Willy sipped wine and tried to fight off the disorienting signals from the potent dope. He felt a vulnerable moment was slipping away and he absolutely had to make love to this woman . . . now, tonight, as soon as possible.

"Yeah, Ricky . . . I guess I did. Can we talk about something else?"

He hooked their wineglasses in the fingers of one hand and led her toward an overstuffed couch in a dark corner of the room. Maybe some body heat would change the course of conversation. She draped her long legs over his knees and contemplated his profile.

"So why don't you tell me about it?"

"You know why . . . you hate the war. I get to talkin' about it and you might wind up hatin' me."

"I won't hate you, Willy. Maybe it'll help me understand what's happening . . . why men have to play such bullshit games all the time."

"It ain't easy to talk about . . ."

"Why not . . . you can tell me."

"No, I can't!"

"Why not?"

"Goddammit, Ricky . . ." Was it the dope? Or the wine? Or some contrary kink in her personality? Surely she could feel the erection pressing through his jeans into the tender flesh at the back of her knees. "Probably for the same reasons you never told me Lucinda was a lesbian!"

She smiled like a well-fed cat and closed her eyes. As she scrunched around to seat her shoulders in a lumpy cushion, her calves seemed to massage Willy's throbbing crotch. On purpose? More kid games?

"You mean shame? I'm not ashamed of Lu. Are you ashamed of what you did in Vietnam?"

"Not ashamed . . . no. But it makes me nervous sometimes. Like bein' locked up in here with a lesbian ought to make you nervous."

"Why? I'm not locked up in here . . . or anyplace else. Lu does her thing and I do mine."

"Yeah . . . I signed the petition too." The heat from his crotch seemed to surge upward toward his face. Willy realized he was angry and grabbed for a gulp of wine.

She chuckled deep in her throat, curled her legs under her, and began to nuzzle at his neck. Painful nips, salved by the warm perfume of her breath. He could feel the rubbery texture of her nipples on his bicep. It was exquisite torture and Willy thought he was bound to explode. Such a short length of fast-burning fuse between sexual tension and rage.

"It's just that . . . well, I was thinkin' about it the other day, Ricky. I get this horrible picture of her trying to get you into the rack . . ."

She giggled into his ear. "She's mentioned it . . . but I'm not ready for that, Willy . . ."

He maneuvered madly, brushing the sweat from his upper lip along her cheekbone until he managed to find her lips. They kissed and tasted each other, flowing back and forth between tension and relaxation. She gently but firmly refused to let him push her into a prone position.

"I'm not ready for you either, Willy. Not yet . . ."

"Jesus, Ricky. I'm fairly strong . . . but this shit is ridiculous. I can't wait much longer . . ."

She blew out the candles and flowed back into his arms. In a moment he felt her hand fumbling at the zipper of his jeans. He tried to maneuver again when she had him free of his underwear, but she pinned his shoulders and began to stroke him with a free hand, pausing at irregular intervals to tease at his tenderest parts with her fingernails. When the explosion finally came, it lifted him off the couch in a horrendous, moaning muscular spasm.

Ricky seemed pleased at the intensity of his orgasm, but Willy couldn't shake a certain sense of humiliation. What was wrong with her? Or him? She kissed him tenderly and lingeringly at the door and asked him to call tomorrow.

He said he would, but as he walked home through the crystal-clear night, Willy Pud thought maybe he'd had enough frustrations and complications in his life. He thought maybe he'd wait on the call, find someone else to fuck, and see if it felt as good as he thought it might when he stopped bashing his head against a brick wall.

Willy Pud hadn't seen Ricky other than casual classroom encounters for nearly two weeks. During that morose time, he'd dated different women with mixed results. A redheaded Earth Mother from his English Lit class helped him consume a large pizza and two bottles of wine and then introduced him to her dope connection, borrowing money for a grab bag of acid tabs, meth, ludes, and hash. He kept the meth and the hash and sat with her for four agonizing hours while she rode the acid roller coaster from wall-melting hysteria through a monumental crying jag into bleary-eyed oblivion. They were naked in the middle of a candle-lit room for most of the trip but Willy never got closer than three feet without sending her into a fetal position.

He was hitting the speed fairly hard when he let his second date take him to a local disco. He couldn't abandon himself on the dance floor and the pulsing strobe lights made him so panicky he had to dip into the ludes to handle the situation. She led him to her bedroom when they got home but Willy was too wasted to function. He staggered out to make room for a guy from the apartment next door who practically pole-vaulted in to take his place.

He sought refuge at Hogan's, staring at himself in the mirror, trying not to think about Ricky, and fighting to ignore the stentorian tones from the TV mounted over the bar. A strange, twisted new world was carrying him along in an unfamiliar orbit. There were no Americans left in Vietnam. He couldn't imagine that. There was no more Commander, United States Military Assistance Command Vietnam, leaving unanswered the bush-beast refrain: "Oh, who can he be, this COMUSMACV?" The news was full of gut-wrenching images as 590 American POWs finally came home to a nation that didn't believe—or didn't want to hear—the horror stories about their brutal treatment in captivity. No sign of Salt or Pepper. Willy wondered if they might try to slip back home disguised as prisoners. He'd been prepared to blow a long, loud whistle if they climbed off a plane at Clark Air Force Base in the Philippines. But they were elsewhere . . . either dead or waiting for the inevitable Big Moment when they could claim their fame as heroes of the revolution that murdered Indochina and disemboweled America. Willy hoped they were dead, but the willpower he focused on the image of their rotting corpses left him feeling uneasy. Assholes always seemed to survive against the odds.

It just went along with all the other proof that there was no justice. Just as there didn't seem to be any familiar social patterns. No one seemed to give a fuck about football or any other apolitical sport on college campuses. Now what kind of shit was that? Willy remembered the quasi-religious reverence for the Fighting Illini among the hopeful seniors on his high school teams. Why did everything have to be fraught with social or political import? You had to make some kind of half-assed statement with everything from the clothes you wore, to the music you liked, to the classes you took. Join this group . . . protest the actions of that group . . . take a stand on this or that issue . . . be this or be that . . . you can't wander around in between. Pursuing an education didn't mean getting smart; it meant getting *involved*.

You take dating, romance, shit like that, Willy Pud mused as he signaled for more beer. It ought to be played by the same rules as when he was in high school, before the Marine Corps, before Vietnam. It still seemed to be aimed at the same target, after all. People were still sweating, straining, doing everything short of shitting themselves to get laid. But the rules of the game had changed radically. There was still no free lunch, but there was plenty of free love. It's OK to get involved in peace, love, and harmony as long as you stay on an aesthetic plane and don't lower yourself to cheesy stuff like going steady or getting married. Where the hell was the emotional commitment that provided reassurance to insecure young men and women? There's something shallow about fucking just because it feels good. Willy Pud's mother had warned him, one teary night after a Valentine gift was rejected by his first great love, not to wear his heart on his sleeve. Fine. But what happens . . . what does it mean . . . when people get their genitals confused with their hearts? Maybe his old company gunny had been more perceptive than profane. *Love ain't shit! If God wanted you to fall in love he'd have made women in the shape of a rifle.*

In the middle of his third week without so much as a phone call to Ricky, Willy Pud decided booze caused him to contemplate while speed allowed him to accelerate beyond the imponderables; go for the moon like the astronauts. Light off and launch from topic to subject without having to pause for extravehicular activity. He looked up the dope connection and paid top dollar for a large stash of Dex and meth tabs.

He was in a speed-fueled orbit around the living room at four in the morning—his breath coming in short snorts that tasted like base metal—when Stosh Pudarski snapped on a lamp and dropped himself into the ratty armchair across from the television. The old man stared angrily at his son's frenetic pacing for a minute and then slung a skinny ankle over the side of his favorite perch.

"Any chance of you slowin' down long enough to tell me what the hell's botherin' you?"

Willy stopped by the window and stared at the misty streetlights through the slats of yellowed blinds. He fought desperately at the demon that was urging him to bite his father's head off.

"Nothin', Pop. Go back to bed."

Stosh sauntered into the kitchen. Willy heard the rasp of his slippers on the worn linoleum. Soft tinks as the old man tapped a church key on the tops of two beer cans. A hiss of escaping air and then he was back holding one of the beers out to his son. Willy Pud stretched his hand toward his father and felt the cold sweat of the beer against his palm.

"Jesus, Vilhelm . . . you're shakin' like a dog shittin' peach pits."

Willy clenched his jaws and felt the demon recede. He rolled the cold metal of the can across his forehead.

"Can't sleep. Don't let me keep you up."

Stosh returned to his chair and sucked at his teeth for a while. The noise shot through Willy like a sharp bayonet. Why didn't the old man just shut the fuck up and go to sleep?

"Story in *The Sun* yestiddy . . . guy back from Vietnam . . . they had to put him in a goddamn hospital because he couldn't sleep. Nightmares about . . . what he seen . . . damned near killed him, I guess."

"So fuckin' what? He ain't got no monopoly on war sweats."

"Guess not. I heard you talkin' in yer sleep the other night. Thought you went to bed hungry or somethin'. Carryin' on about passin' the salt and pepper or somethin' like that . . ."

Willy Pud cringed. So . . . he was letting the images eat into his subconscious guts. Ricky fucking over his mind in the day and those bastards taking her place at night.

"It's nothin', Pop. I don't think about the war so much anymore."

"Then maybe it's that gal . . . Ricky. Thought you two was a hot item."

"She's worse fucked up than I am."

"Seemed like a pretty good old gal to me, Vilhelm. What happened?"

"Nothin' happened, Pop. Not a goddamn thing."

"Well, somethin's eatin' at you, Vilhelm. You ain't been right for a while now. If it ain't Ricky, then what is it?"

Willy slammed the empty beer can into a trash can. The noise sounded like a shot in the still apartment and his nerves responded with an angry buzz.

"Just shut the fuck up, Pop. Leave it alone!"

"I ain't gonna leave it alone, goddammit! You're my son, ain'tcha? If you ain't frettin' over a woman, then, by God, it's gotta be them fuckin' pills . . ."

Willy whirled to face his father but the old man had a horny hand raised to fend off the denials. "You think I'm stupid, Vilhelm? I know about that kind of stuff. I'm a damn sight over thirty but I ain't unconscious. You keep takin' that shit and you'll wind up dead. I seen enough guys do it in my time. Come to work hung over like a horsefly and then take them pills to get through the day. A man's system ain't geared to take that much punishment."

"It's just a little to keep me goin' with the studies, Pop. Jesus, I'm no fuckin' speed freak. I used to take the shit in 'Nam when times got hard."

Stosh Pudarski drained his beer and stood to face his son. The look in his grey eyes said he heard what was said but didn't believe it for a minute. Willy Pud felt like a kid caught masturbating.

"I don't understand what's so hard about these times, Vilhelm. You say the war ain't botherin' you . . . you say you ain't pinin' over Ricky . . . you say them fuckin' pills ain't a problem . . ." Stosh headed for his bedroom, leaving Willy standing in the shadows. "I ain't so far gone I can't smell bullshit no more."

It was shortly after noon on Saturday when a persistent jangling woke Willy Pud. His sheets and pillowcase smelled of stale sweat and he lay still for a moment trying to remember when he'd last showered. There was a dull hum in his ears that kept him from concentrating on anything but the strident phone ringing in the next room. When his bare feet slapped onto the cold floor a bolt of pain shot up through his knees and brought greasy sweat from his armpits. He ached all over, like he'd finished a fifty-mile forced march on nothing but guts. The phone stopped ringing before he could unfold himself and stand.

Stosh Pudarski stuck his head through the curtain that separated Willy's room from the rest of the old tenement flat and glared at his son. "There's eggs in the fridge. I'm goin' down to Hogan's and watch the game. That phone's for you."

He was gone before Willy could ask who called. Maybe it was

Ricky wondering why she was on ice these days. Maybe she was missing him as much as he was missing her. Maybe she's ready to stop playing games. He staggered into the small living room, squinting against the sun that bleached the room with a white glow. The phone was lying off its cradle and he grabbed at it, croaking into the mouthpiece.

"Is this Wilhelm Johannes Pudarski?" Unless she'd developed a whiskey growl in the past three weeks, the voice on the other end didn't belong to Ricky Roberts. Willy swore under his breath and scrabbled around on the coffee table for a cigarette.

"Yeah. Who's this?"

"Are you former Staff Sergeant Pudarski, Marine Corps, Medal of Honor winner?"

"Depends on who's askin'." Willy heard a warm chuckle burble over the phone line. There was something familiar in the tone if not the voice.

"Listen, I'm sorry if I caught you at a bad time. My name is Sam Shaeffer, sergeant major, USMC type, one each, retired. I represent the American Medal of Honor Society. We sent you a letter last month . . ."

The bark in Shaeffer's voice was habitual and unintentional but it served to blow away the cobwebs constricting Willy Pud's brain. The tape-loop of Marine Corps history began to roll. Shifty Shaeffer. Seventh Marines in Korea. Frozen Chosin Reservoir. Sole survivor of a platoon that fought off a marauding Chinese regiment on some hilltop. Fought hand-to-hand through the night and gave his battalion time to slip out of a death trap.

He cleared his throat and felt himself stiffening into the position of attention. "Sorry, Sarn't Major . . . I been . . . I had the flu the last couple of days . . ."

"No problem, Sarn't Pudarski. I can call back later if you'd like."

Willy rolled his shoulders, wondering at the effect of being called by his old rank. His palms were sweating and he tumbled easily, automatically into a modified parade rest.

"What can I do for you, Sarn't Major?"

"Well, like we said in the letter, you've been nominated and invited to join the Medal of Honor Society. I'm sure you understand it's a fairly prestigious group of Americans . . ."

"Fact of the matter, Sarn't Major . . . I don't know much about it at all. I was sorta surprised when I got the letter."

"It's all about *Semper Fidelis,* Sarn't Pudarski. You haven't forgotten that, have you?"

"No, Sarn't Major . . ."

"That's what I expected. Anyway, it's all too damn complicated to explain on the ding-wa. I'm in town and part of the reason is to see you. Can I come by sometime today?"

Willy Pud glanced around the disheveled flat. It looked and smelled like a couple of winos had holed up inside for a four-day toot. His old man never cleaned anything he wasn't going to eat. It had always been Willy's job to keep the place squared away, but lately . . .

"Look, Sarn't Major . . . I'd rather come see you if that's OK."

"Good deal. How about sixteen hundred? They got a Happy Hour in the bar down here."

"Where are you stayin'?"

"Sheraton Blackstone . . . down on the Loop."

"I know where it is. See you there at sixteen hundred."

Willy Pud hung up, did an about-face in bare feet, and headed directly for the shower. He was halfway dry before he realized the lead had melted out of his belly. His mind was clear and clicking through random but distinct mental images. For the first time in nearly a month, he was holding his wings straight and level: neither climbing on speed nor diving into depression over Ricky. Whatever the Medal of Honor Society was offering, he ought to be buying.

Willy Pud winced at the strobe effect of sunlight through the grimy bus windows as he rode downtown to keep his appointment. Getting squared away for the first time in weeks felt good. Clean clothes and a neatly knotted tie firmed up the rubber in his knees like a shower and a fresh set of jungle utilities after a long stay in the bush. A plate of fried eggs bounced hard off his shrunken stomach and he'd had to fight the temptation to dip into his pill stash for relief. But that would have meant more staggering mood swings—lows chasing highs in steady, sickening amplitude—and another lost day. He didn't know what Sergeant Major Shaeffer and the Medal of Honor Society wanted of him, but he knew finding out was good for his health and welfare. The more he thought about it, the less he argued with himself over Ricky.

The real problem, he supposed as the bus jerked and roared along its route toward State Street, was dignity—or a lack of it. He was fighting to keep his head up, to float with some semblance of pride through the sea of breast-beating and collective guilt that was sweeping the country over the war in Vietnam. Not so hard if you turned a blind eye to the clamoring crowd of Monday morning quarterbacks looking to blame someone else for losing the game.

Fuck a bunch of conscience-stricken vets and the bandwagon they were all clamboring aboard.

There were still carrier battle groups off the coast of Southeast Asia. There were still strike aircraft launching from bases in Thailand. There was still Marvin the ARVN, taking his lumps but keeping the NVA wolves at bay. It wasn't much but it was enough to indicate the Greater Southeast Asia War Games were not over yet. It was enough to keep a strong man from writing the whole ten years off as a waste of time and lives . . . if he concentrated . . . if he threw the right rationale at the problem.

Then you fuck around and fall in love and it's hard to concentrate. It's hard to think straight and act dignified when all those emotional maggots are crawling around inside your body. He'd tried to think it through; mellow and maudlin on a bellyful of beer; steaming hard in a sea of speed-induced paranoia; even straight, in the cold light of several sober mornings. Still, he couldn't fight his way through the emotional roadblocks.

These were the facts: He met a woman at a time when he desperately needed to meet one. He fell hopelessly in love with that woman after spending too little time with her and the more she held him at bay, the more he lusted after her in body, mind, and spirit. He was, in spite of all the arguments he could muster against such a thing, mired and virtually immobilized by a passion unlike anything he'd known since Vietnam. Ricky gave a sweet purpose to life that had been missing since his Marine Corps days. She gave him a purpose, an objective, a goal, and he loved her with an all-consuming fire. It was undignified to be so emotionally dependent on a woman who resisted a similar commitment. It hurt to be a love-struck shit-heel ready to be bludgeoned, embarrassed, and frustrated just so you won't be thrown out of the game. Mix a potful of pride into that equation and you arrived at stasis. He was—in the end—a stubborn, hardheaded Polack who would eventually moon himself to death. Or maybe Ricky would finally get the goddamn message, wise up, and give him a call.

Sergeant Major Shaeffer wasn't hard to spot among the affluent Chicago businessmen and the out-of-town power brokers who dealt with them over generous drinks in the darkened bar of the Sheraton Blackstone. His was the only waxy expanse of freshly shorn scalp showing under the muted amber bar lights. Willy Pud pegged him at sixty or better but the solid sheet of steel tempered in Korea and elsewhere was still very much in evidence. He was medium height with a bull neck and barrel chest that seemed to distort an expensive, immaculately pressed civilian suit. When they shook hands, Willy felt the bite of a large ring on his right hand. Even before the stone flashed as they ordered drinks and toasted each other, he knew it was one of those old-time Marine Corps rings: worn, polished, and revered like an icon; the proud symbol of a Parris Island Ph.D.

Willy Pud stared over the rim of a tall pilsner while flinty grey eyes crawled up and down his frame. He wished he'd stopped for a haircut before reporting to this man who was—no matter what uniform hung on his wiry frame—obviously and unequivocally—a sergeant major.

"Welcome to Chicago, Sarn't Major."

"Thank you, Sarn't Pudarski. *Semper Fi.*"

"*Semper Fi,* Sarn't Major. It's good to hear that again."

They carried their drinks to a quiet corner table and sat examining each other for a few minutes. Both wound up smiling. Willy Pud realized he'd been sized up by an expert at evaluating men. Had he been found wanting, there would be no friendly grin creasing Sergeant Major Shaeffer's rugged map.

"Let's get this off on the right foot. How about I call you Willy Pud?"

Willy stared at the man across from him and noticed the small, understated lapel pin. Pale blue. Infantry blue with five tiny stars and a roseate cluster. He had one just like it in the big box containing his Medal of Honor. Handsome thing. He'd thought about wearing it for the first time to this meeting . . . but with Shifty Shaeffer? Jesus, he'd heard that name in boot camp history classes. It takes balls to put yourself in the same class with a legend.

"Call me anything but late to chow . . . but I just don't think I'm gonna be able to manage anything but sarn't major in return."

The laugh was a rich, throaty wheeze that turned a few heads in the bar, but Sergeant Major Shaeffer didn't seem to mind. He waved at a passing waitress with one hand and balled the other into a fist that he drove painfully into Willy Pud's shoulder.

"Spoken like a heavily hung enlisted man, Willy Pud. I'd have been surprised at anything else." They tasted the imported beer and swapped information for a few minutes on people in the Corps they both knew. It was warm and comfortable. Willy found himself wondering how he might turn this meeting into a night on the town. Just two old Marines doing Chicago . . . steamin' hard, forty knots, no smoke.

"So how's school goin'?"

"OK, Sarn't Major. I'm gettin' a new slant on some things—that's interesting—but sometimes I miss it, y'know? Civilian life is . . ."

"It's a necessary evil . . . that's what it is. I'm glad to hear you miss the Corps. There's more than a few Marines who miss you, y'know. Some of my old *panyos* really wanted you to stick around."

"Yeah, well, it wasn't an easy decision to make. But my dad was all alone and he was worried about me and all . . ."

"Damn glad to hear it wasn't Vietnam that drove you out. We're losing enough young talent over that as it is."

"I figger if you take the long view, Sarn't Major, if you look at it from the professional standpoint, Vietnam is just another war like the Boxer Rebellion or Korea."

"Yeah. But it's hard to take the long view when you're losing, Willy Pud."

"We ain't lost it yet, Sarn't Major."

"Hmmmm . . ." Their fresh drinks arrived and there were more toasts to old friends. Eventually, Sergeant Major Shaeffer shifted in his seat and leaned his elbows on the table.

"I get the feeling this might turn into a long night, so let me get the business out of the way here. We want to hold an installation dinner for you, Willy Pud. Right here in Chicago. As many members of the Medal of Honor Society as can make it will be here to welcome you aboard. We do this sort of thing because membership in the Society ain't automatic. You don't become a member just because the President hangs a medal around your neck."

"You mean there's guys who've got the Medal and they don't want to be members of the Society?"

"A few. Sometimes they rebel against the military and all it stands for . . . or all they think it stands for. Sometimes they think we're a bunch of old warhorse hawks who'll use our clout to push for more wars. Sometimes they just want to forget it ever happened."

"Well, I ain't likely to forget . . . ever."

"Didn't think so, Willy Pud. That's why I nominated you for membership. See, there's all kinds of guys who win the Medal of Honor for all kinds of incidents and accidents. We got one guy jumped on a Jap grenade to save his buddies on Okinawa. The grenade was an incomplete detonation. Went off OK and tore him up pretty bad, but it never killed him like it does most

guys who do something like that. To this day, he wanders around
wondering why he ain't dead."

"I've spent some time wondering the same thing."

"Yeah, hell yes. So have I. But we come to grips with it, see?
He'll die wondering what he was thinking in that frozen moment
of time. You and me . . . well, we made a conscious decision to
take a shitty-odds chance on dyin' for one reason or another. The
reason don't matter. The fact that we thought about it—and then
done it—that's what matters."

"So, if I'm a member, what do I have to do?"

"You don't have to do anything, Willy Pud. We may call
on you from time to time to lend your name to some project.
Or we might ask if you're interested in working on something
important . . . usually something to do with veterans affairs, or
support for the active military, things like that. We avoid being
overly political. What we got is clout. And we want it used for
important things, things that impact on the country as a whole.
Like now, I'm working on support for refugees from Southeast
Asia. It's a legacy this country's got to own up to . . . no matter
how the war finally turns out."

"And there ain't no dues or anything like that?"

"You paid your dues in Vietnam, Willy Pud."

Willy Pud considered the man across the table from him. If
Shifty Shaeffer traveled all the way to Chicago to ask him to join
a club, then, by God, the least he could do was join. It would be
nice to claim exclusive membership in something again. It would
be nice to belong where you're wanted and welcomed. He raised
his beer glass and nodded.

"Ship me over, Sarn't Major."

"I think you want more than I'm willing to give right now,
Willy Pud . . ."

Her voice sounded distant, as if she were whispering into a
phone in Tokyo rather than sitting in her apartment a couple
of blocks away from him on a sweltering evening when the
muggy air in Chicago seemed to hold more water than Lake
Michigan.

He tightened his sweaty grip on the phone and shot a startled
glance out the window as a white light flickered and dimmed
over West Calumet Avenue. The dry lightning that crackled and
stabbed down out of the midwestern skies during the drought-
plagued summer of 1974 seemed to reflect the electrifying political and social events that were causing short circuits across the

country. But none of that was on Willy Pud's mind as he fought to put the right ring of passion in his voice.

"Look, Ricky . . . I'm sorry, OK? It's been a long time . . . but I can't forget about you. I figured you were just stringin' me along, you know? Like you didn't want to make a commitment. That's hard to take . . ."

"Maybe I *don't* want to make a commitment. Maybe I'm not ready. Like I told you . . ."

He interrupted, trying to keep his voice mellow and level, fighting the panic and running down the mental script he'd prepared so carefully for this moment.

"No, no. It's OK. You don't owe me anything. I just want to see you again . . . to be around you. If something develops, OK. If it doesn't, no harm done, right?"

"You know what it sounds like to me, Willy Pud? It sounds like you're a man who can't figure out why he didn't get laid in spite of his best efforts."

The words struck him dumb for a moment and he fumbled for a cigarette, squeezing the old black phone against his ear to keep from losing even momentary contact with the sound of her voice, her breathing.

"No, look . . . like I said, you don't owe me anything. If we get together—if it happens between us—then that's good, right? If not, OK. I'm just askin' for a chance here, an opportunity. The way I feel about you . . . it goes beyond the physical stuff. Fact is . . . I'm in love with you, Ricky."

Silence. Was that a sigh, the wind in the wires, static on the line? Willy Pud shut his eyes against the sweat seeping through his brows and prayed for any sound other than the terminal drone of a dial tone.

"You don't mean that, Willy Pud. You don't know what love is."

"Yes, I do. It's what I'm feeling for you right now."

"We come from different worlds . . ."

"What? You're from Evanston; I'm from Chicago. Your old man's a dentist; mine's a carpenter. We go to the same school, for Christ's sake!"

"That's not what I mean . . ."

"You mean I'm ten years older than you . . . I went to Vietnam?"

"That's part of it . . ."

"I can't change that. What's the other part?"

"We just see things differently, Willy Pud. You paid your dues.

Now you want a little house out in La Grange, kids, and a wife waiting at the door with nothing on her mind but dinner and domestic problems . . . your basic *Leave It to Beaver* scene. I don't want to wake up one morning and discover I've become Donna Reed. There's more to life these days . . . or hadn't you noticed?"

"I noticed. It don't alter the fact that I love you, Ricky. I want you . . ."

"Not on your terms, Willy Pud."

"On any terms you say, Ricky. All I want is a fair shot . . . and I'm not gonna give up 'til I get it."

Her laughter was like a refreshing breeze. It swept over the phone line and across his body like a stimulating mist. He felt himself gaining strength, confidence.

"You're hardheaded, Willy Pud. Is that your Marine Corps training?"

"Well, they never mentioned retreat. The emphasis was always on the attack."

"OK, I surrender . . ."

"No shit?"

"No shit . . . Lu's having a little celebration tomorrow. Why don't you come by the apartment around eight?"

"What kinda celebration? Should I bring something?"

"Wine, beer, grass . . . whatever. It's a victory party."

"I don't get it . . ."

"Don't get what? Where have you been all day?"

"Over in Cicero . . . working with my old man."

"They don't have radios or TV in Cicero?"

"C'mon, Ricky. I just got in a half hour ago."

"Nixon resigned! All the bullshit's finally coming to an end."

"Damn . . ." Willy Pud felt a strange itch and reached up to scratch the spot at the base of his throat where a now-disgraced Chief Executive had hung the Medal of Honor. He wrinkled his nose, remembering the man's promises, his high-sounding words about an honorable peace, justice for all who did—and didn't—do their duty in Vietnam, the putrid smell of bunion-crusted feet . . . feet of clay.

"Willy Pud . . ."

"Yeah . . ." He cleared his throat and tried to focus on the task at hand. He was levering himself back into Ricky's orbit. Poor, troubled Earth and all the rest of the planets would have to spin on minus his concern for now. "That's some fairly heavy shit."

"It's really sad, y'know. First the Pentagon Papers and now

this. It was all such a terrible waste, wasn't it?"

"Depends, I guess. The South Vietnamese are still putting up a fight . . ."

"Oh, Willy, c'mon . . . Jesus Christ . . ."

He heard the exasperation in her voice and cringed. Why couldn't he shrug it off? Why was Vietnam still kicking his ass, squeezing his nuts, years after he left it? Why did everything in his life seem to ricochet off Vietnam like a badly aimed round of ball ammo?

"Yeah, sorry . . . you're right. Bad news all around. The good news is you and me, right? Back together tomorrow night."

"No strings, Willy. No promises."

"What?"

"What did you say before? If it happens, groovy. If not, oh, well."

"Yeah, sorry. I got the word . . . lighten up."

Stosh Pudarski was in the kitchen alternating his attention between the front page of the *Sun-Times* and a bottle of Blue Ribbon. Willy snagged two more beers from the noisy old refrigerator and sat across from him at the table. The old man's eyes never left the paper as he reached for the fresh beer. His lips moved as he devoured the details of Richard Nixon's resignation and the appointment of Gerald Ford as the new President of the United States.

Willy reached for a stack of mail. All ads and bills, except for the embossed envelope bearing the dignified seal of the Medal of Honor Society. It was a note from Sergeant Major Shaeffer. His installation dinner was set for September 15 at the Sheraton Blackstone. Less than six weeks to rent a tux and prepare a speech.

"Ain't this a kick in the ass?" Stosh rattled the newspaper and looked up at his son. His expression contorted around a half-raised beer bottle. He held the drink at a precarious angle as though he was torn between the solace of a sip and an urgent need to keep his mouth free for a torrent of angry words.

"This is the man who gave you the Medal of Honor. I shook his fuckin' hand right there in the fuckin' White House! We got his fuckin' picture hangin' out there in the livin' room, for Christ's sake!"

Willy shrugged. "Goes to show you, Pop. You fuck with the bull, you get the horn."

"That ain't what it goes to show you. What it goes to show you is them fuckin' communists in Washington are takin' control.

Them pansy-assed cocksuckers can even kick a President out of office nowadays!"

Stosh brought the beer the rest of the way to his mouth and sucked it dry but his eyes never left his son. He seemed to demand a similar emotional reaction. They did, after all, have some vested family interest in this particular President.

Willy reached for the paper. "I ain't had a chance to read anything about it yet, Pop."

Stosh stood and reached into his old khakis for the money from the paycheck they'd cashed on the way home from the job in Cicero. He counted carefully and then went to the kitchen cupboard where the tin coffee can on the second shelf held cash committed to rent and regular bills. Tomorrow Willy would convert the cash to money orders and meet their financial obligations. Stosh had closed their checking account the day after his wife died.

"Maybe we ought to just take this cash and buy us a ticket to somewhere out of this goddamn country. No tellin' what's gonna happen around here anymore."

"C'mon, Pop. That's bullshit and you know it. This is where we belong. You fought for this country; I fought for this country. We gonna just split because some President gets shit-canned?"

"He's the fuckin' President, Vilhelm! He shouldn't never have been shit-canned. Who the hell you gonna trust now? Who the fuck is in charge of this goddamn country anyway?"

"I dunno, Pop. What fuckin' difference does it make? We work, I go to school; all kinds of heavy shit happens around us. It don't stop me from goin' to class or you from swingin' a goddamn hammer, does it?"

"That's pretty shortsighted comin' from a man who won the Medal of Honor. Wasn't you over there fightin' for the American way of doin' things?"

"I was killin' gooks, Pop, tryin' to stay alive. Who the fuck knows why?"

His father fingered a twenty out of the coffee can, shoved it in his pocket, and reached for the old Cubs hat covered with a patina of the day's sawdust. "I never asked them kinda questions when I come home to see you for the first time back in '45. You never used to say shit like that either. If that's what they're teachin' you in college, you ought to get yer fuckin' money back!"

Stosh glared at his son, ignoring the shower of sawdust that cascaded around his face as he jammed the ball cap on his head. Willy returned the glare, fighting the instinctual urge to hit back.

"C'mon, Pop. You ain't pissed off at me. You're just pissed off."

Stosh shook a Camel out of the pack in his T-shirt pocket, clicked his Zippo, and followed the smoke with his eyes as it drifted toward the grease-stained ceiling.

"Fuckin' right I'm pissed off. Let's go down to Hogan's and douse the fire."

"Maybe later . . ." Willy held up the embossed envelope. "I got to make a speech at this Medal of Honor Society deal. I was gonna make some notes."

Stosh nodded and reached for the doorknob. He was still in a sour mood. "Do me one favor, sonny-buck. You come down to Hogan's tonight, don't be takin' any of them fuckin' pills. Hogan don't say nothin', but I can't stand it when you go bouncin' around, lit up like a fuckin' pinball machine."

Willy wandered to the refrigerator and grabbed a beer. "We had this conversation before, Pop. I ain't had any speed since the day I talked to Sarn't Major Shaeffer. I felt better then. I feel better now. No problem."

Stosh Pudarski grunted and slammed the door behind him. Willy heard his heavy work boots thumping on the stairs. He retrieved the coffee can and counted their net worth. It was enough to make the rent, gas, electric, and phone plus a little for extras. Tuition and books for the upcoming semester would be covered by the GI Bill check. Maybe he could squeeze out enough for a new pair of pants and some good wine for the party. Hogan's was out for tonight if he wanted to look good for Ricky tomorrow.

An old Republican campaign poster covered one wall of the apartment. Richard M. Nixon, confident and charismatic in a pre-Watergate pose, beamed tolerantly down on the stoned and stoked college crowd that hated his guts. Lu Harris was proud of the modification she'd made to the poster and dragged new arrivals over to admire her sense of humor. On one side of his head she'd drawn a speech bubble that had Nixon saying "I am not a crook." On the other side, she'd drawn a thought bubble that had him thinking "I am, however, a crooked, war-mongering sonofabitch."

Willy stood, hitching self-consciously at a new pair of Sears & Roebuck double-knit hip-huggers, and tried to catch the clamorous mood of the party. Ricky had answered his knock on the door with a peck on the cheek, thanked him for the wine, and then run off to some unfinished conversation with a guy wearing shades and a suede vest covered with anti-war buttons. Lu Harris wandered through the crowd and handed him a beer in a plastic cup.

"Here's to truth, justice, and the American way."

Willy Pud tasted the beer. It was flat. Beneath the campaign poster, two hard-edged women sucked on a joint and then kissed to pass the potent smoke. He hit the beer again.

"Thanks for havin' me. Been a long time."

"Yeah. Ricky said she was, uh, surprised when you called." Lu Harris was inspecting him again. She didn't look happy at the prospect of having him around on anything like a permanent basis.

He listened to party noise for a while, trying to avoid Lu's eyes. The Beatles were chanting mantras from their Magical Mystery Tour. Pipes were passing around the room and the dope smoke was becoming a purple haze. Ricky was giggling with two girls he recognized from a Poly Sci class. Her cheeks were flushed and she'd stripped down to a loose tank top that let her breasts bobble and shift as she laughed.

Lu moved to avoid a couple of uninhibited, energetic dancers and Willy Pud found himself crushed against her. She made no move to back off and he was surprised to discover she generated her own sort of sexual heat.

"So, you gonna try to get back in the saddle again or what?"

"Ricky means a lot to me, Lu. I found that out by staying out of the saddle."

"Man, you need to lighten up. She doesn't want what you're offering. How come you can't see that?"

"How come you keep runnin' interference?"

There was a frosty smile on Lu's face as she backed off slightly and studied him. They stood immersed in party noise for a long moment and then she seemed to notice their glasses were empty. Lu grabbed Willy Pud by the belt and dragged him over to a long table groaning under a sweaty beer keg and assorted liquor bottles. She poured heavy hits of Wild Turkey into their beer glasses and turned toward the stereo in a dark corner. Bob Dylan was whining through his nose.

"You dig Dylan?"

Willy was caught off guard and sipped at the whiskey to cover his surprise. "What . . . . yeah . . . what I hear of him, he's pretty good."

"They should have appointed *him* President when Tricky Dick bit the big weenie." She sipped and listened for a while, catching up with the lyrics. Then she sang to him in a sturdy alto: *"The times they are a'changin'."*

"Are you tryin' to tell me somethin', Lu?"

"I'm saying you're out of step, Mr. Marine. Can you dig it? Women today don't want what you want, you know? There's more to life—there's gotta be."

"How the hell do you know what I want?"

"You are who you are, man."

"And you're stoned."

"Nope. You want a job and a house and a wife and some kids. All the apple-pie American bullshit. Don't tell me you didn't think about that while you were in Vietnam."

"I thought about all kinds of shit when I was in the 'Nam. What's wrong with that?"

"What's wrong is you come home expecting to get what you were thinking about. See, the world spun around a few times while you were over there in the jungle. It's not the same place. People found out there was more to it. You don't have to marry a dentist and go to PTA meetings in fucking Evanston for the rest of your life."

"That's not what I want."

"So what? It's what you're gonna get. It's the American way. It's what you fought for, isn't it? And you're gonna drag some simpleminded woman into the swamp with you."

Willy looked around the room but the lights had been dimmed to accommodate dope smokers' dilated pupils and he couldn't see Ricky. Lu's cheeks were flushed as she splashed more bourbon into her glass.

"Jesus Christ. You're really on the rag tonight. Who cocked your pistol?"

"I'm a caring person, OK? I just don't want to see Ricky throw her life away."

"You know what I think, Lu? I think you're pissed off because she won't swing your way."

There was a hard glint in her eyes as she studied him, turning her head from side to side like a confused puppy. "You know what I think, Pudarski? I think the VC would have done us all a favor if they'd shot your cock off."

Willy Pud polished off his drink and grinned at her. "Well, just fuck you, Lu . . ."

She grinned back at him and then reached for a full glass of beer that someone had been using for an ashtray. She poured the drink into his crotch, spun the empty glass onto her upraised middle finger, and then shoved off into the crowd, laughing over the pulsing beat of Big Brother and the Holding Company.

Willy Pud found Ricky in the flicker of a strobe light and pulled her into a corner. She snuggled against him and noticed the soggy condition of his trousers. He mumbled something about spilling a drink, avoiding any mention of the argument with her roommate.

"There's a pair of my dad's old shorts in the bedroom. We can hang your pants in the shower until they dry."

Willy emerged from the back bedroom feeling silly and embarrassed in nothing but an old pair of Northwestern University Athletic Department shorts, but the sight of a bare-chested woman and a hairy-chested man sucking on a hookah in a corner reassured him he was not out of place in the abbreviated costume. No one seemed to notice as he threaded his way through the crowd and into the kitchen to search for a cold beer.

Ricky distractedly retrieved a beer for him from the refrigerator and then returned to conversation with a small man whose neatly trimmed hair and beard were shot through with grey. The man seemed to hold himself aloof from the swirl of activity that ebbed and flowed through the kitchen. He was intense, tightly wound, and his eyes flashed behind wire-rimmed glasses as he stared at Ricky. She mirrored his intensity, hung on his words, nodding and grunting when he paused for breath. Willy hung around on the periphery of it all, trying to listen and be unobtrusive at the same time.

"I'd like to think it will have a healing effect, but I just can't see it." The man cut a glance at Willy. The corners of his mouth twitched slightly in an imitation smile and he returned to rivet Ricky with his thoughts on some weighty matter.

"It's been going on for nearly ten years, for God's sake. Nixon didn't start it and his resignation won't finish it. It's time to cut the losses, bring people home from Canada without penalty. We've got to heal this nation, Ricky, and that's going to be a difficult task."

Willy belted from his beer bottle and shook his head sadly. Another bullshit conversation about Vietnam. Another bullshit artist mounts his soapbox. The motion didn't end when he held his head still. The booze was starting to work on him. He leaned to prop his shoulder on the refrigerator, miscalculated the distance and nearly fell.

"You disagree?"

The man had caught Willy's reaction. Ricky jumped into the void with a giggle. She was getting stoned or drunk. Maybe both. Her voice slurred like an off-speed record when she introduced him.

"Willy Pudarski . . . Dr. John Stanton. John teaches at SIU in Carbondale. Willy was in Vietnam . . ."

Stanton shook his hand and slowly eyed the scars on his body. "Looks like you had a rough time of it. Are all those from Vietnam?"

"All except this one . . ." Willy pointed to his right eyebrow. "This one I got in a losing argument with a '47 Oldsmobile. That was back before they issued me an M-16."

"Well, I'd say it's all over but the shouting at this point."

"Not soon enough. Too many fuckin' guys bought a farm they didn't want."

Stanton was sure he was talking to a kindred spirit. He sipped from a glass of something or other and shook his head sadly. Willy picked up the bottle of whatever Stanton was drinking and slugged furiously from it. The fiery liquid tasted like walnuts and made his stomach convulse.

"Yes, and that's not the worst of it. So many young men, such potential for future progress, all on the road, in Canada, or running from the draft . . ."

"Well, fuck 'em." Willy Pud drank again, chasing the liquor with beer. His eyes were watering when he tried to wink at Ricky. From the shocked look on her face she must have thought he was crying.

"Surely you can't blame draft-resisters for having the courage of their convictions."

"Naw . . . fuck no. I can't blame guys for not wantin' to get shot up or greased. But I can blame 'em for bein' gutless cocksuckers."

A flush appeared on Stanton's cheeks above the line of his beard. He peeled the glasses off his face and pinched the bridge of his nose. "So anyone who didn't go to Vietnam is a gutless cocksucker?"

"So anyone who doesn't go where he's gotta go and do what he's gotta do is a gutless cocksucker."

"And that includes going to kill innocent women and children in a putrid, illegal, genocidal war?"

Ricky was pulling on his arm but Willy Pud was locked in place, feeling the anger build and boil as he stared into Stanton's placid face. "And that includes doing whatever this country asks you to do, shit-head! See, some people understand the world don't owe 'em no fuckin' living. Some people understand you got to pay some dues."

Stanton wrapped his mouth into a wry smile and cocked an eyebrow at Ricky. "Maybe your friend should go back to Vietnam."

"Maybe I should. I been missin' the kind of people I served with over there." Willy reached out to snatch at the lapels of Stanton's corduroy jacket. "And maybe I ought to take your ass with me. Let's see how much courage you got, motherfucker!"

"Please, Willy. Don't do this. Don't start something here. Let's go in the bedroom and lie down." Ricky was trying to break his hold on Stanton but Willy just dragged the man closer. He was delighted to see Stanton cringe.

"Take your hands off me!"

Willy gently unwrapped his fists and smoothed Stanton's lapels. Then he took half a step backward and snapped a kick into the man's left kneecap. "You said hands, man. You didn't say nothin' about feet."

Stanton began to hop around the kitchen clutching his knee. He looked absurd and ungainly, like a berserk flamingo. Willy was startled when he heard Ricky hooting gales of delight into the smoky air. She was bent over a counter wiping tears from her eyes, laughing hysterically as Stanton hobbled out of the kitchen.

First she frets like a nanny and then she cracks up when he actually nails the guy. Willy glanced at his watch. Two hours. He'd managed to get drunk, get in a pissing contest with a lesbian, start a fight, and alienate Ricky in just under two hours. Possibly a new record.

"I guess I'd better get the fuck out of Dodge." He spoke to her heaving back. She was either still laughing . . . or crying. "I didn't mean for this to happen, Ricky."

He'd retrieved most of his clothes and stood in the bathroom splashing cold water on his face when she walked in and locked the door behind her. He straightened and stared at her image in the mirror. It was hard to read the expression on her face. The tiny arrows appeared at the corners of her eyes as she squinted and scrutinized the scars on his back. Her lips were parted slightly; she seemed to be breathing deeply and heavily as though she'd been through some exertion.

"I'll be outta here in a few minutes. I'm really sorry."

She put her hands on his back and began to worm her thumbs into scar tissue. "We haven't been able to spend any time together."

"Yeah, my fault. I was trying to lighten up . . . not bother you."

She giggled and wrapped her arms around his chest. "You sure as hell bothered John Stanton. He says he'll never walk straight again."

"Yeah. Like I said, I'm really sorry about that."

She spun him gently and folded herself into his embrace. Willy felt the heat from her crotch and watched in wonder as she peeled off the tank top. There was a sheen of sweat on her breasts and the nipples were taut.

"I met him when I went down to SIU for a seminar. He tried to feel me up in an elevator at the Holiday Inn. I kicked him in the same place and got the same reaction." She buried her face in his chest and started to giggle again.

Willy put his hands on her buttocks and lifted her off the floor. She wrapped her legs around his waist as he spun slowly and planted her on the counter. She watched, wearing a wicked smile, as he slipped off her panties and his underwear. And then he was in her, standing on trembling legs, sliding easily through her juices, grunting in exquisite pain each time his balls slapped against the marble countertop.

She arched her back and squirmed, bringing them into closer contact. As the friction increased, she began to moan and squeezed so hard with her muscular calves that Willy's eyes were bulging when he glanced at himself in the mirror. He tried to keep his eyes open during the climax—wondering in a detached manner what expression he would wear in a moment like that—but the pleasure was so intense when he thrust and felt the muscles in his scrotum begin to contract that tears obscured his vision.

He panted into her breasts and listened as her heartbeat slowed. "I love you, Ricky. I fuckin' love you." It seemed inadequate yet inescapable at that moment.

"You love fucking me, Willy Pud. Leave it at that."

She had her eyes closed against his planned protest. He wanted to correct that idea. He wanted her to believe him, to love him. But it didn't seem like a time to press the issue. It was enough that she'd offered her body. In time, he felt sure, she'd offer all the rest.

Sergeant Major Shifty Shaeffer parted the lobby crowd like a destroyer steaming through an oil slick. Most of the well-dressed civilians, gathered for Chicago society functions in the Sheraton Blackstone, had probably never seen a live Marine in dress-blue uniform. Even those that had were visibly impressed at the martial splendor of the squatty man with gold chevrons and hashmarks covering his sleeves, three clanking banks of gleaming medals on his left breast, and the pale blue, star-spangled pendant wrapped around the high collar of his uniform blouse.

Even Willy Pud found it hard not to stop and stare as he stood blocking traffic just inside the revolving door off State Street. The rented tux—a midnight-black ensemble with muted maroon tie and cummerbund that caused the old man to tear up the house searching for his old Kodak—suddenly felt like a faded pair of jeans and a ratty T-shirt. Willy shifted the box and papers he carried and shook the sergeant major's proffered hand.

"Holy shit, Sarn't Major . . . you look . . . spectacular."

"About once a year I get the chance to break out the old rig and suit up. Feels fuckin' great." He grabbed Willy by the elbow and led him toward a dark, wood-paneled banquet room. A photographer, standing outside the closed doors near a sign announcing the Medal of Honor Society Installation Dinner, aimed and fired his strobe at them.

"We got time for a drink. Couple of reporters—*Sun-Times* and *Daily News*—want to talk to you before dinner."

They pushed through the doors and into a large room lit by muted chandeliers that gave the polished wood and gleaming crystal of the banquet setup a warm amber glow. Willy saw several men standing in small clutches around the periphery of the room. Some wore medal-encrusted uniforms; some tuxedos. All had the same Medal around their necks.

"Jesus, I forgot . . ." Willy stopped and handed Sergeant Major Shaeffer the felt-covered box containing his Medal of Honor. "I didn't know how to put this on with a tuxedo."

Shaeffer spun him around, fished the Medal out of the box, and fumbled with the catch until it hung around Willy's neck, nestled neatly beneath his clip-on bow tie. He admired his work critically for a moment and then smiled.

"Ain't no regulation for it out of uniform. Guess they figger a guy's got the Medal, he'll wear it any fuckin' way he wants to."

Willy stood self-consciously looking around the room while Sergeant Major Shaeffer went for drinks. Except for the Medal, there didn't seem to be any common denominator among assembled Society members. In fact, most of the men Willy saw looked like accident victims consulting with high-class lawyers.

There were overweight guys with gleaming jowls and Wall Street pallors as well as lanky, silver-maned patrician types with bone-deep Palm Springs tans. Short, sweaty guys with the last remaining strands of hair swept over their skulls like shipyard heaving lines stood casually around the room, smoking, sipping, chatting. Mixed into the bag were men who supported crooked bodies on canes or crutches. Two were in wheelchairs, wearing tuxedo trousers cuffed and folded neatly where legs were missing. A blinded hero in dark glasses crossed to the bar on the only remaining arm of another man who wore a cluster of miniature medals proclaiming service in Korea pinned to the lapel of his tux.

Willy nodded, smiled, and mumbled his name as a few of them stopped to introduce themselves and welcome him to the fold. He felt alien and unworthy, fighting an urge to tear off his pleated shirt and expose some scar tissue, to demonstrate that he, too, had paid some painful dues to be here tonight. Sergeant Major Shaeffer was over by the bar, holding two drinks but anchored in conversation with two undecorated men who must be the reporters.

He began to edge away in the opposite direction until a voice nailed him in place. "Pudarski, right? First Marine Division in 'Nam?"

Willy Pud spun to face a lean individual with dark hair and sparkling green eyes. The voice marked its owner as a longtime resident of Queens. There was something vaguely familiar about the pug Irish face. Willy smiled and offered his hand.

"Bob O'Meara, Third MarDiv, Operation Starlight . . . back in '65?"

Memories hit Willy Pud like a jackhammer. Starlight had been his first combat operation. He arrived in Vietnam as part of the Special Landing Force brought down from Okinawa and hit the beach right behind another unit that had been shot up and pinned down by gooks in a contested tree line. One Marine had broken the deadly log jam on the bloody beach south of Chu Lai that day in August. One sergeant from 3d Marines had fought his way into the trenches and single-handedly killed twenty-five or thirty Main Force VC. One man had broken through the stiff, unexpected enemy resistance to a full-scale amphibious assault and kept Red Beach from reflecting its designation in Marine blood. That man took nine rounds before he fell. That man was standing in front of Willy Pud.

"Jesus Christ! I helped 'em load you on a chopper that day. We thought . . ."

"You thought I was dead meat, right? Shit, so did I."

"I was only a lance corporal, first time I ever got shot at. Scared shitless . . . but you . . . you were somethin' that day. I gotta tell you, man."

O'Meara shrugged and pulled at his drink. "Just wasn't my time to check out, I guess. And somebody had to get us moving off that goddamn beach. You know how it is. You do what you gotta do, right?"

Sergeant Major Shaeffer made his way across the room with the reporters in tow. He made introductions and handed Willy a stiff drink. O'Meara made no move to leave as an uncomfortable silence settled over the group.

"Hey, Sarn't Major, turns out me and Pudarski was on the beach together on Starlight. He was one of the guys that policed me up after the gooks ventilated my ass."

"My first op . . ." Willy mumbled into his drink. "They hit the AmTrac I was riding with a B-40 and killed a couple of guys. Thought I was gonna shit myself right there."

The reporters muttered and shook their heads as the silence descended once more. "Can we have a word or two with you, Mr. Pudarski? We got deadlines."

Sergeant Major Shaeffer grabbed O'Meara by the elbow and started to lead him toward the bar. O'Meara resisted for a moment, sloshing his drink and pointing at the newsmen. "I got somethin' you oughtta put in yer story. I think what Ford did today stinks. I think it dishonors me and every other man who served in Vietnam."

"C'mon, Bob, this ain't yer interview. Let the hometown boy answer the questions." Sergeant Major Shaeffer led O'Meara away as the reporters retrieved their notebooks and circled Willy Pud.

"Guess we might as well start with the hard stuff. How do you feel about the President's announcement?"

"Is that what you're here to write about?"

"No, not originally, but it's kind of hard to ignore reaction from veterans when the President signs a proclamation offering clemency to draft evaders and deserters."

Willy took a deep breath and fought to stay in control. He'd argued most of the day with the old man about the news, trying to keep it in some kind of perspective. "My reaction's about the same as Bob O'Meara's, I guess. I don't know how we're gonna convince veterans they did the right thing by going if we just shrug it off and forgive the guys who broke the law and ran off to Canada."

"Ford said it was time to heal the wounds of war . . ."

"A guy don't get wounded unless he gets shot at. For my money, I'd like to see 'em concentrate on takin' care of the guys who went. Let the guys who ran deal with their lives the best they can. Nobody forced 'em to run."

"There's a lot of people would disagree with that. There's a lot of people who say the threat of being drafted to fight in an illegal war forced them to run."

"Yeah, well, it's still a free country. They can say what they want. It don't make it right."

"So you'd say the President's granting of clemency was wrong?"

Willy polished off his drink and glanced around the room, trying to gauge the proximity of dinner. "Look, I think this country was founded and prospered on certain principles. One of those is that nobody gets something for nothing, you know? You do what the country asks you to do and you earn your rights as a citizen. You make a choice to duck out on that obligation and the country don't owe you shit, not clemency, not anything else."

"What kind of message does that send to Vietnam veterans who have joined the anti-war movement?"

"I don't know . . . maybe they should stop whinin' and get on with their lives. Can we talk about something else?"

"How do you feel about being asked to join one of the most prestigious organizations in America?"

"Very honored . . . and humble." Willy swept his hand across the room. "These guys are legends, you know? They represent everything that's good about us—spirit, determination—all that kind of stuff. I'm not sure where I fit in, but it's great to be asked to join them."

Willy was saved from further torment by the dinner bell. Sergeant Major Shaeffer hustled the reporters out of the room and then led Willy Pud to his seat on a raised dais. There was a prayer for the repose of the souls of all of the nation's war dead and then a sumptuous dinner made more comfortable for Willy by the presence of Shaeffer and O'Meara at his elbows. Sensitive to the need for common ground in an organization with members of diverse backgrounds and pursuits, the Medal of Honor Society arranged dinner partners by branch of service. There were fairly large groupings of soldiers and Marines around smaller assemblies of sailors, airmen, and even a Coast Guardsman or two.

At the end of the meal, Sergeant Major Shaeffer approached a small speaker's podium and waited for the room to quiet. He switched on a green-shaded reading light and began to intone the words of Willy Pud's Medal of Honor citation. Images began to flicker on his dinner plate like muzzle flashes from a concealed bunker. Willy closed his eyes and tried to ignore the haunting of old ghosts.

When he heard the part about "steadfastly and courageously holding the hill alone while his men attempted an escape," Willy saw Fowler. The old shit-kicker was slumped, bleeding from a rash of bullet holes in his torso. His head lolled back and he stared up in agony at the men who were supporting him. Salt and Pepper stood like smiling bookends, their NVA uniforms covered with more medals than Sergeant Major Shaeffer had on his dress blues.

O'Meara quietly but firmly shook him out of it and pointed him toward the podium. He adjusted the light and parroted the words of his prepared speech, saying all the right things about honor, humility, dedication to higher ideals, the unsinkable human spirit in the face of great odds; all the things he'd copied from the modest pamphlet prepared by the Medal of Honor Society to let the uninitiated know why such an organization existed beyond the obvious.

It was over before Willy Pud even realized he'd finished. There was a thunderous round of applause and then he was standing in a reception line with his laminated membership card in his pocket and a fresh drink in his left hand. The right hand was being grasped, gripped, and pumped by a conga line of consummate warriors. Willy stared into their faces and suddenly realized there *was* a common thread here.

Each of them—even the blind man in his blackened glasses— had a mysterious depth to his eyes, as if there was no bottom to the dark pools inside the pupils. If you could dive into those liquid centers, you'd sink like a rock, beyond pain, beyond suffering, past all the images of death and destruction, and you'd never hit bottom. There was in all those eyes, some dark, lurking menace; a great white shark prowling the deep ready to bite, tear, and rip. Willy nodded, mumbled, grinned, and wondered what was swimming in his own eyes.

O'Meara found him in a dark corner of the lobby bar sucking bourbon through ice cubes. The old man had promised to drive over and pick him up but Willy hadn't called. It was hard to apply the brakes and swing back onto the low road, down there among all the people who didn't have the Medal, those who didn't understand the addictive business of being out of the ordinary.

They negotiated fresh drinks and a silent toast. "You sorta went away for a while there at dinner." O'Meara squinted at him through the smoke from a dangling cigarette.

"Yeah. You hear those words . . . from the citation, you know. And all kinds of weird shit starts to happen."

"Uh-huh. I get the same reaction. You sit there wonderin' who the fuck they're talkin' about, right?"

Willy nodded into his drink. "Fucked-up times we're livin' in, you know? You sit in there with guys who have laid their lives on the line—guys who would do it again in a goddamn heartbeat—and outside you got . . ."

"And outside you got a President who wants to pardon all the draft evaders and protesters . . . which is to say what we did—and all them guys who got shot up or killed—don't mean shit. Am I right?"

"There it is. Makes me wonder how come more of our guys aren't upset about it."

"What? Medal of Honor guys, you mean?" O'Meara slugged from his drink and shrugged. "Ain't their war, pally. You, me, couple of others—we're the only ones from Vietnam. Most of the guys who got the Medal over there, they don't want to join . . . just like they don't want to join the VFW or the American Legion."

"Yeah. Nobody wants to be remembered as the outstanding player on the losing team."

"There it is. And we ain't seen the worst yet. The whole fuckin' shootin' match will be down the crapper by Christmas . . . soon as the ARVN realize we ain't comin' back to rescue them. The vets are gonna go in the toilet and all the fuckin' Monday morning quarterbacks are gonna have a field day."

They sipped in silence for a while, relying on the whiskey to fend off different demons. "You suppose there's any Americans left over there?"

O'Meara cut a glance across the table and signaled for refills. "What? POWs? Yeah, sure. They didn't give all of 'em back . . ."

"Not POWs."

"Whaddaya talkin' about?"

There was no holding it back. The whole story came belching out of Willy Pud in a stream of disjointed phrases. He jumped around, skipped over parts, and backtracked trying at once to shock O'Meara and purge the bitter memories. When it was all over, he found himself tense, angry, leaning over the low table and poking O'Meara in the chest with a stiff finger.

"Jesus H. Christ—and you actually seen those two mother-fuckers?"

"Just like Howard says, up close and personal."

"And you never said nothin' . . . to nobody in all this time?"

"Hey, man. It was classified. Far as I know, it's still classified!"

"What fuckin' difference does that make now? The outfit that classified it don't even exist anymore."

"We still got a government. If it wasn't classified, they'd have said something about it."

"They got enough trouble without droppin' that kinda bombshell, man."

"What do you think I ought to do about it?"

"Christ, I don't know. They gotta be dead, right?"

"Who knows? The thought of them two assholes alive makes my fuckin' skin crawl."

"They're dead, man. Or else the gooks would be makin' all kinds of noise about the great white heroes of the revolution. You know how they act about shit like that. Look what they done with the POWs."

"I just feel like people ought to know it happened, you know? I feel like they oughtta be exposed . . . or else they get away with it. Ain't we had enough bullshit stuffed down our throat? Ain't there no fuckin' justice?"

"Best justice for assholes like Salt and Pepper is death, Willy Pud. They gotta be rottin' under some goddamn rice paddy. They got what they deserved, so fuck 'em. Let it rest, man."

Stosh Pudarski and Frank Hovitz were terrorizing both loose women and wives when Willy Pud walked into the VFW Post on Steadman Avenue with Ricky on his arm. In a red velvet minidress trimmed with fake fur, she was a drop-dead package of explosive sex appeal. Stosh and Frank were hitting on her—sprigs of mistletoe dangling from their VFW pisscutters—before she was five feet inside the door.

A couple of kisses kept them at bay briefly, but they drew a new bead and went to flank speed when she hopped up on a bar stool and crossed her legs revealing a fleshy curve of thigh and Jolly Old St. Nick on a flashy green garter.

Willy watched them cavort around her while he ordered beer and ran his eyes over the tall Christmas tree that winked and blinked in a corner of the cavernous hall. He'd rather have taken her where the crowd was younger, but the VFW flyer was the only Christmas party invitation he got and dating opportunities had been spotty since school started. Every time he chased, she dodged, blaming a heavy course load. Lighten up, cool it, relax; don't get heavy, man. Worst of all, that fabulous, first knee-wobbling sexual encounter had so far remained a one-shot deal.

A wheezy old six-piece band, fronted by a Brylcreemed bohunk whose dentures matched the mother-of-pearl inlay on his accordion, was dragging tempo on junior prom classics. When they segued from "Stardust" into "Moonglow," Frank Hovitz went nuts and practically carried Ricky out onto the dance floor.

Willy handed his father a fresh beer. "Nice pisscutter, Pop."

Stosh cocked the hat down over his eyes and ran his fingers along the fabric to insure it had the appropriate catch-me-fuck-me rake. It was embroidered in gold, covered with pins and gewgaws including the pewter rendering of a twin-stack tin can Willy picked up for him in some Navy Exchange before he got out of the Corps.

"You oughtta be wearin' one too, boy. The fuckin' membership committee's been on my ass again."

"C'mon, Pop. Not tonight. I told you how I feel about that shit. One membership is enough for a while."

"There's a big push on to get you Vietnam guys into the VFW. You kids think we're just a bunch of old farts who sit around gettin' drunk and tellin' lies."

Willy Pud snagged a passing bottle of Old Overholt rye and poured shots on top of their beers. "I been comin' down to the hall with you for . . . what? Fifteen years or more. When did you ever do anything more than get drunk and tell lies?"

Stosh cocked a brow at his son. There was an angry glint in the off-eye . . . and then it was gone. It took a lot to piss the old man off at a party and this needle was old and dull. "Well, where the fuck else you gonna get away with them kinda lies? Huh? By God, we have a good time and there ain't no harm in that."

Ricky returned, laughing and hanging on Frank Hovitz's arm. "My God, where did you guys get that band?"

Stosh cranked an arm around her shoulders and signaled to one of the busy barkeeps for more drinks. "Well, we called up to Woodstock but all them assholes was too stoned to make the trip."

"Polacks all got tin ears and two left feet anyway. How the hell you think they invented the polka?" Frank Hovitz made a grab for Ricky as the music started again and wound up in a shoving match with Stosh. Ricky ducked under the storm and came up in Willy's arms.

"Wanna dance or drink?"

Willy canted an ear toward the crowd noise. The drunks were in full voice, singing anything that came to mind in direct competition with the band. "Either way we ought to pace ourselves. I got a feeling it's gonna be a long evening."

The pace Ricky set was fast and furious. She seemed driven to jam full hits of fun down her gullet like tasty canapes. Willy alternated between a beating on the crowded dance floor and the brutal flying-wedge required by frequent trips from their table to the bowl of potent vodka punch across the room. Ricky was flushed and sweaty by the time the band packed up to leave around midnight. Her dress was askew by two fur-covered buttons revealing enticing twin mounds of veined flesh and she'd stuffed her panty hose in her purse during the last trip to the ladies' room.

Willy sat watching her twitch as she shifted her weight from foot to foot, selecting tunes from the VFW's aging Wurlitzer. He breathed hard through his nose and fought to concentrate through the haze. He could almost feel the alcohol coursing through his veins and scorching into his brain. She looked so good and he wanted her so badly. If he didn't get a grip, he'd wind up bending her over the jukebox and giving the thinning crowd a real finale.

She danced her way back to their table and pulled her chair close to his. When she dangled her hand in his lap and let her fingertips graze gently under the table, he thought about the aspirin box full of Dex in his pocket. He'd been off the stuff entirely for some time now. Something about the Christmas party—some vague plan about outlasting her and winding up in bed; in control, able to plow through the semicomatose stage of a debilitating drunk—something had made him gather the last of his stash and bring it along to the VFW. He gave her hand a reassuring squeeze and headed for the bathroom at the back of the building.

When he returned, the crowd was sparse. Wives and other survivors were policing up the battlefield, tending the walking wounded or calling Yellow Cab medevacs for the KIAs. At their table, Ricky sat wolfing thick ham sandwiches beside Stosh and Frank Hovitz with Andy and Maggie Hogan from the neighborhood hangout.

The speed hit took the edge off a nagging attack of munchies but Willy slathered hot mustard on a slab of ham and grinned at the bloodshot eyes and gnashing jaws around the table. He'd forgotten the ritual. Maggie Hogan was a wizard with sugar-cured baked ham. When the Hogans ventured out from behind their own bar to hoist a few with friends, she made a ham and took it along for the traditional post-pisseroo feed for those still able to find their mouths with one or both hands.

Ricky was wearing Stosh's VFW pisscutter and Maggie had Hogan's bent over her permanent wave like a comic-opera commodore. She sliced more ham and offered it to Ricky.

"You finally got yerself a nice lady, Willy Pud . . . pretty too. Better take her off the market in a hurry."

"Got to stay light afoot, Mag. She don't like the thought of anybody riggin' an anchor on her ass."

Stosh sucked mustard off his thumb and swallowed. He seemed to be having trouble getting his gaze to focus and kept closing one eye. "He ain't no anchor. Pain in the keester a lotta times . . . but he ain't no fuckin' dead weight . . . I'll tell ya that. Got the goddamn Medal of Honor in Vietnam . . ."

"Pop . . . cool it. Eat some more ham."

Frank Hovitz poured lethal doses of vodka punch from a plastic pitcher and shook his stubby finger in Willy's face. "If you ain't gonna run off and get married, how about joinin' the VFW? I'm tellin' ya, Willy, you got the Medal and all, you come in and the rest of them Vietnam shit-heels might straighten up and fly right for a change."

Ricky swiped the pisscutter off her head and draped it over Willy's brow. "Looks great, doesn't it?" She cut a catty smile around the table but no one except Willy seemed to notice it wasn't sincere. "Out of one uniform and into another. Can't keep a good cowboy down."

Willy tossed the hat at Stosh and tore off a chunk of ham. He could feel the speed sparking and snapping behind his eyes. He needed a mouthful of something to keep his teeth from gnashing. Andy Hogan swallowed and tried unsuccessfully to cover a hollow belch. Maggie swatted at him and he ducked without ever taking his eyes off Willy Pud.

"How come you think that is, Willy? How come the Vietnam guys don't want anything to do with the VFW or the Legion or shit like that?"

"You're a bunch of old poops who like to sit around and drink, that's why. They're kids. They want to go out, dance and have some laughs . . . like we used to do when you came home from Korea." Maggie swatted at her husband again.

Frank Hovitz was having trouble keeping his face out of his paper plate. "Goddamn beer ain't good enough for 'em. They wanna take that fuckin' dope alla time."

Ricky fumbled with a pile of change on the table, found some quarters, and headed for the jukebox. Willy watched her go and wanted to find a way out of the crowd. He wanted her somewhere . . . anywhere . . . alone . . . now. His heart was throbbing against his rib cage and his lungs were working like bellows.

"We gotta go . . ." He drained his glass of fruit-flavored vodka and started to rise. Maggie Hogan poked at her ham and leaned over to whisper across the table. "She wants to dance some more, Willy Pud. Can't you see that? Go on over there and pick out some slow ones."

He hesitated just long enough to see Stosh's eyes glaze over. The right eyeball drifted slowly toward the left, the imminent danger signal. Stosh grabbed him by the wrist and barked. "You just tell me one gahdamn thing, Vilhelm. You just tell me how come the Vietnam guys won't come down here with us? That's all I wanna know. How come they gotta run off to the fuckin' woods, or stand around pissin' and moanin' about how tough they had it over there? War ain't never easy. You fuckin' kids . . ."

Willy Pud snapped his wrist free of Stosh's grasp. There was a terrible drone spreading out from the center of his brain, resonating on the wrong side of his eardrums. He gulped air and tried to bite his tongue, but the words came gushing out like great gouts of vomit.

"You fuckin' people are . . . drunk . . . nuts . . . fucked up! You piss me off! You know that? Huh?"

He stared at the soft, fuzzy faces trying to register shock. "You wanna know why guys from Vietnam won't join your fuckin' outfit? They've had enough organizational bullshit, that's why! The last organization they joined lied to 'em and then tried to get 'em killed. Think about it, goddammit! They come in here and you tell 'em how it was in *your* war . . . and how it *should have been* in ours. It don't work that fuckin' way!

"You came home and joined the VFW and sat around cryin' on each other's shoulders. It was a good fight and you won the motherfuckin' thing so everybody was happy. We come home and nobody wants to talk to the losers unless it's to tell 'em how fucked up it all was and how they shoulda won. I don't wanna hear that! What the fuck have we got to celebrate? What the fuck have we got to be proud of?"

He kicked over a chair and grabbed for Ricky who stood frozen where his tirade had stopped her on the way back from the jukebox. She ducked and coiled like a snake when he grabbed for her wrist. "Leave me alone, goddammit!"

"We're gettin' the fuck outta here!"

"You don't take me anywhere I don't want to go, asshole! You wanna leave . . . go . . . get outta my sight!"

Willy Pud tried to say more, but there was a painful knot in his throat where the vocal cords constricted and cut off communication. A series of bleats and grunts was all he could manage before he stormed across the VFW hall and out the door.

Christmas morning was an hour gone when Willy Pud forced himself to open his eyes. The pain was terrible, debilitating, devastating. A bullet in the belly would have been blessed relief from the biological chaos that ravaged him from his scalp down to a painful throbbing underneath both big toenails.

Stosh Pudarski clumped into the room wrapped in his old pinstripe bathrobe, his skinny shins full of barks and bites from raw two-by-fours. It was as if he'd been waiting for a cue to go on stage. He rattled a cup of black coffee down on the nightstand near Willy's pillow and then backed off, searching for his key light. Showtime.

"Merry Christmas, Pop."

"Bullshit, Vilhelm."

"We got any Alka-Seltzer?"

"I took your girlfriend home. She said you could call her . . . but I wouldn't do that for a while."

"I fucked up, Pop. I'm sorry, OK?"

"Vilhelm . . . don't you ever . . . not never . . . talk like that in front of our friends again!"

Willy tried to swing his legs free of the sweaty sheets but the effort drove him back down into the mattress.

"You were takin' them goddamn pills, weren't you? Don't lie! I know you were takin' them pills. And you told me you quit!"

"I'm sorry, Pop . . . we got any Alka-Seltzer?"

"You got a lot of acid eatin' at your guts, Vilhelm. I never realized it before. Alka-Seltzer ain't gonna help."

Willy Pud got his feet on the floor finally. He didn't have the strength to lift them out of the pile of puke near his bedside.

He stayed in classes during the week, at work on the weekends, and out of Hogan's completely for the rest of the winter. Ricky refused to take his calls at all during January and February. When he finally ambushed her on campus the last week in April, she was civil but cold. He apologized profusely, saying he'd clean up his act, never do anything like that again, if she'd just give him another chance.

She said he could call . . . to talk . . . but it was probably better if they didn't see each other again socially. Ricky seemed clear-headed and committed to ending their relationship. All the good reasons were ticked off on her fingers as she sat beside him on a stone bench near the main campus quadrangle. She felt constricted and constrained around Willy Pud, as if she were being marched toward some objective with no time out for picnics en route. They saw things so differently: she in terms of bright horizons, uncharted waters, the world an inviting, unshucked oyster. He in terms of dates, deadlines and commitments, pragmatic priorities, peep-sight point of view; the world as a tough place to dig a foxhole. Say what he may and try as he might, Ricky told Willy, he was what the war in Vietnam had made him . . . and . . . sorry, really . . . but that wasn't something she wanted to have to deal with for the rest of her life.

Willy sat stunned, trying to hawk up some anger from down deep but finding nothing in his guts to grip and throw back at her. Another tripwire, another booby trap; somehow, the 'Nam had ambushed him again. He felt numb, shell-shocked, as if he were dangling his muddy boots off the edge of a bunker; going weepy over friends lost in the fight. Lu Harris called and waved from across the quadrangle. Ricky stood and put a cool hand on his flushed cheek.

"It's over, Willy Pud. You lost. Try and forget about it."

He was on the el, halfway to his stop on the way home when he picked up an evening paper and realized Ricky wasn't talking about them. She was talking about the endless, agonizing war in Vietnam that, according to the front-page report, had ended for all intents and purposes that morning on the other side of the world. He scanned the story for sketchy details about Operation Frequent Wind, the full-scale, chaotic Navy and Marine evacuation of all Americans remaining in Saigon; he studied the pictures of desperate Vietnamese snarling and scrambling to escape the looming NVA blitzkrieg. And looking around the car, he saw the solid citizens of Chicago studying the story as they completed yet another leg in the race from cradle to grave. No pain, no regret, no anger . . . not one towering snit or blue funk in the whole carload. The war in Vietnam is over—finally—after ten years and fifty-eight thousand lives . . . so what's new? How 'bout them Cubs this year?

Willy Pud tumbled off the train two blocks short of his regular stop and began walking toward Hogan's Bar.

Pale blue ghosts danced in the shadows along Hogan's Bar, flickering across the upturned faces of early drinkers who sat mesmerized by the special news feed coming to them from Saigon via Hogan's new Sony Trinitron. Willy found a dark hole downrange on the TV's blind flank and slid into it. He studied two trembling hands on the bar in front of him—wondering why they were bunched and balled into knuckle-studded bludgeons—until Andy Hogan followed his cigar out of the dark and nudged him with a cold beer bottle.

"This OK? Or you want something stronger?"

Hogan knew. He understood. Willy could tell. The muted growl, the same pained expression Hogan wore at wakes and funerals. The strong, silent man with a cultural canopy spread taut over his emotions. Hogan was desperately searching but he couldn't find the words. Willy stared down at the white knuckles on his right hand and willed them to relax. Hogan covered the hand with his own for just a second, bobbed slightly, and then banged a bottle of Jack Daniel's down on the bar.

"It's on me . . . me and Maggie . . . no hard feelin's or nothin', Willy. You know we love you, boy. I'm sorry . . . I'm really sorry." Hogan waved off a customer and pulled the soggy cigar from the corner of his mouth. "You want me to turn the TV off?"

Willy uncapped the whiskey, realizing he didn't know much about the situation in Southeast Asia beyond what he read in the paper. He should hear the rest of it . . . bad, good, or indifferent. "Don't matter . . . leave it on."

"Look, you just sit here. Relax. Your old man should be comin' by in an hour or so."

As Hogan disappeared into the dark, Willy could feel the old-timers, Hogan's regulars who knew him and his background, sneaking furtive looks down the bar. This was not a crowd to suffer indignities in silence, not from an out-of-town ball club, not from the mayor or the IRS, not from the cops or some glib candy-ass on TV. Yet they held their peace, alternating attention between the nagging news updates from Hogan's TV and the cold, comforting beer from his reefer. They'd let him suffer in silence, at least until it all got to be just *too* goddamn much.

Willy watched the TV and threw a wall of liquid sandbags around his position at the bar. At commercial breaks and during other periods of stunned silence, when even the rattle-assed correspondents reporting live from the South China Sea had no words to match the agonizing pictures of a monumental rout, he could hear the whispers.

"Jesus Christ, we never shoulda got involved in that stinkin' mess over there . . ."

"Think about Wally Karpinsky's boy, huh? How's he feelin' with no legs and watchin' all this shit?"

"Them goddamn South Veetneese rolled over and ran like a buncha scared rabbits. After all we done for 'em too."

"I told you so, didn't I? Huh? We shoulda nuked them fuckers up in Hanoi and turned the whole goddamn place into a parkin' lot."

The comments rolled down toward him like a quiet wave lapping at a sandy beach. Each drinker added his thoughts, turning subconsciously toward Willy, looking for a response from the only man among them who had a personal stake in the sore subject at hand. And Willy sat quietly, his brain floating like a soggy log, heavy with fungus, moss, and moisture; threatening to sink from his skull, down through his neck, and disappear into the dark depths where his heart used to be. It was still down there now; quiet as the dark and deadly depths where the blind sharks wait to rip and tear at anything floating by on sluggish currents.

He was drowning, going down for the last time with no energy left to resist the awful pressure on his chest. And still the waves of panicky images from the TV smashed at him. Speed would help. He could swim to the surface on a burst of Dexedrine bubbles. Willy gulped beer and ached for a chemical life jacket. He jammed his feet under the foot rail and shook, fighting the urge to leave and head for an off-campus coffee shop where he could score something—anything to keep his head above water. He was off the stuff; had been for months. Promised the old man, promised himself, promised God—whoever had an interest—that he'd leave the speed alone. No more crutches; no more catalysts or catapults. Still, promises and the honor involved in keeping them didn't seem to mean much as Willy Pud dragged deeply on a cigarette and tried to keep himself planted safely on one of Hogan's bar stools.

Whispers washed over him again and he turned to stare at the TV screen. A VNAF helicopter, crammed with wives, kids, old women, pigs and chickens, staggered to a landing on some carrier deck. Sailors rushed to off-load refugees and shove the bird over the side, making room for swarms of other aircraft in a frenetic, uncoordinated landing pattern around the American evacuation fleet. Splash, deep-six, down the tubes. One of the helicopters he'd waited for, *prayed* for at times out in the bush, ejected over the side like just another round of expended ammo.

He saw panicky Vietnamese, soldiers and civilians terrified at the prospect of being associated with soldiers, clawing and biting—fighting harder than they ever had on a battlefield—to escape the unstoppable communist wave crashing at the gates of Saigon. Oriental mothers and fathers—elfin faces distorted into grotesque masks by fear of inevitable slaughter—pushing, packing, and tossing their children onto overloaded aircraft. American aircrewmen beating and kicking at the desperate hands trying to hold them on the ground at Ton Son Nhut. Fists and feet and faces; terror took its ugly toll in the Land of the Lotus Petal, the lair of the Snake-Eater, the Home of the Bush-Beast. And in the background of it all—keening as it sliced through the muggy air of South Vietnam—the thin whistle of the headsman's ax descending.

There was a flash of fading sunlight and the muted rumble of traffic as Stosh Pudarski and Frank Hovitz pushed through the door. The old man caught Hogan's nod as he stood listening to the hush, feeling the anxious eyes that flashed between him and the man hunched over the bar.

All the way home from work, he'd half listened to the radio and hoped for a healthy reaction. Frank Hovitz suggested they stop by the house to see if Willy had trashed the place, tossed the TV set out the window or something. But Willy wasn't home and the silence of the house, the familiar, undisturbed squalor, seemed ominous. They speculated over a beer and then arrived at the same conclusion. Like all the neighborhood kids his age, Willy Pud had been baptized and confirmed in the same church. He'd seek solace in the congregation down at Hogan's.

On the drive over, Stosh loaded up for an emotional grizzly bear. He knew this otherwise unremarkable day at the end of April was potentially lethal. He'd *seen* strong men lose it all. He'd *watched* guys get pushed over the edge and begin that long, tough tumble toward the bottom. You never knew where the edge was and you never knew what horror was waiting down there. All Stosh Pudarski knew as he cranked the truck toward Hogan's Bar was that guys rarely—if ever—crawled back out of that black hole.

He slid onto a bar stool at Willy's left elbow, motioned for Frank Hovitz to keep his distance, and stared at the image in the mirror. It was like watching one of those close-up corner shots on the *Friday Night Fights*. The staggered and stunned contender slumped and stared, weak and wobbly on his stool with all the fight gone out of him. Order the beer, pay off the bets, this guy is never gonna answer the bell for another round. Stosh Pudarski felt like the cut-man in that corner, swabbing at blood, muscle, and meat, staring at exposed bone, and sensing vital nerve damage. He watched himself place a comforting hand on his son's shoulder.

"You got nothin' to be ashamed of, Vilhelm. You didn't start it . . . and they wasn't never gonna let you finish it."

"Don't tell *me* that, Pop." His voice was soft, slightly slurred but clear, as if he was chewing on each word and tasting the bile. "Tell all the guys who died or got their balls blown off. Put up some fuckin' signs at the cemeteries."

"Vilhelm, listen . . . you got to be *proud* of what you did over there. You should be! You volunteered when they said they needed you."

"That just makes me a dip-shit, Pop. Me and all them other guys."

"It was them fuckin' politicians, and you know—"

"What I *know* is that I'm sittin' here as a Vietnam veteran, a newly certified member of the first generation of Americans to *lose* a goddamn war! You're the one who taught me losin' sucks, Pop. How do you want me to act?"

"I want you to hold your head up, Vilhelm. Be proud. An old Chief told me one time . . . the worse the war is, the better the soldiers got to be. Get pissed off at the right people; don't let this thing fuck up your life. You got too much to lose!"

"Yeah, Pop. I know all about losin'. And it don't make me proud. It makes me ashamed."

"You just listen to me for once in your life, Vilhelm . . ." Stosh Pudarski, the contender's corner man, the gnarled and scarred old hand, popped the smelling salts and prayed for a comeback round. "Think about all them stories you told me. Think about all them guys in your outfit who looked up to you. Think about all them real tight friends you made . . . the ones who made it back home and the ones who didn't. Remember what you said? You said it was the highest time of your life. Am I right?"

Willy blinked and stared. There was an uncomfortable, self-conscious hush along the bar. Willy ignored it, glancing over his father's skinny shoulder to the TV where a lone Huey helicopter was hovering, perched on the roof of the U.S. Embassy in Saigon. The last rat was safely over the side. The boilers on the sinking ship were about to explode. The End, music up, roll credits . . .

and Willy Pud just *could not* bring himself to believe it.

"Listen to me, Vilhelm! You don't want to let all those buddies down! You don't want to go crawlin' under a rock somewhere. That ain't what they'd want for you. That ain't what they died for!"

Willy Pud couldn't see the television anymore. He was surrounded by bodies. Hard hands tenderly touched his back, his shoulders, his elbows. Maggie Hogan swiped at tears and kissed his cheek. Frank Hovitz hugged him like he was manhandling a refrigerator. Guys he couldn't name, people he barely knew beyond a casual round of beers, were stacked up around him like sturdy tent pegs. He heard the words he needed to hear.

"Ain't nobody blamin' you, Willy."

"You done what you could, boy."

"You done what you had to do, that's all."

"Thank God it's over."

"God bless you for what you done, Willy Pud."

"Time to get on with your life, son."

Willy Pud looked into his father's rheumy old eyes and saw the pain there. The old man was hurting for him, with him, and there had been enough of that over the years. He forced a smile and found Andy Hogan in the crowd.

"Hogan, you gonna be a cheap sonofabitch all your life?" A large bubble of tension burst and the entire bar seemed to swell and gasp like a swimmer struggling for breath.

"On the house!" Andy and Maggie Hogan scrambled to mix drinks and pull draft beer. The TV died in a burst of electronic bullets from Hogan's remote control and there was a chorus of ragged cheers along the bar. A party fire was being ignited by Maggie Hogan's declaration of payday stakes for the regulars. People who hadn't planned on it were reaching deep into their wallets, wanting to savor the moment, share in the dramatic rescue from the abyss they'd just witnessed.

Tears streamed down Stosh Pudarski's face and he tried to hide them in a beer mug. Willy knew that wouldn't last long. The old man's friends were sliding down the bar in his direction. Willy made room and walked toward the corridor at the back of the bar that led to the toilets and a pay phone stuck in a tiny alcove between the Men's and Women's. He pulled the laminated card out of his wallet, dug for change, and dialed.

"Shaeffer . . ."

"Sergeant Major? It's Pudarski . . ."

"Uh-huh. Figured you might call. Where you been watchin' it?"

"In a bar . . ."

"Nice place? Or just some joint you ducked into to get out of the shitstorm?"

"Nice place. Neighborhood place. They know me here."

"Good place to be right now, Sarn't Pudarski. I'd recommend you stay there and get yerself tighter than a tick."

"Just one question, Sarn't Major . . ."

"That all? I got about a million fuckin' questions myself . . ."

"All the pain and bullshit, Sarn't Major . . . all the guys who died. What the fuck does it all mean now?"

"What the fuck's it supposed to mean, Willy Pud? What's it ever mean when good men die in war?"

"It's supposed to mean *something,* goddammit! What did they die for?"

"They died for the same thing soldiers have died for since the first shot was fired. They died for themselves, trying to prove something. They died for each other, for me and for you; tryin' to do what's expected of 'em, tryin' not to let a buddy down."

"Jesus, it's hard to just sit here drinkin' beer, you know? I feel like . . . like I ought to be dead too, you know?"

"I know, Willy Pud. It's called survivor guilt. And it's another thing that's been around since the first shot was fired. It'll get bearable after a while."

"So what do I do now?"

"I told you . . . get drunk. Forget about it for a while until you can reason the whole thing out."

"That's it? That's all I can do?"

"No. You can do one other thing."

"What?"

"You can do your best not to let 'em down, Willy Pud. *Now's* the time to be a hero."

NEW YORK—1975

Justin Bates Halley, Colonel, United States Army, Retired, eyed a bank of buttons on his phone console and punched himself clear of the contact in Dallas. Five minutes on the line revealed all he wanted to know just now about Emory Technology's big switch from Defense-related production to commercial satellite work at the Texas plant. Things were progressing nicely. Most of the machinery built to efficiently generate communications equipment for the military would produce civilian circuitry without further costly modification.

He'd known five years ago that the boom would bust—this day would come sooner or later—and that's when he ordered the subtle changes in research direction, in software, in tool and die patterns so that Emory Technology could double-clutch and shift gears ahead of the competition when the lucrative flow of Pentagon demands for high-tech military gadgets finally dried up. Halley smiled, allowing himself a long moment of sensual self-congratulation. The great river of war-related revenue was about to become drier than a popcorn fart, but Emory Technology would sail on unaffected.

Justin's foresight, his contacts, and the leverage only a man like him could apply to subtle pressure points in the convoluted Defense procurement system insured that the Pentagon paid the tab for ET's timely conversion to a civilian-oriented industrial base. Conservative estimates from the bean-counters on Cleve Emory's management staff indicated ET was at least three years and thirty million dollars ahead of the pack that would soon be clamoring for NASA contracts and export licenses, trying to duck the samurai swords that were hacking away at their market share.

The new Mercedes 350SL and the office on the fortieth floor with a panoramic view of the East River were two of many tokens bestowed on Justin in recognition of his business acumen. There would be others. A grand post-Vietnam strategy was already floating around the rarefied atmosphere of ET corporate head-quarters. A sizable chunk of conversion change would be sunk into acquiring flash-in-the-pan engineering and research outfits caught shortsighted by the end of a seemingly endless Pentagon patronage. Justin was an intimate of Cleveland Herbert Emory, Senior—as close as anyone could be to the corporate monolith known in the back channels of international commerce as The Iceman—and there was no doubt in his mind about who would get the regal nod to head the newest enterprise under the Emory Technology umbrella.

His attractive Director of Administration darted in with a stack of spread sheets, fresh coffee, and a note that said she'd be waiting for him in the Montauk condo on Saturday. Her name was Eileen Winter but she'd ended the note with the initials

"B.J." Justin felt stirrings in his groin at the thought of what their secret code promised for his weekend. Mrs. Halley—loyal Army wife but terminally gauche in a shimmering cesspool where business and family were just two turds floating side by side—had walked out years ago . . . about the time Eileen walked in, equipped with a Penn State MBA and unfettered breasts that had everyone on the management levels of the ET building—where she was immediately propelled by an astute personnel officer—making pointed comparisons with Dolly Parton. He'd won her services by invoking Cleve Emory's sweeping mandate to "give Mr. Halley whatever he needs" and her personal favors by moving her steadily, unobtrusively up the corporate ladder. Life was good, Justin reflected as he inhaled steam from the hot, cinnamon-flavored coffee, and it was about to get a damn sight better.

He sipped coffee and trailed his fingers across the pages of *The New York Times* spread open on his desk. The first ten news pages had all screamed a version of the same message to a war-weary audience. It's over. Win, lose, or draw, you paid your money; now take your choice. From the ashes of Saigon, a communist phoenix rises, called Ho Chi Minh City after the man who craved it but did not live to lead the victory parade down Le Loi Street. On the extra editorial pages, quarterbacks from both sides of the field were scrambling, trying to fade, pass, lateral or ground the political football. Everybody with an editorial voice was crying the politico-military poor-ass. All trying to be the one who told us so right from the start.

Justin chuckled and turned the page. Finally, something interesting; an ironic, sentimental footnote to the chapter telling how the American dinosaur died after ten years of struggle in an Asian branch of the La Brea tar pits. The faces of two young American Marines stared from a photo tombstone at the upper-right corner of the page. The caption identified them as Corporal Charles McMahon, Jr., and Lance Corporal Darwin Judge, the last two U.S. military personnel killed in action in Vietnam; struck by shrapnel from an NVA rocket during the final withdrawal.

They beamed post-boot camp confidence, resplendent in Marine dress blues, the same uniform they would wear in the grave. Justin sighed over his coffee. *Good-looking kids. Yeah, it figures. The Marines always got the best models for their mold. One of them even looked a little like that clown . . . what was his name? Pudarski?*

Justin doodled a heavy black line around the photos and propped his chin on his hand. His thoughts drifted slowly backward to Vietnam, to Danang, to the beat-up bohunk babbling into a tape recorder.

What's Pudarski doing these days? Crying in his beer, probably. Wondering what went wrong. Down at the VFW with all the other drunks cursing and shaking an impotent fist at the politicians who just wouldn't let them win. Or maybe Pudarski stayed in the Marine Corps. No surprise there . . . Medal of Honor and all . . .

Guy like Pudarski . . . where was he from . . . Chicago? Yeah, another red-blooded transfusion from the heart of America. Probably got greased on a third or fourth tour. Or maybe not . . . maybe Pudarski was lurking out there . . . ticking away, about to explode with anger and frustration . . . about to scream bloody murder about . . .

Justin felt his shoulder muscles spasm and found himself hunched over his desk, like a man expecting a hard blow from behind. He shivered and swiveled to stare out over New York. Clear sky; no haze. Then why the feeling that a shadow had floated in through his light-reflective office window? Atmospheric quirk or old ghosts?

He blinked and tried to clear his mental slate. The old ghosts shimmered into focus. *Salt and Pepper. If the North Vietnamese wanted to gloat . . . wanted to rub salt in a fresh wound just to make it fester . . . Nah! No way. They had to be dead. Had to be! No way they could have survived. Even if Pudarski made a stink . . .*

Justin felt the gooseflesh prickle near his spine. The air-conditioned office felt like a meat locker. He punched a button on his console.

"Eileen . . . call maintenance and have 'em turn down the A.C. in my office. Then step in for a minute please."

She wedged her back into a corner of his sofa and swung her legs onto the cushions allowing him a lingering look at a length of thigh. It was Friday and she was getting into a wanton mind-set, preparing to restructure the power base in their relationship.

"I need a quiet trace on a guy, Eileen." She reached for a notepad on the glass-and-chrome coffee table. "How are we fixed for contacts in the military records business?"

"There's that guy Ludlow in DIA . . ."

"Give it a shot . . . and get hold of Jake Arquette at the records office in St. Louis. Guy I want may be out of the service."

"Have you got a name, rank, and serial number?"

"Pudarski . . . Willy . . . or Wilhelm . . . a Marine sergeant. Polack from Chicago, if I remember right. He got the Medal of Honor sometime in '70. That should help."

"What do we want to know?"

"Where he is . . . what's he been doing . . . that kind of thing."

Eileen Winter tore a page off the notepad and crossed the room to prop herself on a corner of Justin's desk. She was slightly surprised when his gaze did not travel to the spot where her skirt hiked to midthigh.

"Is this business? Something I should know about to back you up on the requests?"

"Nah. Just call in a favor for me, Eileen. I worked on a deal with this guy in Vietnam. I'm just interested in what happened to him . . ."

She began to dangle her leg, letting the skirt ride higher, waiting for the rest of the story. Justin seemed irritated momentarily and then he tossed the morning newspaper in a can behind his desk.

"It's no big deal, Eileen. Just interested in a kid I met in Vietnam, OK? All this shit in the papers reminded me of him. I wanna know if he made it . . . if he's OK. That kind of thing."

She started to rise but Justin pulled at her elbow. Then he ran his hand up under her skirt.

CHICAGO

Willy refolded the paper and stared again at the faces staring back at him from the upper right corner of the third page. He was mildly shocked to learn that both Corporal McMahon and Lance Corporal Judge had been in elementary school when he first served in Vietnam back in 1965.

And now they were preserved in the national memory in a way they could not fathom when they were smiling through adolescent dreams of glory. They were subscripted to italics somewhere down at the bottom of the page, an ironic footnote to a dark chapter of American history. The last two boys from the block to come home from Vietnam in a box.

He stubbed out his cigarette and slid the paper away from him but it didn't help. Those dark eyes staring out from under dress uniform caps kept seeking contact. "I'm sorry . . ." Willy Pud lit another smoke and spoke to the newspaper. "No shit . . . I . . . I don't know why it had to be you two . . . I don't know why you had to die when it was almost over . . . I don't know why we lost . . . I did the best I knew how . . ."

It wasn't enough. McMahon and Judge continued to stare at him. Willy closed his eyes and tried again to think of something productive to do or say, some way to get himself off the mark, back to the land of the living. He tried not to mope, told the old man he was just taking some time to get his poop in a group. When Maggie Hogan or other friends dropped by the apartment to check on him, Willy posed and postured, grinning and bearing it, playing the stoic to insulate himself from pity peddlers. Still, he couldn't find the strength to outwrestle the powerful war demons that were shredding his soul.

Night sweats were the worst. Drunk or sober, he thrashed in his bed, his mind unspooling vivid images like a film projector stuck in high-speed reverse. The last frames were always the worst. Salt and Pepper strutted around his prostrate form, laughing, jeering, and jabbing dirty fingers into his eye sockets, flashing the vee for victory sign.

One turbulent night when a warm rain swept down West Calumet Avenue, Willy breathed the fresh, cool air and decided an exorcism might help. He sat down and began to scribble all the details about Salt and Pepper he could remember. He examined the notes over coffee the next morning, wondering how he might get the information published. The more he thought, the more it seemed like sour grapes, the whining screed of a disgruntled vet looking for someone besides himself to blame for finishing flat last in the Greater Southeast Asia War Games.

Now, the sad story of the war's last casualties made it all seem trite and trivial. It was bad enough that they died in the final spasms of a lost cause. McMahon and Judge didn't need angry vets pissing on their graves, no matter what the justification. The huge black cloud shading the image of Vietnam veterans would not be dispelled by salting it with disgraceful memories.

He got up and wandered into the bathroom. In the midst of brushing the taste of stale beer from his mouth, he paused to study the mirror. There was an image burning back at him; a signal beamed from behind the bloodshot eyes. It was a familiar message, one he'd sent and received a thousand times in the

toughest of situations, when he was trembling, weak in the knees
out there on the edge. The same one he'd heard at the Citadel in
Hue City, at Khe Sanh, in the A Shau Valley, and up on that
bloody hill near Quang Tri.

*Strength, courage, don't mind-fuck yourself, ignore the pain, it
don't mean nothin', continue the mission, drive on . . . all I need
is an indig rucksack and half a shoulder to carry it on . . .*

It translated clearly through the hard set to his stubbed jaw. If
fighting a war couldn't kill him, then losing one shouldn't either.
Life, Willy Pud decided as he rinsed his toothbrush and reached
for his razor, was always a better option than death. And there
had been enough—too many—deaths over Vietnam.

*God bless the ones who died. God help the ones who were
ripped and torn in body or mind. But God knows I did my best.
And goddammit, it just wasn't good enough . . . so I'll continue
the march.*

When he'd showered and dressed, Willy went to the phone
and dialed Ricky's number. If she'd see him; if she'd listen and
understand that he was bound and determined to put Vietnam
behind him once and for all. She could help him get on with
his life. Ricky was the first step he needed to take back from
the war.

Lucinda Harris answered the phone after a long series of rings.
She seemed surprised by his call at first and then warmed to conversation when he told her he wanted to wipe the slate clean.

"Ricky can't come to the phone right now. She's, uh, she's in
the loo . . ."

"Well, look, I was really thinking of dropping by in an hour or
so . . . try to square things away, you know? I really need to see
her, to explain . . . it's over and that's it. I want to get on with
life . . . forget about Vietnam."

"And you want to come over here and tell her that?"

"Yes. I really need to. Is it OK, you think?"

"I don't think Ricky wants to be your crutch, man."

"I'm not askin' her to be a crutch. Look, Lu, would you just
ask her if it's OK if I come by?"

She was away from the phone for a minute and then he heard
what he wanted to hear. "Yeah, come on over. We're uh, we're
working on something in the kitchen. I'll leave the door unlocked.
Just come on in."

Willy Pud paused at the bottom of the stoop. He lit a smoke,
inhaled, and tried to slow his heartbeat. He'd have to make it quick
and effective once he was face-to-face with her again. She'd have

to believe that he truly wanted to flush the virus out of his system. He'd have to convince her it was worthwhile to help him do that. For all the bumps and brawls in their mercurial relationship, he loved her and he felt she loved him. He took a final drag and flipped the cigarette into the street. It was all a matter of getting her to touch that emotion. He walked up the stairs confident he could convince Ricky that she really loved him and that she really wanted him in her life.

The apartment door swung open easily. Willy Pud stepped inside and cringed at a pungent cloud of marijuana smoke. Whatever Lu and Ricky were doing in the kitchen, they'd better be able to handle it stoned. He called out to announce his arrival, but the bass rumble of the stereo drowned him out, so Willy painted on a smile and walked toward the narrow kitchen area.

A large ice cream container sat on the table in the middle of a sticky puddle next to an empty wine bottle but there was no one in the kitchen. He called again, raising his voice against the throb of the music. Nothing. If Lu and Ricky were home, they were elsewhere. He followed his nose to Ricky's bedroom and saw speaker wires trailing under the door. No response to his knock, so Willy Pud pushed the door open a crack and peeked.

She was spread-eagled on the bed, naked, stoned, vulnerable, and clearly enjoying the ministrations of Lucinda Harris. It took Willy Pud a minute to recognize the scene for what it was. Ambush. A big, bright artillery attack designed to crush him into the ground, to pin him down, time-on-target, and lash him with sizzling shrapnel.

Ricky kept her eyes on him as she moved her head and flicked her tongue at one of Lu's breasts. She looked serpentine and cruel like a beady-eyed snake teasing prey. Lu waved a Vaseline-slick vibrator at him and pointed at Ricky's belly. The message was spelled out in whipped cream on a slate between her navel and a line of soft black pubic hair. Off Limits.

"Find someone else to fuck over, man." Lucinda Harris flipped a switch and Willy became vaguely aware of a low-pitched electronic hum from the vibrator in her hand.

He wanted to leave but the scene had a strange magnetism. His voice sounded strangled and strange.

"This is what kept us apart, Ricky? Jesus Christ, it was going on all the time."

She giggled again and massaged Lu's meaty thigh. "A-C, D-C, double your pleasure . . . double your fun."

"Thanks a lot, Ricky."

"Fuck you, man."

"No . . . fuck you, bitch!"

"Never again in your lifetime, man. You are a loser."

Laughter chased him down the staircase and out onto the street. He ran a full block before he stopped hearing it. And then he got very angry.

PART THREE

SINKER

ST. LOUIS, MISSOURI—1975

The gate area of the grimy old bus station at 10th and Pine streets was a howling wind tunnel when Willy Pud stepped down off the Greyhound. He milled around waiting for the driver to unload his seabag, shuffling his feet and wishing he'd managed to beat the Marine Corps out of a fleece liner for his beat-up old field jacket.

Wind-driven sleet stung his ears as he shouldered through the sleepy crowd outside the terminal, searching for a phone. His watch said 11:15]P.M. He dropped change in the slot, turned his back to the wind, and dialed the number for Hogan's Bar in Chicago. Andy Hogan made polite inquiries and then went to fetch the old man.

"Vilhelm? Where are you?"

"St. Louis, Pop. Right on time. Everything's OK. I'm gonna find a hotel and get some sleep."

"You got enough money and everything? You left in a big hurry."

"I got what I need for now, Pop. When I get set up here, I'll let you know."

"Vilhelm, this ain't a good idea. You was gonna finish school . . . at least get some local work."

"Pop, we been through all that. I gotta get away for a while and . . . I need to see a guy down here."

"How come you didn't just give him a call? He don't even know . . ."

"Pop, I gotta go . . . time's runnin' out on this dime. Take care of yourself. I'll call later in the week."

Willy Pud fought the winter wind up Pine Street until he spotted the Laclede Hotel. It looked run-down and seedy, which seemed appropriate both for the blighted inner-city neighborhood and for Willy's current mood.

Outside the hotel, on the dim edge of a pale pool of light spilling from the doors, a pair of razor-thin black men in military surplus clothing smoked, shivered, and nailed him with yellow eyes. The one who'd been a Spec Four in the 11th Armored

Cavalry Regiment according to his overcoat slid left into Willy's path and lowered his head to suck at the Kool cupped in his hand. His buddy, wearing a field jacket from the Big Red One and a Combat Infantryman's Badge, closed the right flank. Willy shrugged at the roadblock and lowered his seabag to the slushy sidewalk.

"You want somethin'? Too cold to be shootin' the shit out here."

A spark of anger flickered across the hard ebony faces. Willy decided these were men unaccustomed to direct confrontation in their downtown TAOR, particularly by white guys without benefit of badge and gun. When the former 11th ACR trooper finally spoke, Willy smelled cheap wine on the wind at their backs. He slid his left foot back for balance and tensed.

"Take off yer pack, bro. We jes be lookin' for a little huss . . ."

The 1st Infantry vet flicked his smoke into the wind and rolled his shoulders. "You a vet, ain'tcha, Chuck? 'Nam . . . Marines . . . I can dig it. You dudes was up north of me."

"There it is."

Willy could feel the touch coming but there wasn't much use arguing given his jacket and the stencils on his old seabag. He shrugged and fought the wind to get a cigarette lit.

"How 'bout that huss, my man? Been some hard times since the 'Nam. How 'bout a coupla bucks for a taste?"

He had exactly $78.50 in his pocket with no idea how much a hotel might cost or how long he'd be in St. Louis. The trip had been spur of the moment, driven by anger, frustration, and the crumpled newspaper article tucked inside his jacket. A meager bankroll might have to stretch a long way.

"Jing is tight. Just got into town."

Both black men nodded, pondering, sliding a step closer. When the 11th ACR vet dropped his right hand to his pocket, Willy casually reached for the strap of his seabag. If he was quick enough, the bag would shield him from a knife thrust. If a pistol played in the developing situation, he might be able to block the first shot.

"Don't seem right, do it, man?" The 11th ACR vet fumbled menacingly in his overcoat pocket and shook his head. "Shouldn't be no vets havin' to stick up no other vet for bread. You oughtta give it up easy, Chuck."

The 1st Infantry grunt blew hot breath on his hands and then aimed down his forefinger at Willy Pud. "Share the rations, Chuck . . ."

Willy hefted the bag and pointed his chin at the hotel entry. "No score, man. I'm headed inside to . . ."

"Freeze! Stay where you are and show me your hands!"

A hot cone of white light burned over Willy's shoulder and turned the angry black faces a pale tan. Out of the corner of his eye, he saw two dark figures approaching slowly from the right and caught a flash of light off a policeman's cap badge. Slowly lowering the seabag, Willy raised his hands and stood still. Across from him, the black vets turned into flood-lit zombies as they raised their arms in a casual, practiced gesture. The expressions said it all. This wasn't the first roust and it wouldn't be the last.

They stood in a shivering tableau listening to radio squawks until a squad car pulled up and bathed the scene in flashing red light. Car doors slammed and the St. Louis Metro cops— now adequately backed up by a patrol unit—moved in to see what they bagged on the chilly street outside the Laclede Hotel. A firm hand gripped the collar of Willy's field jacket and propelled him across the sidewalk. A voice told him to "hit it" and he glanced over his shoulder for an explanation. He was promptly slammed into the rough concrete wall. "Face front . . . assume the position!"

Willy noted the two black vets were spread-eagled, leaning on the wall and undergoing a thorough pat search. He awkwardly molded himself into the same position and felt hands running over his shoulders, down his arms, and back to his armpits. The search was quick and professional, ending when the cop plucked the worn wallet from the left rear pocket of Willy's jeans.

He started to explain his presence to the cop at his back but was interrupted by a whoop from another officer who struck it rich in the elastic top of a sock. Willy inclined his head slightly and saw two white cops examining a cellophane bag under the beam of a long black flashlight.

"Well, just what the fuck have we here?" The cop with the flashlight tapped the 11th ACR vet on the shoulder and held the plastic bag under his eyes. "You just fucked up badly, my man. You just bought yourself a warm room in the cross-bar hotel."

Both black vets knew enough to keep their mouths shut, but Willy could see them seething as they ignored the litany of Miranda rights. A chill ran through his guts that had nothing to do with the weather. If he didn't start explaining, the cops would presume he was a buyer who got burned in a street deal.

"Listen, I didn't have nothin' to do with . . ."

He felt the hand on his jacket again and a voice interrupted his effort. "Cool it! Just keep your mouth shut. Stand up and turn around slowly."

Willy did as he was told and found himself facing a cop in a heavy uniform pea coat, holding a big blue Colt Python in one hand and his wallet in the other. A metal name tag opposite the badge identified the patrolman as E. J. Miller. There was a crooked smile on the man's ruddy face that might indicate empathy or anticipation of a solid narcotics bust.

"I just got into town tonight, man. I was gonna check in at this . . ."

The cop put a finger to his lips and inclined his head toward the black vets who were now being handcuffed and folded into the rear of the patrol car. One of the escorts held the door and pointed at Willy and Patrolman Miller.

"Room for one more monkey in this cage."

Miller made a chopping motion with his hand and holstered his pistol. "Take 'em in and start the paperwork. I'll take care of this one."

When the patrol car was fishtailing down Pine Street toward the local precinct house, Miller tossed Willy Pud his wallet. Then he smiled and fired off a salute that Willy immediately recognized as inspired by the ministrations of a Marine drill instructor. Before Willy could get the wallet back in his pocket, the cop pointed at the lights of a White Castle hamburger joint on the corner.

"You wouldn't want to eat at one of those places, but they got coffee that'll knock your dick stiffer'n a squeegee handle. Let's you and me get some of it and then you can tell me what brings a Medal of Honor man to our fair city."

"Had a chance to play ball at Mizzou after I graduated high school here, but . . . fuck. War was on and I didn't wanta miss it, you know? Anyway, standard route . . . boot camp at Dago . . . ITR at Pendleton . . . then O-C-S . . . Over the Choppy Seas. Oh-three-eleven . . . fucking grunt to the max. Got a bellyful of 'Nam right quick. Blew my ass away at LZ Baldy south of Danang. Got back and couldn't decide whether I was glad I went or disgusted with the whole thing. Never had nothin' but respect for the Corps though. Guess that's why I'm a cop today."

Coffee was free in downtown White Castle joints for Patrolman Eddie Miller and the other St. Louis beat cops who kept the infamous cheap food emporiums from becoming constant rip-off targets. They were on a second cup and Willy had yet to say anything much. Miller was a fan.

"Lessee, I joined Hotel Two-Five right after Hue City. Something like March or April '68. Wasn't that many bush vets left, but what there were . . . man, they were still talking about you. Willy Pud, right?"

Willy smiled and nodded, getting to know and like this guy who—like so many other cops in cities across the country—found his way back to the action after Vietnam by pinning on a badge. "Damn fine outfit . . . Captain Christmas, Gunny Thomas . . . but they were probably gone when you got there."

"Not Gunny Thomas. He extended . . . kickin' ass and takin' names. He's the one who told me about you bein' put in for the Medal of Honor. Glad to see you got it."

"Spotted the card in my wallet, huh?"

"Yeah. But I'd already recognized the name from yer driver's license. Even if I didn't know about the Medal, I ain't about to believe a Marine like you would be involved in a drug deal with them two spooks. We been watchin' those guys for some time now. Lots of 'Nam vets—especially black vets in the projects—dealin' the stuff they got used to over there."

Willy Pud sipped coffee and silently thanked everyone from God on down the pipeline of his life for the strength it took to keep him from going off on a chemical binge when Ricky stuck a bayonet into his heart. He'd been fighting, straining, arguing with himself daily to stay on an even keel when Maggie Hogan brought him the two-page article from a Sunday edition of the *St. Louis Post-Dispatch*. A cousin who lived in the St. Louis suburbs had sent it along as an example of how the city was going to hell in a handbasket.

Miller motioned for more coffee while Willy—against the policeman's advice—decided to try a plateful of the diminutive White Castle hamburgers. Miller cringed as Willy polished off two burgers in four bites.

"Jesus, you're gonna need a stomach pump . . . or a shitload of Augie Bush's finest beer. I'm off tomorrow, if you wanna let me show you around."

Willy glanced at the bare ring finger on Miller's left hand. "No problem with wife and kids?"

Miller shrugged and sipped coffee. "Had one of each there for a while. Not no more. Got married and had a little girl right after I came home, you know? Two years later she tells me I ain't the same guy I was before I went to 'Nam. I sez somethin' like—well, no fuckin' shit, Sherlock—or words to that effect. Anyway, she split. I got visitation rights for my little girl but that don't include tomorrow."

Willy Pud thought for a moment, staring at the smiling face across the table. He needed a friend in St. Louis and former Marine Corporal Eddie Miller was highly qualified for the billet. He reached inside his jacket and spread the newspaper article on the table. It was the first in what was touted as a series on St. Louis's growing problems with angry, disenfranchised Vietnam veterans. It was a poignant, hard-hitting, insightful piece of photo-journalism, but that's not what prompted Willy Pud to read it and take off heading south along the Mississippi River.

He tapped a finger on the byline and looked up at Miller. "You know this guy?"

"Spike Benjamin? Fuckin' A, I know him. We both belong to the local chapter of the 1st MarDiv Association. Shit, he rode with me in a unit when he took most of these flicks. You know him?"

"Yeah. Good dude. We used to run together in the 'Nam. Never heard from him or anything but . . . well, I just need to talk to him . . . about . . . about something that happened to us over there."

Eddie Miller was a good street cop. His ability to read people, to decipher messages in unspoken codes, had kept him alive for the past seven years. He checked his watch and stared into Willy Pud's eyes.

"I get the feeling this ain't just old home week with a buddy from the 'Nam, but that's not my concern unless you say it is. I can hook you up with Spike and then hit the bricks."

Willy Pud stared back and chewed on his lip. "Why don't you deal yourself in on this, Eddie? There's somethin' been eatin' at me for a long time . . . a couple of Americans . . . guys in Vietnam that . . . well, it's a story . . . you probably won't believe but you earned the right to hear it."

Miller nodded, slid out of the booth, and shrugged into his coat. "Decent. Meanwhile, you ain't checking into no fuckin' fleabag down here. My shift's over in less than an hour. Lemme sign off at the station and we'll head for my apartment."

"You gotta be shittin' me! He's here? In St. Louis?" Spike Benjamin swiveled away from his computer terminal and reached for a pencil. His hand was shaking and he snapped the point. Reaching for a replacement, he upset a half cup of cold coffee. *My God,* he thought, listening to Eddie Miller laughing on the other end of the line, *this is a blast from the past!*

"Where are you gonna be in, say, a half hour? OK, lemme shut down around here and I'll be right over." Miller responded as he'd been told, with Willy Pud's strict instructions not to interfere with Spike's routine in any way that wasn't welcome.

"Is he fucking crazy? I can't wait to see him again . . . shit, let me talk to him!"

Eddie Miller said personal communication would have to wait for a while. Willy Pud had set an alarm and gotten up early to run some errands. They could meet for lunch.

"Fuck a buncha lunch! This is gonna go on all night . . . as long as that ugly Polack can hack it anyway. Police him up and meet me ASAP at—how about the Car Barn down on Broadway—just the other side of Baden Circle?"

Spike Benjamin hung up and tried to get himself organized. The appointment calendar on his cluttered desk posed no pressing problems. He was due at his lawyer's office for an alimony adjustment meeting with Wife Number Two at four P.M. He punched a number on his speed-dial console and told a legal assistant that the meeting was postponed indefinitely. Press of business. He'd get back with her about rescheduling.

That cleared the top decks. His editors at the *Post-Dispatch* had two of his popular features on the spike complete with photo selections. His agent was still negotiating with the *Time* magazine people over the piece they wanted him to do on urban blight. There was a flock of congratulatory letters from his National Press Association Award that needed answering but . . .

"Piss on that!" Benjamin stabbed a button and shut down his PC, then mashed the intercom switch and called his young assistant into his cluttered office. She poked her head inside to catch him shadow-boxing in front of his desk.

"Don't tell me . . . you got the Pulitzer, right?" She frowned at the puddle of coffee on his desk and moved to mop it up with a roll of paper towels she'd learned to keep handy.

"Fuck a buncha Pulitzers, Julie! I just got a call . . . Jesus, you won't believe this. A guy I used to know in 'Nam . . . great guy . . . really hot shit . . . won the Medal of Honor, for Christ's sake! He's here . . . in St. Louis and wants to get together . . . haven't seen him in—what? Five, six years anyway. What a fuckin' guy . . . we went on some operations that would knot your panty hose, lemme tell ya!"

Julie was nearly finished salvaging copy paper from the coffee spill. "Does this mean we hit the hold button?"

"This means you haven't seen me, you don't know where I am, and you don't know when I'll be back." Benjamin grabbed his coat and headed for the door. "I'll call you later today. You gotta meet this guy!"

Willy Pud and Eddie Miller were mopping up the remnants of a bratwurst and sauerkraut special at a back booth when Spike Benjamin shouldered his way through the lunchtime gaggle. Willy buried his face in a beer mug, peeking over the rim, wondering how long it would take his old running mate to pick him out of the crowd.

Benjamin's ruddy face looked the same despite a halo of shaggy, grey-flecked hair: intense, probing, always leading with his nose. His flinty green eyes still sparkled despite a pair of wire-rimmed glasses that were new since 'Nam. He was still lean and moved with the same offhanded grace he'd displayed jinking through the jungle. Give him a high-and-tight haircut, a sweaty set of utilities, hang a brace of beat-up cameras around his neck, and he'd be back in the saddle . . . the 1st Marine Division's number-one propaganda peddler and consummate bush-beast.

Willy felt his heartbeat accelerate while his breathing became slow, relaxed, and regular. The deep shit suddenly got shallow. Emotional reinforcements were rushing in and the burden got lighter. It was the same feeling he got in Vietnam when Benjamin—usually unexpected and always unannounced—tumbled off a helicopter or shoved his way forward from the CP to join Willy's platoon on an operation. Spike was never able to make it better but he damn sure made it more bearable.

"Chew tobacco . . . spit . . ."

A hush swept over the noisy crowd at Benjamin's loud bark. Willy watched him hit an assault-fire brace and aim down an extended forefinger. They'd been spotted.

"If you ain't Mah-reen Corps, you ain't shit!"

Willy rose, taller than his old friend by three inches and broader by thirty pounds, but that didn't stop Benjamin from hitting him like a berserk linebacker. They hugged silently, ignoring the stares, transfusing each other with raw emotion, sharing by feel those things that can't be said.

Eddie Miller used the time to order foamy pitchers of cold beer. He poured as they sat across from each other, staring, smiling, searching for subtle changes. Miller filled the void with a rendition of Willy Pud's arrest on his first night in St. Louis. It set them all laughing and prompted Benjamin to recount their first brush with garrison MPs in an infamous skivvy-house at Number 19 Doc Lap Street in Danang.

"Willy Pud's in the rear and staying with me in Hooch 13, see?" Spike polished off his beer and poured around the table. "I figure to cut him a huss and take him on a skivvy-run. So we get out to Number 19, drunk, dodging MP patrols through Dogpatch . . . fucked up like Hogan's goat . . . crawling through the *benjo* ditches like a goddamn recon team.

"Now, this is no shit . . . we finally get to the skivvy-house, and Mama-san trots out two of her finest . . ." Miller was giggling, getting into the story, feeling like he was back there with them, primed and ready for a little boom-boom after too long in the bush. Willy Pud hooted and spit beer all over the table.

"Horseshit, Spike . . . don't believe it, Eddie. *One* of her finest, yeah . . . the other one looked like she'd been pullin' butts for a flamethrower."

"OK, OK . . . I'm on a roll here. So, there's only two skivvy-girls available this time of night, see. One of 'em is fucking drop-dead beautiful and the other looks like she got into a grenade fight and lost. Naturally, the beauty perches on my lap and the hog goes after Willy. About this time, the sonofabitch tells me he's dead broke.

"Like an asshole, I ask him what happened to all his jing . . . and he gives me this goddamn story about his dad needing an operation . . . cancer, or some such shit . . . tells me he had to send all his pay home . . . and he needs more, see. So, shit, I fall for it and pull out a roll of MPC that would choke a fucking horse and—right there on the spot—I lend him two hundred dollars! Now it only costs twenty MPC or ten green to get laid in Danang at going rates, so I only hold back a twenty MPC. Nothing's too much when a buddy's in trouble, right?"

Two waitresses had taken over the chore of replenishing and pouring the beer. They hovered around, grinning, missing some of the jargon but digging the story and the joy telling it seemed to bring their customers. Nobody at the table minded. They were all in Danang, back in '68.

"Anyway, fucking Willy Pud . . . he gets all teary-eyed and thanks me . . . for him . . . for his dad . . . for the Corps . . . the whole schmaltzy deal . . . and *then* . . . the asshole . . . he leans over to my girl . . . the good-lookin' little honey . . . and he promises her the whole two hundred if she'll spend the night with *him*!"

The waitresses were laughing out loud now, shrieking, ignoring their other customers. Spike Benjamin shook his head and tried to finish. "Now, see, I'm in fucking shock here . . . the good-lookin' little thing . . . she jumps off me, hauls the hog off his lap, and wraps herself around Pudarski like a fucking boa constrictor. They disappear inside . . . with my two hundred! Here I am with this goddamn female Fu Manchu grinnin' at me with betel-nut stains all over what's left of her teeth . . . and I hear the meat start slappin' in the next room.

"I'm lookin' around for my .45 . . . I'm gonna go in there and shoot the sonofabitch right in his naked ass, see . . . and this hog snatches my last twenty and hauls me inside. Fortunately, I brought along a canteen full of gin . . . anyway, I must have got drunk enough to mount this beast . . ."

Benjamin shook his head and snorted into his beer. Willy Pud wiped at his eyes and nodded at Miller. "Ask him how he knows he got laid that night."

Miller pressed but Benjamin refused to finish the story until even the waitresses insisted. Finally, Spike let himself be talked into it. "I wake up back in Hooch 13 the next day, see. Hungover bad. Don't know where I been . . . what happened . . . nothin' . . . except I'm stone-broke. Pudarski leaves me a fuckin' thank-you note and disappears back into the bush. I'm figurin' . . . you know, we had a good time . . . what the hell . . . except two days later, I find out I got a case of the fucking crabs!"

The stories began to roll out of them in a joyous rush. Fortunately, Eddie Miller knew enough people of common acquaintance to hold up his end with tales from beyond Willy's and Spike's tours with the "Pogey Rope Fifth" Marines. It was nearly an hour before Willy Pud remembered the gift he'd brought for Benjamin. A St. Louis shoemaker, recommended by Eddie Miller, did a rush job on it, and Willy haunted surplus stores all morning until he found just the right gift box. He reached into his jacket and gently placed his gift on the table in front of Spike Benjamin.

"What the hell is this?" Benjamin picked up the cardboard canister and read the stencil: Grenade, Hand, Fragmentation, M-26, HE Comp B. Willy grinned and winked at Miller who was in on the surprise.

"It's a grenade canister. Don't you remember what they look like? You seen enough of 'em."

"Yeah, I remember. Hated the fucking things."

"Well, open it up. Maybe you'll like what's inside better than a frag."

Inside the canister was a handsome belt made of black ostrich hide that cost Willy Pud thirty dollars. Fortunately for his bankroll, the shoemaker threw his snap and clasp work in for the price of the exotic leather. Willy wanted the special buckle attached to something worthy and realized he'd made the right decision when he saw the look on Spike's face.

Benjamin showed the square, nickel alloy, interlocking buckle with the raised, five-pointed star to Eddie Miller. Smaller and more well made than the standard NVA trooper's equipment belt buckle, it was one of the rarest and most coveted war souvenirs among Vietnam combat vets. Miller leaned in for a better look and whistled softly.

"Hey, man . . . that's a goddamn NVA *officer's* buckle. I tried to get one of them for eighteen fucking months. Only guy I knew had one wanted two SKS carbines before he'd even start talking trade."

Benjamin looked up at Willy and caught the nod. "Yeah, it's the same one. I told you I'd get it for you and here it is."

While Spike laced the belt through the loops of his khaki trousers, Willy Pud filled in the blanks for Eddie Miller. "We were on a sweep down near Go Noi Island, see . . . one of those quick-insert deals where you're supposed to be reactin' to hot intelligence."

Miller snorted into his beer but Willy Pud continued the story. "Yeah, I know . . . only this time, the intel was right. We ran up on a goddamn regimental CP and caught the fuckers kicked back cookin' rice. Anyway, shit hits the fan . . . we're way over our heads, outnumbered for a fat-man's ass, screamin' for air and arty and tryin' to hang on. Ammo's runnin' low, so me and Spike are diggin' around, collectin' up spare magazines, grenades, and shit when they hit us with eighty-deuce mortars . . .

"We head into this big-ass bunker to get out of the fire and—no shit—we run smack into two NVA officers. One of the bastards has got a pistol and cranks a round right in my face. Don't know how the round missed, but I get knocked asshole-over-teakettle. Spike smashes the guy in the gourd with one of his cameras, grabs the pistol, and wastes the fucker. Meanwhile, the other officer is headin' for the exit. He wings a shot over his shoulder and catches Spike right below the ribs."

Willy Pud poked Benjamin in the approximate spot and elicited a grunt. "Anyway, Spike empties the first gook's pistol and nails the other one halfway out the bunker. Now he's down and I'm still tryin' to get my shit together but he hauls ass out to deliver the ammo. On the way back to police me up, he gets hit by mortar shrapnel and the next time I see him, he's shot fulla morphine and waitin' for a medevac."

Benjamin took his eyes off his new belt just long enough to pour beer for all of them. "Bad fuckin' day at Black Rock, dudes."

"I hope to shit in your mess kit. Anyway, I go up to the LZ to see if he's OK . . . bullet in a fuckin' lung, shrapnel all over his ass . . . and all he wants to know is will I make sure he gets this Tokarev pistol he used to shoot the gook officers.

"Naturally, I can't find anybody willin' to say they found a souvenir like that and volunteerin' to give it back, so I promised him I'd see that he got one of the officers' belt buckles. Been packin' that bastard around for six or seven years, waitin' for the right time and place."

The race of conversation lulled—like the moment in a firefight when everyone seems to change magazines at the same time— and then Eddie Miller tapped the table for attention. "How about that story you mentioned in the White Castle last night? You said it was gonna blow my socks off, right?"

Benjamin glanced up sharply and saw the look in Willy Pud's eyes. What he'd missed earlier—in the excitement of seeing his old friend, in the momentum of long-suppressed adventure stories—was obvious in that moment. Willy Pudarski remained haunted and haggard; some part of him remained in Vietnam, an affair unrequited and unresolved. Five—nearly six—years since he'd left Vietnam behind, and he still had that look in his eyes; the same ghostly stare that chilled Benjamin the last time he saw his friend after the Recon insert, when they went out after . . .

"Salt and Pepper?"

"Yeah. It's time we talked about it, Spike. Shit's been botherin' me for a long time . . . I need to talk about it . . . you're the only one . . ."

Benjamin held up his hand and glanced at Miller. The cop's grin was fading rapidly.

"Hey, look . . . it's like I said to Willy Pud . . . if this is something just between you two . . . no sweat." He stared at his new friends, sensing their uneasiness. "Besides, if it's some kinda atrocity shit—like My Lai, or something—I don't think I want to hear it anyway. Good times, that's one thing. All that other horseshit—well, who needs to remember it?"

"There's *some* stuff you can't forget . . ."

Benjamin sipped beer and shrugged. "Whatever . . . but last I heard, it was classified higher than the plans for a fucking H-bomb."

Willy shook his head and leaned across the table. "Look, Spike, it's like a guy told me one time back in Chicago, it *can't* still be classified. The outfit that classified it *don't exist anymore.*"

"We still got a government . . . such as it is."

"Spike, this has been kickin' my ass, makin' me crazy. It's like there's no fucking justice, you know? If somebody don't say something about those guys, they get away with it! Goddammit, man, people ought to know!"

"Why?"

"Why? Are you shittin' me? C'mon, Spike. You read the papers . . . shit, you help write 'em, for Christ's sake! All of us are livin' under a goddamn cloud! Babykillers, junkies, psychotics, ticking time bombs, losers, all that kinda bullshit. And the truth is, most guys who served over there are just like us three: good warriors who fought a bad war. We get this shit out and people can see . . ."

"See what, Willy? See that we had a couple of genuine turncoats to go along with the junkies and psychos? See that there were people who did worse things than kill babies and fuck over farmers? What's the point?"

Eddie Miller gulped beer as the subject became clearer. "Holy shit . . . I heard something about a couple of guys who fought with the gooks one time . . ."

"Yeah, so did practically everybody else who was any kind of line-dog in the 'Nam." Benjamin shook his head and opened a fresh pack of smokes. "It got to be a legend after a while—Vietnam folklore—and every motherfucker who could find an audience of new guys swore he'd seen round-eyes fighting with the gooks."

"Yeah, there it is . . ." Willy Pud spoke to Miller but he was staring deep into Spike Benjamin's eyes. "Except, this story is true. We know . . . we saw 'em."

"No shit?"

"No shit. Spike took pictures and I gave a sworn statement. MACV scarfed up everything and classified the hell out of it, but they existed! Two turncoats—white guy and a black guy— Salt and Pepper."

"I'll be kiss my ass! Now, that's a story you'd have a hard time sellin'."

"We *need* to sell that story. Those two bastards are probably dead—gotta be dead—but they shouldn't get away with what they done."

"Willy, we don't even know who they were!" Spike Benjamin blew smoke toward a ceiling fan. "Even if we could get somebody interested in this . . . Shit, man, the whole country is tryin' to ignore Vietnam!"

"I ain't tryin' to ignore it! You ain't tryin' to ignore it! Neither is Eddie . . . and about a million other guys who are tryin' to hold their heads up out of the shit! We owe it to them. We owe it to ourselves . . ."

"Look, man . . . I've seen Spike's pictures, so I know he's no bullshit artist . . . and dudes don't get the Medal of Honor for stayin' in the rear with the gear, but you ask me . . . you ain't got a whore's chance in hell of convincing anybody that counts that this story is true."

"That don't mean we shouldn't try. I come down here to see Spike because I thought he could show me how to do it."

"I'm a cop, you know? I deal in evidence. Let me run it down like a crime we're tryin' to prosecute here. What have we got? We got two eyewitnesses—very credible—but we got no bodies to point a finger at or interrogate, not even names so we could run some kind of records check. We got no other physical evidence— no photos, no battlefield sighting reports. All that's classified, right? There's not even a group of upright citizens screaming for justice. The way I see it, you might get a one-shot story in the papers—some vets might come out of the woodwork and say they heard the story too—but you're never gonna turn it into a big deal or set any kind of record straight. There ain't no record! My advice is forget about it."

"Bullshit, Eddie. I'm not gonna forget about it. I can't! And I'm not gonna quit until this story gets told."

Miller shrugged and pointed at Benjamin. "Well, there's the man to see . . ."

"Lemme tell you what I think . . ." Spike had been silent through most of the exchange. Now he drew a deep breath and drummed the tabletop with his fingernails. "I think over the next decade or so, there's gonna be a concerted effort in this country to forget there ever was a Vietnam, or a war there, or Americans who fought and died there. That's a shame . . . and the poor bastards who will have to live with the shame are the veterans.

"I think this country fucked around in Southeast Asia and gave birth to a brood of bastard children . . . literally and figuratively.

Every big city in 'Nam is full of half-gook, half-round-eye kids that get treated like rice paddy scum. Stateside we're trying to cope with shit like amnesty for draft dodgers, broken-up families, the fucking hordes of Vietnamese refugees being settled all over the country, the bad rap most vets are ducking through booze and smack and hard-living of one kind or another . . . and most of all the flat fucking ignorance that might just get us involved in another Vietnam somewhere down the line. I think we ought to do something about that ignorance . . ."

"Get some!" Willy Pud nearly overturned a beer pitcher as he reached across the table to grab at Spike Benjamin's elbow. "You're sayin' we tell the story, right?"

Benjamin blinked at the glitter of passion in Willy Pud's eyes. It blinded him to practical problems.

"I'm saying we use this case to focus some light on the straight veterans. We use it to take some of the heat off the good guys. It's spectacular enough to generate some high-level interest if we do it right. I'm saying we start to investigate. We compile what evidence we can. We look for the other guys who were on that patrol with us. And—most importantly—we try to *identify* Salt and Pepper."

"Tough fucking job . . ." Eddie Miller shrugged and flagged down a passing waitress.

"Maybe not so tough . . ." Spike Benjamin laid his notebook on the table and clicked a pen into action. "We got a veteran cop, we got a True Believer with the Medal of Honor . . . and we got the one photo of Salt and Pepper that MACV *didn't* get."

Heat from Spike Benjamin's bombshell galvanized them into a dedicated task force. The next morning, Eddie Miller moved Willy Pud into Spike's apartment and sat nursing a hangover with him while Spike puttered in a loft that he'd converted into a custom darkroom.

"Jesus, we gotta slow down . . ." Eddie rummaged in a kitchen drawer looking for aspirin. "You want a couple of these?"

"Fuck a buncha aspirin, Miller. The entire Russian army may have dug a slit trench in my mouth, but I feel great. Like I'm back in the saddle, you know?"

"Man with a mission." Miller sipped coffee and read over Willy's shoulder. "That the list of the guys who were on the patrol?"

"Yeah . . . this one and this one were KIA. We know that. The other three could be anywhere."

"What about your company commander? You said he was there when you got back in . . ."

"Shit! I forgot about the skipper." Willy Pud chewed on his pencil for a moment and then began to scribble. "Name was Stacey . . . Phillip A., I think. He was from some place in Oklahoma . . . near Ardmore. Anyway, he was a mustang, so he musta stayed in after the 'Nam. I can work my bolt with the Marine Corps to find him."

Eddie picked up the list and scanned it. "There's some guys over at the Federal Building who owe me. I can get the FBI to run a check on these names and request a search through NCIC. If they fucked up anywhere along the line, we'll get some leads . . . presuming they didn't get blown away after you left."

"I don't think so, Eddie. It was a Recon unit, you know? Pretty tight. I'd have heard something . . ."

A lock rattled in the loft and both men moved toward the short flight of spiral stairs that led to Spike Benjamin's home work space. He emerged blinking and wiping his hands on an old shop towel.

"Well, I've got the bastards framed. C'mon up and take a look."

Inside the cramped, pungent darkroom, they blinked against dim red light and watched as eerie images shimmered toward focus in a pan of developer. Willy threw a steadying arm over Spike's back and felt the accelerated rise and fall of the man's shoulders as he fought to control his breathing and concentrate. There was an ominous, nearly palpable tension in the tiny room as the ghosts of Salt and Pepper responded to the chemical seance.

"There they are . . . the motherfuckers." Willy jabbed a finger at the eight-by-ten photo as Spike rinsed it in stop-bath and hung it to drip dry. "Now you tell me that ain't something the world ought to know about."

Eddie Miller leaned in and squinted. Hard to believe, but there it was in black-and-white . . . literally. The hulking black man humping extra RPG rounds, towering over two NVA troopers. The white man with badly repaired GI glasses teetering on his nose and wearing a VC bush hat. The details of their mixed uniforms and weapons were clear despite the dissolution of enlargement from a 35mm negative. No manacles, no weapons pointed at their backs, and no doubt about what the photo showed. These guys were playing on the other team when Spike Benjamin's camera caught them at it.

"You know . . ." Eddie whispered into the dark, "that just pisses me the fuck off."

Spike ran a soft sponge over the enlargement and then snapped it with his fingernail. "I took a hell of a chance when I stole this neg. Thought I might need some kind of major scoop to get a job, you know? Then I got home and got some work right away. Shit, I forgot . . . well, I forgot how intense it was."

"When do we publish it?" Willy Pud felt himself streaming sweat as he stared at the images that had haunted him for so long. "It's time these cocksuckers got what they deserved."

Spike herded them toward the door. "Let's let the print dry first, Willy Pud. There's a lot of planning to do."

When they were seated at his dining-room table, Spike fetched cold beer and a yellow legal pad. "OK, you guys were scheming while I was in the dark. Where do we stand on this thing?"

"Eddie's gonna run Ledsome, Goodman, and Purdy through his cop sources to see if we can find 'em. I'm gonna check out Captain Stacey through the Marine Corps. I don't know who else . . ."

Benjamin looked up from his notes. "What about that MACV colonel who interviewed you on tape? Remember his name?"

"Nah. Shit, I don't know if he ever told me his name. He must have told the skipper. Major league MACV spook, if you ask me. Even if we found him, a guy like that wouldn't say shit if he had a mouth full of it."

"Never can tell, Willy Pud. It's been a while since the war ended. Lots of hyper-lifers are looking around to tell their stories." Benjamin smiled and scribbled a note. "Let's hear a cop's assessment."

"Well, I gotta tell ya . . ." Eddie shook his head and slugged at his beer bottle. "It's the goddamnedest thing I ever saw. Hard to believe, you know? Not that I don't believe it but . . . shit, for instance . . . ask yourself how do we know those guys in the picture are Americans? How do we know the picture was taken where and when you say it was. It's a hell of a deal but it ain't iron-clad evidence of two traitors. There's a lot of loopholes. A guy—or an organization—that wanted to discredit the story wouldn't have much trouble coming up with plausible angles of attack."

Willy Pud began to sputter and fume, but Spike waved off the storm of protest. "Listen, buddy, Miller is right. We can't go off half-cocked on this thing. We can't just run a fucking ad in all the major dailies and ask anyone who recognizes those guys to give us a call. See what I mean? We've got to build the evidence if this is gonna be anything more than a fart in a windstorm."

"So how do we proceed?"

"I see it like a homicide investigation, I guess. We build a case. We go after all the surviving witnesses to prove a crime was, indeed, committed. Then we nail down the identity of the perpetrators, which just might give us motive, opportunity, and means . . . although two of those elements seem obvious to me."

"Goddammit! This ain't a murder investigation!"

"But it is a good way to approach the problem." Spike tapped his pencil against a tooth and smiled at Willy Pud. "Just relax, man. We're gonna get this thing nailed. As I see it, the key is to tie names and personal histories to these guys. We've gotta find out who Salt and Pepper were. Once we've got that, we can support the story in a number of credible ways."

"Look, Willy Pud, most times when a long-shot investigation like this one pays off, it's due to a lot of grunt work by the investigators. To get started, we gotta make some basic assumptions. These guys were probably in the service and the service almost certainly sent them to Vietnam where they defected to the gooks, right?"

Eddie Miller tore a sheet from Spike's pad and began to make his own notes. "OK, that means their status might be MIA . . . Missing In Action. I figure we start the process of elimination by trying to get pictures of every American that's currently listed as MIA by the Pentagon. We do a comparison and—just maybe— we spot Salt or Pepper."

"Lemme try it." Willy nodded around the table. "The Medal ought to buy me some pull in that area."

"Let's not overlook the obvious either. We should trace this mysterious MACV colonel. He might already know who Salt and Pepper were. And—you never know—he might be willing to point us in the right direction."

Eddie Miller shrugged and glanced at his watch. "I gotta go to work in a couple of hours. I'll start making some phone calls. Looks like we're on the case . . ."

Willy Pud was at the kitchen table, eating eggs and running a red pen through the classified ads when Spike Benjamin wandered out of his bedroom dressed for work. He poured coffee and sat inhaling scented steam.

"What the hell are you doing?"

"Looking for a job."

"You *got* a job."

"Hey, Spike, it ain't gonna work that way. This thing is gonna cost money, not to mention the fact that I'm bummin' room and board offa you."

"Lemme tell you how it's gonna work, you hardheaded Polack. This morning I'm gonna have my assistant start paperwork to put you on salary as a research assistant. Figure you'll get a paycheck that comes to around $350 a week. That oughtta cut it since beer and a bed are free around here."

"I didn't come to St. Louis and contact you because I was lookin' for a fuckin' handout, Spike."

"You ain't getting a handout, Willy Pud. You're cutting a deal, see? You actually have to *work* on this investigation . . . and you have to promise me all rights to your story when we break it."

Willy Pud shoved scrambled eggs around his plate and pondered. "How about you promise any money you make from the story goes to help Vietnam vets?"

"How about *half* of any money I make on the story?"

They were nose-to-nose across the table, horse-trading, challenging, maneuvering, the way they used to over favorite C-rations in the bush. Willy felt the laughter bubbling up from his gut even as he tried to brow-beat Benjamin. When it exploded, they both sat shaking, bouncing around in the kitchen chairs, pounding the table with tears streaming from their eyes.

When the deal was done and Spike Benjamin left him alone in the huge suburban apartment, Willy Pud found himself roaming—fairly dancing—around the empty rooms. He caught his reflection in a long vertical mirror near the double entry doors and stared in wonder. Morning sunlight blazed through an arched window at his back but the flattering rays weren't responsible for his transformation.

He took a step closer to the mirror and leaned in to look at his face. What an extraordinary thing, he thought, running fingers across his forehead and down his stubbled cheeks. It was the same . . . but different. A certain sagginess was missing, as if someone had run an iron over him and steamed out some of the wrinkles. The face in the mirror looked keen, lean and hungry, like a tomahawk slicing through the air toward a target.

The eyes—pupils dilating and contracting as they focused on surrounding features—glittered with interest and acumen. In a moment of stunning awe, Willy Pud recalled the last time he'd seen that face . . . in Vietnam, in a scratched and rusting metal mirror he used for shaving in the field. After a long stint in the rear with all the unnecessary gear, Willy Pudarski was back in the bush, on patrol and head-hunting.

He smiled and rolled his shoulders, feeling for the weight of harness, canteens, magazines, and grenades. "Salt and Pepper," he whispered as he raised an imaginary M-16 and squinted through the rear sight, "Willy Pud is back on the track . . . and you mother-fuckers are mine!"

When coffee, smokes, notepad, and extension telephone were planted on the kitchen table, Willy Pud had an office. He called Andy Hogan's home number and spoke to Maggie. She promised to give the old man his St. Louis number and have him call back collect when he came by the bar.

He hung up, made a careful note of time and charges for the call, and dialed a number on the West Coast.

"Shaeffer."

"Sergeant Major, it's me, Pudarski, callin' from St. Louis."

"Hey, Sarn't Pudarski, you PCS down there or just visitin'?"

"Stayin' with a buddy from the 'Nam, Sarn't Major. We're workin' on a project—it's got to do with, uh, veterans . . . in a way. That's how come I called."

"You may be a Polack, Willy Pud, but you got the luck of the Irish. I'm leavin' in about an hour for the airport."

"Where you headed?"

"Bangkok. It's a nasty job, but somebody's gotta go over there among all them bars and nubile young women . . ."

Willy snorted at the image of Sergeant Major Shifty Shaeffer organizing a platoon of Thai hookers for a little close-order drill down Patpong Street. "You scarf up somebody's R&R quota, Sarn't Major?"

"Nah, shit, it's business. Lookin' into reports of live POWs still in-country. They got a regular goddamn industry over there sellin' bones, artifacts, and information. I'm supposed to sift through all the shit and see if any of the rumors bear lookin' into. Officially, I'm workin' for the Medal of Honor Society. Unofficially . . . well, I got some heavy hitters in Congress and the Pentagon backin' the trip."

"No shit? That's sorta related to why I called. This buddy I'm stayin' with, former Marine, ISO sergeant who ran with me in First MarDiv, he's a big-time journalist out here now. Anyway, we're—uh—hold on . . ." Willy Pud lit a smoke and thought about Spike's warning, wondering how much to tell the Sergeant Major. Keep it tight, he decided, need-to-know only. If they scored, he could bring Shaeffer into the fold and use his influence to spread the word.

"Anyway, we're lookin' into this MIA situation. You know, guys who get sent to 'Nam and then just fucking disappear off the face of the earth."

"Yeah, that's a crock of shit. Somebody's got to be account-able . . . either us or the goddamn gooks."

"There it is, Sarn't Major. So we figure maybe we can ID a couple of these guys given a network of vets and all. Anyway, what I need is photographs of everyone that DOD has got on the current MIA list . . ."

Even over long-distance phone lines Shaeffer's staccato laugh sounded precise, like the rhythm of a well-tuned heavy machine gun. "Shit, Willy Pud! You know what you're askin'? There's somethin' like twenty-three or twenty-four hundred guys on that list."

"I know, Sarn't Major, but goddammit, this is important. We might actually be able to do some good here. Ain't there a way to use the Society and muscle the Pentagon? We'll pay the admin costs and everything, but if this is gonna work, we gotta put some faces to the names."

"Well, there is a special office in the Pentagon that does nothin' but handle POW and MIA affairs. I'm wired into them pretty tight. Maybe I can make it happen. Gimme an address there in St. Louis."

Willy Pud dictated Spike Benjamin's home address, wished the Sergeant Major good luck on his trip, and started to hang up when an underlined note on the pad in front of him caught his eye. He shouted to hold Shaeffer on the line.

"Just one more thing, Sarn't Major."

"C'mon, Pudarski, I got to *hiaku* out to the airport."

"I need to find my old Recon CO, Sarn't Major. His name was Captain Stacey, Phillip A., and I think he was from someplace in Oklahoma."

There was a long moment of silence before Willy Pud heard the quiet growl of Shaeffer's response. "He was from Ceiling, Oklahoma."

"Oh, shit! You know him?"

"Knew him, Willy Pud. We were *panyos* from the Camp Schwab Staff Club back before he got commissioned. He got killed a few weeks after you left."

Now the stunned silence was on the St. Louis end of the line. Shaeffer tried to soften his tone, but the stupid way in which a

Marine like Phil Stacey had been killed still pissed him off.

"There was a major investigation over it, Willy Pud. Dumb fucking deal. Marine Corps was pullin' out. No big ops, you know, gettin' ready to leave Vietnam. Anyway, somebody fucked up royal. Horseshit security, if you ask me. One lone gook with a goddamn B-40 rocket launcher got into a spot overlooking the LZ at An Hoa. He fires one round and blows one helicopter out of the fucking sky. Naturally, a guy like Phil Stacey has got to be on that chopper."

"He's dead."

"Not many people gonna survive a thing like that, Willy Pud. Not even a hard-dick like old Stace. They never found much of him to bury. I'm sorry. I thought you knew about it."

Willy wished the Sergeant Major luck, hung up, and began to doodle on the pad. Midwestern sun streamed in through the kitchen windows and Spike Benjamin's forced-air heating system whispered warmth through the apartment, but Willy Pud felt a cold chill. His bush senses began to click on-line for no reason he could identify. He felt that odd prickle of intuition that always told him of enemy in the area.

"I found it!"

Retired Master Gunnery Sergeant Bud DeVries chuckled and hoisted his wingtips onto a hissing radiator behind his desk. Over his toes he could see ice chunks floating in the Potomac where it flowed by the Naval Photographic Center at Anacostia.

"Hey, that's great, Bud! No shit, thanks a lot. I know it was a pain in the ass."

"No sweat, Spike. A guy retires from the Marine Corps and becomes a Civil Service puke, he's got nothin' better to do than fuck around with old files. Besides, I got a kick out of seeing some of the names on the photo work orders. Brought back a lot of memories . . . good and bad."

Spike Benjamin tapped the keyboard of his office computer and brought up the Salt and Pepper file. He cradled the phone receiver on his shoulder and congratulated himself on a stroke of genius. Bud DeVries had retired as the senior enlisted photographer and now ran the Corps' photo archives stored at the Anacostia Naval Station outside Washington, D.C.

Spike thought of his old NCOiC while trying to get an angle on locating the MACV colonel. It occurred to him that the archives might contain more than prints and negatives. Given the Corps' penchant for precise record-keeping, they might also contain the official documents that generated photographs and photographic work at every Marine lab around the world.

"I'da had a hell of a time if you couldn't remember the year and date." Not fucking likely to forget, Spike thought as he typed in a new heading for the MACV colonel. "Anyway, it was there, filed under jobs for First Recon Battalion, where you said it might be. You're listed as the shooter . . . location, I Corps, R-V-N . . . subject, just says Recon Mission . . . everything else is blacked out the way they do with shit that's still on hold, you know?"

"Yeah, I know, Bud, but they usually leave the signature block alone."

"Fuckin' A . . . names ain't secret, right? And every work order has got to have an authorized signature—or no photo work. That's policy."

"I remember. That was supposed to keep us snuffy photographers from doing *cumshaw* work, trading photos for favors."

"Not that it ever worked worth a shit." DeVries chuckled warmly. "Anyway, it took me a while to decipher this asshole's scrawl but near as I can read it, your man is J. B. Halley, Colonel, M-I, You-ess-fuckin' Army. He signed for all prints and negs."

Benjamin typed furiously until DeVries finally asked if he was still on the line. "Yeah, Bud, sorry. I wanted to get it down on the computer. Listen, I owe you. I'll probably be back your way in a few weeks."

"Like I said, Spike, no sweat. You were a fuckin' rascal, but you were a good one. We still print some of your stuff for shows and displays. Too bad we can't pay royalties."

Spike hung up the phone and punched his intercom button. "Julie, put a call through to Jake Arquette at the Military Records Center over on North Broadway. See if you can get an address on an Army colonel, or maybe brigadier general, named Halley. H-A-L-L-E-Y, initials are J. B."

Eileen Winter greeted the caller warmly. It was the second time in just over a week that she'd spoken to the friendly voice from St. Louis. The first call had put Justin Halley in a good enough mood to approve a pay raise and put her name on the authorized list for space-available travel on Emory Technology's fleet of corporate jets.

She buzzed her boss and heard a muted click as he keyed the blinking line. "Mr. Arquette is calling from St. Louis."

"Thanks, Eileen. I'll take it." Justin Halley frowned at the red light on his phone console and stabbed a button. "Jake, what can I do for you?"

"Hi, Justin. Before I forget, thanks for the stereo stuff. The kids went nuts over it."

"No better way to advertise the Emory line of products, Jake. Glad to send 'em along."

"Listen, I know you're busy, so I'll get to the point. We got this reporter out here in St. Louis—popular guy, lots of press awards, he's a veteran, does a lot of stuff concerning Vietnam vets, that kind of thing.

"Anyway, this guy calls out of the blue yesterday with a request for your last known address. I didn't talk with him personally. Seemed like a routine thing from a local reporter so one of my assistants handled it. He said it was in connection with some story he was doing. I thought you should know about it in case you get a call."

Justin Halley uncapped his pen and reached for a piece of notepaper. "Good deal, Jake. These days a guy needs to watch out for ambushes. What's this reporter's name?"

"Spike Benjamin."

Halley's fingers froze. He watched the thick paper soak up an ink blot and distractedly noticed he was pinching his pen tight enough to turn the first two fingers of his right hand white at the knuckles. Cutting his eyes around the office fixtures, he took stock of where he was, who he was . . . and tried to convince himself it was coincidence.

"Benjamin? I may have heard that name somewhere, Jake. Do you happen to know what service he was in?"

"Oh, yeah. He refers to it all the time in the stories he writes. He was a Marine photographer in Vietnam. First Marine Division, I think."

Justin Halley felt the prickle and pinch in his armpits as his glands reacted to mental alarm signals. He struggled to control the timbre of his voice.

"Listen, Jake. I don't think I want to do any interviews. Cleve Emory gets testy about that stuff, you know? His boy was killed over there and all. If this Benjamin makes any more inquiries about me, shut him down, will you?"

For the next hour, Justin Bates Halley walked around his spacious office and talked to himself. No matter how many angles he computed, no matter how he squinted and twisted for different points of view, he couldn't convince himself it was all just post-war happenstance.

Benjamin? Jesus Christ! Benjamin was the name of the photographer who shot the pictures of Salt and Pepper. So he survived . . . and now he's a reporter. Does that mean he's going to write a story about Salt and Pepper? Maybe not. If he'd wanted to do that—if he thought he could prove it—he'd have made his move long ago. So why is the guy on my trail? How does he know who I am . . . who I was?

Maybe he's fishing, testing the waters, probing for a way to break the turncoat story. He must know there's no evidence . . . none at all. All that could be left in the official archives are secondhand sighting reports and my investigation report saying it was all smoke and mirrors . . . and that's still classified. So why is Benjamin looking for me?

The company commander is dead. Emory's got the only photos and all the negatives Benjamin shot. Why is he looking for me? Emory's got the only copy of the Pudarski interview . . . Pudarski?

Halley buzzed for Eileen Winter and tried to compose himself during the short time it took her to leave her office and knock on the door of his. He was shuffling through a stack of memos at his desk when she entered.

"Sorry to bother you, Eileen, but I'm tying up some loose ends. Did you get anything out of that call to Chicago?"

"Name, address, and particulars are in one of those memos, Justin. As of last week, Pudarski's low-profile . . . a City College student and part-time carpenter." She approached the desk and saw the distracted frown. Something was eating at him. And it wasn't the mundane report concerning the post-Vietnam life and times of Wilhelm Johannes Pudarski.

"I saw the fucking memo, Eileen!" His bark startled her. "If that's all I wanted, I wouldn't have had you call Chicago."

"I was just dictating an update for you, Justin. No need to bite my head off."

He waved her to a seat and tried to relax. She'd see he was upset, try to fuck him out of a funk and that wouldn't do . . . not now. He needed to concentrate. "Sorry. Just fill me in . . ."

"It took me a while, but I finally talked to his father. Real old coot. Suspicious, but proud. I told him I was a reporter wanting to do a story on his son . . . Medal of Honor winner after the war, that kind of thing. He laughed at that. Said his boy had gone to St. Louis to visit a reporter, apparently an old buddy from Vietnam. Seems he quit school and left town in a hurry. I've got a St. Louis number . . ."

Halley swiveled abruptly in his chair and sat staring out the window of his office. His heart was pounding and he could feel long strands of sweat crawling down his rib cage.

Oh, my God! Loose ends. Emory was right. I should have had them all killed. It would have been easy enough to get away with. There was plenty of time ... even after Pudarski got the Medal ... but I didn't think ... I never thought ...

He cleared his throat and ran his hand through his thinning hair. The movement let him know the sleeves of his shirt were soaked. He was sweating like a pig; sitting here stewing in his own juices when the situation called for clear, prompt action.

"Eileen, Mr. Emory is due back from Los Angeles on, uh, Tuesday of next week. Get hold of his personal appointments secretary. I want to see him immediately when he gets back to New York."

He was still staring out the window when she slid behind his chair and began to massage his shoulders. Her thumbs had barely touched his spine when he spun on her and bit hard.

"Goddammit, Eileen! Get out of here and do what I told you to do!"

CAMP 413, SOCIALIST REPUBLIC OF VIETNAM, 4 APRIL 1976

Now that Tet celebrations were over Comrade Cleveland Herbert Emory, Junior, thought he might finally get the audience with the regional political officer he'd been requesting for the past six months. Army patrols were sweeping through Pou Phang and such activity usually meant a Revolutionary Education and Assistance Team was making rounds.

The officer leading one patrol that paused at Camp 413 was a young *Thi Uy* from the Red River Delta region who managed to acquire a passable English vocabulary somewhere. He'd heard there was a "foreign volunteer" in this remote camp and sought him out to hone his language skills ... and to freeload a dinner of fresh fish from the teeming stream that flowed near the communal hut where Emory lived with nineteen other "student workers."

The People's Army lieutenant was grateful for the smoked fish and vegetables, lingering over green tea long enough to give the emaciated American a look at his map. It was a startling revelation for Emory who assumed he was marking time somewhere near the capital until his health was fully restored. But the map showed Camp 413—the third such education and work center for "special category citizens" that he'd been in over the past four years—was in a remote northwestern corner of the Socialist Republic, some eight kilometers from Laos and ten kilometers from China.

That baffled Comrade Emory, but he did not bother to question the lieutenant who would have no knowledge of policy decisions outside his platoon. He simply added a question to the list of topics for discussion with the regional political officer. *Why,* he would ask, *am I being moved* away *from the heart of revolutionary ideology? And what,* he'd continue, *is being done about my request for a more active role in the task of nation-building that I earned on the battlefield?*

The unspoken truth of the matter was that after seven years of struggle and toil on and off the battlefield, Comrade Cleveland Herbert Emory, Junior, was sick, tired, and suffering a loss of faith in the sincerity of his revolutionary hosts. He was either being mistreated or ignored. Assignment to Camp 413, a den of political vipers and rootless reactionaries, proved one or the other. The time had clearly come to find out which . . . and to demand his just deserts.

Since 1970 when he was wounded near the Mu Gia Pass, he'd spent two years in a series of hospitals around Hanoi. That was understandable. His injuries were extensive, requiring long periods of painful treatment and therapy. Even now, he did not have full use of his right arm and leg, which were withering at an alarming rate. Still, he kept his medical complaints to a minimum.

A limp, coupled with limited flexion in the right arm and shoulder, usually resulted in less physically demanding work, such as his current job tending a series of seine and gill nets strung along what the lieutenant's map told him was a tributary of the Black River flowing south from China. It was easier and more rewarding than toiling in the paddies or vegetable gardens between the twice daily political classes required of all persons training for important roles in the process of creating a new world order. Tonight, Comrade Emory promised himself, during the constructive criticism session, he'd take a stand as a Hero of the Revolution. Tonight he would demand a transfer; perhaps even refuse to work until his complaints were addressed by appropriate authority.

He sat and scraped scales from a basket of small, bony perch, carefully crafting words. It would not be an easy speech. Despite seven years of almost total immersion in Vietnamese culture, he still had difficulty with the language. He was glib with simple phrases required to survive in the camps but the subtleties of the language, especially those phrases and intonations commonly used in political discussions, eluded and frustrated him. During the required lectures and classes, he wrestled with the language, turning phrases over in his mind, picking them apart word by word, looking for comparable terms in English. He was generally disoriented, lost in convoluted thought, and so far behind the flow of the lecture that he did a halting, uninspired job when called on to stand for self-criticism.

Comrade Emory had never seen the fat file maintained on him in the cadre hut under the name *Di Anh,* so he had no way of knowing his political instructors had consistently evaluated him as "slow, unstable, and unreliable outside communal groups. Perhaps even mentally defective; probably as a result of wounds suffered during an attack by Yankee air pirates." Since it had been more than a year since he'd seen a representative of the politburo in Hanoi, Di Anh—loosely translated as "fleeing foreigner"—had no way of knowing his only value to the Socialist Republic was as a potential pawn in the continuing efforts to end a painful American trade embargo against Vietnam.

Failing that end, the distracted handful of government officials in Hanoi who even knew of Comrade Emory's pitiful existence in Camp 413 had no interest at all in whether he lived or died, much less in his claim to a share in the meager spoils of a Pyrrhic victory.

He was so engrossed in fish-cleaning and speech-writing that Comrade Emory did not notice Sergeant Ngo Xa Dinh of the Provincial People's Militia when he arrived for the weekly barter session. Dinh waited quietly to be noticed, then coughed politely and squatted on his haunches. Emory finished gutting a fish and then rinsed his hands before offering a gnarled, unruly paw for Dinh to shake.

Dinh was a former NVA sergeant, wounded in the Central Highlands of the south, and one of only a few from his remote home province who made it back to recover. Sometime during his combat tour, Dinh's family disappeared. It took him nearly a year of searching for scattered friends to confirm that the Dinh clan had fled as refugees when the Hanoi government confiscated the fertile fields of their ancestral home for a communal farm.

Having neither the health nor wealth to follow, Ngo Xa Dinh applied for a slot in the local militia that, among its other duties, provided security for Camp 413. As Dinh told the story during his regular dealings with residents of the camp, the militia's job was to insure marauding H'mong bandits left the student-workers in peace. True enough, but everyone who walked the camp perimeter at night or wandered off into the surrounding jungle discovered that the militia were also posted to keep residents of Camp 413 from going anyplace but back to work.

Still, Emory didn't think of old Dinh as a prison guard. In fact, up until the camp cadre began ignoring his regular demands to see the regional political officer, Emory suspected Dinh was his quasi-official bodyguard. He was, after all, a Hero of the Revolution, an unusual and important person who required special security to protect him from reactionary elements who thought of all westerners as mortal enemies.

While Dinh rummaged in his raggedy knapsack for trade goods, Emory opened a bamboo hamper and began to assemble market staples. There were fillets of smoked perch, freshwater eel jerky, turtle meat, fresh onions, turnips, and banana squash. He laid a little of each on a pile of banana leaves that served as butcher-paper to wrap purchases.

Dinh wheeled the worn stock of his Simonov carbine around to serve as a rude platform and laid out his first offering: a half can of East German tooth powder. It brought some perch and three turnips. There were two more minor exchanges before Dinh got around to the serious business he always saved for last. Like all economic systems, the commodities market at Camp 413 found its own levels of supply and demand. It always took Dinh a few preliminary forays to determine his strength vis-à-vis the American cigarettes he obtained on the black market downstream at the Lai Chau ferry landing.

Emory did his best to hide the craving when Dinh plunked two unopened packs of L&M filters on the table. He'd never been offered more than a single pack in previous visits and usually only five or ten stale cigarettes wrapped in rice paper. As casually as he could, Emory reached into the hamper and pulled out half a filleted catfish. Old Dinh's eyes sparkled at the delicacy, but he expressed his regrets with a small sigh and pointed at the eel jerky and the chunks of rich turtle meat.

Emory let his face cloud over and tugged at an earlobe. "You ask too much, *Trung Si* Dinh."

Dinh stared at the dirt beneath his feet. He was generally a playful trader, always ready to mix banter with barter, but Emory could see something was bothering the old man to the point of distraction. Intuition told him to up the ante or he'd lose the precious cigarettes to another camp resident. He reached into the hamper, but Dinh stopped him with an upraised hand.

"We have done business for a long time. Now, I wish to speak privately . . . as a friend."

Emory settled into a more comfortable squat and nodded.

Dinh glanced at the rear of the hut where two student-workers were cleaning farm tools and leaned toward Emory to speak in a quiet voice.

"I think you will understand my feelings, being a foreigner in this land . . ."

"We are all brothers in the great struggle . . ."

Dinh hissed like a snake and spat between his knees. "Don't lecture, Di Anh. I've heard enough of that. Haven't you?"

Emory paused to light the last of his remaining cigarettes. This was dangerous ground. It might be a test. On the other hand, it might be something he could use to advantage.

"Tell me what you wish."

"I want vegetables and fish . . . smoked, salted, and wrapped . . . enough for a long journey . . . perhaps three weeks or more."

Emory studied Dinh's rheumy eyes. There was a hint of desperation. A man setting a trap would be more confident and casual.

"That amount of food, prepared for travel . . . I think it would require some explanation . . ."

"No one must know of it. I will make another trip to Lai Chau next week and get more cigarettes for you—as many as I can afford—if you will help me."

As the camp's primary fisherman, Emory knew it was possible for him to supply the commodities Dinh wanted. Everyone at Camp 413 kept a secret stock of staples and the barter system was well established even among the cadre. Still . . .

"Please, Di Anh, I think I have found . . . there is word of my family . . . in Thailand . . ."

Family. The word startled Emory momentarily. He sat contemplating the concept, rolling the foreign word around on his tongue, chewing on forgotten fodder. *So long ago . . . father, aunts, uncles, and cousins. Do they think of me as hero . . . or whore? Do they think of me at all?*

"Di Anh, we are veterans . . . you can understand."

Comrade Emory reached for the cigarettes with his left hand and offered his misshapen right to *Trung Si* Dinh. "Come to see me when you return from Lai Chau. I will have the provisions you require."

When old Dinh departed, Emory restashed his hamper in the cache between the roots of a tall teak tree on the east side of the camp perimeter and headed for the stream to check his turtle traps before dark. An odd, familiar tune whirled in his head as he limped along a rice paddy dyke and he struggled to identify it. A march of some kind . . . flutes and snare drums.

He began to whistle mindlessly and then the words came in a rush. "When Johnny comes marchin' home again, hoorah, hoorah! We'll give him a hearty welcome then, hoorah, hoorah! The bands will play and the children shout, and we'll all feel gay when Johnny comes marchin' home . . ."

There was a picture he'd painted long ago; a self-portrait he'd contemplated long and hard . . . when he was so full of himself; so sure of his decisions. The image was crystal clear and glorious back when he was proving something to the world . . . back before Mu Gia Pass.

The image had fizzled and flared since then. It fizzled when the great parade found him ingloriously ripped and torn; incapable of standing much less marching among the diminutive victors who vanquished the greedy American giant. It rarely flared anymore; except when he was feeling depressed and conjured the image up to contemplate it in the haze of smoke from an opium-laced marijuana cigarette.

Comrade Emory reached the low mesa above the bend in the stream where he set his most productive turtle traps and reached for a flat white rock wedged into the cliffside. Behind the rock was a plastic bag containing three joints of potent smoke. Such potentially subversive substances had to be covertly purchased from the militiamen and concealed from the camp cadre but Emory had become expert at both those endeavors. He lit one of the joints and sucked the pungent smoke deep into his lungs.

The image flared in the looming shadows of the jungle night and for a moment Cleveland Herbert Emory, Junior, saw himself hailed as the conquering hero. He saw all the Army assholes and crackers and shit-heels toss a friendly punch at his shoulder, embarrassed, admitting he'd been right all along. He saw a scruffy gaggle of motor-mouthed Berkeley intellectuals parading him around on their shoulders, celebrating the one among them who showed the courage of his convictions. He saw his father, divested of mega-buck trappings, dressed in jeans and faded chambray shirt, shouting "power to the people!" He even saw Stinson—the rabid, raging SDS revolutionary who bombed the campus ROTC building—with his fist in the air, saluting Cleve Emory, tears in his wild eyes, saying . . . alright, brother . . . you are really cool, man . . . you are so fucking cool . . . to do what you did . . . oh, man . . . you are an inspiration . . .

The dope wasn't nearly as potent, but he'd smoked enough of it to significantly lower his inhibitions that day when he had the first fistfight of his life. It was delicious, a real slug-fest featuring balled fists, bare knuckles, blood, snot, and spit. It was the day in 1968 when he brought Julie Dandridge to the Students for a Democratic Society council meeting, the day Stinson stood up in front of everyone and called him a bourgeois maggot.

There was just no excuse for it. And when it happened, it demanded decisive action. He might have gone a different route if she hadn't been there. He might have challenged Stinson—everyone was getting tired of his wild plots anyway. He might have cut off the money or the logistical support for SDS operations that he was providing, but she *was* there and she laughed when Stinson put him down just for urging caution.

Everyone at Berkeley knew they were walking a tightrope. The feds had busted Angela Davis; Huey Newton and the Panthers were all on the run or in hiding. Hoffman and the brothers in Chicago were in jail. FBI rats and moles were all over the place making everyone paranoid. You had to be careful. Rhetoric was one thing but revolutionary fires banked quickly when you got busted on a felony rap and Stinson—that anarchist mother-fucker—was talking about conspiracy, arson, maybe even murder if some fucking Rot-cee Nazi got caught in the blast.

And who the fuck was Stinson to be calling him names, any-way? Nobody made a bigger sacrifice to support the exploited masses than Cleve Emory, Junior. Nobody risked being cut off from anything like the fortune he stood to inherit. And nobody poured more money into the cause of world solidarity than he did. But would Stinson acknowledge any of that? Fuck no! *He calls me gutless; all tough talk and no balls to back up my beliefs.*

That's when he shucked off his glasses and hit Stinson like a ton of goddamn bricks. And that's when he first formulated the idea that made him famous in certain radical circles. It came rushing out of him in a torrent—right after the inconclusive fight was broken up by the council members—as if he'd been planning

it all along, rather than firing random shots in self-defense. He'd
likely have forgotten it; gone ahead with his SDS activities and his
graduate school deferment plans, but Julie Dandridge and several
others called it the wildest thing they'd ever heard.

The liaison guy from the Syracuse Solidarity Movement blew
Stinson away when he called Cleve's half-formed scheme the
most audacious show of commitment and self-sacrifice he'd ever
seen. They'd all been talking about moral and economic support
for the National Liberation Front. Hell, Jane Fonda even went to
Hanoi to show her solidarity with the poor people of Vietnam,
but no one as yet had found a way to join the oppressed brothers *on the battlefield*. It seemed so . . . outrageous . . . so fucking
radical . . . so fucking perfect when he told them he'd actually join
the goddamn Army, get sent to Vietnam . . . and then defect to the
other side!

*Oh, wow, man . . . we're not talking speeches and moratoriums
and subversive activities just to give the establishment a pain
in the ass here, people! We're talking about the jungle, in the
swamps with the peasants, under the fucking fascist bombs and
napalm! We're talking about laying your motherfucking life on
the line to show solidarity with oppressed people struggling to
be free!*

After it was said, back at his apartment when the dope-buzz
was fading and Julie Dandridge was slithering across the brass-rail
bed, rewarding his fervor with a luxurious blow job, Cleve Emory
decided he'd actually try to pull it off. If something went wrong, if
he got caught, or blocked, or hurt, at least he'd be in the Army, in
Vietnam, and it would be hard to challenge his motives.

If he made it . . . and if he was correct in his estimate of domestic and foreign opposition to this immoral, illegal war . . . the Viet
Cong would win in a big way . . . and so would he . . . on his own
terms, without his father's help. And Johnny would *indeed* come
marching home, vindicated in his beliefs, a conquering hero of
the new world order.

A turtle struggling in a bamboo trap below his perch brought
Comrade Emory back to Camp 413. He slid down the bank and
checked the catch. It was a nice one and he picked it up, admiring
the amphibian's tenacity as he clenched the morsel of rotten fish in
his powerful jaws. Bending closer to the water he saw the captive
turtle turn a murderous, malevolent eye on him.

He shivered and thought for the first time in a long time of
Theron Clay. Dead and buried, he decided as he walked back

to his hut with the turtle in a sack hanging from his hip. They said Comrade Theron "Mustafa" Clay was unlikely to survive his injuries. Just as well, Emory speculated. The man was too fucking mean to live.

CAMP 401

As she had every morning for the past three weeks, Trinh Thi Thai squatted in the shade of the coconut palms near the well and watched the two hulking black shapes churn through the cloying mud of the rice paddy. The one in front of the plow—the one with horns and a ring in its nose—was a water buffalo. She might be a city girl—born and later abandoned on the streets near Ton Son Nhut—but she knew a water buffalo when she saw one.

What she could not understand was the strange allure of the taller black beast—the one with the horrible scars and hard eyes—who stalked silently behind the water buffalo, all day, every day. It was a man—no doubt about that—a foreigner like the American GIs who enjoyed themselves in the bar where her mother once worked. Beyond that obvious fact, Thai knew very little.

She noticed the man on her first day in camp when Grandmother Ba stationed her by the central well and taught her to operate the crude bamboo device that somehow sucked water right out of the ground. Thai had seen no others like him, not since the Americans all ran away from Vietnam, only a few short months before the Army patrol caught her stealing rice from the market on Lai Khe Street and sent her off to work in the fields.

Camp 401, at a place called Nam Poc on the banks of the Black River some eighteen kilometers equidistant from the borders with Laos and China, was her second home away from Ho Chi Minh City, the place she always thought of as Saigon. In the first camp, farther to the south near An Khe, she was beaten severely and forced to sleep with guards who gave her a liberal education in sexual activities that far surpassed anything she'd experienced in her seventeen years of survival on the teeming streets of Saigon.

All that was back in the early days, when she'd still allowed herself to cry. At the first camp, she was suspended like a captured monkey in a bamboo cage, crying and bleeding between her legs when Grandmother Ba found her. The old woman nursed her back to health, feeding her extra rations of rice and hot leek soup; cackling and crowing as she told stories of her days as a Viet Cong saboteur, infiltrating the American base at Cu Chi. Grandmother Ba's venerable age and influence in the camp kept Thai safe for a while, long enough for her to learn the important facts of life under the new regime.

"If you fought with the Viet Cong, Grandmother Ba, why are you here in this place?" Thai had never been afraid to ask impertinent questions. The camp cadre said it was one of the reasons for the beatings. They called her uncultured, a mongrel dog, but Grandmother Ba was patient with explanations.

"I am here because the northerners have big appetites and small memories," Grandmother Ba sniffed. "When the northerners won, the Viet Cong lost. I knew it would happen. I always said you cannot trust the northerners, but no one would listen to an old woman."

"But I don't understand . . . you are Vietnamese . . . we are all Vietnamese."

"Bah, child!" Grandmother Ba spit a stream of betel-nut juice between the stumps of her teeth. "Don't add stupidity to your problems. I am Vietnamese, yes . . . but not the right *kind* of Vietnamese. I am like you, Co Thai . . . a mongrel. My father was a Chinese from Cholon. Your father was an American. The new regime has no use for us other than to work the land and keep them fed."

Thai realized in that moment that she would never leave the camps. No matter what the cadre said in classes and lectures, she would never be a part of the new Vietnamese society. They were true, those terrible things she'd heard from the other children. She was tainted with monkey's blood; an ugly, evil spore of the American occupation of Vietnam.

She'd never known a father, although she realized hers must have been different than others. The long string of aunts and cousins who kept her and fed her until she was turned out to fend for herself shushed her questions about family, saying she had only to look in a mirror if she wished to know about her ancestors.

The mirror told her she was different, ugly as a water buffalo if she listened to the taunts of the other children on the streets. They mocked her tightly curled hair and dusky skin. Even the allure of dark, delicately slanted eyes was not enough to overcome the stigma of the broad, flat nose that separated them.

One night just before she was arrested, Thai took refuge in an old prostitute's apartment near Le Loi Street. Under the sleeping mat she discovered a photo album stuffed with pictures of American GIs, posing and posturing, draped over Vietnamese women with gaudy faces and vacant eyes. The Americans all had dark skin, black, kinky hair, and broad, flat noses. They were all black men . . . and any one of them could have been her father.

She hung her head and never again looked another person in the eye, except for Grandmother Ba who got only a disinterested shrug from the authorities when she asked permission to take Thai along with her to Camp 401. The old woman had become her savior, her strength, her solace, her only source of reliable information.

Thai stood and tugged at her conical straw hat, shading her eyes from the glare of noontime sun glinting off the flooded paddies. She noticed that the black man wore no hat. His hair was cropped to a tight skull cap and his skin was burned a rich ebony color except where welts of scar tissue ran like a nest of snakes across his head and down over his shoulders.

She kept her eyes on the black man as she carefully negotiated a muddy dyke, headed for the place on the other side of the paddy where Grandmother Ba would be supervising preparation of the first of two meals served each day at Camp 401. Viewed from another angle, his head seemed slightly distorted, flattened in back, forcing his ears to stick out and creating a rounded point at the crown of his skull.

Several Vietnamese words meaning ugly in one variation or another came to mind, but Thai forced them all out and settled on a word meaning curious . . . in an attractive way. She stopped in the middle of the dyke and squatted, slyly tipping her hat up away from her face, so the black man would be sure to notice her when he reached the end of the furrow. He passed her and turned behind the wallowing buffalo, but there was no sign that he saw her smile, no sign of life at all in his vacant expression.

Thai recognized that mask. She'd worn it herself to hide hurt from her tormentors and conceal pain from herself. When you are born different from everyone else, she'd discovered early in life, you can never hope to be the same. You can only hope to hide, to wear an effective mask, to come as close as possible to absolutely neutral.

Grandmother Ba was squatting near the cook-fire, squawking at the other women working on the noon meal, and puffing clouds of acrid smoke into the air from one of her foul-smelling, handmade cigarettes. Thai caught her eye and then squatted some distance away, waiting for the old woman to join her where they could talk privately.

"You should not leave the well until it is time to eat, daughter. Some of the guards may want their canteens filled."

"I filled all the canteens and left them in the shade, Grandmother."

Grandmother Ba squatted beside her and clucked when she noticed the object of Thai's rapt attention. "You must be very hungry today . . ."

"No . . . just curious."

"It is better not to wonder about some things."

"But I do wonder, Grandmother. I can't help that, can I?" Thai inclined her chin in the direction of the man who continued to churn through the paddy like a huge black beetle. "Tell me about him."

"There is not much to know . . ." Grandmother Ba sighed, hacked and began to roll another slug of raw tobacco into a dried corn shuck. "He is a foreign volunteer, an American who fought with the Liberation Front during the war. They say he was wounded in a bombing raid. He spent many years in hospitals . . . and when he came out, he was wild . . . like a tiger, they say."

"What else do they say, Grandmother."

"Only that he went crazy and killed a guard when they sent him to the reeducation camps. No one knows why he still lives. Perhaps they do not kill him because he is crazy . . . or because he is an American. I don't know and the cadre will not talk about it. He does not speak . . . except a few words in our language. He does nothing but walk behind the plow." Grandmother Ba cackled and spat.

"I think they are afraid of him." She pointed at a shady spot near the far corner of the paddy. "This one merits his own guard." A militiaman with a rifle kept a watchful eye on the black man. All the other militia guards remained outside the perimeter of Camp 401, leaving the interior police of docile workers to the lightly armed political cadre.

"I feel . . . sorry for him, Grandmother."

"Bah! As you would a pet monkey, I suppose? He is not a man. He is skin and bone with no brain. See his head? I think there is no room for a brain in there."

"I think he is like me."

"Aha! Now it comes out. He is a black one . . . like your father." She cackled and coughed, reaching for Thai's left breast with her horny hand. "Do you feel for him here?" Thai turned away but not quick enough to escape Grandmother Ba's hand on her crotch. "Or do you feel for him here?"

In the distance they heard the cadre officer's whistle. Workers began to straggle out of the paddies, walking toward the cooking fire. Thai watched as the black man continued to mush along behind the water buffalo, heaving on the bow of the plow while his militia guard shouldered his rifle and went to get his meal.

"I will take him his food, Grandmother."

"If you wish to feed dumb animals, I cannot stop you, daughter. Just be careful he does not bite your hand off."

Thai beat the crowd to the serving line and helped herself to a large bowl of vegetable soup and rice. She poured hot, green tea into a bamboo container and then walked toward the paddy where the black man worked. She stood directly in his line of sight, and for just a moment, Thai thought she saw a glimmer of recognition, just a flicker, perhaps only a series of rapid blinks, but it was enough to encourage her.

"I have a meal for you, sir. Stop and eat."

His expression remained blank, placid and uncomprehending like the water buffalo he followed in endless lines up and down the flooded paddy. He needed to eat. Thai felt her heart thump. No matter what, people needed to eat, to live. She swallowed a dry lump in her throat and stepped cautiously into the paddy.

The black giant slowly turned at the sound of her splash and glowered from under brows ridged with scar tissue. He stopped as she approached, jerking effortlessly on the reins around his neck and bringing the buffalo to a halt. She stood, knee-deep in warm, muddy water and shivered. He was so huge. His skin was slick and gleamed with the deep, soft glow of polished teak. His scarred chest seemed as broad as the buffalo's back. Taut lines of muscle heaved and rolled as he slowly, distractedly passed a muddy hand across his face.

"Ciao, Ong. Kham co thi?"

Nothing . . . but his mouth sagged slightly. He was missing four or five of his front teeth. Thai thought he might respond. There was *something* there in those eyes, as dark and cold as the night sky after monsoon. It was like the sad expressions of the young dogs displayed in the butcher's shop on Nam Phuong Street. She felt a sting at the corner of her eyes and realized for the first time in many years, she wanted to cry. Instead, she extended the soup and rice toward him, lowering her eyes to show she meant no challenge.

Thai was startled to find him so near when she looked up from under the broad brim of her hat. She felt the way she had in the first camp, once when she was harvesting yams and encountered a poisonous snake: paralyzed, fearful, yet tremendously curious and excited by the encounter.

She heard a rumble . . . a deep growl and something else. A word that sounded like . . . "go?" She craned her neck to stare up at his face. His broad nose twitched slightly and he repeated the word, flicking a bright red tongue through the gap in his teeth.

"Gao," she said. "Rice? Yes, it is rice . . . and vegetable soup. For you."

She turned toward the shady spot vacated by the guard and began to wade through the paddy. She could feel the pressure of water on the back of her knees as he clumped along in her wake. Thai climbed out of the paddy, removed her hat, and unfolded a clean cloth she kept there to serve as a platform for his meal. He stood still, towering over the paddy dyke. She motioned for him to come, sit and eat, watching as his dark face contorted, jaw muscles bunching, eyes squinting as if he were smarting at some painful irritation.

"Hunh . . . hunh . . . hunh." He grunted and winced, reaching for the string that held baggy trousers around his waist. As Thai watched in shock, the black giant pulled a knot from the string and dropped the trousers down to his knees. His penis was huge, veined and swollen like a purple snake. It twitched once and spat a stream of yellow urine that rattled and hissed into the muddy dyke.

When he was finished, he reached for his trousers and grunted again, his vacant eyes boring into hers. She struggled to look away from his crotch and patted the ground next to her. The giant squished up out of the rice paddy, squatted next to her, and began to eat, scooping huge globs of food into his mouth with muddy hands.

Grandmother Ba scolded and squawked, telling Thai it was a terrible idea, sure to get them all punished or sent to another camp that would be even worse than this one. Thai explained herself patiently, using phrases that just came to her, saying things from her heart and stumbling on the words.

"He needs someone . . . I can tell. I can feel it. As I felt when you came to help me in the first camp. And he is like me . . . alone . . . different from everyone else. They fear him as they hate me . . . because we are different."

Grandmother Ba stuffed her gums with betel nut and wrung her hands over the night fire in the center of the women's communal hut. "They will not allow it. You will be punished . . . and I will be punished."

"Grandmother, you taught me the way of the camps. You know I will never be allowed to leave. Why should I not make a life for myself here? The cadre will not object. Many men and women in the camps live together as husband and wife."

"But this one . . . he is different."

"Yes. He is black . . . and I am half-black. I will never get a Vietnamese husband. Never. And this man is like a child. I can teach him. Make a life that is bearable for both of us."

"But the guard . . ."

"I will find a way past the guard. Once we are together, I think he will protect me. You said yourself they are afraid of him."

"They will kill both of you!"

"Yes, perhaps . . . either now or later. But it is better to take a chance than to have no life at all."

Trinh Thi Thai bathed carefully in the stream at dusk and busied herself until dark with packing a few meager belongings. Rain-swollen clouds rolled across a full moon as she slipped out of the women's communal hut and made her way to the north end of Camp 401, past the pigpens, beyond the melon patch, to the thatched hut where the black man lived alone, isolated from the rest of the camp residents. There was no light from the hut but she could make out the dark form of a militia guard leaning against a coconut palm near the open door.

When the clouds parted, spilling silver slivers of moonlight into the clearing around the hut, she emerged from the shadows and approached the guard. He stiffened and slid the rifle off his shoulder. She continued to approach, keeping the wind at her back so he would catch the aroma of the fresh limes she'd squeezed into her hair.

She was very close when he growled at her to halt, but Thai could see the smile on his face. She returned his smile and softly dropped the sack of belongings at her feet.

"What is your business here?" The guard clipped his challenge with stiff formality but he was still smiling.

"I wish to see the one inside . . ." Thai raised a graceful hand and gestured at the door of the hut.

The guard lowered his rifle, leaned against the tree, and chuckled. "It's not allowed. This area is off-limits to everyone."

She took a step closer, shaking her head to jostle her hair and stimulate the scent. "Why? I only wish to bring him some food."

The guard inhaled deeply and his smile widened. He shook his head and pointed. "That one is crazy. He might bite your head off. He sees no one. He's *dinky-dau.*"

Thai knew it would not be easy. She steeled herself, thinking of a new situation, a partner, someone to care for, someone like her, someone who needed her. She began to unbutton her blouse and felt the wet wind stimulate her nipples.

He took her from behind, leaning his rifle against the tree and holding onto her hair for leverage against a series of savage thrusts. It was over quickly and they bargained while he buttoned his pants and lit a cigarette.

"I know nothing about this," he warned. "You waited until I had to piss and then you sneaked in. Understand?"

Thai agreed and walked toward the hut. She faltered at the door, pausing, peering into the gloom, and wondering if she was making a fatal mistake. What did she know of the black giant other than what she felt in the savage beating of her heart? They said he was crazy and he'd killed a guard. What if he killed her? What if the cadre killed them both? What if he rejected her?

From the dark interior of the hut she heard the squeak of a bamboo sleeping platform and the ragged sibilance of the giant's breathing. As he inhaled, she entered, feeling herself being sucked in, sensing the fecund warmth of his body. He was naked on the sleeping mat, lying on his back, dark and still in the pale moonlight that peeked in through a single narrow window.

She undressed silently and moved toward the sleeping platform. As she stood over him, watching, trembling, fighting the fear in her belly, she saw the ebony eyes open and roll slowly toward her. The giant stared, his eyes widening until she could see full circles of white around the black centers. Still, he did not move, did not start or acknowledge her presence in any way. She took it as a good sign and slid down next to him, letting her flesh mold to the contours of his hard body.

Suddenly a shadow blocked the moonlight. He stiffened, sprang, and straddled her in an instant. Thai felt his hard hands squeezing her neck. She wheezed and choked, trying to reassure him, but his huge thumbs pressed hard against her windpipe. She felt her eyeballs bulging as tears rolled down her cheeks and onto his fingers.

The pressure eased just enough to let a hoarse whisper escape. *"Anh ngu ong nhu lam,"* she croaked. I love you. The pressure eased a bit more. She felt the massive weight of his chest flatten her breasts. Thai brushed at a teardrop dribbling across his cheek with her left hand. With her right hand, she reached between his legs and began to stroke and squeeze. When he was rigid and throbbing under her caress, he took his hands away from her throat and began to stroke her hair.

"Hunh . . . hunh . . . hunh." He whined and grunted as she splayed herself wide and wrapped her legs around his thrusting hips. She didn't understand, but it didn't matter. For Trinh Thi Thai in that moment life had either started or ended.

A harsh, white beam of light stabbed through the door just before dawn. She bolted upright in fear, but the black giant pushed her back down on the sleeping mat, rolled over her, and sprang to his feet. He was massive, angry, and ominous as he stood coiled and growling in the cone from the cadre's flashlight. There were some muted words as the light played around the room and settled on her. She couldn't hear clearly over the guttural growls of her giant.

The floorboards squeaked as one of the cadre moved to enter the hut. The giant drew himself up to full height and barked. *"Dung lai! Di! Di, mau lin!"*

Floorboards squeaked again and the cone of light receded into a dull glow. She heard footsteps as the cadre walked away from his . . . from their . . . hut. Trinh Thi Thai felt the crushing weight of her giant as he poised over her, grinding into her with his hips, and knew she was safe . . . at least for tonight. Tomorrow? Well, that was out of her hands now.

The cadre commander of Camp 401 offered the visiting political officer a cigarette as they walked away from the black American's hut back toward their quarters near the center of the camp. He smoked in silence for a while contemplating the situation and then probed for position.

"The militia guard must be disciplined. His story can't be true. He had to know. They nearly woke the rest of the camp with the noise they were making in there."

"Of course. There is a work detail, clearing brush up near the Chinese border. Hard work. Lots of snakes, I'm told."

"He leaves in the morning then."

"And what of the woman?"

"Something, I suppose . . . she is a mongrel, a half-breed whore . . . and a thief . . . an enemy of the people."

"Yes. And perhaps she will get what she deserves."

The cadre commander smoked, smiled, and let Truong Li Xuan, the Regional Political Officer, finish his thought.

"Perhaps her lust has solved a problem for us, Comrade. We

are not allowed to dispose of this man Clay despite his obvious infirmity. We are forced to guard him . . . to feed him . . . to deal with a madman . . . constantly alert in case he becomes unhinged and tries to kill someone again. Now he has a concubine to keep him calm and passive . . ."

"What do you suggest, Comrade?"

"I suggest we leave them alone. A moron and a mongrel . . . hardly a threat to the State. Perhaps we move them farther into the country—banish them—and wash our hands of the affair entirely."

The cadre commander smiled into the night and felt a weight lift from his sagging shoulders. "As usual, Comrade, your sage counsel is both wise and welcome."

CAMP 413

"Furthermore, Comrade Xuan, I demand to know why I am kept like a prisoner in this remote camp. You must know that my role in the revolution was very special? No other American had the courage to fight alongside the victorious Liberation Front forces . . ."

Comrade Emory sipped green tea to hide a smug smile. His thoroughly rehearsed words were flowing with just the right mix of gritty sand and soothing fluid. Despite the blank expression on the Regional Political Officer's narrow face, despite the critical cast of his hooded eyes, Emory thought the rhetorical questions and subtle demands were hitting home.

"There *was* one other, Comrade . . ." Xuan paused to light a cigarette, sensing the man across the low table from him, judging his reactions, ignoring his stilted speeches. This was a difficult case.

"He was killed in the fighting . . . the same air raid in which I myself was . . ."

Xuan waved his hand in the air as if he were swatting mosquitoes, an impolite gesture designed to let the whining American know the courteous parlay was coming to an end.

"You are wrong about that, Di Anh . . . as you are wrong about many other things. Comrade Clay is alive. He lives not far from here, with a wife, perhaps children soon. He farms and works diligently . . . a productive member of our new society."

"But . . . but . . . they said . . . I was told . . ." Emory seemed startled and staggered by the news. Good, Xuan thought, an excellent tactic; a revelation, a subtle shift in leverage.

"You seem upset, Comrade. A star does not shine so bright when its light must be shared, eh? Comrade Clay assimilates the new order, becomes one with the people and the land . . . while you complain about your treatment and fall behind in political education."

"I have a special value, Comrade . . . to the revolution . . . to the building of a new world order . . ." Emory's tone had changed, Xuan noted. The pompous bleats and honks of his mispronounced Vietnamese had softened to a pleading drone. "If I were sent to Hanoi . . . if I were, uh, used . . . exploited by the politburo. I could . . . should serve as an example to western imperialists. I could tour the emerging countries as a symbol of solidarity . . ."

Xuan let a veil of stone drop over his face, turning a mental knob to tune out Emory's nasal whine. Anger roiled inside him, building like pressure in a boiling pot. He struggled to keep the lid on, to decide on a way of keeping Comrade Cleveland Herbert Emory, Junior, locked securely in his country's reserve ammunition locker.

Those were the orders from the politburo. Xuan's briefing had been clear and concise, delivered by a senior party official, a deputy minister of State Security, relayed directly from the prime minister.

Deal with the black one as the situation dictates; anything short of having him killed. He will never be whole again, or useful except perhaps as a pawn.

As for this man Emory at Camp 413 . . . he must be handled in a more subtle fashion. He wishes to be exploited for propaganda purposes . . . or so he says when anyone of influence will listen . . . but that is impossible. It would only serve to reopen old wounds among the Americans just when the scars are beginning to heal.

His father is a man of great power, a rich industrialist with worldwide influence. There is always the possibility that in time his son can be used in one fashion or another to help with current economic problems. We doubt that this man has—or ever had— any genuine political motivations, but the illusion is useful. Keep him isolated, and pacified to the extent that is possible.

Xuan briefly twisted the mental tuning knob. " . . . and so, don't you see, Comrade? I would be of great value as a symbol, in places where the revolution pits the masses against westerners who . . ." Xuan tuned out again, feeling the adrenaline-charged blood surge from his chest to his extremities. His body was screaming for violent action. He wanted to smash the pasty white face that served as host for a constantly flapping mouth! He *hated* Americans; hated them for their smug, superior attitude, for their false pride, for their weakness in the face of adversity, for their rootless political convictions, for their hideous polyglot faces, for their foul, shit-smelling breath, for their bombs that killed his sister, brother-in-law, and nephews near Haiphong, for their . . .

Xuan could no longer sit still and hope to control his emotions. He rose stiffly and began to pace around the small hut borrowed for this meeting from the cadre commander of Camp 413.

"I have listened to your petty complaints and foolish plans, Comrade. Now you listen to the truth of these matters! Your usefulness as a propaganda weapon ended when the last of your former countrymen left Vietnam. If the State is to use you again, you must have demonstrated the depth and validity of your commitment to the new order. You must become a functional citizen of the Socialist Republic! No special treatment; no special privileges. Such things weaken your resolve . . . and your value. You must learn to subjugate your ego, Comrade . . . for the greater good of the people!"

Emory flinched under the impact of Xuan's harsh words. He caught the anger in Xuan's gestures, the finality in his tone. There would be no appeal in the matter before this court. He closed his eyes, sucked his lower lip between his teeth, and bit hard, trying to conjure up the image. It would not come. He tried again, harder, but the approving roar of the revolutionary crowd muted to a disinterested rumble.

He saw himself then, in a flash of frightening clarity: an old, angry man, sun-blistered and bent from labor, squatting like a frog, leaning on a homemade rake, spitting through the stumps of rotten teeth. He saw himself forgotten in the backwater of time, doomed to poverty, perversity, and oblivion. It was not *at all* what he had in mind.

"No one can say I did not do my part for the oppressed people of Vietnam . . ." Emory flapped his withered right hand in the air and summoned all his remaining resolve. "Now I wish to be repatriated."

Xuan tamped a cigarette on his lighter violently before trusting himself to speak. "You wish what?"

Cleve Emory stared straight ahead and spat the words at the bamboo wall of the hut. "I wish to be returned to the United States. I wish to go home!"

Xuan forced himself to lean close to the sweating American. He hissed into the man's dirty ear. "You cannot go home, Comrade. You have no home . . ."

"I have influence, Xuan. My father is . . ."

Xuan snatched at the map case on the table and tossed a pile of papers onto Emory's lap. "Read those! Your father is a dupe, a servant of a corrupt system that means more to him than his only son!"

Emory stared at the clippings, read his own obituary, digested the reports of his father's press conference on the occasion of the death of PFC Cleveland Herbert Emory, Junior, KIA on a mission in Cambodia. He'd never been anywhere near Cambodia. Apparently his family had no idea about his decision, his defection to fight *against* America in Vietnam. Someone lied to his father. And his father lied to the people. He'd never made a call to the old man or said any of the words quoted in all the stories.

Going to Vietnam . . . my duty? The war . . . right or wrong . . . not the point? No fracturing of social and moral structures will ever destroy America? Cleve Emory realized as he read the weathered clippings that he'd gotten his wish. He'd been exploited, become a propaganda tool . . . for the wrong side. *Wasted. It was all wasted!*

His stomach contracted violently and he struggled to keep from puking rice gruel on Comrade Xuan's sandal-shod feet. Slowly, as he fought the wave of nausea, a spark of Emory's camp-survivor cunning kindled. Developed as a protective device against the pain, adversity, and disillusionment of the new socialist system, it was just what he needed to slap his shocky system into survival mode.

Xuan snatched at the newspaper clippings and stuffed them back into his map case. "Ignore the fact that you would be marked as a traitor and likely spend the rest of your life in an imperialist prison, Di Anh. Think of your father . . . think of your family. Conditions may be harsh, but here you have honor. In America you have only dishonor and disgrace for your family."

Honor . . . pride . . . ancestors. Emory put his elbows on his knees and lowered his head. *Socialist self-sacrifice for the good*

of the whole versus the age-old oriental business of saving face.
It was the wrong appeal. He'd just as soon the next look he
got at his father was through rifle sights. He knew what was
behind the carefully staged press conference, the lies, the false
emotions. He understood about exploiting situations. He was,
after all, his father's son, trained from the cradle to go for the
throat.

"You are right, Comrade Xuan. It is very hard to accept, but I
begin to see the situation as it really is . . ."

"You are not alone in the struggle for enlightenment, Comrade
Di Anh. Many Vietnamese—particularly those from the south—
have been tainted by western imperialism. It is the mission of the
camps to cleanse them of bad influences and false philosophies.
We struggle for regeneration through our own efforts."

Emory struggled to his feet, favoring the injured leg. "I will
make a better effort in the future . . ." The veil began to descend
over Xuan's face but Emory caught the signal and finessed.
"Meanwhile, Comrade . . . if you would speak to your superiors
in Hanoi. I would make sure of swift improvement in another
camp, closer to the capital."

"I will, of course, make your wishes known to my superiors."
Xuan watched the American limp out of the hut and smiled
at his back. Typical, he thought. *Weak-willed; no strength of
conviction. Tells me what I want to hear. Anything to get what
he wants; to make life more pleasant. You may be set free to
live as a citizen of the Socialist Republic of Vietnam, Comrade
Emory . . . but I would not hold my breath waiting for the day
to come.*

The entrance door was closed only a moment before the Camp
413 cadre commander entered, jerking a thumb over his shoulder.
"I hope you will tell me he goes, Comrade. I am sick of hearing
him whine."

Xuan looked up from the entry he was making in Di Anh's
file. "You have my sympathy, Comrade . . . but he stays at this
camp. He will try to convince you that he has seen the error of
his ways, that he will strive to become a productive citizen, that
he can be a guiding light of socialist theory. Don't be fooled. You
are to requisition permanent guards from the local militia and keep
a watch on him."

Xuan finished the notes, capped his pen, and stood with his
hand extended to the cadre commander. "Keep this in mind,
Comrade. A man who betrays once will not hesitate to do it
again."

"So he is to be treated like a prisoner?"

"Yes, Comrade . . . a prisoner who will bolt at the first opportunity."

Emory was not surprised when he was moved from the communal hut to an isolated dwelling near the center of Camp 413. He was not surprised when an armed guard accompanied him on his morning rounds to check the fishnets and turtle traps. Xuan was also cunning, Emory realized, but he didn't live in the camps. He didn't know how the system worked.

Trung Si Dinh showed up for a shift as Emory's guard around dusk. He leaned against the side of the hut and surveyed the surrounding jungle as Emory squatted by his side, smoking and mumbling in what appeared to be idle conversation.

"The provisions are ready . . . enough for a month if you conserve."

"I have cigarettes, ten packs, American brands."

"You still plan on going to Thailand?"

"Yes. My family is in a refugee camp there."

"What will you do when you find them, Dinh?"

"I don't know. Live with them in the camps . . ."

"To live a good life in Thailand, with your family, that would require money."

"I know . . . but there is no money. We will survive."

"I could tell you of a way to make money—lots of money—for a favor . . ."

"You are a prisoner now, my friend. Helping you to escape would get me killed."

"You could help me *after* you reach Thailand, Dinh. There are people there—Americans—who would pay you money for information about me. There would be no risk."

"Who are these people? Where would I find them?"

"Just find an American, Dinh. Tell him you saw me here. I will give you something . . . proof that I am alive. They will give you great rewards for this information."

Dinh walked with him to check the turtle traps along the stream. On the way back to camp, Emory pointed out the cache where his larder was stored. It was dark when they returned to the solitary hut. Dinh positioned himself below the window and listened carefully to Emory's whispered instructions.

"There is a gold ring with my initials on it. Take it to any American you find. Get a translator. Tell him you know of an American prisoner in Vietnam . . . that you have seen him. Don't mention that I fought for the Liberation Front. Simply say you saw me in a prison camp. Tell him where the camp is and say that I gave you the ring."

Dinh reached over his shoulder and felt Emory's hand groping for his in the dark. He closed his fist around a small, hard object wrapped in rice paper and bound with a scrap of cloth. Shoving the object into his pocket, he walked wordlessly away from the hut and disappeared into the jungle.

Cleveland Herbert Emory, Junior, bided his time nervously through two long days and four complete guard cycles before he finally relaxed, certain that Ngo Xa Dinh was gone . . . on his way to Thailand.

NEW YORK

"I'm a little surprised, Justin. It's not like you to panic."

Halley pointed at Cleve Emory's empty snifter, got a nod, and poured a generous dollop of strong ruby port. He stirred his own wine with the clipped end of an after-dinner cigar and stared out at the rhythmic Atlantic breakers as they washed the beach fronting Emory's private Long Island estate.

"It's not panic, Cleve. Call it caution. I'm merely concerned that we don't wind up haunted by old ghosts."

Cleve Emory fogged the salt-scented air with cigar smoke for long, silent minutes, waiting for his houseboy to clear the dinner dishes and disappear. Justin's vague call had made him edgy. He stayed awake the entire trip from Los Angeles posing and discounting possibilities.

By the time the jet shut down outside the private hangar at La Guardia, he was convinced they were bulletproof on this thing. Unless, of course, his son had somehow miraculously survived the war . . . but that was impossible. The goddamn gooks would be rubbing American noses in a thing like that by now.

"Let's play it out, Justin. Give me the benefit of your military thinking on this."

"I'm a cautious man, Cleve. My training and background in military intelligence taught me to recognize and assess threats. Some bells began to ring when Saigon fell. The POWs came home . . . there was all this business about live Americans still in Vietnam—the MIAs—all the speculation in the papers. It set me to thinking about our, uh, enterprise about six years back. We took a helluva a risk . . ."

"A risk you assured me was absolutely safe."

"That's correct, Cleve. I still believe we're on solid ground here, but some interesting facts began to surface. I checked on Pudarski. He'd been out of sight; out of mind in Chicago . . . going to school, working at odd jobs. Strictly low-profile, no obvious interest in the war. And then he quits school and heads for St. Louis . . ."

"And there's a reunion of old comrades?"

"Precisely. These days he's living with a photojournalist . . . the same guy who took the pictures of your son and that nigger in Vietnam. That's followed by a tip from a friend of mine who tells me this Spike Benjamin is making inquiries, trying to find me."

"Which leads you to believe . . ."

"Which leads me to believe they might be collaborating on a story. I think they may be trying to locate me for information about the Salt and Pepper case. You've got to understand, Cleve. There's a lot of knee-jerk reaction going on among the veterans— from Westmoreland on down—looking to hit back, to lay the blame for the debacle in Vietnam on someone else's shoulders. It's entirely conceivable that Pudarski and Benjamin intend to go public with the story of the turncoats they saw serving with the enemy in Vietnam."

"So what, Justin?" Cleve Emory relit his cigar and savored the rich smoke.

"So what? So . . . well, I don't want to see this mess become a cause célèbre. I can imagine certain politicians sharpening their bayonets on it, Cleve. I can see some right-wing zealot with clout on The Hill pressing the issue now that the war's over. There may be bases we didn't cover . . ."

Cleve Emory pushed his chair away from the table and trailed cigar smoke to the picture window overlooking the rolling velvet surface of the Atlantic. He stood admiring the view for a while and then turned to point an accusing finger at Justin Halley.

"That's bullshit, Justin. You know it . . . and I know it. You're not afraid of some cockamamie investigative report in the press. You're not afraid of some shit-heel politician probing into the case. You've got the wind up your ass for another reason.

"So Pudarski and this guy Benjamin swear on a stack of Bibles they saw two Americans fighting with the VC in Vietnam. There's no proof, is there? We've got the only evidence that the story is true, don't we? They don't have names, do they? They don't have the foggiest notion who Salt and Pepper might have been, so what's the sweat here? Where's the goddamn connection to us? It's a fucking tempest in a leaky teapot, Justin."

Cleve Emory moved to hover over Justin Halley. He grinned like a shark, showing strong white teeth around the stub of his cigar, and then bent to rest his weight on the arms of Halley's chair.

"I know what you're really afraid of, Justin. You're afraid a newspaper story—credited to eyewitnesses—might force the Pentagon to declassify the official records on this thing. You're afraid they'll catch up with *you* and start asking questions *you* don't want to answer.

"You don't want to be put on a Congressional witness stand where your word is pitted against a fucking hero who won the Medal of Honor. You're pissing your pants over that thought right now, Justin . . . you can't stand that kind of heat . . . because you left some loose ends."

Halley straightened in his chair bringing his face close to Emory's. Their cigars crossed like fencing foils until they were both wreathed in smoke.

"You're omitting an important consideration in that scenario, Cleve. What happens if these two guys push and prod until they build a genuine goddamn bandwagon? What happens if they start digging on tangents and come across a picture of Private First Class Cleveland Herbert Emory, Junior? What happens if they recognize Salt from his service record or some old high school yearbook? Are *you* ready for that kind of heat, Cleve?"

"What the fuck are you talking about, Justin? Huh? What are the goddamn chances of a thing like that happening?"

"It's a loose end, Cleve. Do you want to take the chance?"

Cleve Emory dropped the cigar into a crystal ashtray and slugged at his port. *Insurance,* he thought. *It's all about minimizing the goddamn risk.*

"How's the Houston retooling project?"

"Fine, Cleve. On track, on budget. We'll be ready to bid before Christmas."

"Leave it alone. Get on this other situation. Use whatever money and juice you need. I want it put to rest—forever—no chance of us ever hearing about it again. You clear on that, Justin?"

"Crystal clear, Cleve."

ST. LOUIS

Willy Pud wandered into the kitchen as quietly as possible and put a cold coffeepot on the stove. It was early Saturday and Spike Benjamin was upstairs in bed where he usually stayed on weekend mornings, fighting off the fatigue of long nights in his darkroom.

Waiting for the coffee to heat, Willy went into the living room and climbed three stairs, to a spot where he could get some perspective on the work that had kept them all on the bitter edge of brain failure for the past six months. Crammed against a long wall of Spike's apartment was an eighteen-foot length of quarter-inch plywood that they'd muscled into place when the paper finally started flowing from the Pentagon. Even supported by six sawhorses, the makeshift worktable groaned under the load.

Willy Pud stared at the gargantuan pile of paper and photographs, arranged in neat, organized stacks, and cursed under his breath. It was a monumental effort; one that had kept himself, Miller, and Benjamin churned up and charging like bloodhounds on a scent for the first half of 1976. Right down to the last pass on the last photo, around three this morning, they kept hoping for paydirt. Hard as it was for them to accept, it appeared the MIA search was a dry hole.

He was puttering idly around the kitchen looking for something to eat when the note taped to the door of the refrigerator caught his eye. It was covered with Miller's spiky scrawl. "Be back sometime in midafternoon. Should have FBI report on Ledsome by then. Off Sunday. Your turn to buy beer." It was signed Miller, E. J., Cpl. USMC (Retarded).

Willy Pud chuckled over the way they'd fallen right back into their old Marine Corps mannerisms, the old chain of command and rank structure with a wry spin added for laughs. It made for a satisfactory, familiar way to handle a difficult and demanding chore to which no one but himself could devote full-time effort. And Sergeant Pudarski was getting about as much mileage out of the mission as a butter-bar with a broken compass.

They needed a shot in the arm. Maybe Ledsome would come crawling out of the woodwork. He went into the living room, rummaged for a second, and then plucked out the "Patrol" file. Weighting one side of the manila folder with his coffee cup, he began to browse through familiar information; the easy stuff that Miller brought in while they were still hassling with the Pentagon over the MIA information request.

Stacey, Phillip A., Captain, USMC, 28, Ceiling, Oklahoma. Commanding Officer, Alpha Company, 1st Reconnaissance Battalion, 1st MarDiv. KIA in helicopter crash as a result of hostile ground fire, 23 June 70, Quang Nam Province, RVN. A cryptic confirmation of what he'd learned from Sergeant Major Shaeffer at the start of their investigation.

Henderson, Orville L., Sergeant, USMC, 21, Mussel Shoals, Alabama. Last unit, Alpha Company, 1st Reconnaissance Battalion, 1st MarDiv. KIA as result of enemy explosive device, 17 May 70, Quang Tri Province, RVN. That was bullshit for the record, of course. Hamhock got blown away five klicks over the line in Laos.

Wyatt, Steven B., Lance Corporal, USMC, 20, Bingham, Virginia. Last unit, Alpha Company, 1st Reconnaissance Battalion, 1st MarDiv. KIA as a result of multiple gunshot wounds, 17 May 70, Quang Tri Province, RVN. More crapola, but no Americans were even supposed to be in Laos, much less blown away on a cross-border op.

The next two entries were a sad testament to hard times turned up through Miller's access to the National Crime Information Computer. Willy Pud took a deep breath, slugged at his coffee, and read on.

Goodman, Sterling T., Lance Corporal, USMC, 19, Sacramento, California. Last unit, Marine Barracks, Naval Base, Treasure Island, California, for release from active duty. Honorable Discharge 23 December 70 to Home of Record. And from the NCIC: Arrested 19 March 72, interstate transportation of stolen vehicle. Sentenced to 3–5 years at California State Penitentiary, Chino. Died 4 April 74 of stab wounds received in cell-block fight with another prisoner.

Purdy, James Lee, Lance Corporal, 20, Spartansburg, South Carolina. Last unit, Headquarters Battalion, Marine Corps Base, Camp Lejeune, North Carolina, for release from active duty. Honorable Discharge 20 February 1971 to Home of Record. NCIC: Multiple arrests (71–73) possession and possession for sale of controlled substances (narcotics). One conviction. Served six months, Agricultural Work Program, Valdosta, Georgia. Released to parole board in Atlanta, Georgia. Died 19 January 75, drug overdose, in Savannah, Georgia.

Willy Pud fought the depression he felt each time he looked at the file. *Such good Marines: fuckers, fighters, wild bull riders, and heavily hung enlisted men, every one of them. What the hell happened?* It was a rhetorical question. He knew damn well what happened, knew fucking well from his own experience what went wrong with Cherry Boy Goodman and Poke Purdy. *Died of Bush-Beast Disease, decompression sickness. Trying to crawl back out there on the edge of the envelope and they fell off.*

There but for the grace of God, he thought, go Wilhelm Pudarski and Spike Benjamin. The roll call was complete except for Booger Ledsome, the last unaccounted for member of the Salt and Pepper recon patrol. His name skated through the NCIC computer. All they had was Marine Corps information indicating he was discharged honorably in September 1970 at Camp Pendleton and released to his home of record in Lancaster, Pennsylvania. A stepmother in Lancaster said she had no idea where he went. Drunk and fighting all the time, she complained. He disappeared without a word one day in '71 with the cops and a pregnant girlfriend hot on his trail.

Willy Pud closed the file and went to refill his coffee cup. Maybe Eddie Miller would turn up something through his pals in the regional FBI office. If not, they were fresh out of corroborating eyewitnesses beyond himself and Spike.

When he got back to the living room, Spike Benjamin was standing in front of the worktable, scratching his ass with one hand and his tousled hair with the other. Willy did an about-face and got another cup of coffee.

Spike nodded his thanks and prodded at a pile of photographs. "Christ on a rubber crutch, man! Takes us months to get the best available photos of all 2,483 guys Missing in Action in 'Nam or Laos. We finally force the issue and not one of them looks even remotely like Salt or Pepper."

Willy Pud nodded at the fourteen-by-twenty wide shot and the two grainy eight-by-ten individual enlargements pinned prominently over the table as their standard for comparison. "It wasn't for lack of trying."

Spike worked all night for four nights to create the best possible head and shoulders images of Salt and Pepper from the tiny 35mm negative. They were soft-focus ghosts, vague and blurry, but Willy and Spike had fleshed out the photos for Miller with detailed descriptions. They all felt certain they would recognize any likeness they came across in the material shoe-horned out of the Defense Department by Willy's influential friends in the Medal of Honor Society.

That material began to arrive in a flood shortly after Christmas. Willy Pud worked as organizer and record-keeper while Spike and Eddie Miller set up a system to sort through the deluge. Obvious Hispanics were the first to go on the rejection pile. Then came men who were too old, those who had disappeared very early in the war, and the vast majority of aviators. Willy's gut told him Salt and Pepper had been ground troops of one ilk or another. Since many of the MIAs were pilots or aircrew, that pared their case-load down to a reasonable size.

Unfortunately, the photos sent along by the Pentagon were of dubious quality almost across the board. Most were goggle-eyed boot camp or basic training shots, bearing little resemblance to what a man might look like after a few months in the bush. Spike went to work in his darkroom making copy negatives and trying to improve or alter the images. It was exhausting, painstaking work and this morning they'd finally finished it with zero results. Nothing seemed even close. Salt and Pepper—the traitors Spike and Willy saw in the bush with the NVA—were not among the American servicemen officially listed as Missing In Action.

Spike put his coffee on the table and stretched muscles cramped from long hours spent stooped over his enlarger. "Maybe we should go back and take another look at the white guys we eliminated because they didn't wear glasses."

"We can look, but it's pissin' in the wind, Spike. You saw that asshole's specs. He must have been wearing 'em since he was a kid. Ain't no grunt gonna run off into the jungle wearin' contact lenses. It doesn't figure . . ."

"Yeah. And how come we didn't hit something among the black dudes, you know? There weren't that many of them."

"Most of 'em were pilots or aircrew. None of 'em looked anything like that mean motherfucker we saw in Laos. You get a feelin', you know? Gut instinct is usually right on the money and that dude had U.S. Army draftee written all over him. He's a broke-dick eleven-bravo grunt or I'll kiss your ass."

"Well, shit. What now, Sarge?"

"I been thinkin', Spike . . . what if we're lookin' in the wrong hole here? What if the Pentagon covered this shit up by just declarin' whoever these guys were KIA. You know, send home a closed coffin fulla rocks—remains unviewable—who the hell is gonna ask questions?"

Spike shook his head. "Doesn't seem likely, Willy Pud. I mean, you've got to give them *some* credit for integrity. What about the families? If they declared Salt and Pepper KIA and one of them showed up, they'd never live it down. I don't see them taking that kind of chance."

"You sayin' this whole thing is too hard?"

"Negative. I'm just saying there are other avenues to pursue before we make ourselves *dinky*-fucking-*dau* trying to obtain and compare photos of fifty-eight thousand goddamn dead guys."

"What about the colonel from MACV?"

"Still ducking my calls. Even the goddamn source in military records dried up, but not before I found out where Halley works. Big shot with Emory Technology in New York. My guy on the *Times* tells me we got the right man, though. He retired as a full-bird colonel in Military Intelligence. Last combat tour was MACV staff, Saigon. He's the one who put you through the debrief."

"You figure he knows what we want?"

"He ain't dumb, Willy Pud. I told his assistant my name . . . said I was a reporter looking into something that happened in Vietnam. He's probably got a strong clue it has to do with Salt and Pepper."

"I guess I could fly to New York . . . get right in his face."

"No need . . . and it might spook him anyway. He'll wind up on the hot spot when we break the story. We name him as a substantiating source and he'll find his ass subpoenaed to appear in front of a congressional committee. What we need to concentrate on right now is the official records. We need a way to crack the classification on this thing, Willy Pud. We need to get ourselves a look at that file, see what's in there that we can use, and then force the whole thing out in the open."

NEW YORK

"Mrs. Fielding? How are you? My name is John Bradley. I knew your stepson in Vietnam."

"My God, you people keep turning up like bad pennies."

"Excuse me? I was just trying to locate Bill for a reunion we're having next month . . ."

"Veterans' reunion, huh? Well, he'd be interested alright. Anyplace there's a free drink . . ."

"Yeah, that's old Bill Ledsome for you. Uh, Mrs. Fielding, have you got a number for him?"

"It's like I told those other fellas that called, Mr. Bradley. I ain't got no idea where Bill Ledsome might be. Went wild after his daddy died. If I was you, I'd check with the police."

"Some other guys were looking for Bill? Maybe I know them. Did you get a name?"

"Yeah, some kinda Polack . . . ski-something . . . ain't they all? I believe it was . . . Plutarski . . . something close to that. Said he was in Vietnam with Bill too."

"I know the guy. Thanks, Mrs. Fielding."

Justin Bates Halley stabbed the long-distance line dead and punched another button on his phone console. "Two things in a hurry, Eileen. Get Mike Ludlow at Defense Intelligence Agency in Washington on the phone for me . . . and book me on something into St. Louis tonight or tomorrow morning."

While he waited for the call to Washington, Halley barged into his private bathroom and splashed cold water on his face. He liked what he saw in the mirror peeking over the pristine edge of a towel. The old soldier was on parade again. The old warhorse was back in harness. He winked at the sparkle in his eye and the firm clench in his jaw. *No guts, no glory . . . no balls, no blue chips.* When he stood to answer the buzz from his phone, his shoulders were square and solid. Colonel Halley stepped out of the bathroom with a full 30-inch stride at 120 steps per minute.

"Hey, Mike!"

"Justin . . . last week you promised the next time I heard your voice you'd be standing at attention in front of my desk."

"Yeah, figures, doesn't it? I've gotta go out of town for a week or two but soon as I get back, I'll catch the red-eye up there and we can reminisce at the Fort Meyer O Club. No shit, I promise."

"Looking forward to it. I suppose you're calling to see what we turned up on the Marines?"

"Yeah . . . I don't mean to push but the Special Ops Association is giving me fits. Gotta find these Recon Marines . . . you know how it is . . ."

"Well, let me get my notes here. We found all five but it's not gonna make the SOA very happy, I'm afraid. Let's see . . . Henderson and Wyatt, KIA in Vietnam. Goodman and Purdy . . .

both dead sometime after discharge. Sad story. One died in prison and the other from a drug overdose. The only one from your list that's still alive is William B. Ledsome."

Halley managed a convincing sigh of regret for his old friend from the instructor staff at Fort Holabird, Maryland.

"Hell of a deal, Mike. That goddamn war killed us over there and it's still killing us. So, what have you got on Ledsome?"

"Well, I guess he's available . . . provided the SOA is prepared to fly him back from Corsica."

ST. LOUIS

Eddie Miller dropped the case of cold Budweiser on top of Spike Benjamin's cluttered coffee table. "You assholes can cheer up now. I found Ledsome."

"No shit?" Willy Pud bounced up off the couch.

Spike Benjamin hooked a beer and took a long drink. "We were beginning to feel like the Lone Ranger and Tonto. It's about time for some good news."

"Well, there's good news . . . and there's bad news. The good news is that he's alive. The bad news . . ."

Willy Pud collapsed back onto the couch with a loud groan. "Don't tell me. The bad news is that Booger Ledsome is in a Trappist monastery under a vow of silence."

"Not quite. My guy in the FBI played hell getting a line on him until he finally shot off a query to InterPol."

"Oh, shit . . . he defected to the Russians!"

"You guys wanna hear this or not? William B. Ledsome, former corporal of Recon Marines, is in the French Foreign Legion."

"He's what?"

"Yeah, no shit. He wound up in Marseilles, France, and enlisted in the goddamn Foreign Legion. Can you believe that?"

Willy Pud shook his head and smiled. "Yeah, I can believe it. Booger Ledsome always said he was gonna give civilian life *one* shot. If it pissed him off, he was gonna find another war to fight."

"He's in the right outfit then. The FBI says he's with the Second Parachute Regiment at a place called Calvi on Corsica. No wants, no warrants, but they're keeping an eye on him anyway."

"Now what the hell do we do?"

Spike Benjamin rummaged under the beer case for his worn and battered phone file. "We get a sworn deposition about what he saw out in the bush with us. If the shit hits the fan after we break the story, maybe he'll fly back to testify in person. Let me get hold of a buddy who works for *Agence France Presse*. Let's see if we can get a message to Ledsome and let him know we're looking for him."

Colonel Halley was staring out his hotel window, admiring the magnificent view of the muddy Mississippi and the Gateway Arch when a phone in the sitting room of his suite warbled demurely. He slid into the leather chair behind the desk, opened his notebook, and reached for the receiver.

"Call from Mr. Fontagne in Paris, Mr. Bradley."

"Put him on, please."

"*Bonjour,* Justin. Can you hear alright?"

"Good enough, Henri. What have you got for me?"

"My man just returned from Corsica. Consider the job taken care of, *mon ami.*"

"No screwups on this, Henri. Are you dealing with reliable people?"

"Everyone in *La Légion Étrangère* is reliable, Justin, given the right amount of money."

"You need more?"

"No, no. What you sent was entirely adequate. As I said, consider the job done . . . in the next few days."

"I'll leave it in your hands then, Henri. Call me back when you have confirmation."

"And the guidance system contract?"

"Consider it yours, Henri. Good-bye."

Halley hung up the phone and flipped a page in his notebook. He ran a finger down a list of numbers, cradled the receiver on his shoulder, and got an outside line.

"SatCo Security. Carver."

"Freddy? It's Colonel Halley."

"You in town, sir?"

"Yeah. Suite 1412 at the Hyatt. Did you do the recon?"

"Yessir. He uses a standard IBM office model. Probably doesn't even code-lock his stuff. Piece of cake."

"Can you come by and see me tonight?"

"Roger that, Colonel. Bring anybody along?"

"Negative, Freddy. Solo mission. You can handle this one unless you've lost your touch."

"Nevah hoppen, boss. Like they say, you can take the boy out of the Projects, but you can't take the Projects out of the boy."

"Twenty hundred hours, Freddy."

Colonel Halley was an organized man. He printed a few terse lines in the notebook that he'd taken to considering his Op Plan and Mission Diary, then checked to be sure he had Spike Benjamin's office address.

Time for dinner and a drink, he told himself as he rummaged in the desk drawer for a room service menu. *It's all coming together nicely. In a day or two, I'll know what Benjamin's got. There's not a computer made to withstand the ministrations of Special Forces Master Sergeant Freddy Carver. That's how the man got to be the top crypto expert in MACV Studies and Observations Group.*

CALVI, CORSICA

Sergent-chef Leon Wolfinger ran the prejump equipment check for the twelve-man right door stick with practiced precision. He'd been a Legionnaire for fifteen years and a certified 2nd REP Jump Master for the past four of those. He had an outstanding record including citations for service in Chad, Djibouti, and Kolwezi.

More importantly, he told himself, as he watched *Caporal-chef* Ledsome assume the hands-on-head position for the jump master's personnel inspection, he had a perfect parachuting record from all aircraft types. Never a major malfunction nor a Legionnaire killed or injured on one of Wolfinger's jumps. The accident investigation would be cursory and routine.

"*Bonjour, Ledsome. Comment allez-vous?*"

"*Bien. Et vous, Sergent-chef?*"

Wolfinger grinned and nodded, running his hands over the front of Ledsome's T-10 troop harness. Helmet . . . canopy release assemblies . . . cheststraps . . . harness quick-release assembly . . . waistband . . . reserve parachute.

Reserve? Wolfinger smiled reassuringly at the American. *Won't help you, mon ami. This is a LALO jump, Low Altitude-Low*

Opening ... the reserve is window dressing. He spun Ledsome in place and continued the checklist.

Helmet ... riser assemblies ... diagonal backstraps ... horizontal backstrap ... saddle ... and static line. Wolfinger took the snaphook from the pack-closing tie of Ledsome's main chute and routed it over the jumper's right shoulder. He traced the static line with his fingers, looking for frays or cuts, and found none.

It was just a drill. The fifteen-foot length of Type XIII nylon webbing would never do its job of pulling the MC1-1B maneuverable parachute from the backpack. *Sergent-chef* Leon Wolfinger had seen to that last night in the Rigger's Loft.

He tapped Ledsome on the helmet and reached around to snap the static line snaphook on the top carrying handle of his reserve parachute. *"Bonne chance ... "* He looked into Ledsome's grey eyes and forced a tight smile through a twinge of regret.

A good Legionnaire ... a veteran of combat with his own devils ... but it is the destiny of all Legionnaires to die ... one way or the other ... sooner or later ... there is no escaping it. Wolfinger sidestepped to the next paratrooper and began his check. His sharp eyes and quick hands didn't miss a thing, but his mind was elsewhere.

His mind was on the ten thousand francs deposited that morning in his personal bank account in Brussels, and on a lovely little house on the eastern shore of Papeete with a veranda that overlooked the South Pacific.

Booger Ledsome struggled to his feet and executed a left face on the jump master's hand signal. He loved this part of it; loved the numbing vibration of the aircraft engines through the thick soles of his boots and the stinging rush of cold air through the jump door. He loved the jangling jolt of adrenaline when his heart told him to put his knees in the breeze and his brain called him a motherfucking lunatic for leaving a perfectly good aircraft in midflight. Not quite like a firefight, but right up there on the scale of activities that provide a plus-four pucker factor.

He snapped his static line onto the anchor cable, took a six-inch bight in the line, and focused on the red light gleaming beside the yawning maw of the C-130's paratroop door. *Sergent-chef* Wolfinger caught his eye, standing in the center section of the aircraft with his arms extended pointing at both doors. Stand in the door. Just seconds to go. Altitude six hundred feet over Dee-Zed Camerone. Ledsome wished it were a high-altitude jump so he'd have more time hanging under the canopy . . . up there free and clear of all the bullshit. Sometimes he thought of Willy Pud when he was up in that silent sky.

"Go . . . go . . . go!" Green light. *You should be here, Willy Pud. You'd really dig this shit.* Ledsome assumed the position for a vigorous exit and felt the slap on his thigh. He locked his eyes onto the inside rim of his helmet and launched into the slipstream, driven back and down by the combined forces of gravity and propwash from the 130's four giant turboprops.

ONE THOUSAND, TWO THOUSAND, THREE THOUSAND, FOUR . . . Oh, my God! Booger Ledsome was unintentionally free-falling on his thirty-fourth static line jump. He knew death was imminent when he missed the familiar rip of pack-closing ties and the stomach-churning lurch of initial opening shock.

"Why now? Jesus God, why now . . . after all I've been through?" There was no one to hear it. Ledsome was alone in his final moments. He felt himself falling, spiraling without main chute deployment at thirty-two feet-per-second-per-second. There was just enough time to open the reserve— he automatically pulled the ripcord with his right hand—but not nearly enough time for the canopy to deploy and slow his descent. It took less than 18 seconds for his 186-pound body to reach terminal velocity of more than 18,000 feet per second.

Booger Ledsome cratered into the rocky soil of the drop zone, feeling only a sharp flash of excruciating pain before his spine snapped and a leg bone—driven upward by the impact—penetrated his skull and smashed his brain.

ST. LOUIS

Security in this fern-shrouded hothouse, thought former Master Sergeant Freddy Carver, *is about as tight as Aunt Polly's pussy.* He chuckled softly, climbing carefully up the back staircase of the high-rent downtown office building, wondering about the genius who convinced American businesses they were safe with rent-a-cops. Worse than the fucking ARVN and just as predictable, he thought as he reached the eleventh floor and checked the access door for alarms.

You want to get by a St. Louis rent-a-cop in summertime? Just pick a night when the Cardinals are on TV. You could haul a fucking nuke through the front door anytime before the seventh inning. No alarms. Carver cracked the door and beamed an electronic signal from his hand transmitter at the video camera overlooking the corridor. The jolt would throw the electrons in the camera's vidicon tube into a tizzy for about one minute.

The guard in the lobby—if he bothered to check his monitors at all—would notice snow and static. It would clear up before he could tear himself away from the game and investigate. By that time, Freddy Carver would be inside the editorial offices of Major Features Syndicate and out of sight. He snapped open a leather case, popped three small tools between his teeth, and sprinted down the corridor.

The suite door tumbled to a shim, pick, and tumbler wrench in less than fifteen seconds. Carver ducked inside, shut the door, and put his tools away while his eyes adjusted to the dark. The recon, performed the previous week under the guise of a free security check leading up to a sales pitch, told him where Benjamin worked. He picked up his black canvas satchel and moved in that direction.

In Benjamin's cluttered office, Carver seated himself in front of the computer and booted the machine to life. He stared at the soft green glow of the terminal screen, waiting for a sequence of command queries, estimating he'd be back on the street in less than thirty minutes. And he'd be five grand richer when he hit those streets.

Asshole Halley. Always the big-time high roller. James-fucking-Bond. Guy thought the war in Vietnam was all about sneaky-pete espionage bullshit. But he could spend the money . . . whatever it took to do the job. And that's why none of the noncoms in MACV SOG ever took him out to the bush and disabused Colonel "007" Halley of his romantic notions.

Benjamin's computer beeped softly, asking Carver what he wanted to recall from its 640-kilobyte memory. He tapped the keyboard, experimenting with a few access patterns. A lengthy menu came up on his fourth try. He examined the alphabetized list of slug lines. Arson . . . aviation . . . beat-cops . . . blizzard . . . C-rations? Carver punched it up and recognized several of the recipes from Vietnam that Benjamin had recorded for one reason or another. Interesting, but not what Halley wanted.

"Look for anything under the name Emory. If you don't find that listing, look for seasonings, condiments, salt and/or pepper . . . that kind of thing." Carver shrugged and tapped the screen, running his fingernail down the menu list. *NaCl. What's that? Na . . . chemical symbol for sodium. Cl . . . chloride . . . sodium chloride . . . and that is . . . salt. Yeah.*

Carver twisted his penlight into a soft glow and found the activating controls of Benjamin's printer. He tapped the keyboard a few strokes, waited a few seconds, and then nodded as the printer began to transcribe all of the reporter's notes in the NaCl file from electronic signals to hard copy.

It took the better part of fifteen minutes before Carver could tear out the perforated sheets and fold them into his satchel. He shut down the power to the display screen and carefully hauled the computer mainframe from its slot in the desk. Holding his penlight between his teeth, he supported the bulky box on his lap and twisted out six small screws. That let him into the heart of the machine where all the data was stored. He pulled the powerful degaussing wand from his satchel and plugged it into an outlet. When it was vibrating in his hand, he began to poke it into the guts of the computer. The generated magnetic field would work like a big art-gum eraser on the machine's hard-disk memory banks. In a few minutes, there would be absolutely nothing left on Spike Benjamin's computer, not even the basic program that controlled its logic.

With the machine reassembled, Carver stood at the door of the office wondering if he'd left any trace of the subtle raid. Halley's orders were specific in that regard. *The more it looks like a simple case of catastrophic computer crash, the better. Be thorough but discreet.*

Thorough? Yeah. Missing something here. A guy like Benjamin doesn't take chances with this stuff. Information is meat and potatoes to him. Gotta be a backup somewhere.

Carver rummaged carefully in a credenza behind the tidy desk occupied during the workday by Benjamin's assistant. He found three thin boxes full of floppy disks in a locked drawer that he opened with a bent paperclip. The second box held the disk marked NaCl. Carver removed it, marked a blank floppy with the same label, and replaced everything.

Checking his digital watch, he cracked the door, extended his hand transmitter, and futzed the surveillance camera with a second burst of electronic hash. He was back on North Kingshighway fumbling for car keys just as his watch trilled to announce the preset thirty minutes had elapsed.

Eddie Miller tossed his uniform cap and duty belt on Spike Benjamin's kitchen table. Willy Pud held a coffee cup in one hand and a beer can in the other. Miller dug around in his patrolman's portfolio, inclining his head toward the beer.

"You off duty?"

"As much as I ever am since you blew into town. I got that report for Spike. Where is he?"

"In the living room. Still trying to reconnect on that call to Paris." Willy handed Eddie a beer and went to find Spike.

Benjamin slumped into the kitchen command post with a disgusted look on his face. "It's the wine and cheese hour over there. He'll call back as soon as his palate is cleansed. You got the report?"

"Yeah. The burglary guys said to tell you they got better things to do. No prints, no sign of forced entry, and the security guy in the lobby swears nobody was in the building after close of business. Maybe some kind of electrical surge or something. Buy a better computer . . ."

"That's bullshit, Eddie. If it was a power thing, how come nobody else's machine was affected?" Willy Pud had been hearing alarms ever since Spike reported the massive computer glitch in his office.

"And how come we drew a blank on the Salt and Pepper file when we checked the backups? I'm telling you, Eddie, somebody got into the office and into my computer. Somebody who either knows or wants to know what we're working on."

"I ain't gonna argue. But who the hell would it be? Nobody but us three knows about Salt and Pepper."

"Us three and Colonel J. B. Halley." Willy Pud flopped into a padded kitchen chair, cupped his chin in his hand, and stared at the starlings digging seeds out of Spike's window boxes. "I still think we need to talk to that shitbird."

Benjamin rapped a knuckle on the windowpane but the birds ignored him. "I put another call through to his office yesterday. His assistant says he's in London on company business. She also said I shouldn't bother to call again . . . Mr. Halley is not interested in talking to reporters."

The phone rang but Spike ignored the kitchen extension. "That's gotta be Paris. I'll take it in the other room where I can hear." When the ringing stopped, Willy Pud walked to the sink and leaned next to Eddie Miller.

"I been gettin' signals, Eddie. That kinda spooky shit that crawls up and down your backbone out on point or flank when there's gooks in the grid-square?"

"Yeah. Something ain't right . . . half a bubble off plumb everywhere we look. We should have turned up something in those MIA files."

"You suppose somewhere out there is a sonofabitch that would *kill* to keep this information from going public?"

"Shit, I don't know, Willy Pud. Why? Even if the story does get out, so what? They can say they just kept it under wraps to avoid embarrassment or some such shit. I mean you had the Pentagon Papers, that fiasco at My Lai, Hamburger Hill, that fucking doggie outfit refusing orders, heroin epidemic, guys shipping smack home in body bags, they owned up to all that once the press got hold of the stories. Why get crazy over two stinking assholes who turned traitor out of a half million or so?"

"Beats me. Unless there's a whole hell of a lot more to the Salt and Pepper story than we know right now. Anyway, I think you oughtta keep a close eye on Spike from now on . . ."

Benjamin wandered into the kitchen wearing a puzzled frown. He retrieved a beer from the refrigerator, pondered it briefly, then put the bottle back on the shelf and poured a stiff slug of bourbon.

"Uh-oh . . ." Willy Pud shot a glance at Eddie Miller. "I think we're about to get some more bad news."

Spike handed over the bottle and sat at the kitchen table contemplating the liquor in his glass. "Booger Ledsome is dead."

"What?"

"That was my friend from AFP. He worked his bolt and finally got onto a Legion source on Corsica. They were gonna set up a meet for my guy to get a message to Booger and then this morning . . ."

Willy tensed, gripping the edge of the table hard. His senses were screaming like sirens. "What the hell happened?"

"Parachuting accident apparently. My guy says Booger was killed last Tuesday during a regular training exercise. Chute didn't open for some reason. They investigated and decided it was equipment malfunction."

Eddie Miller splashed whiskey into glasses and joined his friends at the table. "Look, I been a cop long enough to know when coincidences add up and when they don't. We got this deal with your computer . . . and now Ledsome buys the farm halfway around the world just when we're trying to get to him. I don't like it . . ."

"Well, whoever the motherfucker is that's plantin' the mines, he's in for a fight." Willy Pud reached for the phone and dialed.

"Yes, ma'am . . . name's Pudarski . . . round-trip coach to Washington National, please. Yeah, that's fine . . . hang on a minute." He covered the mouthpiece and plucked a pen out of Spike Benjamin's pocket. "Gimme yer credit card number . . ."

Colonel Halley opened a window against the putrid fumes from the acetate computer disk smoldering in his waste can and settled in to reread the printout of Spike Benjamin's notes on Salt and Pepper. His name appeared prominently—capitalized and underscored—as a source of corroboration. No doubt about what was planned. Benjamin and Pudarski were on some sort of holy crusade to make the story public.

He noted with satisfaction that their information concerning other patrol members jibed with his . . . and Ledsome was now eliminated as a potential problem. If they went ahead with their plans, it would eventually boil down to their words against his. Even the records, should they become public, would only reveal secondhand sightings, an in-depth investigation, and his conclusion that Salt and Pepper were apocryphal grunt-lore; nothing more.

Even as he ran down that mental checklist, Halley knew the game was not ended. He was standing in the path of a potential avalanche. The mood of the country, the angry veterans, the clamor for dirt, the search for scapegoats and excuses . . . all that was very real. And those were forces that might bring people to their feet, screaming for truth and justice. Those were forces that might set influential people to digging up old graves.

Halley was not an odds player, not when the game meant his life and livelihood. Perhaps it was a long shot that Pudarski or Benjamin might ever run across a picture of Cleveland Herbert Emory, Junior—or even the nigger—but the chance was there, waiting to be stumbled on like a deadly booby trap.

And that can of worms must be kept tightly, permanently sealed. He reached for his phone.

"Freddy? Who do we have locally that might be able to handle some wet work?"

"Uh-oh . . . expensive proposition, Colonel . . ."

"We can afford to think big, Freddy."

"What kind of cut-out?"

"Solid. No connection to Forces. Has to look like street stuff."

"What can I offer?"

"Whatever it takes."

"Gimme a day or two, sir."

"I'll be waiting for your call, Freddy."

WASHINGTON, D.C.

Willy Pud hailed a cab outside his hotel in Arlington, Virginia, and told the driver to take the Key Bridge over the Potomac into D.C. The rumble of Georgetown's cobblestone streets reminded him of his trip to the White House the day he got the Medal of Honor.

He was on his way to meet the man primarily responsible for that decoration at the Old Ebbitt Grill on 14th Street, Northwest. Major General Clayton Matthews had been delighted to hear from one of his favorite Marines when Willy finally managed to fight his way through the maze of palace guards at the National Security Agency. As he'd told the general on the phone, it wasn't easy for Joe Shit the Ragman to reach the Deputy Director of NSA, even if they were old war buddies.

"Joe Shit doesn't wear the Medal of Honor," General Matthews had barked into his phone. "You do, Willy Pud. And when the day comes that your old battalion commander can't find time to buy you a beer, that's the day they can roll up the goddamn ladder on me!"

"Semper Fi, sir . . ."

"Semper Fi, Willy Pud. Let's have some chow and a drink or two tonight."

They'd spent four hours over chow and drinks. One of the first items on Willy's agenda was something he'd been meaning to say for a long time.

"You know, sir . . . I never did get a chance to thank you for writing me up for the Medal."

"And there's no need to do it now. It was one of the high points of my career the day you got it, Willy. I believe a leader is best judged by the successes of the men he leads. You were a success.

And I was proud to lead you. That's all that needs to be said. Now tell me what brings you to Washington."

Willy lifted his drink in tribute, washed away the lump in his throat, and launched into the story of Salt and Pepper. The general listened quietly, his sharp mind registering all the main points of the tale. When it was done, he pondered the ice in his glass for a long moment.

"You know I can't get that file for you."

"I just want to know what's in it, sir. We need to know how to put a name to these guys. We need to know where to look."

General Matthews had promised nothing more than a phone call later in the week. When he made it, Willy Pud got the invitation to meet him at the Old Ebbitt for dinner.

He paid the cab fare and strolled into the venerable Washington watering hole. General Matthews was sitting at a back booth, looking comfortable in a tweed blazer and regimental striped tie. He caught Willy's eye, waved, and spoke briefly to a passing waiter. Willy slid into the booth and shook his hand.

They chatted about life and changing times until the drinks arrived, then ordered dinner. When the waiter left, the general leaned his elbows on the table and lowered his voice. "Well, I've seen the file."

"Yessir?"

"I think you're pissing in the wind, Willy Pud."

"Sir?"

"There's nothing in the file, Willy. No transcript of a post-op interview with you, no photos, nothing like what you described."

"It's gotta be there, sir!"

"It isn't. I examined the whole thing and it's pretty thick. What it boils down to is a shit-pot full of secondhand sighting reports, some vague statements, lots of negative search reports . . . including one from a Special Forces team out of Danang that was supposedly tasked with no other mission than to find Salt and Pepper. They gave up after three months of chasing shadows."

"That's all? Nothing else?"

"Just a summary investigation report signed by this Colonel Halley that you mentioned. His conclusion is that Salt and Pepper never existed. They were propaganda perpetuated by grunts because it made a good story. That's all."

"General, I didn't lie to you or make this whole thing up. Spike Benjamin will back every word. There were pictures and a tape of my interview with Colonel Halley."

"No doubt in my military mind what you say is true, Willy Pud. But in fact *none* of that stuff is in the classified files. So, it disappeared . . . somewhere between Saigon and the Pentagon."

"What the hell . . . ?"

"I don't know, old friend, but I think I'd be wanting to ask Colonel Halley some probing questions."

When a cab dropped him at his hotel across the Potomac, Willy Pud stopped in the lobby and had the woman at the travel desk book him on an early Amtrak shuttle to New York.

BANGKOK

Sergeant Major Shifty Shaeffer scowled over his reading glasses at the offending phone. It screeched again and he began to shove a path through the unruly pile of notebooks, maps, and photographs that had accumulated in his room at the Peninsula Hotel on Prabang Street. He'd been trying to organize, screen, reduce, and pack a useful record of his activities and discoveries but he was convinced on the eve of departure from Thailand that he was about to throw the baby out with the bathwater.

"Shaeffer . . ." He snarled into the receiver hoping his tone would prompt whoever was on the other end to keep it short and simple. What he needed now was time and solitude to reflect on the unnerving events of a month spent in Thailand's teeming refugee camps.

"Hey, Shifty, it's Bob Terranova. I get you up off the crapper or something?"

"Sorry, Bob. I'm just swamped here. All this stuff to organize. I don't know how the hell anybody's gonna make sense of it."

"Well, you can't say I didn't warn you." Terranova had, in fact, told Shaeffer shortly after his arrival that the most productive thing he could do with the substantial amount of unofficial cash he'd transferred into the country was buy a small business or build a Buddhist shrine. An old Air Force NCO with half a lifetime invested in Southeast Asia, Terranova was currently the overworked and underfunded post-war U.S. Agency for International Development representative in Thailand. If anyone understood the vagaries and double-dealing involved in the high-stakes information auction that flourished in the camps, he did.

"Yeah . . . can't say I believed you back then, but I didn't get blindsided either. What's on your mind this morning?"

"Got any of that spare change left?"

"Bob, I'll *give* you everything I've got left but I can't listen to another fucking horror story."

"You might want to make an exception for this one. Guy's fresh in and he's got People's Militia papers. Says he was a guard at a camp where they're keeping a round-eye."

"C'mon, Bob, that's story 14-A with a Type B twist. I got fifty goddamn transcripts that say—"

"This yahoo brought some proof. Claims a round-eye gave it to him and told him to find the nearest American. It's an interesting story."

Shaeffer glanced at the chaos of his hotel room and shuddered. He passed a hand through what was left of his hair and decided he was obliged to roll the dice. "So this is worth listening to . . . in your opinion?"

"I'll be by in fifteen minutes . . . water-taxi . . . meet me at the back of your hotel."

The snarl of a modified VW engine mounted on the aft end of a long, slender Thai water-taxi made communication difficult, so Shaeffer and Terranova motioned for the driver to throttle back and moved forward where they could confer. Shaeffer felt the after-action report he was due to deliver in the States would have to begin with a description of the current situation or no one would understand the apparent contradictions and convolutions. Terranova did his best to encapsulate.

"It's fucking Southeast Asia, man. The history of the whole region is one long example of making a silk purse out of a sow's ear, you know? You walk in and start blowing the shit out of their country with artillery. What do they do? They build a whole goddamn economy based on making trinkets out of your discarded brass shell casings. Am I right?

"OK, so we pull out of Vietnam and the NVA ball-busters take over in the South. You got pogroms and gulags and even the hard-core VC are running for the escape hatches. Those on the coast become boat-people . . . those who live inland head for the jungle and just keep going until they die or they hit Thailand. Now you got swivets of refugees fucking all over the Thai economy. Thais don't want to piss away money on border camps for refugee foreigners and we ain't pumping the big bucks this way anymore. So what happens?

"The gooners survey the marketplace and come up with their own currency. We got every ilk of government-sponsored organization and private party over here trying to find out about POWs or get solid information on MIAs. You got wives and grown kids who won't believe a guy's dead until they can kiss a cold corpse in a Stateside funeral parlor; you got former military and special ops assholes scamming big bucks and promising to lead some sort of Terry and the Pirates rescue mission; you got preachers and pundits and bureaucrats, all convinced they can buy a clue and bring some poor bastard out of the jungle . . ."

"Take it easy, Bob. This is an emotional issue back home. The fucking war ain't never gonna be over for a lot of Americans until we deal with this thing one way or the other."

"I know that, Shifty . . . and so do these little rice farmer refugees and former VC in the camps. Hell, they lived with us for ten years. They know which buttons to push. Old aircraft parts, diaries, IDs, dog tags, or bones they find one day while they're plowing; any kind of wild story they think we'll buy for cold cash. It's the only economy they got and it's a seller's market."

"So, what makes you think this guy we're going to see is legit?"

Terranova shrugged and trailed a hand in the muddy water as the taxi pilot steered smoothly into a shallow Mekong tributary. "Hunch, gut feeling, instinct, I don't know . . . but my people in the camp say he's not run-of-the-mill. He found most of his family, you know? Happy as a clam but he keeps asking to speak to an American. Says a round-eye gave him a message and promised an American would pay big bucks for it."

Shaeffer spotted the refugee camp landing in the distance and stood to stretch his legs. "You believe it, don't you, Bob? You think there's still some Americans left inside."

Terranova reached for the bowline and fiddled with the wet rope. "I think the Vietnamese learned how to play poker from the experts, Shifty. I think they know enough to keep an ace or two in the hole."

Ngo Xa Dinh bounced his grandson on his knobby knee and eyed the USAID translator sitting beside him in the camp's clapboard administration hut. The woman was a southerner and spoke an uncultured, accented Vietnamese that marked her as a farm girl from somewhere in the Mekong Delta. He glanced at the two sweaty Americans seated across the table from him and then asked the woman to insure she translated his words exactly as he spoke them.

She sniffed, opened her notebook, and began to speak to the visitors in English. As he listened to the nasal whine of the foreign words, Dinh marveled at how different these men looked from Di Anh, the only Americans he had ever seen inside the effective range of an RPD machine gun. They were thick and hard, wearing the bored expressions of old soldiers. He decided to tell his story straight, with no embellishments.

"Ngo Xa Dinh . . ." The translator mispronounced his name. "Forty-six years old, born in the northwestern part of Vietnam in Thuy Binh Province. A farmer until he enlisted in the Army. Fought in the south. Wounded and evacuated in 1969. Joined the People's Militia and served with a security unit guarding a reeducation camp near the borders with China and Laos. Mr. Dinh says he ran away to find his family."

She turned to him and switched to Vietnamese. "I have told these Americans of your background. You may say what you wish now."

Dinh set his grandson on the dirt floor to play with a doll made of rice straw and nodded at the Americans. "I was with a People's Militia unit that guarded a camp—Camp 413—where people went for political indoctrination . . ." He cut himself off nervously as the translator converted his words to English.

"At the camp was an American. He was wounded, in his right arm and leg." Dinh demonstrated Di Anh's stiff leg and withered right hand before he continued. "He had been in many camps before, I think, since he spoke in Vietnamese. I know nothing more about him, except that we became friends and he told me he wanted to get out of the camp. He said I should tell this to any American I meet when I get to Thailand."

When the translator finished, the shorter of the two Americans leaned his elbows on the rickety table and spoke directly to him. "How do you know this man was an American?"

"He looked like you."

"That doesn't mean he was an American . . . a soldier, a prisoner of war . . ."

Dinh hesitated. This was dangerous ground. Di Anh had specifically directed him not to mention that he had fought for the Liberation Front.

"I know Americans. I fought against them in the war. This man is an American. He has been a long time in the camps, but he is an American."

"Many people have told such stories to get money. Why should we believe you?"

Dinh understood the translation but he was confused. Did the Americans suspect he would lie about such an important thing? Perhaps they simply expected everyone to lie as they did. He shrugged and reached into the pocket of his baggy shorts.

"You should believe me because I am telling you the truth . . . and because the American at Camp 413 gave me this." Dinh unwrapped the gold ring and placed it in the center of the table.

Shaeffer picked up the ring, read the initials, and handed it to Terranova. "It's in good shape. Probably wouldn't be that nice if it'd been buried in some rice paddy for years."

"Maybe . . . and maybe he got it on the black market from some NVA vet who took it off a dead guy's finger. Who the fuck knows?"

Shaeffer turned to Dinh and drilled into the old man's eyes looking for deception. Dinh simply stared back without blinking.

"When was the last time you saw this American?"

"Only one month ago . . . just before I left the camp."

"Did he tell you his name?"

"Not his given name. In the camp he is known as Di Anh."

The translator stifled a giggle and lowered her eyes. "It would be something like 'Running Foreigner' in English."

Shaeffer made a note and toyed with his pencil. "Can you describe this man for me?"

"Tall . . . taller than you but not as tall as him. Very thin. A long face with a thin nose and green eyes. He wears glasses."

"If this man is a prisoner of war, why wasn't he returned with the other American prisoners?"

Dinh dropped his eyes for the first time. He shifted in his chair and watched his grandson for a moment. He was not prepared to answer this question and took some time to formulate a response he hoped would satisfy.

"I don't know why he was not returned. Perhaps he has some important information the government wants. They make him go to the political lectures every day. Maybe they wish to make him a communist."

"Did you ever hear this man speak English or see him in an American uniform?"

"He speaks Vietnamese. If he spoke your language, no one would understand. He is the only round-eye. He wears the same clothes they give to everyone in the camps."

"Is this man guarded so that he can't escape?"

Dinh smiled and shook his head. "He is guarded. I myself was his guard for a while. But even if he was left alone, he could not escape from Camp 413. Where would he go?"

Terranova leaned into the conversation. "Tell us anything else you can about this man."

"I know nothing else. He is an American . . . and he wants to go home."

"Did this man tell the cadre he wants to go home?"

"I think he is like everyone else they send to the camps. He tells the cadre what they wish to hear. Everyone wants to go home, but it is not wise to speak of such things around the cadre."

Shaeffer dug in his briefcase and retrieved one of his large-scale map sheets. He spread it on the table facing Ngo Xa Dinh. "This map shows the part of Vietnam near the borders with Laos and China. Do you recognize the area?"

Dinh studied the map carefully, nodding and pointing at locations he knew. He traced a tributary of the Black River north from the ferry landing at Lai Chau and inscribed a circle with a dirty fingernail. "Camp 413 is near this place. There you will find the American."

Shaeffer made more notes including the coordinates of the camp and then stood to fold the map. All that remained between him and Ngo Xa Dinh was the gold ring. He picked it up and weighed it in his hand. "Thank you, Mr. Dinh. I will take this to my superiors in the United States."

Dinh glanced at the translator and mumbled. She sniffed again and relayed the message. "Mr. Dinh says the American who gave him the ring promised that he would be paid for delivering it to another American. He wishes money so that he may take his family out of the refugee camp."

Terranova stood and stretched. "There's the bite, Shifty. What's it worth?"

Shaeffer popped the ring into his briefcase and glanced briefly at the baby crawling around in the dirt at Dinh's feet. He fumbled with a fat envelope and then counted out the equivalent of a hundred U.S. dollars in baht. Dinh accepted the cash, wrapped it carefully in a bandanna, and walked out of the hut with his grandson on his hip.

As they boarded the water-taxi, Terranova spotted Dinh watching them from the door of a communal hut and waved. "Seemed like a pretty straight shooter. Hope I didn't bring you out here on a wild goose chase."

"I like the way he looked us dead in the eye, Bob. Most of the bullshit artists are constantly trying to read you, trying to figure out what you want to hear before they answer any questions."

"He's new to the game. Maybe he just doesn't know the rules yet."

"Yeah . . . and maybe he's telling the truth as he knows it. Anyway, this ring did belong to an American at one time or another. There's a New York jeweler's mark on the inside that won't be hard to trace. He didn't bullshit around about the location of the camp either. Knew where it was and pointed right to it. Maybe we got something here. Worth a hundred bucks anyway. Thanks."

Ngo Xa Dinh watched the two Americans roar away in the water-taxi. Perhaps Di Anh would be free soon, he mused, standing on one leg, watching the spreading wake of the boat and touching the thick wad of money in his pocket. Then he began to laugh.

His daughter asked what brought him happiness in this miserable place, but Dinh could not explain. Di Anh might get out of Camp 413, he might leave Vietnam at long last and return to America, but he would never be free. No one—not even the Americans—would let a traitor go unpunished.

NEW YORK

Eileen Winter plopped her oversize purse on one of the free-standing tables that dotted the dark interior of the Camelot Bar on West 65th Street and told a passing waiter to bring her a quick Finlandia on the rocks. She slid onto a stool and glanced at the well-dressed business crowd trying to decompress before heading out of Manhattan. There was enough beef at the bar to help her out if things got nasty.

He strolled in off the street just as her drink arrived and stood inside the door, letting his eyes adjust to the gloom. She sipped and smiled as he made his way through the crowd toward the bar. *OK, asshole, here I am. You want to start something in here, just give it a try.*

He sipped dark beer from a thin pilsner and turned to look at her. There was a grin on his face but it didn't look menacing.

Eileen ordered another drink and sized him up in a series of quick, disinterested glances.

Tall, broad-shouldered, straight, trim, and tan. Definitely not a native. Clothes right out of Sears basement. Maybe a cop . . . or some dumb-ass soldier pole-vaulting through a leave in the Big Apple; looking for a little class action. Doesn't look much like a pervert or serial killer . . . but they never do. So why the hell is he following me?

The man snagged the waiter, dumped some bills on his tray, and picked up her drink. Eileen spotted him weaving toward her through the crowd and casually reached inside her purse where she kept a small aerosol dispenser of Mace.

"Excuse me, are you Miss Eileen Winter?"

Oh, shit, he knows my name! She covered her surprise with a hit of vodka and quickly drew a version of the standard New York subway veil over her face.

"Listen, I'm not some kind of street creep and I'm not trying to pick you up." His expression was open and honest, based on a loose, lopsided grin. Eileen arched her eyebrows and released her grip on the Mace.

"You've got until I finish this drink to tell me how you got my name and why you're following me."

"That's time enough for a simple story." He shrugged and sipped at his beer but made no move to sit. "I got your name from the security guy on your floor at the Emory Building. He tossed me out so many times we got to know each other . . . and it turns out we did some time overseas together. I'm following you because I'd like to know why your boss refuses to see me."

Wilhelm Johannes Pudarski . . . in the flesh. Eileen nodded and pointed to the stool across from her. She was intrigued. After all the curt refusals, she thought surely he'd have gone back to Chicago or St. Louis by now.

"So you're Pudarski?"

"I am." He extended a hand and she shook it. "Mr. Halley and I had some brief acquaintance in Vietnam."

"I'm aware of that, Mr., uh, what should I call you?"

"Willy or Willy Pud, whatever's comfortable."

"Mr. Halley mentioned that he'd run across you when he was in the Army. He's not very anxious to relive those days, I guess."

"Did he say anything else about me?"

"He said you were highly decorated. Medal of Honor, I believe?"

"I'm really interested in talking to him about something that happened back in 1970. He debriefed me, uh, after an important mission . . . and I'd like to kind of pick his brain about that."

Eileen stared at him over the rim of her glass. He really was handsome, in an open, airy, non-New York fashion. Justin was out of town . . . and he'd been treating her like a hooker since this man's name had popped up out of the blue. She wasn't even briefed on his new project, except that it had the full weight of Cleve Emory behind it . . . and it took him out of town for extended periods. Might just serve the sonofabitch right . . .

"There's two things you should know, Willy Pud." Eileen ticked off the points on her manicured nails. "First, Mr. Halley is out of town—no, he really is. He's on an extended trip doing business for Mr. Emory. Second, he wouldn't see you if he were in town. Vietnam is a sensitive subject in the higher echelons of our firm. Mr. Emory's only son was killed over there."

Willy nodded and toyed with his beer. "I didn't know that. But if I could just talk to Halley for a minute or two, let him know what I'm after, I think he'd make an exception."

"And take a chance on upsetting the chairman of the board of Emory Technology? Why would he do that?"

"He's a soldier, Eileen, or he was one for a lot of years. What I want to talk to him about . . . well, it's an important issue for all soldiers."

"I'm his personal assistant, Willy Pud. Take it from me, Justin Halley would not make an exception."

"Well, I'll trust your judgment on that." He smiled and tugged at an earlobe. He really was intriguing. There was an aura about him . . . a sort of pent-up power, a magnetism that made her squirm inside. Eileen pointed at both their glasses when the waiter made his rounds and then stared into his green eyes. The subdued lighting made them sparkle with tiny gold flecks. She wondered idly how many men he'd killed, what sort of extraordinary things he'd done to win the Medal of Honor.

"Anyway, I'm determined to talk to the man. If you'll tell me, confidentially, where he is, I'm ready to travel."

She reached across the table and tapped his hand with a fingernail. He didn't look down or move the hand. "I might let something like that slip, Willy Pud, but we'd have to get to know each other better."

The waiter brought the drinks. Eileen talked around his quest, trying to get a feel for the subject. Inside information was always valuable, especially when it was the kind of thing that might yield leverage. When the piano started to tinkle, they retired to a couch in a dark corner of the bar, near a crackling fire. She sat close and let him feel the flesh of her thigh.

"When were you planning on leaving New York?" Her voice was a suggestive purr. She retransmitted, just in case he was missing the message.

"Well, that depends, there's not much to keep me here now. I've got an open reservation back to St. Louis." He scooted around on the couch, cocking his head to one side and letting his hand fall on her knee.

"We could spend some time together . . . and maybe I could give you a number to call in St. Louis."

"A number in St. Louis?"

"You want to talk to Mr. Halley, right?"

"Oh, shit! He's in St. Louis?"

"I didn't say that . . ."

"Goddammit!" Willy Pud glanced at his watch and then stormed out of the bar, leaving Eileen Winter with a healthy drink tab and an unhealthy dose of sexual frustration.

"Hi! This is Spike Benjamin. I'm not in to take your call. Leave a name and number when you hear the tone."

"Goddammit!" Willy Pud checked his watch and glanced down the airport corridor searching for the right gate number. Ten minutes to make the plane. "Spike, it's me. Are you there?" Nothing but long-distance static.

"OK, look . . . I'm at LaGuardia about to catch a plane back to St. Louis. There's some shit you should know. The file is a washout. There's none of our stuff in it. You can guess what that means . . . we'll talk about it when I get in. More importantly, Halley is in St. Louis! Put Eddie on it . . . see if we can find him. And watch your ass, man. Check six o'clock at all times. Gotta go."

ST. LOUIS

"He down near Boyle Street now, man . . . shootin' flicks like a motherfucker and headin' dis way." Andre Kingston lit a joint, sucked on it, and pointed the wet end at Shack Burton.

"How many times I gotta tell you 'bout dat shit, bro?" Burton spun the cylinder of the nickel-finish Ruger revolver and reached into an open box of .44 Magnum jacketed hollowpoints on the coffee table. "Dat's how come you got blown away on dat op up by Tam Ky. Ain't nothin' but a motherfuckin' fool goes smokin' dope in the bush."

"This ain't the bush, mah man . . ." Andre swallowed smoke and moved to gaze down through a taped-over window at the Pruitt-Igoe Housing Project's decaying recreational area. A swarm of black kids crawled around the rusting playground equipment like the roaches that infested their tenement homes.

"Tell you like it is, bro . . . anyplace you go after a dude with a weapon . . . that's the bush." Shack moved to a dark corner where two recently stolen shotguns waited to be loaded. "Yer piece ready, Andre? We ain't got as much ammo as we need for the scatterguns."

Andre Kingston expertly racked the slide on his Smith & Wesson semiauto, watched a round of 9mm Federal Hydra-Shok snick into the chamber, and thumbed the safety. "Cocked and locked, mah man. Where you plannin' on settin' the ambush?"

"Just inside the alcove. The dude likes to take pictures of winos . . . and we gonna oblige his ass." Shack picked up a spool of electrician's tape and began to pad rough edges left by the hacksaw used to remove the stocks of the Ithaca ten-gauge Magnum Roadblocker shotguns. "And remember what the man said. He got to be deader'n a motherfucker and we got to take his bread and his cameras."

Andre Kingston nodded and rolled the other shotgun upside down, sliding double-ought buckshot shells into the tubular magazine. "Check it out . . . this is one *bad* motherfucker!" The heavy shotgun felt solid and substantial in his hands like the M-79 blooper he carried for the Americal Division in southern I Corps.

"Don't get attached. When mah man Mistah Benjamin is down to stay, we drop the fuckin' weapons, go right down to Snook's parkin' lot, get the car, and head for the airport."

"There it is. And the motherfucker that finds mah ass in Jamaica best be ready to fight."

Spike Benjamin ducked into the gloom of the alcove covering the riverside access to the Projects and automatically racked his camera open two f-stops. He kept his eye to the viewfinder of a scarred and world-weary Nikon F, duck-walking forward until a comatose black man drooling heavily on a bottle of Thunderbird wine filled the wide vista of a fast 35mm lens. He shifted the lens through a parabola, letting the motor-drive crank Tri-X past the shutter. Somewhere in this roll or the one he'd just finished shooting on the street outside Pruitt-Igoe should be a frame that snarls and barks loudly enough to make the cover of *Time*.

The guarantee his agent nailed down was substantial but the cover shot carried a healthy bonus in both money and prestige that Spike was determined to earn with his photo-essay on urban blight. St. Louis would stand in nicely for a hundred other places across the nation where the decay of abandonment and hopelessness had finally eaten through the pearly white enamel of American inner cities.

Spike popped open the back of his camera when the rewind mechanism whirred to a stop and reached in his shoulder bag for more film. He blinked and stared into the gloom, seeking the rheumy red and yellow eyes that glared from half a dozen black faces. He could almost feel the hate wash over him. Only the numbing, emasculating effect of cheap wine kept these angry, befuddled, desperate men from carving him up like a Mississippi catfish.

Spike twisted an 85mm telephoto onto the camera body and racked it open to inspect the frame. The long lens brought angry eyes into startling proximity. He put his back against a cold concrete wall and wished for a moment he'd taken Eddie Miller up on the offer of a police escort. But a uniformed cop had the same effect on the people in this low-income housing project that bright light has on cockroaches. If he wanted a look at the despair, if he wanted to catch the hostility that pervades the black ghetto of the inner city, he'd have to stand alone, hoping his camera and his interest were enough to keep him alive.

An angry man jealously guarding a half pint of Early Times looked up from the chore of folding newspaper into his shoes when Spike's camera intruded. He snarled, showing Benjamin a ratty row of yellow teeth and a lanky middle finger. Five frames cranked through his camera before Spike's peripheral vision alerted him to motion in another part of the dark alcove.

He swung the camera without taking his eye from behind the viewfinder. Had he looked with a naked eye or framed the two new arrivals with a wider lens, he'd have missed the shotgun barrel lancing up through the tails of a ratty overcoat. He barely had time to react, spinning behind a rack of abused metal mailboxes as the first round boomed like a howitzer in the alcove.

Spike saw the winos scatter, some rolling on the ground, some scrambling away on all fours, and heard another big-bore shotgun begin to broadcast. *Two of the bastards with goose-guns! Jesus Christ, what did I do?*

The alcove was belching and bellowing with the echo of rapid gunfire as Spike low-crawled and scrambled for cover, ignoring the questions for the moment and desperately trying to save his life. In the glare of muzzle flash, he got a quick glimpse of the attackers. Minor league disguises for major league hitters; they were good. Hugging left and right sides of the alcove, firing in steady rhythm. Each man in a close-combat crouch, using opposite hands to expose as little as possible of their bodies to . . . what?

I'm unarmed . . . they gotta know that. Why all the fancy shit? Unless they can't help it. Unless they're pros, doing what comes naturally . . .

One of the men tossed his shotgun and whipped a nickel-plated revolver from under a leather jacket while his partner pumped final slugs into a brick wall just above Spike's head and then maneuvered to cut off the interior exit from the alcove. Spike took advantage of a slight pause in the hail of fire to sprint desperately for a short, dark corridor he knew ended at the door to a maintenance storage area. The crack of close handgun rounds chased him into the gloom and he felt the bite of debris from ricochets. As he grabbed and fumbled for the doorknob, Benjamin was oozing blood from several cuts. One at the base of his scalp gushed a curtain of red into his eyes.

When the door rattled but refused to budge, Spike realized he was trapped. He pulled a sleeve across his stinging eyes and spun to look for an escape route. The gunmen stood shoulder-to-shoulder at the corridor entrance. As he pressed his back into the unyielding door, Benjamin saw one of the men crank a speed-loader into his revolver while the other dropped to one knee and sighted down the barrel of a semiautomatic.

Ripping a Nikon from his neck, Spike heaved the camera at his assailants and then launched his body after it, hoping to bull through before they could get a steady sight-picture. He felt a round rip painfully across his back as he stretched for the deadly blossoms spearing from the muzzles.

Breath blasted from Benjamin's lungs as he belly flopped onto the concrete and curled to absorb the impact of bullets. He heard an uncoordinated volley, a muffled grunt, and then something heavy fell, crushing him into the ground. It was quiet for a moment and then two more shots echoed in the alcove. The heavy object pinning him to the pavement twitched and he realized it was a body. Spike rolled the man away and felt for a hand, hoping it held a weapon he could use to blast himself out of the ambush.

His fingers contacted hot metal and he ripped the pistol from a flaccid grip. He was on his knees and aiming into the gloom before he realized the slide was locked to the rear over an empty magazine.

"Spike! Spike? You OK in there?"

Benjamin blinked into the glare of a flashlight and lowered the empty pistol. He was shaking too badly to stand. Eddie Miller and his partner had to help him to his feet. They propped him against a wall and he heard the wail of sirens as Miller checked his injuries.

"Lucky goddamn thing I decided to tail you in here. We were just across the playground when the bastards opened up."

"How bad am I hit?"

Miller lit a smoke and poked it between Benjamin's trembling lips. Spike was cut up around the face and arms from stone shards; a .44 round had seared a bloody channel diagonally from his shoulder across his spine, but Miller could find no penetrating wounds.

"Cheap heart, buddy. And that makes you one lucky sonofabitch. These guys were loaded for serious shit."

As backup cops began to flood the area in response to Miller's radio call, Spike looked around at the bloody concrete battlefield. Miller's partner leaned on his shotgun and made a thumbs-down gesture over the gunman who had fallen on Benjamin. "This one's gone."

Miller nodded and holstered his revolver. "Get the medics for the other one. Don't move anything until the shooting team gets here."

Spike tried to stand but Miller pushed him down and patted his shoulder. "Take it easy. We got an ambulance coming for you."

"Who the fuck were these guys?"

"Beats me . . . but we'll find out pretty damn quick." He gestured at the groaning body under the muzzle of his partner's shotgun. "That one took two rounds but he's gonna be able to answer questions before long."

Two paramedics arrived with a gurney and Miller waved for them to come his way. Benjamin felt himself hoisted onto the litter and grabbed Miller's elbow, pointing at the surviving gunman being attended by two police medics.

"Listen, Eddie, this wasn't just some rip-off. These guys were good. It was . . . like fucking 'Nam, you know? They made all the right moves. If you hadn't . . ."

"Yeah, but I did. We'll talk it over after my shift. And I got a shit-pot of paperwork to do before that happens." Miller signaled to the medics and the gurney began to roll.

He was watching his friend being loaded into the ambulance, silently thanking Willy Pud for tripping his danger alarm, when the watch commander put a hand on his shoulder.

"Looks like a righteous shooting, Eddie. No problem that I can see."

Miller turned and nodded. "Listen, Lieutenant. This was a setup and these guys were designated hitters. I need to talk to the homicide guys ASAP."

"Eddie, if there's some kinda hidden agenda here, I'm gonna want to know about it."

"It'll be in my report . . . at least as much as I think anybody's gonna believe. Meanwhile, can I talk to the homicide guys?"

The St. Louis Police lieutenant had been Patrolman Miller's watch commander for the past three years. He consistently evaluated Miller as one of his top cops. If the man had a key to this thing, there was no use hiding the lock in a departmental file drawer.

"You got a week of desk duty until the shooting board meets. Far as I'm concerned, you can shuffle papers at homicide. They'll be glad to have the help."

With the exception of the long, painful .44 run across his back, Spike Benjamin felt good . . . even healthy, fresh, and vital. He commented on the wonder of that, but the attending physician at Deaconess Hospital's Emergency Room shrugged and mumbled something about an unaccustomed adrenaline jolt.

All it took to get Spike back on the road was eight stitches, several yards of gauze bandage, and some tape. After two hours at a precinct house where he dictated a detailed statement and identified his assailants from mug shots, he was free to go home. A young *Post-Dispatch* beat reporter who looked vaguely familiar intercepted him on his way to the parking lot where the police had left Spike's car.

"Hey, Mr. Benjamin . . . OK if I call you later?"

"Yeah, OK . . . you gonna do a piece on this?"

"Nah . . . just checkin' facts for the police blotter column, you know?"

Spike nodded and tried to smile. He felt slighted, as if his close brush with violent death didn't merit public attention.

"Nothing in an attempted murder, huh?"

The kid shrugged and sucked on a cigarette, looking old and frazzled far beyond his years. "Hey, it's St. Louis, right? The Projects? Business as usual . . ."

Spike slid gingerly behind the wheel of his new Pontiac, maneuvering for a comfortable driving position and wishing he'd bought a more conservative model with less engine and more leg room. He wheeled carefully out of the parking lot, into rush-hour traffic, and drove, thinking about the men who tried to kill him, asking himself questions that had no ready answers.

Andre Leon Kingston. Edwin Meshach Burton. Two bad-ass black dudes; well-known and universally feared enforcers around Pruitt-Igoe. Rap sheets stretching back out of sight. Armed robbery, assault, weapons charges, drugs, B and E . . . and what the hell did they want with me?

Steal my cameras, toss me for my wallet? OK . . . but why the goddamn artillery? They walked in with everything but a fucking air strike! Had to be a hit . . . a deliberate attempt to take me out for good. They were obviously hired by someone. But who . . . and why, why, why?

Spike was in his driveway before he finished running down the list of major stories he'd done over the past five years. There were a few possibilities he could suggest to Miller and the other cops investigating the case. The labor versus coal-mine operators thing in West Virginia, the Memphis police payola deal, the heroin pipeline on Mississippi tugboats . . . all stories involving people who played for big-time stakes.

From the stairs leading to his front door, Spike spotted a St. Louis PD black and white parked across the street. Two cops smiled and waved. He waved back and limped toward his door. It hadn't taken long for Eddie Miller to get the word out among his friends.

The red light on his telephone answering machine pulsed in the gloom. Spike bolted the door, flipped on a bank of muted lights, and cued the recorder. He noted names and numbers for a few minutes and then recognized Willy Pud's voice. As the disembodied drone from New York accelerated through the message, Spike's smile faded.

He was fairly sure by the time he played the message again that he knew who was behind the assault. He was also sure it had suddenly become more important than ever to investigate and expose Salt and Pepper. Evidence of collusion and conspiracy was building rapidly from circumstantial to concrete. Someone—for some serious reason—did not want anyone probing into the Salt and Pepper story.

Benjamin wandered into his living room, stared at the pictures of Salt and Pepper on the wall, and then began to climb the stairs toward his darkroom, mulling the situation over in his mind.

Spike Benjamin is heading an investigation into the Salt and Pepper story; the connection between Spike Benjamin and Salt and Pepper is known by only one outsider . . . former Colonel Justin Bates Halley . . . Halley is now in St. Louis . . . res ipsa fucking loquitor. Somewhere in the bushes, weeds, and smokescreens surrounding Salt and Pepper, there was a deadly, poisonous snake, coiled to strike.

He slipped the negative out of its hiding place in his darkroom procedures manual and carried it down to his desk. He flipped open his address book, then got an envelope from the desk drawer. When it was properly addressed and stamped, he carried it outside and down to the loitering police car.

"I appreciate you guys hanging around out here. Rough fucking day for me."

"Glad to do it, Mr. Benjamin. Cops like to take care of their own and we figure you qualify in that regard."

The cop riding shotgun got out of the car and smiled at Spike over the rack of emergency lights. "By the way, Eddie Miller called about ten minutes ago, Mr. Benjamin. He's gonna pick up your buddy at the airport. Said they should be here a little after nine."

"Yeah? OK, thanks. Listen, will one of you guys stick this in the mail for me?"

"Glad to . . . and we'll keep an eye on you until Eddie gets here."

Benjamin nodded and turned to head back toward his apartment. It was nice to have a couple of cops guarding the gate, but that didn't mean he could stack arms. Spike bolted the door and headed for his bedroom thinking of the general orders for sentries he'd learned so long ago at Parris Island. *Sir, my second general order is . . . to walk my post in a military manner, keeping always on the alert and observing everything that takes place within sight or hearing . . . yes, and back your bets.*

Spike reached for the phone and dialed Stanislaus Pudarski's number on West Calumet Street in Chicago. The insurance policy was in the mail and they might need someone reliable to make a claim in the near future.

"I can't fucking believe it."

"Believe it. My partner hadn't thought to bring the shotgun along, they'd have nailed him before we could do any good."

Eddie Miller steered his cream-puff Oldsmobile, a legacy of his days as a family man, onto I-70 and maneuvered into the slow traffic lane. He and Willy Pud had a lot to talk about and there were some things that needed to be said before Spike Benjamin joined the conversation.

Willy Pud stretched in the roomy front seat, glancing idly at the blinking blue ribbon of the duty runway at Lambert-St. Louis Airport and the yellow blur of halogen security lights around the McDonnell-Douglas aircraft plant.

"Well, it don't take a calculator to add it up. We're in St. Louis . . . so is J. B. Halley. Spike makes inquiries about J. B. Halley . . . a couple of knee-cappers try to take him out . . ."

"Roger that . . . and you know the rip-off story is a blind. Fucking goons like Kingston and Burton don't bother with heavy artillery for a simple shakedown. They came in under orders to blow Spike away—pure and simple."

"*Halley's* orders . . . or I'll kiss your ass."

"Another rog . . . I talked to the homicide detectives for a few minutes just before I left for the airport. They know it was a hit all the way. Car in a grocery store parking lot down the block was registered to Kingston's mother. They found beaucoup cash and two tickets to Jamaica in the trunk."

"It's Halley, goddammit! I fucking know it's him. Did you tell the detectives?"

"Yeah, I told them they ought to check on the guy. Of course, I didn't know he was here in St. Louis at the time."

"What did they have to say?"

"Well, shit, what would you expect 'em to say? I got some funny looks when they asked about motive. It's hard to get them to take it seriously, Willy. Think about it. These are city cops and they deal in relatively straightforward crime, you know? They're gonna believe some high roller from New York comes all the way to St. Louis and hires two splibs to whack out a respected journalist? And all because the guy is looking into some story about American deserters in Vietnam?"

"And nobody's even dead yet . . ." Willy Pud rubbed his eyes and leaned back in the car seat. It was becoming clear that they'd have to deal with this firefight minus reinforcements.

"There it is. They got higher priorities in homicide right now."

"So you gonna be able to check around? See if we can locate Colonel Halley?"

"No problem. I'm riding a desk in homicide for the next week. Plenty of time to check the hotels and some other sources."

"Good deal . . ."

"Probably not. You gotta figure he won't be staying in town under his own name. And Halley's got enough bucks to keep himself out of sight if that's what he wants."

"Shit!"

"Don't panic. The docs say Shack Burton is gonna be ready for questioning day after tomorrow, and the homicide guys are gonna let me spend all the time I want with him. If I can tie those two up with Halley, we can likely indict the sonofabitch."

"Well, I ain't gonna hold my breath."

"OK . . . what *are* you gonna do?"

"Look, Eddie . . . we gotta deal with the real world here. This ain't the great crusade for truth and justice anymore. There's a bastard out there ready to kill us over it. We gotta drop this Salt and Pepper thing for a while and just watch out for each other until the heat is off."

"Never thought I'd hear that."

"What the hell do *you* suggest? I ain't gonna risk gettin' my friends killed over this. It ain't worth it."

"Yeah, it is. Goddammit, it's worth it." Eddie Miller swung off the highway, jammed the Olds into Park, and turned to face Willy Pud. "What you gotta do is let me and Spike make our own decisions about whether we quit or continue the march. Fuck Halley! I'm not afraid of that sonofabitch—and I know Spike isn't either."

Eddie Miller offered Willy Pud a cigarette and punched the lighter on the dashboard. "Now, you started this shit. You want me to wheel around so you can catch a plane back to Chicago or what?"

Willy Pud's smile was radiant in the dull red glow of the lighter's coil. "Here's the plan. You stay on this Burton thing. I'll call in some heavy hitters and see if I can pin Halley down. We both watch Spike's back while he gets down to writing the story. What do you think?"

Eddie Miller popped the Olds into gear and swung back into the fast lane. "I think Chesty Puller would be right fucking proud of us."

LOS ANGELES

"Shaeffer . . ."

"Dick Simpson at the Pentagon, Sergeant Major. Welcome back to the World."

"Thanks, Dick. Glad to be back. Thailand ain't quite the R&R center it used to be."

"Yeah. We've been hearing some hair-raising stories from over that way."

Sergeant Major Shaeffer twisted to glance over his shoulder at the stacks of boxes, files, photographs, and items of evidence that filled every spare inch in the small office he kept in his San Fernando Valley home. He still had no good idea how to get it all, intact and organized enough to be useful, into Dick Simpson's hands at the DOD Office of POW and MIA Affairs.

"I'm up to my ass in alligators with the stuff I brought back, Dick. Soon as I get it organized, I thought maybe I'd just bring it all to Washington."

"That's the way to do it, Shifty. We need your eyewitness evaluations more than anything else. There's just so much bullshit floating around, you know?"

"If I didn't know before I went to Bangkok, Dick, I sure as hell know now. I got some stories that'll tie your skivvies in a knot! Twilight Zone, you know? Goddamn ghouls over there . . ."

"Yep . . . and still the same hardheaded attitude up here. We won't be held up for ransom. The Geneva Convention requires strict accounting . . . information and remains will not be used as bargaining chips . . . yakkety-yak."

"Well, we can't do anything less than keep working on it, can we? By the way, did you get anything on that ring?"

"Oh, hell, that's why I called . . . sorry to get sidetracked. I think we found your guy."

Shifty Shaeffer stiffened in his chair and groped around his cluttered desk for a pencil. "Nice work, Dick! Any chance we've got a live one?"

"Don't think so, Shifty. Nobody on the MIA list has the right initials. Of course, that doesn't necessarily disprove the story, so we traced the jeweler in New York. The ring was one of two made for a customer."

"Yeah? What else, Dick?"

"One of the rings is presumably still on the finger of the man who had them made. He's Cleveland Herbert Emory, Senior, president and CEO of Emory Technology, New York and the world."

Shaeffer whistled softly into the phone. "Jesus Christ."

"Yeah, almost. Anyway, the other ring was a gift from Emory to his son, Cleveland Herbert Emory, Junior, who was . . ."

"KIA in Vietnam."

"You got it. Records indicate he was killed on a recon mission in April of '70, just prior to the Cambodian thing. Remains consigned to his father and buried in a private family plot on Long Island."

"Goddammit! I thought we had something here. That old dude, the guy I got the ring from, he seemed . . . well, I thought surely he was telling the truth. Maybe I'm losing my touch."

"Not a chance, Shifty. Hell, everybody wants to believe there's some left alive. Nobody wants to just write it off . . . at least not any of us who fought over there. We just keep hoping . . ."

"Yeah, I guess. Thanks anyway, Dick."

"You want me to forward the ring to Cleve Emory?"

"No . . . a man shouldn't get something like this in the mail with a form letter. Listen, I'll pack up what I've got ready for you and catch a late plane tonight. Can you book me on something out of Washington to New York, say, tomorrow afternoon?"

"Can do easy."

"OK. I'll pick up the ring and deliver it to Mr. Emory personally."

"Roger, I'll call his office and get you an appointment."

NEW YORK

"He left St. Louis yesterday, sir." Eileen Winter rocked back in her chair and grinned at the angry tone in Cleve Emory's voice. She'd spoken with him enough in the past to recognize the signs. Mister I'm-On-A-Mission-From-God Halley would soon be losing a large chunk of his ass.

"Where is he, Eileen?"

"He said something about contacting some friends in the Special Operations Association, Mr. Emory. He's supposed to call me from Houston and leave a number."

"Listen, Eileen . . . you get on the goddamn phone and you *find* Mr. Halley. When you do, you tell him I want him here in New York tomorrow for a ten A.M. meeting. Understood?"

"Yessir. I'll do my best."

"You do better than that, Eileen. You find Mr. Halley and you make whatever arrangements are necessary to have him in my office at ten tomorrow morning. And you tell Mr. Halley he's to make the meeting or else—tell him I said that—and tell him it has to do with the project he's working on."

Eileen punched the line dead and stabbed her intercom button, which brought two secretaries on the run.

"Mr. Halley is somewhere in Houston and we've got to find him. Get a phone book from central files and start making calls . . . every hotel in the city. Get him on the line for me before lunch."

ST. LOUIS

"You need to get down here before they put this asshole back to sleep."

"I hate to leave Spike alone."

"Forget about it. I've got a black and white on the way to relieve you."

"OK. I'll take off as soon as they get here."

"Take off now, Willy Pud . . . security wing at Deaconess Hospital . . . and bring the blowup of Pepper with you."

Eddie Miller hung up before Willy could question the strange request. He unpinned the grainy headshot from the wall over the worktable in the living room and slipped it into a folder. From the loft area outside Spike's darkroom, he heard the muted click of computer keys.

"Miller wants me to meet him down at Deaconess. There's gonna be a squad car parked outside."

"He get anything on who hired those two bastards?"

"Standard shit. This guy Burton gave 'em a name and description. Name's phony and the description could fit a thousand or so white guys."

"But not Halley?"

"Right. They got a picture of him from the newspaper files. Not even close."

"Figures . . . the sonofabitch would cover his ass."

"Hey, you wanna know how much you're worth?"

"Can't wait to hear."

"Ten grand and two coach-class tickets to Jamaica."

"Cheap bastard. I'm gonna nail his fucking ass."

"How's the story going?"

"Hard sledding, man. It just doesn't want to come together for me without names, you know?"

"Yeah . . . gotta go."

A uniformed cop cut Willy off at the entrance to the hospital's security wing on the third floor. He phoned into the reception area and spoke to Eddie Miller before pressing the red button that unlocked the door.

Miller was talking to a couple of plainclothes cops, doing some kind of high-pressure sales job while they waited for fresh coffee to perk. He patted one of the detectives on the shoulder, winked at the other, and motioned for Willy Pud to join him on a sagging couch.

"Those guys are the detectives assigned to this case. Good men."

"They still giving you a hassle about Halley."

"Yeah. The fucking guy's got a lot of juice. Big bucks . . . big business . . . nobody wants to piss off the Pope without a damn good reason."

"Are they even gonna talk to him?"

"Can't . . . at least not directly. He's out of our jurisdiction. He was staying at the Hyatt under a different name, but he checked out yesterday."

"The day it happened."

"Yep. But you gotta figure he's got himself well covered. He hired somebody . . . who hired somebody . . . who hired somebody . . . et cetera, et cetera. Anyway, I talked 'em into making some inquiries through NYPD. That's about the best we can do right now."

Willy Pud flipped open the folder and spun it around so Miller could look at the picture of Pepper. "What about this?"

"I think our man Shack Burton knows Pepper."

"What?" Willy nearly spilled hot coffee in his lap. "How did you get to that?"

"It was something Spike said just before we loaded him into the ambulance. He said Burton and the other guy acted like soldiers in a firefight. It set me to thinking and I ran a check. Both of those assholes were with the Americal Division around Chu Lai in '68 and '69."

"Another Vietnam veteran success story . . ."

"Well, it gave me something to work with anyway. So I sat up all night with Burton and played Let's Make a Deal. Just us two vets against the world. He talks . . . I listen and maybe put some good words in for him at sentencing."

"Yeah?"

"So it's early in the morning, this asshole's rapping away about good times and dope and shit like that, and we're playin' who can tell the biggest war story, when he comes up with this tale about a black guy who frags an NCO and runs away, then gets nabbed by the gooks and nobody ever hears of him again. I put two and two together and called you."

"You think he could be talking about Pepper?"

"I think it's worth the time and effort to show him the picture."

"Can we trust this cocksucker to tell the truth?"

"I told him if he even *thinks* of lying to me, I'll sell his ass directly to this big black fag I know doin' life at Joliet."

Shack Burton was propped up in bed, lying on his side, favoring the buttock and thigh where doctors had probed for two of Eddie Miller's .38 Special rounds. Eddie and Willy Pud pulled chairs up to the bed and sat facing him.

"You bring my Kools, dude?"

Miller reached into a jacket pocket and produced the smokes. Burton eyed Willy Pud suspiciously as he fumbled with the pack and fired up a cigarette.

"Was you in the 'Nam, white boy?"

"Yeah. Marines . . . up on the Zee . . . north of you."

"Officer or EM?"

"Sergeant . . . squad leader."

"Grunt?"

"There it is."

Burton sucked on his cigarette and nodded he seemed satisfied with Willy's responses.

"Miller says you want to know about Theron Clay."

Willy opened the folder and handed Burton the photo. "I wanna know if you recognize this man."

"Don't fuck me around on this, Burton. Remember what I said."

"Relax, man. Why am I gonna lie about shit like this?" Burton stared at the photo for a long time to let Miller know he was studying hard, but he'd recognized Theron Clay at first glance. *Ain't no mistakin' that ugly motherfucker. Used to run neighborhood jobs with him over across the river. Yeah. That's mah man Mustafa . . .*

"You recognize that man?"

"Ought to . . . the motherfucker and me used to run with the Panthers over in East St. Louis. His name is Theron Clay. Used to live over on North Florissant with his momma."

Willy Pud glanced at Miller and got a nod. Eddie was buying the story. "And you knew this guy Clay in Vietnam?"

"Yeah. I was in Charlie Company and he was in Bravo, first of the Twentieth, Americal, down at Chu Lai."

"And this guy Theron Clay disappeared over there?"

"Yeah. He fragged this fuckin' cracker sergeant and then split. They was lookin' for him in Chu Lai, but Clay was hidin' out with a couple of brothers in a crib up by Tam Ky ville. They turned his ugly ass out after a while and the fuckin' VC got him. One of the brothers heard it from his woman. Straight shit."

"And nobody ever heard of him again?"

"Musta killed his dumb ass, man. The fuckin' gooks ain't gonna feed that ugly motherfucker for long. And wasn't no Thee-ron Clay climbin' off no fuckin' airplane when the POWs come home. He be six feet under some fuckin' rice paddy . . ."

Willy Pud stood and tapped the photo. "Look again. Are you sure this is a picture of the man you're talkin' about?"

"How many times I gotta say it, dude? This here is Theron Clay, homeboy from the northside. Called hisself Mustafa when he joined the Muslims."

Willy put the photo back in the folder and nodded for Miller to follow him out of Burton's room. They stopped at a phone and Willy dialed with trembling fingers.

"Spike? Yeah, listen, check the MIA list for Theron Clay . . . C-L-A-Y."

"Nope. No Clays at all."

"OK, check the KIAs."

"Here he is. Theron Clay, Missouri, KIA in July '69 . . . who the fuck is this guy?"

"Get your tape recorder, get in the car, and get down here—in a hurry."

"Why?"

"Because we just ID'ed Pepper."

NEW YORK

Cleveland Herbert Emory, Senior, took the ring reverently, compared it with the one on a finger of his right hand, and then laid it gently on the antique coffee table in his office. The yellow gold had been polished respectfully by the jeweler who made the ring so that it glowed with a rich, deep luster.

Sergeant Major Shaeffer stared at the bowed figure across from him and noted the livid flush spreading across Emory's well-barbered neck in sharp contrast with a pristine white collar. "I'm very sorry. I wish I had better news for you, Mr. Emory . . ."

The Iceman wiped a hand down over his face, leaving a sorrowful but stolid expression in its wake. "Call me Cleve, and forgive me for almost losing it there . . ."

"Please don't hold back on my account. I know how it feels, believe me."

"I expect you do, Sergeant Major. All the young boys . . . a waste . . . such an awful thing."

"Yessir, and we continue to hope that some of them are still living." He pointed at the ring and shook his head. "That's what makes a thing like this such a tragedy. We really thought maybe . . ."

"That my son might be alive?" Cleve Emory took a deep breath and then swept his arms to encompass his opulent office. "I'd give anything—all of this right now—if that could be true. But Cleve Junior is dead. I . . . I . . . saw what was left of him when they sent the remains home from Vietnam . . . there could be no mistake."

"Yessir. That's what we found out when we checked the records. Once again, I'm sorry."

"You say a man in a refugee camp gave you this ring?"

"Yessir. He had some cock-and-bull story made up about an American in one of the North Vietnamese reeducation camps. It was good enough to earn him a hundred dollars . . . and that's all he wanted. He probably found the ring somewhere in the jungle, likely close to where your son was killed. Little personal things—watches, rings, religious medals—they often get overlooked on the battlefield."

"Or taken by the enemy as souvenirs?"

"Yessir. Both sides were prone to do that kind of thing. Some part of the warrior mystique . . . like counting coup among the American Indians."

"I'm familiar with the concept, Sergeant Major. It's becoming quite common to count coup in business these days." They shared a wan smile and took advantage of the moment to sip the rich, dark coffee Cleve Emory always served important visitors.

"This man who had the ring . . . he was a North Vietnamese?"

"Yessir. People's Militia, kind of like a National Guard, or State Police Auxiliary. They're often used to provide security at these reeducation camps. He had genuine papers, which is why we tended to buy his story at first. He claimed to have personally guarded an American at this one camp . . . and the American supposedly gave him the ring and a message that he wanted out."

"My God . . ." Cleve Emory, Senior, shrugged, sipped coffee, and stared out his office window as though he was in a mood to ponder imponderables. "But if there really was an American still being held, why wouldn't the North Vietnamese release him with the other POWs, or at least bring him to the bargaining table by now?"

"Well, this is strictly speculation, Cleve. If there are one or more remaining American POWs, the communists have got to be holding on to them as part of a long-range plan. I don't know. It's one of the nagging questions that makes chasing these shadows so frustrating."

"Well, it's quite a story anyway."

"Yeah. And there's a million more just like it for sale in the refugee camps. They'll tell us anything we want to hear, swear to it . . . even provide a little evidence . . . if the price is right."

"Tell me, Sergeant Major, did this man indicate where the camp was?"

"Yessir. He was perfectly clear on that. He pointed it out on a tactical map."

"And do you believe such a camp really exists?"

"Very likely it does, Cleve. The communists have got these so-called reeducation centers all over the country. The camp's probably where he says it is, tucked up there in a corner of Vietnam between China and Laos. But there's no American in it."

"Can you be certain?"

"No, we can't be certain . . ." Shaeffer finished his coffee and then pointed at the signet ring. "But given this situation, we know our source of information is no good. That puts the odds at a thousand to one against there being any truth to it at all . . ."

"Hmmmm . . . I wonder . . ." Cleve Emory rose stiffly and began to stretch his legs, pacing like a caged cat while Shaeffer sat watching him in an uncomfortable silence. "Could you give me the location of this camp, Sergeant Major? I can have somebody with a background in the area give you a call."

"Mr. Emory, Cleve, I know what you're thinking, so let me give you a little advice. The refugees over there are running a con game and getting rich off of other people's grief. You might find some kind of cowboy commando who will charge you a lot of money and swear he'll get into that camp, but even if he does, he won't find anything. Your son is dead and buried . . . God rest his soul. You know that and there's nothing gonna change it."

Cleve Emory showed his visitor to the door and spent some time shaking hands and expressing his gratitude to Shaeffer for seeing a memento of his dead son returned to a proud father. When his office was empty again, he stormed behind his desk and mashed the intercom button.

"Get in here."

Justin Bates Halley pressed the counterweight next to the two-way mirror that allowed him to observe the meeting between Emory and Shaeffer. With a muted click, the wet bar built into the wall rotated on a spindle and he walked into Emory's office. He moved across the room and folded himself into a chair. Several tense moments passed before Emory spoke.

"Your opinion?"

"It's got to be a fabrication. You know and I know . . ."

"Bullshit, Justin. I don't know anything anymore . . . and neither do you!"

"You can't honestly believe he's still alive over there."

"What I can't believe is that some fucking gook *found* this ring in a rice paddy. This is his ring and I've got to believe it came off his finger!"

"Take it easy, Cleve. For Christ's sake, it may have come off his finger, but that doesn't mean he's alive. For God's sake, they know who you are. We'd have heard something by now. And I took extraordinary measures back then. I think it was likely taken from his finger after he was killed."

"But you don't know that, do you, Justin? You can't guarantee me this thing isn't gonna come out and destroy all of us. I want some goddamn insurance and I want it right fucking now."

"What do you suggest?"

"I suggest you stop screwing around and take care of this business . . . for good. I want this to go away or I'll hold you directly responsible. Is that clear enough for you?"

"I don't think it's productive to make threats, Cleve."

"This is not a threat, you sonofabitch. This is a promise. Either you get a handle on this thing right now or . . ."

"Wait just a goddamn minute here. You're as culpable as I am if something happens . . ."

"No, I'm not, Halley. I'm just a grieving parent who got sent a box of rocks in place of his son. I'm just a guy who got taken to the cleaners by you and the U.S. Army. There's no way anybody can prove otherwise."

"You really want to get in that kind of fight—over this thing—something that probably isn't even true?"

"I want you to take that word 'probably' and turn it into 'certainly,' that's what I want from you, Justin. You go where you have to go and you do what you have to do. Call me when it's taken care of—not before."

Shifty Shaeffer shuffled through a stack of phone messages in the elevator headed up to his hotel room. Six of the notes were from people who wanted Shaeffer to know Willy Pudarski was desperate to get hold of him. A seventh indicated Willy Pud had finally tracked him down in New York.

He loosened his tie, got a cold beer from the service bar, and picked up the phone wondering what put Willy Pud so hot on his trail. As he listened to the phone in St. Louis announce his call, Shaeffer recalled Pudarski's interest in the MIA situation. Maybe there was good news . . .

"Hello?"

"Pudarski?"

"Hey, Sarn't Major, I been chasin' you all over the country."

"Yeah . . . so I noticed. You found me in New York. What can I do for you?"

"Sarn't Major, I need a favor, something you could do for me before you leave New York."

"Fire for effect."

"I need to locate a guy, really pin him down, and then get up in his face."

"Yeah? Well, why does it sound like you want to do more than invite him to lunch?"

"Because he tried to kill one of the guys workin' with me on this project."

"What? Wait a minute! You told me you were working on something to do with MIAs."

"Sort of . . ."

"Sort of's dyin' ass, Pudarski! You want anything out of me besides a very hard time, you'd better come clean."

There was a long silence on the St. Louis end of the line. Shaeffer was able to fill, tamp, and light his old briar pipe before Willy Pud spoke again in hushed tones.

"Over in the 'Nam, Sarn't Major, you ever hear of Salt and Pepper?"

"What? That bullshit story about a white guy and a black guy fightin' with the gooks? Supposed to be deserters? Yeah, I heard it. So what?"

"So . . . it's true."

"What's true? That two Americans defected and fought with the other side? C'mon, Willy, I just spent a month hearing wild-ass tales."

"Sarn't Major, there's somethin' I never told you. When I was with Recon back in '70, I went out on an insert and I *saw* Salt and Pepper—I mean, they were literally right on top of me—they spoke to me. Spike Benjamin was along and he took pictures!"

"Jesus! Are you shittin' me?"

"Negative. The whole thing was classified to the max. We thought it was all wrapped up in a neat bundle somewhere in a Pentagon vault, see? Anyway, the war ended and nothin' was ever said about these two guys. It was eatin' on my guts, so I decided to do somethin' about it.

"I came to St. Louis lookin' for Spike because he's a reporter and he was there with me when we saw these guys. I figured to get the story out somehow . . . get it all exposed. Anyway, I didn't know Spike secretly kept one of the negs from the rolls he shot. That gave us some substance. We had faces but no names, so we got on the case of tryin' to find out who these two guys were, you know? That's when I asked you to help me get the dope on all the MIAs, remember?"

"Yeah. And you didn't find your guys in the MIA files, right?"

"Right. Nothing close . . . and it turns out all the information from the classified files—Spike's flicks, the tape they recorded with me after the patrol—all that stuff's gone! We were runnin' out of places to turn and the only other survivor of the patrol has some kind of suspicious accident. He's dead and now there's only Spike and me that actually saw Salt and Pepper. So a few days ago, a couple of jamokes try to make a hit on Spike. We add it all up and it's gotta be one guy . . . the only other guy who knows for a fact that Salt and Pepper were real. He was a colonel with MACV SOG, and he was the guy who signed for the photos and took the tape of my interview."

"And you're tellin' me this guy gives enough of a shit about somethin' like that to try and kill you two? Why?"

"I don't know why, Sarn't Major. There's somethin' more to the story than even we know, somethin' important, that's all we can figure. Anyway, if we don't find this guy—Halley is his name—somebody's gonna die."

"You're serious about this?"

"As a fuckin' heart attack, Sarn't Major."

"So where do I start lookin' for this Halley?"

"Right there in New York. He works for Emory Technology."

Shaeffer nearly bit through his pipe stem. He spent some time fussing with the briar, trying not to let his mind wander down dark trails.

"Sarn't Major? You still there?"

"Yeah, Willy Pud. I'm right here in my hotel room in New York . . . and I just got back from a meeting with the chairman of Emory Technology . . . Mr. Cleve Emory himself."

"Great! You can ask him to help you get a handle on Halley."

"Might take a few days. He was pretty shook up when I left him."

"How come?"

"Painful memories, I guess. Did you know his son was killed over in the 'Nam?"

"Yeah, I found out about it when I was in New York tryin' to find Halley. That how come you went to see him?"

"Sort of. Over in Bangkok, I ran into this former NVA who sold me a line about guarding a round-eye in a camp in North Vietnam. This creep had a gold ring and he swore the round-eye gave it to him along with a message saying he wanted out. I had the story checked. Turns out the ring once belonged to PFC Cleveland Herbert Emory, Junior, and the records indicate he was

KIA in Cambodia. Anyway, I brought the ring back and gave it to the kid's dad."

"Oh, my God."

In Spike Benjamin's apartment in St. Louis, Willy Pud looked up from the paper where he'd doodled the name just dropped by Sergeant Major Shaeffer. He sat dazed, unable to speak, and slowly underlined the first letter in each name.

"Oh, my God . . . oh, holy shit . . ."

Spike Benjamin and Eddie Miller heard the hoarse whisper and looked to see if Willy Pud was alright.

"Willy? You OK, man?" Spike Benjamin put his hand on Willy Pud's elbow. He could hear a similar expression of concern on the New York end of the line.

"Oh, Christ . . . I found him. The ring, the initials . . . were they . . . Sarn't Major? Was it a gold ring . . . with the initials carved right into the gold? Yellow gold? And the initials . . . C-H-E?"

"Yeah, that's right. What the hell's the matter with you, Pudarski?"

"Sarn't Major, do you have pictures of the ring?"

"Yeah, we took a bunch of Polaroids."

"And do you have all the information this NVA gave you concerning the guy he says gave him the ring?"

"Yeah, sure. It's all in my notes."

"Listen, Sarn't Major. We shouldn't say anything more. You need to get out of New York in a hurry. Can you get on a plane and come to St. Louis right away?"

"Well, shit, Pudarski, I got a life, you know?"

"Sarn't Major, this is one of those times."

"What times?"

"This is one of those times to be a hero. Get on a plane and come to St. Louis. Call me back with details, we'll meet you at the airport."

Shaeffer rang off to make flight reservations. Spike Benjamin took the receiver from Willy Pud's hands and hung it up. He glanced across the table and arched his eyebrows at Eddie Miller. The cop shrugged and nudged Willy Pud.

"Hey, you alright?"

Willy Pud shook his head, pinched the bridge of his nose, and took a deep breath. He started to chuckle softly.

"I found the sonofabitch . . . or Sarn't Major Shaeffer did . . . we've got Salt."

"No shit!"

"You know who he was?"

Willy Pud drew a heavy circle around the name he'd printed on the phone message pad. Benjamin and Miller leaned in his direction to read.

"Cleveland Herbert Emory, Junior?" Eddie Miller looked across the table at Spike and frowned.

"The son of the president of Emory Technology? He was in Vietnam? Cleveland Herbert Emory, Junior, was Salt?"

Willy Pud stood and leaned his knuckles on the Formica tabletop. "Wrong tense, Spike. Cleveland Herbert Emory, Junior, *is* Salt! I think the sonofabitch is still alive."

OVER THE PACIFIC

Willy Pud admired the slim figure of the Royal Thai Airlines hostess as she undulated up the aisle and out of sight at the front of the first-class passenger cabin. Sipping the icy bourbon she'd just delivered, Willy stared out the window at the blue-black void below the 727's wings, down toward the invisible black velvet of the ocean.

He was less than an hour into the journey, fourteen more to go before he arrived in Bangkok, but Willy Pud could already feel the excitement swell and throb throughout his body. He snorted into his drink, remembering the last time he'd felt so stimulated on a long flight, recalling that moment all those years ago when the Flying Tiger from Danang finally circled LAX after only sixteen hours of decompression. Some Spad jock turned commercial pilot woke the weary warriors by whistling into the PA system and announcing that the World was now visible through the windows on the left side of the aircraft.

He reached for the overhead controls, turned on the reading light, and twisted the vent to direct air gently over his face as he reclined in the seat. Breathing deeply, he smelled it all: camphor wood cook-fire smoke, frangipani blossoms, decaying foliage on a dank jungle floor, verdant monsoon scent, exhaust fumes, fermenting fish, gas bubbles generated beneath the mud, muck, and mire of centuries, sweat, shit, fear, blood, and bamboo . . . all of it. *And the Snake-Eater tasted the air on his tongue, droning single-mindedly across the Pacific, in pursuit of his prey.*

There was really nothing more to do, at least until he made contact with Ngo Xa Dinh. Sergeant Major Shaeffer's USAID friend had located the former refugee sharecropping a small piece of farmland about twenty-five miles northeast of Bangkok. He'd get final confirmation and some vital details there. Over the phone with Shaeffer in St. Louis, Bob Terranova also promised to get Willy Pud the best available maps and a quick shot across the border from northern Thailand into northern Laos. If he didn't dance on his dick somewhere along the line, if he held to the mission profile, he just might make it back inside the thirty-day deadline they'd established as a cut-off point.

If Willy Pud didn't contact them in a month, Spike and Eddie would fly to Thailand and begin a search. If he completed the mission . . . if he actually came out of the jungle with Cleveland Herbert Emory, Junior, alias Salt the penitent turncoat . . . Benjamin would muster every reporter in the English-speaking world and break the story from Bangkok.

Willy Pud hit the call button and ordered another drink from the doe-eyed flight attendant. She lavished a brilliant smile on him and brought the pencil and paper he requested along with his drink. Funny how the little perks connected with a first-class ticket made the tough business of transporting your ass over long distances in a confined vehicle so much more tolerable. Willy silently thanked Spike Benjamin for insisting on it.

"You're gonna need to hit the deck running," Benjamin explained after he made the flight reservations, "not spend the first week working off jet lag. Besides, we can deduct it from the fucking zillion dollars we're gonna make for rights to the biggest story of the decade."

Willy sipped his drink and tried to get a start on an equipment and supply list. Bob Terranova had told him to prepare one so he could get started finding the necessary items; either legally shopping for them or submitting prepaid requisitions through Bangkok's bustling black market. It was an important task, but Willy couldn't concentrate. He felt uneasy about the situation Stateside.

Sergeant Major Shaeffer was safely back in southern California with a weather-eye out for booby traps or ambushes. Miller was doing what he could to guard Spike while Benjamin ignored everything else and ripped into the story. The plan was to have the background researched and written by the time Willy Pud walked out of the bush with the final chapter. There had been no further contact with Justin Halley. Everyone involved in the Salt and Pepper mission agreed to keep it that way if possible; betting Willy Pud would come up with the trump card needed to force his hand.

They were holding low-profile and watching each other's six o'clock, but Willy was still nervous. Halley was somewhere back there . . . aware that they intended to break the Salt and Pepper story . . . and willing to kill to prevent it. What would the sonofabitch do if he thought Salt was alive . . . and they were actually going to try to bring the bastard home to justice? Whatever it was about the Salt and Pepper situation that made Halley so paranoid would come out with the rest of the story. It was probably some sort of cover-up . . . some sort of deliberate manipulation of the records to hide the facts about the traitors. But why such extreme measures?

Spike's take on the matter held that Halley's high position at Emory Technology was no coincidence. He believed the cover-up involved Emory, Senior, and the desperate measures to keep the story under wraps were examples of a tycoon turning tyrant in time of jeopardy. Benjamin believed Halley was an accomplice certainly . . . as well as Emory's henchman in quashing the revelations they stood to make. But the real criminal was Cleve Emory, Senior, because, as Spike saw it, he had the most to lose.

Sergeant Major Shaeffer found Emory's involvement implausible. "You're talking about a man's only son here," he said during one of the late-night planning sessions in St. Louis, "and traitor or not, a man's not gonna cook up some deal to make it look like his son is dead when he isn't. Nobody's that fucking cold."

"Hey, Sarn't Major . . ." Spike countered, "they call him The Iceman, you know? And what if he genuinely believed the kid *was* dead all these years. Suddenly, you show up and he gets the first clue that maybe that isn't the case. Maybe the guy in the refugee camp is telling the truth. Maybe his kid survived and now he wants out, wants to come home . . . the story's gonna fuck all over Emory's reputation and his business . . . might even put his ass in jail. Now that's some motivation for extreme measures."

Willy Pud shuddered. That kind of wild speculation didn't help his concentration. They'd just have to play the cards as they appeared on the table and try to stay out of the line of fire. Meanwhile, he had a list to make. And when that was done, he'd turn his attention to the simple business of getting into North Vietnam, locating a well-guarded compound, sneaking in and then out with a prize prisoner, and making it back to Thailand alive.

He flopped a spacious tray table across his lap and spread Shifty Shaeffer's tactical map under the light. As he had so many times in his past, he focused hard and tight, running his fingers over the colors and contours lines, absorbing terrain features, probing for a swift route in and a safe route out.

ST. LOUIS

Former Master Sergeant Freddy Carver braked at the airport toll booth and handed the bored cashier a five. She made change mechanically and punched a button, raising a gate and letting them onto the highway. It was nearly three A.M. and they made good time heading for the city.

Carver goosed the gas pedal and glanced at the morose man in the seat next to him. *Got somebody torching your ass big time, Colonel?* Freddy Carver knew it must be the case. He recognized the subtle signs of tension, and Halley's call from New York made it pretty clear he was coming to town to conduct serious business . . . no holds barred and no expense spared.

"What hotel, Colonel?"

"No hotel. Won't be in town long enough to get comfortable. Can you put me up at your place?"

"No problem, sir. I pretty well cleared the decks when you called."

"Good . . . because I'll want you to go with me when we leave."

"Thailand?"

"That's where Pudarski went. That's where we're going . . . just as soon as we clear up this other matter."

"How much money are we talking about here, Colonel?"

"It always comes down to money with you, doesn't it, Freddy?"

"Look, Colonel, I don't give a flyin' fuck about this Salt and Pepper shit." Carver decided it was time to let his old CO know just how this duffel bag was packed. "It don't surprise me that a couple of goddamn draftee pukes switched sides and fought with the gooks. Far as I'm concerned the pussies that brow-beat us outta 'Nam *ought* to know about it. I go along with you on this deal because you got big bucks and you ain't afraid to spend them. Now, I'm not gonna get involved any further unless we reach an understanding on the money."

"I don't shake down easy, Freddy."

"This ain't a shakedown, sir. I'm dog-ass tired of working and stretching a piss-ant retirement check. I go all the way with you on this deal and I don't want to have to work anymore."

"How much would that take, Freddy?"

"Well, I got to cover my ass . . . maybe move back to Germany and set up there . . . pay off all the bullshit here . . . I figure a quarter mil' does it."

Carver expected some haggling but he got none. Halley merely stared out the window and told him to drive.

"So we got a deal?"

"Certainly, Freddy. Who else could I trust in a situation like this? You get your money . . . as soon as Benjamin and Pudarski are out of the picture."

"So when do we move?"

"Soon as possible. Depends on the cop."

"He spends the night with his daughter—Tuesdays and Thursdays and most weekends when he ain't working."

"We go Thursday then, tomorrow night."

"Miller usually has a black and white patrolling the neighborhood when he's not there."

"Well, then, you need to start earning all that money, Freddy. You need to figure something out, don't you?"

"Mr. Pudarski? It's Spike Benjamin calling from St. Louis. Yessir, fine. How are you?"

Spike glanced at his watch. Just after midnight. He probably woke the old man up, but the voice on the other end sounded clear and alert.

"Sorry if I got you out of bed."

"No big deal, Spike. You heard from Wilhelm?"

"Yessir. He called from Thailand about half an hour ago. Said to say hello and give you his best. He's fine . . . drinking beer and chasing women."

"Both of us know that's a crock of shit, don't we?"

"Yessir, he's got a big job on his hands."

"I'm just worried, you know? I don't wanna think about him gettin' killed over there . . . with the war over and shit."

"Willy Pud's a capable man, sir. He wouldn't have lived to get the Medal of Honor if he wasn't."

"Yeah . . . and it's what he wants to do. Never was any stoppin' him when he got a wild hair in his ass. Maybe if he gets this one thing done, he can put it all behind him."

"Uh-huh. We've gotta look into it . . . no matter how it turns out. Even if it's a wild-goose chase, we've gotta know the answer."

"Well, you guys just be careful. Tell Wilhelm to call me from over there."

"OK, Mr. Pudarski, did you take care of the negative like I asked?"

"Yeah. Frank Hovitz has got a safety deposit box down at the bank. We put it in there."

"But you can get to it whenever you need to?"

"Yeah, Frank put me on the list."

"OK, that's great. Now, I'm gonna mail you a big package of papers. It's all our notes and the main part of the story—names, places, dates, background on the two guys involved—the whole schmear."

"I'll be interested in readin' that."

"Just make sure you put it away somewhere safe."

"You oughtta stop worryin' so much, Spike. Some sonofabitch comes after me, he's gonna have his hands full."

"Yeah, I know, Mr. Pudarski, but there's no reason for that to happen. See, you're the insurance policy. There's no way anybody's gonna suspect that you've got this material. Now, there's a letter in with the papers. It's instructions for what to do with all this stuff if anything happens to me and Willy."

"Nothin' gonna happen to either one of you yahoos. You been through too much already."

Buoyed by Stosh Pudarski's tone and reassurance, Spike Benjamin sealed the bulky prepaid envelope, printed the address neatly on the outside, and headed for the door. He was faced with another long night at the computer and the walk around the block to a mailbox would help clear his head.

About halfway there, he was nailed by the spotlight on a police patrol car. He recognized the cops and they waved back at him. Spike felt some of the tension drain as he slipped the bulky envelope into the mailbox and started for home.

Sitting beside Carver in a darkened car parked inconspicuously at the entrance to an alley, Justin Halley jumped at what sounded like gunshots. Freddy Carver looked up from his task of screwing suppressors into the specially threaded muzzles on a pair of sanitized 9mm Walther P-38s.

"Firecrackers."

"What?" Halley heard a rapid series of reports as if some gung-ho gunner were ripping away with an M-60. This was countered by louder blasts and he caught a flash of light somewhere down the block.

"Firecrackers *and* cherry bombs." Carver handed Halley a pistol, indicating it was in Condition One, cocked and locked. "I got a guy up the block who gave one of the nigger gangs a hundred dollars and a shit-load of fireworks last night."

They got out of the car and stood in the shadows while Carver checked his tools. Within a minute they heard the wail of a siren and saw flashing light disappear around the block. Carver gave the signal to move.

"Diversion's working. Them kids will keep the cops hopping for a couple of hours anyway." At the door of Spike Benjamin's apartment, Carver bent to work while Halley covered his back and kept watch for intruders. It was 0125 and they did not expect surprises, but Carver worked swiftly. It took him less than three minutes to deal with a doorknob lock and the dead-bolt mounted above it. When the door was ready to give way, he reached inside his bag and got a pair of narrow-nose bolt-cutters. With Halley pressing at his back, Carver soundlessly pushed open the door and cut the heavy chain of a safety lock.

Standing in the small foyer of Benjamin's apartment, they unlimbered the pistols and stood silently, getting their bearings. Halley thought Benjamin would be asleep at this hour and planned to jump him in bed. A series of nicotine coughs and the muted click of computer keys told him that wouldn't be necessary. He led Carver to a blind corner at the foot of the staircase. Sound indicated Benjamin was working above them on the other end of the stairs. They exchanged nods and then Carver whirled into action, mounting the steps three at a time.

"Freeze, asshole! Don't move! Stand up . . . real easy."

Spike Benjamin recoiled at the shout and the sight of a long barrel pointed at his right eyeball. Wearing a look of profound surprise, he stood up from his chair and saw a second armed intruder slowly mounting the stairs. It took him a minute to force rational thought through the shock, and then he recognized the older man.

With recognition came the realization that Colonel Justin Bates Halley would not let him live through this encounter. A cold jolt hit his spine. He tensed, waiting for the moment when Halley and his goon would be side by side at the top of the staircase.

Halley caught the angry set of Spike Benjamin's jaw and paused a step or two below the landing where Carver was locked into a tight Weaver kneeling position, staring at their victim over the Walther's oily slide. He raised his own pistol and thumbed the safety off.

"Don't do anything stupid, Benjamin. We're just going someplace to talk."

"You're the one who's being stupid, Colonel Halley. Killing me won't get you off the hook."

"Shut up and start moving." Halley gestured a path between himself and Carver, leading down the stairs toward the door. Spike played for time, looking for an opening. He kept his eyes on Halley and took a cautious step forward.

"Tell me something, Colonel. What's the big deal? Why did you cover it up? What's wrong with letting America know two—out of the million or so guys who served in Vietnam—were traitors?" Benjamin took another small step forward. He was lined up squarely between Carver and Halley who motioned again with his pistol.

"Let's go, Benjamin. None of that's any concern to you now."

"Yes it is, Colonel. And you know why the heat's on, don't you? Salt is Emory's son, right? You and Emory schemed to have him blown away after he switched sides, but the plan didn't work." Benjamin shuffled forward another step and jabbed the air with his finger. "Now *your* ass is on the line."

Just for a moment, Freddy Carver shifted his eyes, following Spike's finger to look at Halley. That's when Benjamin launched himself over the banister and took both of them out with a cross-body block. They tumbled down the short flight of carpeted stairs in a tangle of flailing arms and legs.

Spike heard the spit of two silenced shots and felt a hot spear lance into his left hip. He struggled to his feet, grabbing at the wound and limping toward the door. With the deafening roar of blood pumping past his eardrums, there was no way Spike Benjamin could hear Halley shouting for him to stop. He scrambled on, dragging his left leg until Freddy Carver fired three more rounds and blew his spinal cord apart just between the shoulder blades.

"How we gonna handle it?" Halley and Carver stood over Benjamin's corpse. The original plan called for the actual killing to occur elsewhere, outside Benjamin's apartment, somewhere near the Chain of Rocks Bridge where they planned to dump his wrapped and weighted body into the Mississippi.

Halley checked his watch and chewed on his lip. "I'll get some towels and make sure he doesn't bleed all over. We can still dump him in the drink and buy some time. Go get the computer . . ."

Carver retrieved his tool bag and remounted the stairs to wipe out Benjamin's computer files for the second time. Halley selected several thick towels from Benjamin's downstairs bathroom and returned to stare down at the corpse. The subsonic rounds were still inside the body and Benjamin had fallen on his face, so the task was primarily to keep blood seeping out the entry wounds in his back from dripping onto the floor. He placed towels strategically and went to explore the apartment.

In the living room, he froze. Halley stood, rooted before the long worktable containing the MIA files and photos, staring in shock at the enlarged picture pinned to the wall. No question, it was from the same series that Benjamin originally shot in Vietnam. *The ballsy bastard managed to hang on to one photo.* Halley unpinned it from the wall, understanding fully for the first time the sort of danger he was facing. A pro like Spike Benjamin would back himself up all the way down the line.

He hustled for the upstairs landing where Carver was just finishing with the computer. "We've got to search this place thoroughly—top to bottom. Start with the darkroom. We're looking for the negative that produced this picture."

Two hours later they were out of places to look and getting nervous about Benjamin's stiffening body.

"Damn! He's got it hidden someplace else."

"Pudarski or the cop?"

Halley pondered, weighing the odds. "Not the cop. He's only in on this thing by invitation. It's gotta be with Pudarski. That's why he went to Thailand. He's got part of the proof . . . now he wants the rest."

"You mean he really believes this fuckin' geek is still alive?" Carver looked up from the task of tying Benjamin's corpse into a rolled throw rug.

"Yes, he believes it." Halley picked up an end of the carpet roll and began backing toward the door. "And, goddammit, so do I!"

THAILAND

While they negotiated the rain-slick surface of a paddy dyke, Bob Terranova cautioned Willy Pud about offering Ngo Xa Dinh anything more than thirty or forty dollars.

"He gets fifty from you and he can buy himself another fucking rice paddy, see? He'll turn himself into a land-owning tyrant."

Willy promised to keep the cash flow to an absolute minimum. He had plenty of money for the project, from his own savings and the traveler's checks Spike Benjamin handed him before he left the States, but if Bob said to save it, then he'd haggle and scrimp as required. Over the past week, Terranova had proven to be a reliable confidant, friend, and mentor.

Combining the skills of a Wall Street deal-maker and a Mafia Don, the USAID man took Willy's equipment list and began to massage the system. While his shoppers were pumping the markets—black and otherwise—Terranova spent valuable time with Willy going over the current situation in Southeast Asia.

It was all coming together now that he was on his way to meet Dinh. Back in Bangkok, between his hotel room and a secure storage area on the commercial side of the airport, he had nearly everything required to begin the bush phase of the mission. Just as importantly, he had a healthy dose of Bob Terranova's vast feeling for the area, including the situation inside Vietnam.

"How much farther?"

"Not too far . . . anyway, you'd better get your walking muscles back in shape."

"Still no word from your buddies up north? I really need to be closer before I start humping."

"I'm waiting on a messenger. Not many phones work up that way. If a few things click, I might have you a Huey ride. That would be a touch of nostalgia, right?"

"What kind of Huey? Who's it belong to?"

"Don't ask. There's this fucking cowboy up on the border there. Vinh Sanchahorn, used to be a Pathet Lao honcho. He somehow wound up with a Huey when the Air America boys split."

"He's a pilot?"

"Not that I know of . . . just a local wheel who commandeered a helicopter . . . some kind of status symbol, I guess. Anyway, last I heard, the bird was still sitting up there on the border, ready to go."

"What good does that do?"

"Well, I also heard Vinh was trying to teach himself to fly. People say they've actually seen the fucking helicopter airborne. Maybe he's got enough stick time to get you near where you're going."

Willy Pud caught sight of a wood and thatch hut perched on an island of land in the middle of four flooded paddies. He turned to Terranova and got a nod. They were near the manor house of Mr. Dinh's green acre. "Bob, I had it in mind to arrive in one piece."

"Yeah. Look, just check in with Vinh and see if he's become some kind of air commando. If he's capable, you guys can strike a deal and he'll fly you across the border. If not, well, there's always the shoe-leather express. Either way, you need to make friends with him. He's the key to safe passage and intelligence on what's happening inside Laos."

Dinh's daughter took them around to the back of the house where her father was negotiating with another farmer over the price of a water buffalo calf. They reached a stony impasse, glaring at each other over a bamboo fence as Terranova motioned for the translator they brought from Bangkok to interrupt.

The old man was glad for something to divert him from the aggravation of business and led his visitors to a shady spot on the porch of his new house. The oldest daughter swept the kids out from underfoot and then served sweet green tea. Terranova made the introductions through his translator and told Dinh that Willy Pud was inquiring about the American who gave him the gold ring.

"Yes." Dinh nodded over his tea. "I thought perhaps there might be more questions about that one."

"Mr. Dinh, I'm willing to pay you more money for information about this man, but I want the absolute truth. You must tell me everything you know about him and the camp. Is it agreed?"

Dinh eyed the stack of colorful bills on the low table between him and his visitors. His fortunes were improving rapidly, and there was little that could hurt Di Anh from this distance. He nodded and took a deep breath.

"Ask your questions; I will answer."

Willy Pud opened a large envelope and showed Dinh the fuzzy blowup of PFC Cleveland Herbert Emory, Junior. "Please look very carefully. Remember that this photograph was taken several years ago. Is this the man who gave you the ring? Is this the man you call Di Anh?"

Dinh examined the photo closely, even walking out of the shade and looking at it in better light. The picture showed a younger, stronger man but the features and facial structure could easily belong to Di Anh. And the American he knew in Camp 413 was a wounded veteran; a battered survivor of jungle hardships.

The black plastic glasses in the photo had been replaced by Chinese wire-framed spectacles, but the eyes behind the lenses seemed the same. Dinh walked back up on his porch, handed back the photo, and picked up his teacup.

"That is Di Anh. That is the man I knew at Camp 413."

"And why is this American still a prisoner in a camp, Mr. Dinh, when all the other Americans have been returned?"

"As I told the other man who visited me, I do not know why he remains in the camps."

Willy stared into Dinh's eyes until he was sure the old man understood the subterfuge was ended. "Mr. Dinh, I know that this man fought with the Northern Army and Viet Cong. I know that he is a traitor to his country . . . to America."

Dinh glanced up from his contemplation of the tea flakes in the bottom of his cup. He tilted his head and squinted into Willy Pud's direct gaze. *A soldier,* he concluded, *a hard man who has seen the elephant and heard the owl. This one knows the basic nature of right and wrong.*

"You are correct." Dinh tapped the photograph with his index finger. "This one fought with the Liberation Front. According to the stories, there were two of them . . . one white and one black."

Willy's eyebrows arched and he nudged Bob Terranova under the table. "Do you know anything of the black American?"

"No. I know nothing of him. But this one . . ." Dinh tapped the photo again and rinsed his throat with a slug of tea. "This one is said to have been wounded in an air attack. He has a stiff leg and a withered right arm so the cadre do not make him do hard work. Even so, he complains. He wishes to be taken to Hanoi and given a parade, I suppose. He talks as though the government should reward him."

Dinh furrowed his brow and sipped again at his tea. He seemed to be wrestling with difficult concepts. Willy eyed the blank-faced translator and prodded gently.

"It does seem strange that the new government would send so . . . unusual a man to such a remote camp . . ."

Dinh's face brightened. He looked at Willy Pud and began to laugh softly. "That is exactly what Di Anh keeps saying. It is so . . . foreign, so . . . American. A man fights for a new order where all will share equally—rich and poor, farmer and factory manager. Then when his side wins, he wants to be treated *better* than everyone else. This is the kind of thing that got Comrade Di Anh sent to the camps in the first place."

Willy Pud spread the large-scale tactical map of the area on top of the photograph and pointed to the location where Shifty Shaeffer had penciled in a box containing the number 413. "And this is the location of the camp?"

Dinh studied the map, tracing terrain features and water courses. "This is Camp 413. My militia unit was responsible for security here and for patrolling the area around the camp."

"So you know the area well?"

"Yes, it is very near the village where I was born; a remote area as you can see . . . very near the borders."

"How far is the camp from the borders with China and Laos?"

Dinh didn't bother to refer to the map. He closed his eyes and seemed to be counting. "From China . . . perhaps ten kilometers . . . some thick jungle along the border area that is being cleared by engineers . . . two mountain ranges. If you must remain out of sight, I think three or four days march.

"From Laos . . . maybe eight kilometers . . . less jungle and only one mountain range . . . some swamps. An easier march but there is less cover for one who wishes to remain hidden."

Bob Terranova touched Willy's elbow. There was an expression of concern on his face.

"No sweat. He's an old soldier, Bob. He knows damn well what I'm planning to do."

Dinh's daughter brought more tea and they waited for cups to be refilled before turning their attention back to the map. Willy opened a notebook and leaned toward Dinh. The old man also leaned over the table. They sat hunched, concentrating, looking like two veteran field commanders plotting an operation.

"Now you must tell me everything you can remember about Camp 413. Schedules, layout of the buildings, cadre strength, fortifications, alarm systems, lights . . . every detail is very important."

Dinh glanced up at Willy Pud and smiled. "And I am to think like a soldier?"

Willy Pud returned the smile and clicked his pen into action.

An incessant purr from the phone by his bed dragged Willy Pud out of a sound sleep. He'd gone to bed early after a long day of final equipment preparation, planning sessions with Bob Terranova, and several hours on a remote range zeroing a variety of weapons. This would be his last night in a civilized bed and he had intended to make the most of it.

"Willy Pud? It's Eddie, man. You awake? I've got some bad news . . ."

"Yeah, go ahead. What's up?"

Willy swung his legs over the edge of the bed and let the cold jet from a nearby air-conditioner wash over his naked skin. Something about Miller's tone made him instantly alert.

"Look . . . maybe you'd better come home . . ."

"What? I'm leavin' in the morning, this morning, today. What's the problem back there?"

"It's Spike, Willy Pud. He turned up missing a couple of days ago . . . and then . . . well, yesterday the Corps of Engineers scooped up his body in one of their dredges."

"Spike is dead?" Willy felt the bottom drop out of his stomach. There was a numb buzz between his ears that had nothing to do with static on the overseas line.

"Yeah. I identified the body down at the morgue yesterday afternoon. I'm really sorry, man. I loved him and I know you did too."

Willy jammed a cigarette in his mouth, trying to control the heaving in his chest. He was in a war . . . movement to contact phase . . . no doubt about that now.

"What the hell happened, Eddie? Was it Halley?"

"Had to be, man. Had to be. Check this out. Somebody rifled his apartment; the blowup of Salt and Pepper that we had on the wall? That's gone . . . but nothing else. And his goddamn computer files were totally erased again."

"Jesus Christ . . ."

"I got an investigation started right away when I couldn't find him. We prodded NYPD about Halley but before we could get anything going, the engineers found the body. He was shot three times in the back. Nine-millimeter slugs . . . still in the body. They weighted him down and tossed him into the water out near Chain of Rocks."

"Are you gonna get the sonofabitch?"

"Halley? Yeah, we'll get him . . . one way or the other. We got a murder case opened here . . . and I'm gonna bring the FBI in on it. They're gonna want you back in the States for a deposition, man. We gotta give 'em everything we've got on this."

"Can they tie Halley into it?"

"I don't know, but we can sure as shit hand 'em a motive and get 'em to start asking serious questions. You'd better put the mission on hold and get back here."

"No."

"Willy Pud, come on, man. This is a different ball game now."

"Goddamn right it is, Eddie. I'm goin' after Salt and I'm gonna bring that sonofabitch back. We owe it to Spike."

Over Eddie Miller's protests, Willy hung up the phone and headed for the shower. Standing under the hot spray, he let his tears mix with the murky water and opened an old, stand-by communication channel.

God . . . it's Pudarski checkin' in on the net. Please take care of Spike. He was a good man, a good Marine, a guy who cared about right and wrong. Hold him in the palm of your hand, God . . . and help me with what I have to do now . . .

Freddy Carver paid the extra wad of baht required to secure the round table in the "business corner" of Lucy's Tiger's Den. Several of the old hands he'd contacted from the hotel were already bellied up to the long, battered bar but he waved them off and ordered a pair of Singha beers over ice from the waitress.

Two more candidates wandered into the smoky interior of Bangkok's most notorious emigre hangout while he savored the tangy brew and waited for Halley to arrive. Carver knew the men they were here to meet, either personally or by reputation. All were confirmed Asiatics, bush-beasts of varying skill and experience, addicted to the post-war intrigue that permeated Southeast Asia. More importantly for his present purposes, they were all out of productive work, down at the heels, hanging on to a bare-bones existence in Thailand, ravenous for two things: money and a chance to charge fading batteries. Carver and Halley were offering both in irresistible quantities.

Justin Halley entered before Carver had finished his beer. He waved and watched the colonel snake his way over to the table. Carver pointed at a chair, noting that Halley had managed to bribe the hotel tailor into a rush order for a form-fitting khaki safari suit. *Nice cover, Colonel.* Carver shoved the extra beer at Halley and smiled. *You look just like a fucking Stateside spook trying not to look like a Stateside spook.*

"You get your call through?"

"Yes."

"And?"

"And it's not a problem, Freddy. Let's talk to some of these people."

"Colonel, I ain't gonna be kept in the dark."

Halley sipped his beer and pursed his lips. "Well, the New York police have been trying to contact me. Obviously, it's about what happened in St. Louis. Mr. Emory has informed them I'm overseas on a business trip."

"How'd they get onto you?"

"Obviously, our policeman friend in St. Louis is privy to more information than we thought."

"All he's got is a theory . . . provided you've got an alibi."

"There's an itinerary and visa stamp that put me in Taipei on the date in question."

"Mr. Emory is taking good care of you, Colonel."

"We're kindred spirits, Freddy. We value loyalty."

Carver caught the inference but he was not about to turn into Halley's butt-boy on this thing. Knowledge was power and if his theory was right, he might need to influence events somewhere down the line.

"Just how does Emory figure into it?"

"That's need-to-know only, Freddy. Suffice to say he's backing our play . . . *and* paying your salary."

"You owe me the truth, Colonel."

"What was it we used to say in SOG, Freddy? I can tell you, but if I do, I'll have to kill you." Halley's stare was flat and hard. Carver decided to let it rest and wait for a more strategic moment. He was certain the wait wouldn't be long.

The first man to occupy the third chair at the table had a long scar running from somewhere under his scalp down the right side of his face to the point of his chin. He was overweight for a line trooper but his eyes were clear and his grip was firm. Halley eyed him critically while Carver made the introduction.

"Breed Toliver. White Star in Laos. Fifth Group in 'Nam. Mostly A Teams out of III Corps. Some line-jumping stuff in Cambodia for Project Delta late in the war." Carver motioned for a waitress but Toliver shook his head.

"I'm off the sauce, Freddy. Can't afford it anymore."

"That mean you're looking for work, Breed?"

"Depends. What's up?"

Halley shifted in his seat and rattled the ice in his beer glass. "I'm looking for solid men with bush experience, Toliver. One mission, mostly in Laos, probably no more than a week or two."

"Doing what?"

"Waiting for one or two men to approach the border up north. When they do, we ambush them."

"This official or unofficial?"

"Entirely a private enterprise."

"These guys you want to hit . . . gooks or what?"

"Or what, Toliver. I'm offering three thousand U.S. dollars per man. If you've got any more questions, I don't want you along."

Toliver rubbed his chin and cut a glance at Carver. No caution lights from the NCO side of the op. He shrugged and lit a smoke from the pack in front of Carver.

"I need some earnest money up front." Halley reached into an envelope to hand Toliver a stack of brightly colored baht. When he made room at the table, Carver signaled for the next candidate.

It took them the better part of three hours to put together a team of five men from the eight who showed up for an interview. Of the three who failed to pass muster, one was a jaundiced alcoholic, one was a fire-breathing speed freak, and another was overly anxious to avoid the Thai police who wanted to question him concerning a hijacked shipment of Defense Ministry small arms.

"So what's next, Colonel?"

"Standard mission prep, Freddy. You handle logistics and I'll cover intelligence."

"I figure we can be ready in four or five days. How are we gonna get a line on Pudarski?"

"Also SOP, Freddy. We're going to interrogate a gook."

Bob Terranova nodded at something the Thai charter pilot buzzed into his headset and then scrunched around to prod Willy Pud who was asleep in the jumpseat of the drafty old Beechcraft Twin Commander. When Willy struggled his way upright amid a jumble of gear, the USAID man pointed at a spare headset hanging from a hook in the ceiling of the cockpit.

"Almost there. About another ten minutes. You ready?"

"Ready. Let's do it."

There really wasn't much more to say. All the details had been hashed out prior to takeoff from Bangkok. The rudimentary airstrip somewhere ahead of the whirling props was the closest available thing to the Laotian border. It was usually off-limits for civilian aircraft, but Terranova's connections had gotten them clearance for the flight plan, supposedly an aerial delivery of irrigation equipment to an experimental farm in the area.

"Vinh is supposed to meet you, but don't get discouraged if he doesn't show right away. He might get hung up dodging border patrols."

Willy merely nodded. He'd planned for that possibility. If he ran into one of the elite Royal Thai Special Forces units searching for smugglers or refugees, he'd figure Vinh as a no-show and strike off on his own. The distance from the airstrip to the border was only twelve kilometers. The hard part would be finding Vinh in the seventy-five kilometers he had to navigate across Laos to reach Vietnamese soil.

And he needed to find Vinh who was, according to Bob Terranova, a man with a taste for doing business with round-eyes and a spook-sponsored affinity for clandestine ops. The rugged stretch of Laos between the Thai and Vietnamese borders was turf jealously guarded by former Pathet Lao turned opium traffickers and feudal warlords.

The Beechcraft banked into a landing pass and Willy craned out the window to look at a long ribbon of hard-packed red dirt and gravel. A ragged windsock waved in the breeze, otherwise there was no sign of life on the ground. He'd have to grab his gear and disappear in a hurry. A civilian aircraft landing here would surely draw an inquisitive patrol if one was in the area.

Bob Terranova grinned beneath his aviator shades and handed him a laminated calendar advertising a skivvy-bar called "Lips" on Patpong Street. "Be sure and watch the number of days you're inside. It's easy to lose track . . ."

Willy returned the grin and keyed his mike. "Roger, just like we planned. Give me ten days and then start making this run every other day. If you see my signal, pick us up. If not . . ."

"Yeah, yeah . . . if not, call the States and sound the alarm. I'm not worried about that shit. I'm worried about covering all the flight time on my expense reports."

"You won't have to make too many trips, Bob."

Terranova extended a ham-sized hand. "Just bring that bastard out, Willy Pud."

They lurched forward in the seat belts as the pilot threw the props into reverse and stood on his brakes. He taxied the Beech to the far end of the runway near the edge of the encroaching jungle

and stopped. Willy popped the cabin door, feeling the humid
breath of the bush on his back, and began to drag his carefully
packed equipment to the ground. Braced against the wash of
the idling props, he shouldered the heavy rucksack, picked up
a canvas equipment case, and shuffled toward the bush.

Willy Pud was just into the green gloom when he heard the
aircraft engines rev up to takeoff speed. And then he was on his
own. *Cold insert complete. Charlie Mike. Continue Mission.*

Struggling farther into the bush, he located a small clearing and
grounded his gear. From the equipment case came an accurized
Steyr AUG-77 rifle in 5.56mm with an integral 1.5 power opti-
cal sight. The sleek, space-age bullpup from Austria's vaunted
Steyr-Daimler-Puch felt solid yet jumpy in Willy's hands, with
excellent shouldering and pointing characteristics. It was a challenge to find in Bangkok, even for Terranova's veteran black
marketeers, and Willy paid steeply before they came up with
the rifle, four magazines, and five hundred rounds of hot NATO
SS109 ball ammo.

Attached to the synthetic stock material of the weapon was a
special bracket Willy designed to accept his other budget-buster:
a British Pilkington KITE 4X Individual Weapon Sight. The lightweight image-intensifier gave him daylight vision under starlight
conditions out to six hundred meters. At just over two pounds with
a couple of C cell batteries for power and mounted forward of the
weapon's balance to counter the weight of a loaded thirty-round
magazine, the sight was both a tactical and practical asset. It
was also a quantum improvement over the bulky, cranky old
"Starlight Scopes" he'd used in Vietnam, and since Willy Pud
planned to do most of his difficult work at night, it was also a
necessity.

His ruck was packed with a minimum of dehydrated rations
supplemented by riceballs wrapped in foil. There was a medical
kit built around the possibility that Salt was too ill or weak to
make the break. It contained powerful stimulants and depres-
sants, a variety of fast-acting medicines, painkillers, and spirits
of ether . . . in case Emory suddenly decided he'd rather remain
with his current hosts. Willy was fully prepared to drop all or
most of his gear and carry Salt out on his back if necessary.

On his harness were four canteens, magazine pouches, a trusty
old K-Bar he'd brought from the States, six M-33 frag grenades,
battle dressings and a first-aid pouch, signal flares and strobe
light; a utility pouch containing insect repellant, camouflage paint-
sticks, OD tape, parachute cord and matches; as well as a modified

holster and a stubby, handy, hard-hitting Colt Officer's Model
.45 ACP.

The equipment bag also yielded two Claymore mines and firing
devices, two pounds of C-4 plastic explosive, 250 feet of OD rope,
and several snap-links. He stuffed most of it in the ruck on top of
his spare ammo, ponchos, poncho liners, a pair of rubberized air
mattresses, and other life-support equipment. All up, with jungle
boots and an extra set of faded tiger-stripe fatigues like the set
he was wearing, Willy Pud's load ran just under seventy pounds,
but he'd had to plan and pack for two.

It was the prospect of carrying his own gear and most of what
Salt would need—since the American was in poor physical condition according to Dinh—that kept Willy Pud from including a
high-power, long-range radio in his equipment. He had a short-
range, lightweight Fox Mike unit pre-set on an aviation frequency
for use in contacting Terranova once he was out of the bush, but
even that was backed up by a variety of air-panels and flares.
Once he was over the line, inside Indian country, he was beyond
summoning earthly help. Given the situation and terrain, that's
simply the way it had to be. Willy Pud stared around him at the
familiar green walls of the jungle. *Saddle up,* he told himself. *For
a long-odds crapshoot like this there ain't no cheap insurance.*

He donned the gear and pack, shifting his shoulders, settling
the weight, and realizing some of the equipment was superfluous.
He'd overdone the prep on purpose. There was no telling exactly
what he might encounter on the way in or what obstacles he might
have to overcome at Camp 413. The basic plan was to go in quick,
use the element of surprise to facilitate the snatch, and run like
hell. He had no doubt he'd have to kill someone—maybe even
a lot of people—in the process, but once he had Salt in hand, he
was taking no chances on losing the sonofabitch for lack of all
the right stuff to keep them alive.

Checking his compass, Willy faced northeast and spotted a
small piece of high ground that might give him a look at the
airstrip. He'd wait there for a while and give Vinh a chance
to show.

Before he reached the top of the small hill, Willy was praying
that Vinh had managed to teach himself to fly. His back, hips,
and legs were complaining loudly about too much weight and too
little exercise. The first few days of humping would be ass-kickers
until his body settled into the old familiar patterns. He could trust
himself then; when the weight seemed to disappear, when the heat,

thirst, and pain seemed irrelevant, when he was scanning with all his senses, tuned into mission, survival . . . and nothing else.

He was three hours from insert and no closer to the Laotian border. Sitting just below the crest of a small hill, camouflaged and tucked into a stand of thick elephant-ear plants, Willy sipped water and rechecked his compass. No sign of Thai Army patrols and no sign of Vinh. Situation Normal: All Fucked Up. He got a quick bearing on the direction of the border and was about to heft his ruck when he froze in a half crouch. A chill shot up his arms and down his back.

It thrummed, warbled, and whumped, beating the heavy air over the silent jungle like a snare-drummer on a long, rhythmic roll. It was a familiar sound. Only a Huey chopped and bashed through the air like that and this one was coming from his rear, from the direction of the border, out of the sun. He shielded his eyes and scanned the horizon.

The black speck jinking over the treetops grew into recognizable form. A Huey, no markings, flat black where the aluminum skin wasn't glaring through chipped paint. Willy donned his gear and was halfway to the airstrip when he heard the first burst of fire.

Vinh—if it was Vinh at the controls of the droning Huey— was taking ground fire. Willy saw red tracers lance up out of the jungle, reaching for the helicopter, but the man at the controls flew straight through the storm of lead. Willy hitched at his rucksack and jogged toward the edge of the clearing, craning over his shoulder to watch the helicopter.

It staggered left, bucked and bobbled for a moment, the nose of the aircraft pitching up at a steep angle . . . then back down as the pilot corrected the glitch in his flight path. There was smoke coughing from the turbine exhaust and Willy was sure he was about to witness a spectacular crash as the Huey banked hard, clipping branches with its rotor blades.

More small-arms fire erupted from a patch of jungle near the airstrip just as Willy Pud reached the edge of the clearing. He crouched near the surface roots of a teak tree and watched a squad of Thai Special Forces troops on border patrol duty stand like duck hunters in a blind and aim their M-16s into the air. He was about to spin and disappear back into the jungle when a large shadow passed overhead. The Huey was making a fast, flat landing approach! If it was Vinh at the controls, he was doing a respectable imitation of a veteran Air Cav pilot on a hot Combat Assault.

The Thai troops redirected their fire as the bird pranged down onto the strip. Willy saw the skids bend and caught a glimpse of a brown face wearing teardrop shades in the cockpit. A few rounds sparked off the Huey and the pilot lightened up on the skids, driving the helicopter along the edge of the jungle like a taxi searching for a fare.

He was trying to decide what to do when a woman—a girl really, with long black hair whipping in the rotor-wash, wearing shorts and a gaudy plaid shirt—leaned out of the left cargo door and began to crank away at the offending Thai troopers with an M-79 grenade launcher. Her rapid, accurate fire drove the soldiers on the edge of the airstrip to ground, but rounds began to zing into the zone from Willy's rear as a second element of the patrol joined the hunt. He decided his ride had arrived.

Willy sprinted for the helicopter, nearly sprawling flat halfway to the gaping door as the man in the copilot's seat, wearing a kamikaze bandanna around his head, kicked open the cockpit door and cranked a full magazine of AK-47 rounds over his head. The girl showed surprising strength and courage as she leaned out to haul him over the skids and into the cargo compartment. His ass was still hanging over the edge when the pilot pulled pitch and hauled the Huey toward the sun.

His hostess blooped two more HE rounds toward the ground as Willy hauled himself the rest of the way inside the helicopter, scrunching around on his belly, watching in amazement as winking muzzle flashes faded below them. While he was still trying to get his bearings and recover from shock, the bird lurched violently and staggered, straining for lift. He braced for a crash but the woman simply grinned, shook her head, and pointed at something overhead. Her smile said this was SOP; nothing to put one's bowels in an uproar.

She handed him her M-79 and then whipped a red-checked bandanna from her neck. Using the cloth to plug a leaky line that was spitting hydraulic fluid all over them, the Lao woman who apparently served as combination door-gunner and crew chief on this bird made a critical repair and the Huey began to settle into a semblance of straight and level flight. She squatted next to him, grinning to expose a mouth full of gold, and then stuck out a tiny hand. Shake partner . . . we made it.

"Vinh?" She brought her head closer to his mouth to hear what he was shouting over the rattle and roar of the laboring engine. He pointed at the unruly mop of coal-black hair visible over the armored back of the pilot's seat. "Is that Vinh?"

The woman showed him a thumbs-up and then began to roll a cigarette. She wasn't having much luck with the loose tobacco and the gale blowing through the open doors. He shook out a Winston and offered her one. She clapped her hands like a kid on Christmas morning and expertly cupped his Zippo for a light.

Willy insisted she keep the entire pack and then carefully scooted toward the door of the staggering Huey to watch as the familiar shadow of the dragonfly flitted across the border into Laos. There were a hundred questions screaming for answers but it would have to wait until they landed . . . presuming Vinh could manage that maneuver twice in the same day.

Ngo Xa Dinh was absolutely astounded by his good fortune. Less than three months out of the Socialist Republic of Vietnam and he was well on the way to becoming a rich man. His family was shopping in Bangkok so Dinh personally poured green tea for his customers. Next to his new plastic insulated teakettle were three stacks of baht, totaling approximately three times the amount of money he had seen in his entire life.

He picked up a pencil and pondered the tactical map his visitors spread on the table. They wanted the same information as the other two customers. He'd answered all the same questions about poor Di Anh in Camp 413 and now he was asked to mark the camp's location on yet another map. Dinh could almost do it without looking—the maps were all the same—but he delayed, frowning, studying, not wanting to make it seem too easy.

The customer who spoke Vietnamese, the one with the long scar on his face, cleared his throat and asked if Dinh was having trouble.

"No." Dinh smiled and sipped at his tea. "I am just trying to be as accurate as possible."

Actually, Ngo Xa Dinh had been lost in contemplation of the wondrous system under which he now lived. The concept was amazing. Just look around where you are free to move, find something of value—it can be anything as long as someone else wants it—and then offer it for sale. You get money and a better life. You get the chance to look more and find other things people need but don't have. Then you get more money and more fine things. Sometimes, if the thing you find is information, it can be sold three or four times. Amazing!

Dinh marked the map and put down the pencil. He scanned the three hard faces across the table from him, wondering which of his customers Di Anh would choose to take him out of Vietnam.

The first customer seemed kindest. The second customer—the one with the picture—seemed most capable. These men were cold, brisk, businesslike. That was admirable on one hand. On the other hand, Dinh thought, if *he* were Di Anh, he would not choose to escape with these three men.

The man on the left, the one with the scarred face, folded the map and stuffed it in a pocket. Di Anh bowed over the table in gratitude and reached for the money. The tall grey-haired man in the center, the one who had put the money on the table during initial negotiations, clamped a cold hand over Dinh's wrist. The man on the right, the one with the cold grey eyes and the slight pink slash for a mouth, pulled a pistol from his jacket, pointed it at Ngo Xa Dinh's right eye, and fired.

Carver watched Colonel Halley stand and stuff the money in a manila envelope and then drop the package in a new alligator briefcase the hotel shoe and leather shop had made for him. The sight of Dinh's dead body—half the head missing, blood, fluid, and mangled brain tissue draining into the bamboo floor of his house—didn't seem to put him off in the slightest. He stepped carefully over the corpse and down off the porch.

A bright orange sun was dropping toward the western horizon. They would not get back to Bangkok before dark. Carver stared out over the two flooded paddies flanking Dinh's property and decided he was ass-deep in a fairly shitty operation. Even the thought of lifelong financial security was beginning to pale.

"What now, Colonel?"

"You and Toliver burn the house and the body. Then back to Bangkok."

"When do we head up-country?"

"Soon, Freddy. I've got an appointment to keep first."

Ngo Xa Dinh's funeral pyre was visible as a dull red smudge in the rearview mirror of their rented Toyota Land Cruiser as they bounced away toward Bangkok. Freddy Carver was driving, wheeling the vehicle over the treacherous backcountry roads toward civilization with the practiced skill of an old soldier. He steered and shifted mechanically, which gave him time to think.

Murky, dirty, or fucking filthy . . . shades of the same thing, but the differences are significant when you're talking clandestine operations. He'd signed onto a black op—involving wet work, no delusions about that—based on some vague story about nailing a traitor. That tended to justify a lot in Carver's military mind, but all the wrong people seemed to be dying.

• • •

Willy Pud sat on a sort of throne fashioned from artillery ammo crates in the center of Vinh Sanchahorn's empire reacquainting his mouth with the bitter taste of *Bierre LaRue* and trying to decide if the diminutive emperor of this jungle domain looked more like a scaled-down version of Pancho Villa or Ming the Merciless. He was certainly a leader with well-established priorities and that meant the business Willy had come to conduct had to wait.

After a wild, low-level roller-coaster ride over the verdant Laotian bush, Vinh hauled the Huey in a screaming protest up the side of a mountain and then dropped it like a big, flat rock through a small hole in the jungle canopy. As indicated by the splayed and battered skids on his helicopter, Vinh had yet to develop a deft landing touch. Willy wrapped his arms around a stanchion in the cargo compartment and kept his eyes closed as the Huey slammed into the ground, shuddered, wheezed, and settled.

He climbed out on shaky pins while the female crew chief easily shouldered his heavy ruck and hauled it toward a line of thatched huts. Vinh's LZ, sandbagged and well tended with a floor of metal matting, was in the center of his camp that looked a little like a forward firebase and a lot like a jungle slum. Swirling around the heavily armed, bandy-legged Lao troopers was a noisy gaggle of women, kids, pigs, and poultry.

Vinh climbed down from the cockpit, smiling and acknowledging the cheers of his minions. They all seemed quite impressed— as Willy was—to see their leader make it back from another mission. Willy shook the outstretched hand, noting with interest that Vinh's English had a slightly clipped, sort of Jamaican lilt . . . a credit, no doubt, to some Agency subcontractor with a trace of Caribbean blood diluting the ice water in his veins.

"You are Willy? And Bob sent you to see me?" The names sounded like Wee-lee and Boob. He smiled and thanked his host for the exciting ride.

"Hey, no sweat, GI . . . just like in the war. You were in the war?"

"Yeah. Marine Corps in Vietnam . . . but I spent some time in this country too . . ."

Vinh's eyes lit up. He grabbed Willy Pud's elbow and led him out from under the drooping rotor blades. "Ahhh, Marines! Tough troops . . . big bad-ass. Good show!"

A platoon of kids swept around the corner of a large thatched hut, headed for them, shouting and waving. Vinh beamed and held his arms out as if he were waiting to hug the entire group.

"Vinh, is there someplace we can talk?"

He made a motion with his hand and Willy found himself escorted to a chair on the periphery of the LZ. "We talk later . . . plenty of time." One of the older kids was sent scurrying after beer while Vinh herded the rest of them toward his helicopter. There was nothing Willy could do but sit and watch as Sky King entertained the kids of Melody Ranch with tales of aerial daring, using his hands like a fighter jock at a detailed debrief.

The female crew chief brought him another beer. Willy smiled at the dirt and grease ground into her surprisingly delicate hands. Her plaid shirt gaped slightly at the buttons where a pair of full breasts strained for release. Scrubbed and stuffed into an *ao dai* or western clothing she'd be stunning by any standard. Willy wondered where she came by her knowledge of helicopter mechanics, but her English was very poor. He managed to get a name—Sarang—but nothing more. She squatted at the arm of his chair, idly running her fingers through the hair on his arms.

Vinh stood and clapped his hands twice. The kids scattered and he walked toward Willy who stood respectfully. "Now we talk." He said something to Sarang and motioned for Willy Pud to follow him toward a rambling hooch perched on a knoll above the LZ.

"Can she bring my pack, Vinh? I have some things in there for you."

Vinh shouted over his shoulder sending Sarang off in another direction at a trot. He noticed Willy's admiring glance and chuckled.

"She is very beautiful mechanic, no?"

"Yes. Where did she learn about helicopters?"

"Funny story." Vinh did a little dance and laughed in a shrill cackle. "Very funny story. I am trying to learn flying. This is very difficult. I need school. But there is no school and no one to teach me. I pay much money to people in Vientiane for teacher. They take my money and send me Sarang." Vinh couldn't control his laughter. They were nearly at the steps of his hut before he could continue.

"Sarang is only *clean-up girl* at flying school in Vientiane. People think they cheat me, but I am winning in the end. Sarang has learned everything about Bell UH-1 helicopter while she is cleaning. She is better than books. I learn helicopter from her. All the rest is practice, practice, practice . . ."

And a god-awful amount of luck, Willy thought as he followed Vinh up the steps. "Where do you get fuel?"

"Steal it." Vinh laughed again and opened the door of his headquarters. "We raid Vietnamese engineers along the border . . . stop trucks . . . anything. Huey is good bird. Sometimes just piss in fuel tank."

Sarang arrived at the door bearing his rucksack just as they were making themselves comfortable. The term was not particularly relative inside Vinh's sprawling quarters that were festooned with Japanese-made electronic gadgets ranging from a noisy refrigerator to complex stereo components and four or five oscillating fans. No big surprise, Willy told himself. If they can steal enough fuel for a helicopter, they can probably keep one or two generators running.

"You are CIA?" Vinh fired the opening salvo on his way back to the table from fetching beers.

"No, sir. Just a man who needs your help."

"But I understand you wish to cross the border."

"Yes, I do. I want to get as close as possible without being detected, cross, pick up someone, and then get out. You could help me going in both directions."

"But this is not something your government wishes you to do?"

"It's something they don't know about yet, Vinh. I am going in to get a man—an American—and bring him back to Thailand."

Vinh pondered this while he chewed on ice from his beer glass. "I very much wish to help the American government. Changes are coming in Vientiane. I wish to benefit from those changes . . . for my people."

There was an uncomfortable silence as Willy Pud tried to read Vinh's unspoken message. "I think anyone who helps me with this mission will find America very grateful, Vinh. Bob Terranova tells me you are not a bandit. He says you are a strong leader with good ideas . . . for your people. If you help me, I will report that to everyone in America who will listen."

"And if you bring this man back, many people will listen to you?"

"I think so."

Vinh eyed him critically, then placed his beer glass carefully on the table and leaned forward on his elbows. "Good . . . we talk business."

Willy opened his pack and retrieved a leather pouch. He pulled the drawstring and laid the solid gold bar, for which he'd given a black market jeweler $3,800, on the table. It was Bob Terranova's idea. Currency didn't mean much to men like Vinh given the varied markets in which they did business. Gold, however, was still an international standard.

Hefting the ingot in his hand, Vinh reached in his pocket for a rusty can-opener and scraped enough of a gouge to reassure himself that the bar was what it appeared to be even beneath the lustrous surface.

"And for this payment . . . what must I do? Fly you into Vietnam?"

"No. That would be too dangerous. I do not wish to announce my presence until the last moment. Just get me as close to the border as you can. Then return for me when I have done the job and fly me back to where you picked me up."

"There are many dangers . . ." Vinh rocked back in his chair, chewing on the problem. Willy reached into his rucksack and upped the ante. Over the gold ingot, he draped a nomex flight suit, size 36 short, a black baseball cap with "Vinh" embroidered around the silver star of a brigadier general, and a pair of Master Aviator wings.

Vinh's stolid face became a grinning mask. His smile was so wide that the skin of his cheeks nearly closed over his eyes. Willy Pud knew he'd scored. The gifts were the result of an inspiration he got after one of Terranova's background briefings on Vinh Sanchahorn. *Napoleon had it right . . . it is by such baubles that one leads men.*

"Will you help me, Vinh?"

Vinh carefully molded the bill of his new hat and placed it reverently on his head, cocked forward over his eyes in a get-some aviation rake. He cleared the table, pocketed the gold, and grinned.

"You have maps?"

They worked for an hour, pausing only briefly for Vinh to piss and try on his new flight suit. Finally, they agreed on insert coordinates and timing. Vinh had only one final question before dinner.

"Why must you go *into* Vietnam to get the American?"

"Because that's where he is."

Vinh scrutinized the map more closely and then placed a stubby finger on a spot less than a kilometer from the border inside Laos. "He is here. We see him all the time."

"The American is in Laos?" Willy was staggered. "I was told he was here . . . at Camp 413."

"Perhaps they kick him out?" Vinh shrugged but seemed positive about his information. "I don't know. But he is an American . . . this I know. There are no blacks among my people."

Willy's knees crumpled and he sank heavily into the bamboo chair. Vinh was absorbed in experimenting with the zippers on his flight suit and didn't notice the reaction.

"There is a black man . . . living in Laos?"

"Yes, of course . . . as I said . . . at this place. He has a wife. My men say she is fat with a baby."

"Could you take me to him?"

"Of course, Willy." Vinh was pinning the pilot's wings on his hat. "We can go tomorrow if you wish."

Dinner was delicious, egg-flower soup followed by spicy chicken and rice, but Willy Pud barely tasted any of the food Sarang ladled into his bowl. He sat stunned by the sudden realization that Pepper was also alive. It had to be Theron Clay. There was virtually no other explanation. He had a chance to get them both.

Shortly after sundown he crawled onto a bamboo sleeping platform in a hut near Vinh's headquarters, tired but unable to sleep for the stimulating images that kept racketing around inside his head. He stood close to bringing *both* Salt and Pepper to justice. He stood to finally close some heavy doors and open others. Willy was lying still, listening to jungle sounds, staring out the door of the hut at an inky black sky, and hoping Spike was up there somewhere watching.

She whispered her name and bowed when she entered the hut. As Sarang slowly turned, he caught every feature and contour of her naked body in silhouette. When he lifted the nylon poncho liner, she slithered under it with the slow undulation of a snake. And then she sank her tiny, sharp teeth into his earlobe. Willy rolled over on top of her, smelling petroleum products in her hair, and telling himself it was a good omen.

A small, fastidious man with badly cut hair and tinted glasses reached inside the jacket of a cheap suit and handed a card to the headwaiter. Justin Halley watched as the man pointed in his direction and then stood to shake hands with the bureaucrat from the Embassy of the Socialist Republic of Vietnam. He pointed at a seat across the table and accepted another card, printed on one side in Vietnamese and Thai, and on the other side in English.

His phone call had elicited the services of an attaché from the Ministry of Economics and Trade. As good as any, Halley thought as he sat and waved for a waiter, they all sleep in the same bed.

Mr. Le Phuoc Trinh neatly arranged a leatherette notebook and ballpoint pen next to his plate and ordered black coffee.

"I was very happy to hear that you called, Mr. Halley. My country has suffered under the American embargo and we welcome such overtures from private industry."

"Well, you understand this meeting is just preliminary, Mr. Trinh. The feeling at Emory Technology is that we should put the war behind us—heal the wounds, so to speak—and get on with business."

"If American politicians shared that attitude, we would all be better off . . . perhaps even rich." Trinh snorted through his nose, then mopped at it with a napkin. Halley tried not to wince as he watched Trinh dig in a small can of pungent Tiger Balm salve with his little finger and then shove a glob deep into a nostril. He'd have to get down to business with this guy or risk losing his appetite.

"Mr. Trinh, my government does a number of things that are not supported—that are, in fact, opposed—by private industry. I have reason to believe something like that is happening right now, up near the northwestern border of your country."

Trinh paused with his finger halfway to the other nostril. "Are we not here to discuss business, Mr. Halley?"

"Of course we are, Mr. Trinh. And you must know that the basis for all business dealings is honesty and respect. I am merely trying to open some doors here."

Trinh took Halley's meaning, wiped the clot of salve onto his napkin, and flipped open his notebook. "I am prepared to convey any information you may have to my superiors in Hanoi."

"I have reason to believe an American—an ex-soldier who fought in the Vietnam war—will try to violate your border in the next few days, Mr. Trinh. I'm not sure what his purpose is, perhaps sabotage, but he is headed for a place called Camp 413."

Trinh ate with one hand and jotted notes with the other throughout dinner. Halley was careful to remain vague concerning the source of his information. He was more specific in letting Trinh know that careful, discreet handling of this situation would be considered a personal favor by men at the very top of Emory Technology, himself included.

Trinh was packing his nose with Tiger Balm again as the waiter wheeled a dessert tray to their table. Halley made excuses about the press of other business, paid the bill from a thick sheaf of fresh currency, and offered his hand.

"I'm not sure what my superiors will do with this information, Mr. Halley, but I will urge the utmost discretion."

Halley favored the little man with a solemn nod and a sad smile. "I'm sure you, and your government, will do the right thing, Mr. Trinh."

While her giant shoveled food toward his face with the right hand, Trinh Thi Thai picked up his left and laid it gently on her distended belly. The baby was kicking again and she wanted the father to feel it. If he understood there was new life inside her, he would realize they needed more food from the garden.

If he would only work a little harder, be more careful with the planting and weeding, they could produce more than enough fruit and vegetables. Then Thai would have some to take to the market at Yen Xa. Then they could get chickens, maybe even a pig. But the giant could be so difficult to control.

She tried denying him access to her body but he was too strong for that. When the great snake that lived between his legs was hungry she submitted or suffered the consequences. He took her anyplace, anytime; even now with her swollen belly, he simply rolled her over when the mood was on him and battered at her backside. When it was over, he was generally placid and manageable. She could get him to do things by asking.

Otherwise, she had to demonstrate what she wanted done; begin the work and talk to him until he got the idea and took over from her. It was the method she used to get their bamboo and palm-thatch house built and it was likely what needed doing if she wanted it expanded to make room for the baby.

"Feel the baby kick? It is a boy. I am sure. Your son will require more room in this house . . . and more food."

There was a brief spark in the giant's dark eyes. She had come to recognize the rare moments when her words seemed to penetrate his misshapen skull. Thai smiled at him. He chewed silently on a mouthful of squash and then moved his hand over the arc of her belly, down toward her pubic region.

Thai sighed. It was never clear if the giant understood what she said. She spoke to him constantly, using simple words as if she were talking to a child, because she had a lot to say and there was no one else to hear her words. It would be different when the baby arrived. Then they would need the ones called H'mong.

By diligently exploring, farther and farther away from the bamboo house, she discovered they were in a foreign place where the people spoke a strange, barely understandable language and called themselves H'mong. But Yen Xa, where the H'mong operated a market, was a full day's walk from their valley and they could never tell if they would be welcomed or warned away.

So Thai and her giant continued a solitary existence in the narrow green valley close to where the truck from Camp 401 had dropped them off nearly six months ago. Sometimes they saw men with guns, but they were not soldiers or militia. No one seemed to know or care that Thai and her giant barely survived by cultivating wild vegetables, by gathering fruit, by trapping monkeys and jungle lizards for meat.

Certainly no one—perhaps not even the giant whose seed was sprouting inside her—knew how fearful she was for the baby. When the baby kicked, keeping her awake at night, she prayed for Grandmother Ba; for anyone who could help her with the difficult task that lay ahead after the child decided to come into the world.

She moved his hand to another spot on her abdomen and asked if he felt the baby kicking. He barely acknowledged her words but did not withdraw his hand. If only he would speak more, Thai thought. He says a few words when he wants something; otherwise, he grunts or says nothing at all.

And lately he cries, she wondered. During the night when the giant's head rests on her milk-swollen breast, he cries. His pain must run very deep; down where I can never share it or ease it. And so we are alike . . . and so we must shield our baby from such pain.

As he had so many years ago, from a patch of jungle south of this one, Willy Pud lay prone, quietly observing Pepper through binoculars. If such a thing were possible, given the vivid, nightmare quality of Pudarski's recollections, Pepper looked even uglier and more dangerous.

His ebony skin was welted and latticed with the weals of old scar tissue. Pepper had seen some hard times since the day Willy encountered him on the operating end of a Tokarev pistol. His skull, perched above massive shoulders like a pumpkin caught in thick vines of neck muscle, was oddly distorted.

As Pepper moved around his bamboo hooch, Willy gained perspective, realizing Pepper's head was caved in on one side . . . like an underinflated football holding the shape of a kicker's toe. Still, there was no mistaking the hard face on the front of that damaged skull. That man, milling around outside a primitive thatched hut in the remote badlands of northeastern Laos, was Theron "Mustafa" Clay.

The question that bugged Willy Pud—the puzzle that kept him from waltzing out of the bush, capturing Pepper, and stuffing him into Vinh's Huey for safekeeping—was why . . . lots of whys, in fact. Why no guards? Why was he in Laos instead of Vietnam? Why does he just squat and stare like that? If he's a free man, why is he here in such primitive circumstances? Why no weapons in evidence? Why is he living like such a dog-ass peasant? Why is he moving around down there like a goddamn zombie? Why is he alone? Where is the woman Vinh mentioned?

There. Willy Pud adjusted the binoculars as his peripheral vision picked up movement from the rear of the hooch. The woman in question . . . very pregnant and very . . . what? Different somehow. As she moved to take Pepper's thick wrist in her tiny hand, leading him toward the hooch, Willy made the connection. The woman was black . . . half-black anyway . . . so, maybe it had nothing to do with politics. Maybe Theron Clay was tied to the land and the people in the most primitive fashion of all.

Vinh bumped his elbow. "You see? The woman is very near to having a baby. Maybe not so smart we take her for a ride in the helicopter." He was pushing for a decision. Shit or get off the pot. They were only able to bring five men and weapons on the long flight from Vinh's CP to this spot near the SRV border. The Huey, with just about enough fuel to make it back, was parked in a clearing about a kilometer to their rear. His sentries were agile and hostile, but Vinh was worried over being outnumbered and overrun by rivals in the area. He thrived in the guerrilla vagabond business primarily because his was the only team that could field an air force.

"How far are we from the border?" Willy replaced his field glasses and broke out a map.

Vinh didn't bother to consult it. "About a kilometer . . . maybe two but no more."

"Vinh, I did not expect to find this man. The one I came to find is a white man and I believe he is across the border inside Vietnam."

The guerrilla leader shrugged and checked his Seiko. "We must go soon." He pointed at the bamboo hut. "Do you want this one . . . or should we leave him?"

"I *want* this one, but you'll have to keep him for me at your camp until I return with the other one. Will you do that?"

"And the woman?"

"She stays or . . . it's up to you."

Vinh sent a runner back to his security detail saying they'd be returning in two hours and then followed Willy Pud on a circuitous route to flank the little hut. Crouched behind a pulpy banana tree just fifteen meters from the entry to Pepper's hooch, Willy handed Vinh a pair of police handcuffs.

"I'm gonna go in hard and pin him up against the wall. You come right after me and put these around his wrists." Vinh quietly checked the chamber of his AKM and nodded. Willy got a firm grip on the Steyr, locked his eyes on the doorway, and vaulted into action.

He heard the woman scream as his boots slammed the bamboo steps. There was a rumble and bump inside the hooch as if something heavy had been upset, and then Willy Pud was in the door with his back pressed against a wall of thatch. He kept his muzzle sweeping through the gloom as his eyes dilated to accommodate the low-light situation. Pepper was nowhere in sight but the woman was squatted in a corner with her hands wrapped tightly around her belly. Vinh ducked inside with the pistol grip of his AK in one hand and the handcuffs in the other.

"Where is he?"

Before Willy could answer, Pepper appeared, his giant form blocking the midday sun that filtered in through the back door of the hooch. He was grunting and huffing, brandishing a hard, heavy teakwood pole in his hands. Willy swung the AUG and slammed it into his shoulder. Pepper's brutal mask leapt at him through the scope sight.

"Drop it, you sonofabitch!"

"Hunh-hunh-hunh . . ." Pepper snarled, slowly shuffling forward on bare feet. At Willy's side, Vinh tried Vietnamese. It had no effect on Pepper, who arched his broad back, tensing to spring like an angry mastiff, but Thai took the opportunity to influence the action. She came out of her corner like a desperate boxer behind on points, arguing and scuffling with Pepper until she finally got his attention.

He turned dull eyes on her and made a pitiful sort of whining sound. Vinh tossed a translation out of the corner of his mouth, keeping his eyes and his muzzle steady on the giant. "She's telling him to think about the baby. She say don't fight until we see what these men want."

Vinh hung the AK around his neck and cautiously edged forward with the handcuffs extended. Pepper growled like a wounded bear, swiped Thai out of his path, and started to advance. Vinh ducked and disappeared out the back door as Willy Pud thumbed the selector and cranked a five-round burst through the roof of Pepper's hooch. The racket froze the action for a tense moment.

"Goddammit, Clay, take another step and I'll blow your ass away!" But Theron Clay continued to advance, slowly, methodically, as if the man threatening him with a loaded weapon were no more than a bothersome mud clod he intended to knock from the blade of his plow.

Thai instinctively reacted to the tension, leaping between them to block Pepper's path and Willy's line of fire. She begged and pleaded, dancing around in front of Pepper, forcing him to look at her, rubbing her belly against his crotch. Willy Pud watched in amazement as she tugged on his elbows, taking the staff from his hands and pressing him to squat passively in a corner.

She turned and began to speak when Vinh cautiously poked his head back in the door. "She say what you want here? Why you don't go away and leave them alone?"

"Tell her I'm here to take this man back to America. He is a traitor and must stand trial."

She listened to Vinh for a while and then turned an incredulous look on Willy Pud. She pointed to the giant's scars, running a hand over his distorted skull. Pepper didn't seem to mind. In fact, he appeared to have zoned out; taken himself to some place behind his eyeballs where current affairs were meaningless.

"This is a traitor? This is an American? This is nothing! He doesn't even know where he is. How can he know where he came from or what he did before?"

Vinh translated, relaxing into a slouch against the far wall now that the monster seemed sedate. "Willy," he added on his own, "I think we have big trouble with this man in the helicopter."

Willy Pud leaned his rifle against a wall, drew the .45 from its holster, and jacked a round into the chamber. He cautiously approached Pepper and knelt on one knee just out of arm's reach. He aimed the pistol between the black man's eyes and waited until they crossed, staring into the muzzle.

"Take a good look, Clay. I know who you are and you ought to know who I am. Remember a day on a trail in Laos? You were on the other end of the weapon . . . and you probably should have shot me, Clay. There's about a million guys back Stateside waitin' to hang your ass."

Willy lowered the pistol and searched Pepper's dull eyes, looking for recognition, remorse, defiance, shock . . . anything. But there was nothing in those dark orbs. Clay's stare was flat and shallow, as if the driver inside his head couldn't find the switch for the headlights. Some sort of mental glaucoma had spread from his damaged brain to fog over the eyes; to block all but the fuzziest perceptions.

The woman asked for a translation and Vinh gave her a short version. She chewed on her lip, cutting glances between Willy and Pepper. Then she put her hands together as if she were praying, bowed, and spoke in a small voice.

"I ask you to understand me. This man is not the one you call Clay. Perhaps he once was such a person, but not now. He cannot give you the revenge you seek. His only place is here, with me, with the baby in my belly."

Willy Pud waved his hand in front of Clay's dull eyes trying to elicit a blink. He got nothing and—he realized the woman was right—he never would; not from this empty shell. No one would put this hulk on trial. No one could punish this man beyond what he was suffering now. And likely no one could give him anything more—or less—than what he had here.

Willy rose, took a long last look at one half of his worst post-war nightmare, and realized that in this case, the appropriate sentence had been passed. He signaled Vinh to follow him out of the hooch. *Pepper is dead. Good riddance and God help . . . whoever this is.* The woman's voice stopped him before he was completely out the door.

"For her baby . . . she want to know what is his name . . . his real name."

Willy Pud turned to look at the woman, her young face already beginning to sag under the strain of simple survival: half-caste, outcast, orphaned spawn of American failures, foreign and domestic. A name for her baby? A name for a child whose blood will weld iron and steel from two of the world's most tenacious races?

"Tell her it's . . . Mustafa."

Outside, Willy stood smoking, looking east toward the jungle he had yet to traverse. Inside, they could hear the woman crooning softly. Vinh jerked a thumb over his shoulder. "This one stays?"

"That one stays, Vinh. He belongs here. The man I was after is dead."

"And you? Go or stay?"

"Gotta stay, Vinh. I've come too far to turn back now. I'll see you in one week . . . back at the LZ."

"Roger . . . OK . . . see you." Vinh slung his AK and began to walk back in the direction of his helicopter.

"And, Vinh, remember the deal." During negotiations and planning for the mission, the threat had been veiled for face-saving purposes, but clear enough for Vinh to feel the squeeze. If he failed to support Willy Pud as promised, Bob Terranova would burn up the back-channel wires and Vinh Sanchahorn would move immediately to the top spot on the Central Intelligence Agency's shit list.

Vinh showed Willy Pud a thumb and a smile. "No sweat, GI. Taxi be here on time."

CAMP 413

Cadre Commander Nguyen Pho Dang raised a slender finger in the air to emphasize a particularly trenchant remark about rebuilding through frugality and economy. He was gratified to see some light in the dull eyes of his audience. A sea of blank faces swiveled to look where he pointed.

Startled by the reaction to a standard gesture at the standard place in a standard speech, Comrade Dang also raised his eyes. Through a hole in the thatch, he saw a giant shadow cross the sun. The old, dry palm fronds on the roof of the classroom began to bend and flutter. Like the frightening roar of a sudden storm blowing down out of China, the sound buffeted the class and blew Dang's words away on a whipping wind.

Several of the students, particularly those whose wartime experiences made them familiar with marauding helicopters, headed for cover. Dang motioned frantically for his assistants to block the door and then dug his way through the throng. An excited militiaman met him near the mess hall, jabbering and pointing at the sky.

Dang shielded his eyes and saw the helicopter circling low, headed for a landing in the bean field at the rear of his quarters. He recognized the Army markings and the type of aircraft. It was an Mi-8, with five rotor blades, a long tail-boom, and a fat belly. Dang straightened his uniform, slowed to a dignified stride, and headed for the bean field wondering why, for the first time in the three years he had commanded Camp 413, he was being visited by a helicopter.

A hard-faced officer, bundled in combat equipment and wearing the insignia of a captain, stood outside the aircraft organizing a steady stream of heavily armed troops as they jumped to the ground. Dang walked toward him noting with some alarm that the helicopter bristled with rocket pods. His instincts and all the well-maintained weapons in evidence told him this was not an inspection junket.

The Army officer barely touched Dang's outstretched hand before he began to bark orders. While the cadre commander mumbled words of welcome, trying hard to look pleased by the unexpected visit, he heard soldiers being sent off to find the leader of the local militia while others were detailed to begin an inspection of Camp 413's security measures. Finally, the captain turned to Dang, crooking his AK in an elbow and looking his host over from head to toe. It was apparent to Dang that the man was not pleased with what he saw.

"Welcome, Comrade. I am Nguyen Pho Dang, commander of the Reeducation Cadre at Camp 413."

"You are not wearing a weapon."

"There is no need. The people we have here . . ."

"You have an office?"

"Yes."

"We will talk there."

Dang led the way across the bean field, shouting for one of his assistants to bring tea as they stepped into the hut that served as both his office and living quarters. The Army officer took a chair but kept his AK-47 across his lap. When Dang had poured the tea, his visitor lit a cigarette and blew smoke at the ceiling. The man seemed to be composing himself for a speech. Dang opened a notebook and painted an attentive expression on his face.

"I am Captain Loan . . . Fourth Special Operations Company under orders from the Minister of Defense. I have twenty men and the helicopter in which we arrived in my command. You are to provide us with food and other support as required during our stay here."

Dang took his time sipping tea and trying to hide his surprise. Army political officers who visited Camp 413 had mentioned the Special Operations units, trained by Soviet advisers and organized along the lines of KGB border guards. They were tough, resourceful, and ruthless; known to the politburo as General Giap's Avenging Angels.

"And the purpose of your visit, Comrade?"

"As of now, the security of this camp is my responsibility. In all matters relating to operations, you will consult with me."

"Captain, the role of this facility is to reeducate and reform citizens who have engaged in criminal activities, enemies of the party, or those who have been tainted by association with our enemies. For the past three years there have been no escapes, no disorders, no failures . . . and no reason for security measures beyond the militia detachment assigned to us."

Dang was about to put more of his tacit objections on the record, but Captain Loan gulped the last of his tea and moved to the map of Camp 413 pinned to a far wall.

"You have an American here."

"Yes. He defected from the Imperialist forces and fought with us during the war. An insincere convert and a weak-minded man as I have regularly pointed out in my reports to Hanoi. Under orders from the Regional Political Officer, he is being treated as a prisoner."

Loan turned a baleful eye on Dang and lit another cigarette. "And this American has asked to be sent back to the United States?"

"He asked, Comrade . . . his request was denied. He is closely supervised and has made no attempt to escape."

"And he could not have communicated with anyone outside this camp?"

"Of course not, Comrade." Dang felt sweat dribbling down his rib cage. He suddenly remembered the missing militiaman. Dinh had been guarding Di Anh when he deserted his post. And the man was never found. Could there be some connection? He decided to leave that burden with the local militia commander. Dinh was his responsibility.

"Captain, I can be of much greater help to you if I am told the nature of your mission here."

Loan turned from the map, letting smoke dribble out his nostrils, looking at Dang through hooded eyes. "I am here because of a rumor, Comrade Cadre Commander. One of our diplomats heard a rumor and he passed it on to his superiors in Hanoi. They passed it on to the Ministry of Defense and my commanders passed it on to me."

"And this rumor concerns Camp 413?"

"The rumor is that some Americans are headed here to rescue their former countryman." Dang's mouth dropped open in shock. The reaction clearly pleased Captain Loan who flipped his cigarette out a window and headed for the door.

"This camp is now on full security alert. Issue weapons to your cadre . . . and see that they know how to use them."

Clattering rotor blades sent Willy Pud scuttling like a beetle through the silty brown water of a Black River tributary. He struggled to the base of a tall banyan tree, tucking himself into the tangled roots and feeling his boots sink into the muck. Freeze, he told himself . . . stop, stand still, think, don't panic. If he churned up much more mud and silt, if he cut through the water leaving a wake like a fucking destroyer, the aircrew would spot his ass whether they were looking for it or not.

Willy scanned the lattice of pulpy succulent vines that formed a low roof over the mangrove swamp. Through a ragged green hole he caught the flash of whirling blades and a hint of sky-blue belly paint. It was not enough to tell him type, armament, or mission, but there was no doubt in his mind that the helicopter was headed for Camp 413. A solid intersection plot at sunrise put him three klicks from his objective and the area overlay on his map showed no other active installations.

If the helicopter was headed for the Lai Chau ferry landing, the NVA's westernmost logistics point, it would have been flying in another direction; south-to-north, across the sun, or from his right to left. But this bird had come out of the morning sun, banked into a groaning turn over the swamp, and reversed direction while losing altitude, a west-to-east course that put it on line for a landing at Camp 413.

Why a helicopter? Why now? Old Dinh seemed amused when Willy asked about air assets. If the country had an Air Force, it would be news to the simple people of this remote region where things moved by foot, or by boat or by road, or not at all. Was it reconnaissance? Reinforcements? Resupply?

Willy Pud closed his eyes, trying to ignore the pinch and pull of leeches infesting the tender spots around his ankles and at the back of his knees. Two hard days of humping over jungle mountains, probing and picking his way through the thickest of it to avoid obvious patrol routes, had nearly sapped his strength. Shortly after crossing the low range of craggy fingers that jabbed into Vietnam from Laos, he was forced to admit the sturdy torso and piston legs that carried him through the war would be a while returning from civilian exile.

No sweat, he had reassured himself, as he pressed into the murky half-light of dusk and through the night on short legs proscribed by the luminous needle of his compass. Humping—

the mule-headed business of putting one foot in front of the other for interminable periods, ignoring the painful scrape of belts and straps, coping with the irritating snatch and scratch of jungle vines while being pounded into the ground by huge, unbalanced weights on your back and shoulders—was mostly a mind game. To win, you simply had to be convincing and talk yourself out of losing.

While his body worked slowly through numbness to a growing strength, Willy Pud's bush senses came back on line clearly and quickly. They allowed him to take full advantage of the dense terrain, conquer the night, and easily avoid the single People's Militia patrol he encountered during the trek. They were alert but unobtrusive; a band of country boys on a laid-back squirrel hunt who stuck mostly to main trails or large animal tracks. Smugglers filtering across the border or a Chinese recon patrol would likely be spotted, but a lone man determined to stay out of sight could do so easily enough.

Willy Pud chewed idly on a sticky ball of white rice until the drone of aircraft engines gave way to the feral, wet sucking sounds of the mangrove swamp. The helicopter was a dangerous turd in his otherwise placid punchbowl. Plans might have to change. He pushed on, shoving slowly through a raft of lime-green algae, ignoring stinging squadrons of mosquitoes that rose to defend their nest. His malaria could lick their malaria any day of the week and he was on a tight schedule.

Hauling himself onto the relatively dry surface of a matted reed bed, Willy Pud flipped open his compass and consulted the pertinent section of his laminated map. The options were fairly clear. He could continue east through the swamp until he reached the Black River and found the camp fishing holes. Then when Salt showed to check the catch, Willy could make the snatch as planned. That meant ignoring the helicopter as a fluke. Or, he could turn north, head for high ground, and eyeball the situation before he committed to action. That option sacrificed a valuable day he might need on the way out. Vinh would show but he wouldn't wait.

Fighting his impulse to forge ahead and get it over with, Willy Pud decided to go the cautious route. A balls-to-the-wall kamikaze strike might spring Salt but that was only half the mission. This was a one-shot deal—no fallback position—and to succeed, he had to get the bastard back alive.

At dusk, headed up into the tangled underbrush coating a hill about six hundred meters west of Camp 413, Willy Pud cut a trail and nearly ran into the left flank of a militia patrol. Fortunately, the troopers out bulling this particular stand of jungle were pissed off about something. As he planted himself painfully in a patch of prickly vines, he heard them grumbling. A terse command from a voice of obvious authority ended the bitching. In the gathering gloom along the trail below his perch, Willy saw a leader and his radio operator directing the patrol. They were dressed differently than the militiamen, carrying more weapons and better gear.

Strike two, he thought as the last man in the patrol disappeared around a bend in the trail. First the helicopter and now NVA regulars reinforcing the militia. Willy Pud worried the unpleasant surprises over in his mind as he snaked up the hillside and selected a night position. Either Dinh lied or things at Camp 413 had changed since he split for Thailand. He snuggled into a narrow recess beneath a rotting log and stared at the camp, backlit by the last rays of the setting sun.

He set the silent alarm on his wristwatch, deciding to sleep for three hours, before beginning a slow, careful perimeter reconnaissance around the camp. A chilly wind indicated a cloudless night. He should be able to see clearly through the night-vision scope. At his back, some fifty meters away on top of the hill, a stand of bamboo shivered in the wind. The hollow rattle was familiar, an eerie, skeletal sound that regularly spooked men on watch in the jungle. Willy Pud closed his eyes, remembering another odd thing about bamboo, and beginning to get the first faint glimmer of a plan.

The image was ghostly, devoid of dimensional detail, but Willy Pud could plainly see the helicopter, parked in the bean field behind what Dinh had told him was the cadre commander's hooch, was an Mi-8 Hip. The two troopers keeping an alert vigil around it were NVA regulars, not militia. The aircraft could carry maybe fifteen troops with the 57mm rockets in multiple launch pods bolted to the fuselage. So, he was facing that many bad-asses directing about the same number of militiamen.

He panned slowly with the night-vision scope, taking his time, searching for heavy machine-gun positions, mortars, or other support weapons. On the edge of a rice paddy, halfway through his circuit of Camp 413, some of his faith in Dinh was restored. He'd spotted no weapon heavier than an RPD machine gun and there was no wire, security lights, or other impediments beyond the flat, open terrain on three sides of the camp that gave sentries a clear view of any approach from those directions.

As Dinh had shrewdly observed, there was no practical reason for anything more. The guests in Camp 413 might slip away, but where would they go? To Laos? To China? With no food, no equipment, no weapons? They would be quickly killed or recaptured. And defend the camp? Against what? Who would be interested in attacking?

All that worked in Willy Pud's favor, but he was still one man against forty; the cat burglar trying to snatch a pearl out from under the noses of a security force. And like a smart sneak thief, he knew his best chance was in being long gone before the crime was discovered.

He killed power to the scope and carefully moved on, skirting the perimeter counterclockwise, heading for the banks of the river on the east side of the camp. Willy Pud had left his hillside hide lean and clean, girded lightly for night ops, carrying minimal weapons and equipment to reduce noise, with all exposed skin streaked against moonglow. He felt strong and steady, fully committed and capable of pulling it off once he spotted Salt.

On the banks of the Black River, south of the camp, he flattened himself into the mud and dipped a hand in the water. Current was mild but running in the wrong direction. He would have to maneuver against the flow, moving upstream to a position where he could observe the back of the isolated hooch in which Dinh said Salt was kept.

And there were bound to be sentries. Militia might consider the river an effective obstacle against assault from the rear of the camp, but the NVA would allow no such assumptions. He would run out of darkness if he maneuvered back around to the north side of the perimeter and floated downstream to do his recon. There was only one option.

Willy wrapped the Steyr and scope in a poncho and buried it under a clump of soggy leaves. He marked the spot with a recognizable branch and then silently slipped into the water, pulling himself against the current, hugging the bank, feeling for purchase on exposed roots or digging his fingers into the mud to make slow, steady progress. After twenty minutes, he reached a shallow place on the bank and cautiously poked his head over the edge.

A sentry stood smoking and staring into the water about thirty meters upstream. Looking quickly toward the camp, Willy caught the glow from a series of windows. Those would be the windows of three communal barracks buildings where prisoners were housed. Salt's hooch was located upstream another fifty meters, according to Dinh, which meant that Willy would have to pass the sentry in order to approach it.

He heard a soft belch and then caught the flare of the sentry's cigarette butt as it spun toward the river. Was he standing or walking his post? Willy ducked, hugging the bank, keeping only his eyes and nose above water. He impatiently estimated a full five minutes before he chanced another peek. The sentry was still in place but the second look told Willy the man was militia and not NVA.

Slipping silently beneath the surface, he held purchase against the current with one hand and groped along the river bottom with the other. On a second try, his fingers found a baseball-sized rock and he brought it to the surface. When the excess water had dripped off his right arm sufficiently to avoid splash, he checked the sentry again, waited until the man looked away upstream, and then heaved the rock toward one of the barracks. It landed with a satisfying thump and rattled through the thatch to plop down onto the ground.

The sentry unslung his SKS carbine and shouted what must have been challenge. When he got no response, he hefted the weapon to port arms and began to stroll toward the communal hooch. Shouting again, the sentry finally got a muffled response from someone inside. Willy let him take five more steps and then made his move.

He got more than he expected out of the distraction. The militia guard seemed edgy, quite willing to engage in a heated conversation with the disgruntled sleeper inside the communal hooch. The sound of their argument covered his passage as Willy Pud pulled himself through the water toward Salt's solitary residence.

A soft flicker of candlelight spilled through the window that stood propped open at the rear of the building. There was also a door, but it was closed. Willy noted as much detail as possible in a series of quick looks over the edge of the bank. He had to time his bobbing periscope peeks with the passage of two NVA sentries who walked in opposite directions around Salt's hooch. One pissed off militiaman patrolling everything downstream and two very alert NVA guards around this solitary structure? Willy was certain he'd found Salt but he needed to be sure.

There was no way past the sentries without killing them. Willy Pud was willing to do that, but only when it served his purpose. Right now he needed to get a look at Salt, find a way to confirm the target. These pros would not let some idle distraction pull them off their post.

He was crouched in the lee of the riverbank, wondering what might make Salt leave his hooch, when a stray sliver of moonlight flashed on something wet and gleaming: a string . . . or line stretched taut and dripping from the branches of a scraggly tree to . . . what?

Willy slowly turned to stare out over the rolling velvet surface of the river. Something floated near midstream, bobbing against the current. A float . . . fishing float? From Willy's low perspective it looked like an inverted plastic jug of some kind. He swung in the other direction, following the line back toward the bank with his eyes. Tied to the branches was a cluster of rusty tin cans.

He remembered Dinh saying Salt was employed as Camp 413's primary fisherman, saved from coolie work in the paddies and gardens by his war injuries. And then it all came together . . . Salt was running a trot-line from the back of his hooch. He was night-fishing for bottom feeders the way Willy's old man and Frank Hovitz caught mud cats when they took him fishing in the Ozarks. The float held the bait in place and the tin cans rattled when a fish hit the line.

Willy maneuvered slowly upstream, searching with his hands until he found a rotten branch that pulled silently out of the mud. It was long enough to let him jiggle the fishing line. Salt should respond like any fisherman who thinks he's got a big one on the hook and come out to check. He waited until the NVA sentries passed each other headed for the front of Salt's hooch, then snagged the line with his branch and jiggled it. When the cans rattled loudly, he gave the line another shake, then dropped the branch, let go with his anchor hand, and felt the current sweep him downstream.

Salt's back door slammed open just as Willy got a grip and poked his head above the bank. He was only twenty meters from the tree that anchored the fishing line. It was dangerously close but he needed to see some detail in the next few minutes. A tall figure stood silhouetted by the yellow light spilling out the door at his back. As he moved toward the water, both sentries appeared and Willy heard them speaking Vietnamese. He recognized the word "mam" for fish but what caught his ear was the tall man's diction. He garbled the words, speaking in disconnected spurts . . . like a man forced to think hard before uttering sentences in a language not his own.

Willy Pud ducked quickly, blinded for a moment by the beam of a flashlight. When he bobbed up again, he saw one of the sentries probing the black water with a cone of intense light. His beam steadied on the bobbing float and there was some further conversation. The tall man seemed to be arguing against an order to go back inside.

He stumbled through a comment that elicited soft chuckles from the sentries who began to help haul in on the fishing line. Willy watched carefully as the tall man ducked into the cone of light to grope for the float. He swallowed hard, blinking at the tears that threatened to blur his vision.

The man's glasses glittered in the flashlight beam. His crudely cut brown hair was streaked and sun-bleached. Even in the pale light his skin glowed with the reddish tinge of a rawboned Caucasian. And Willy Pud had stared at that face for so long—in his dreams and in his quest for this moment—that there could be no mistake. There was no question. He had found Salt.

The sentries complained about a missed delicacy or wasted time. Willy watched as Cleveland Herbert Emory, Junior, simply shrugged and smiled. *Fisherman's luck, guys.* He was rebaiting the hook with a gob of fat worms when Willy let go of the bank and felt the current sweep him downstream.

He was exhausted, soaked, and shivering two hours before dawn when he reached the sheltered nook under the fallen log and crawled inside to wrap himself tightly in his poncho liner. On the way back up the hill, he carefully cut fresh foliage and stacked it outside the entrance to his hide. Thus camouflaged, he could afford to sleep for a few hours, restoring his energy for the snatch after nightfall.

Bamboo rattled on the hilltop, reminding Willy to check his ruck for a white phosphorus grenade. His fingers touched the canister, feeling for the tapered bottom that differentiated a Willy Pete from the flat-bottomed, tin-can shape of a common smoke grenade. He had the heat. If it didn't rain, he could cook up a solid diversion.

Given the unexpected NVA, who seemed from his observations to be sharp, well-motivated troops, and the helicopter, which multiplied the hell out of their mobility, a single diversion might not be enough cover. He needed to upset the apple cart at Camp 413. He needed some King Hell sensory overload that strained their ability to react. He needed to keep the bastards bouncing around like pinballs.

Claymore ambushes, booby traps, arson, mayhem, murder . . . he needed all of that and more. And then there was the difficult proposition of knocking a helicopter out of the sky. If he hit the aircraft on the ground, the gooks would focus on the camp area and he wanted to pull them out—while he was sneaking in—to snatch Salt. He was massaging the plan in his mind, half asleep when the incoming started.

The grenade tore through the camouflage covering over his hole and caught Willy just above his right ear. He scrambled quickly out of the enclosure and rolled downslope waiting for the missile to explode. *How the hell did they spot me? And how did they get close enough to use a grenade?* His head throbbed as if he'd been bludgeoned and there was a painful knot on his skull, but there was no grenade blast.

When his breathing slowed and he could think clearly, he realized the grenade that hit him on the head must have been a dud. No detonation . . . and no small-arms fire. *What the hell?*

Willy pulled the .45 from his holster and thumbed the safety off. It was something . . . not enough if he had a squad of night fighters out there closing on his position. Slowly he began to crawl upslope, hoping to retrieve his rifle and ruck before shifting harbor sites. There was furtive movement in the bush but he kept crawling, stretching to get his hands on more firepower. Two more missiles hit him in the back and legs before he managed to get back in the hole.

Slipping the Steyr AUG comfortably into his shoulder, Willy cranked power to the night-scope and swept the bush from side to side twice before he finally sighted the enemy. Rock apes! He was being pelted by monkeys throwing stones. There were four, five, six of the little bastards, heaving rocks and then scrambling for cover.

Willy Pud lowered his weapon and grinned. They'd go away in a while. He had experience with rock apes . . . one time back in the summer of '68 when his unit was dug in around a combat base at Ca Lu preparing to relieve the pressure on Khe Sanh. A gaggle of nocturnal monkeys just like these had come down out of the surrounding hills after half-empty ration cans carelessly tossed around the perimeter. A number of Marines were wounded in the god-awful firefight that started when a bunch of new guys on watch thought the rock apes were gooks in the wire pelting them with ChiCom grenades.

Willy Pud checked his watch, set the alarm, and felt in his ruck for rations. He had plenty . . . and he had an idea for another diversion.

At 2300 Willy Pud sat in the stand of bamboo above his hide sucking muggy air into laboring lungs and hoping the six hours left before dawn would stretch long enough for him to get the job done. Rube Goldberg on acid couldn't have come up with more wild-assed variables than he was facing at that moment. He stared up through the mesh of tall stalks and caught only the faintest moonglow. At least he had a dark night with scudding clouds blocking what little light shone from a quarter moon.

Touching the bamboo around him, Willy felt only cool, dry stalks. It would burn brightly and the sudden escape of heated air trapped inside the large bamboo sections would sound like a rifle platoon in the assault. He taped the white phosphorus grenade low on a thick stalk at the center of the stand and then began to check the two Claymore mines he would rig on the way back down the hill to serve as booby traps. He worked quickly, reviewing the preparations already made.

Just after full dark, Willy Pud left his hide and worked his way down the hill to the banks of the Black River where he'd entered the water on the previous night to carry out his reconnaissance. There, he'd stashed his ruck, underinflated two "rubber lady" air mattresses, and fashioned them into a raft. When this "split-kit" was hidden from casual view, he worked slowly along the camp perimeter in a clockwise direction, rigging four of his M-33 frag grenades, anchored in place with monofilament tripwires through the pins, to serve as booby traps. The traps were a bonus, which could be paid by panicky guards or the rock apes he was hoping to lure down out of the hills.

Leading from the camp perimeter and along a winding trail back up the hill, Willy Pud had scattered rations and the pulp of ripe jungle fruit. If he got lucky, if God didn't give up on a bush-beast in need, if Buddha didn't blink, the apes would be driven down off the hill by the fire and noise in the bamboo stand, pick up the food trails, follow them to Camp 413, and begin to harass the guards. If either the apes or the guards tripped his frags, so much the better. He needed mayhem over the next six—Willy checked his watch—make that five and a half hours.

Willy picked up his Claymores—one rigged for standard command detonation and the other set up with a pull-friction detonator for tripwire activation—pocketed a spool of black monofilament, and pulled the pin on the WP grenade. He was just out of the bamboo stand when he felt the hot glow of phosphorus feeding on air. Flames were already beginning to lick at the thick stand when he stopped seventy-five meters below to plant the first Claymore ambush along the trail where he'd nearly run into the militia patrol.

As he'd done so often during the war, Willy Pud felt for
the raised letters on the convex side of the Claymore, popped
the folding legs, and jammed them into the ground, twisting the
3.5-pound mine to aim it down the trail where the 700 steel
spheres embedded in C-4 explosive would cut a devastating swath
through flesh and bone. He pulled the shipping plug, screwed
in the detonator, and paid out electrical line until he reached a
position some fifty meters to the right and slightly above the
trail where he could observe the camp in the distance below
the hill. Plugging the wire into the hand-magneto firing device,
he scrunched down to wait for the first play of the game.

Flames from the roaring fire in the bamboo spread rapidly,
setting up a racket that sounded like a sporadic firefight was
under way on the hilltop. Willy smiled tightly, remembering
the spooky times in South Vietnam when the phenomenon had
scared the hell out of units advancing after a napalm strike or
while torching an enemy ville. He'd fired his share of rounds at
nothing before learning to recognize the sound for what it was.

He heard scrabbling motion in the bush nearby and automatically grabbed for the Claymore firing device. He had the safety
off before he realized it was too early for a reaction from Camp
413. Another facet of his plan was beginning to work. The tribe
of rock apes that lived on the hill were scrambling away from the
fire. *OK, you little shitbirds, go find the chow.*

Willy hit the power switch on his night-sight and scanned the
camp for reaction to his ruse. He could see more than the usual
points of light. They were awake alright, and there was a cluster of
bodies milling around near the cadre commander's hooch. *C'mon,
boys . . . check it out. Is it a fire . . . or a firefight? You gotta come
on up here and see for yourselves.*

Below Willy's perch, Captain Loan was scanning the hillside
from the back porch of the cadre commander's hut. Two men,
stumbling through the rutted bean field in the dark, arrived below
him at the same moment.

"Militia at their posts, Comrade Captain." His senior NCO was
calm as usual. "And I have twenty men ready to go at your
order."

Loan remained silent for a moment, staring at the fire on the
hill, listening to the loud noises that echoed down across the rice
paddies.

"Tell the militia commander to remain calm. The sounds are
probably just burning bamboo."

"And the helicopter, Comrade Captain?" The other voice belonged to the pilot who was clearly not anxious to do any night flying in an aircraft that was minus both night visual aids and radar.

"You may go back to sleep, Comrade . . . after you have put your crew on alert and posted them to guard the aircraft."

Loan heard the door open at his back but did not take his eyes off the flickering horizon above the camp. "A fire on the hill, Comrade, as you can plainly see."

The cadre commander stepped to his side and stared at the glow in the distance. "Will you send someone to investigate?"

"In your time here have you seen many such fires at night, Comrade?"

"No, never. There is no lightning. The jungle is empty all the way to the border. What could cause such a fire?"

Captain Loan lit a cigarette and blew smoke in the cadre commander's face. "I don't know, Comrade. And so I will send a patrol to find out."

"Is there some way I can assist you, Comrade?"

Loan noticed the cadre commander had a revolver stuck in the waistband of his trousers. "I suggest you go and check on the American, Comrade. Stay with him, hold his hand, or try to reeducate him, until my patrol returns from the hill."

Willy Pud screwed his eye into the scope and watched the patrol leave the camp perimeter, meshing into a single file as they traversed the paddy dykes, heading for the high ground. There was plenty of bamboo left to burn and the racket from exploding gas was getting louder. Given the dark and the noise, they'd be shaky as hell by the time they walked into his kill zone.

In forty-seven minutes by Willy's watch, the point-man appeared cautiously threading his way along an edge of the trail with his eyes locked on the glow ahead of him. Must be militia, Willy thought as he slipped the safety wire off the Claymore firing device. A regular would be averting his eyes, scanning the surrounding jungle, saving his night vision.

There was a timing problem and no way to determine if the patrol had shifted formation when they started up the hill. Willy wanted to blow the ambush *before* the patrol leader and his radioman walked into the zone so he wouldn't kill the prospect of a panicky call for rapid reinforcements. He counted three more men visible through his scope, then silently set aside the AUG and picked up the firing device. Ducking to avoid being flash-blinded by the detonation, Willy Pud squeezed hard on the magneto three times in rapid succession sending a jolt of electrical energy through the wire and into the Claymore.

He was already scrambling downhill with the second Claymore in his hands when the ringing in his ears from the thunderous detonation cleared. He heard screams, shouts, and wild shooting as AKs raked the bush ahead and to the flank, searching for targets; and he caught glimpses of survivors surging forward to inspect the carnage in the eerie glow from the bamboo fire.

Behind him was a familiar sight: the meat-grinder effect of a Claymore on a patrol bunched up on a trail to maintain contact on a dark night. He had some time to work while the shocked survivors of the ambush got used to the fact that half their number were now littering the area like bloody, blown-out sandbags.

Working swiftly in the dark, unconcerned with the noise he made being heard over the racket of the fire and the screams of the wounded, Willy planted the second Claymore on the opposite side of the trail pointing downslope, and rigged it with a monofilament tripwire. When the patrol leader called for reinforcements or medical assistance, as he was probably doing right now somewhere up above, the cavalry riding to his rescue was in for another fatal surprise. He pulled the safety pin on the firing device and hustled away toward the east, heading for the Black River and a rendezvous with Cleveland Herbert Emory, Junior.

Captain Loan stormed inside the cadre commander's hut and snatched the radio handset from a bewildered militiaman.

"Report quickly! Calm down and report your situation."

There was a moment of irritating static before his second-in-command came on the line. "We have been hit by some sort of mine, Comrade Captain. Most of the militiamen are dead . . . and five of our men. Many others are wounded."

"And the enemy? Did you receive small-arms fire?"

"I don't know, Comrade Captain. Everyone was firing into the jungle after the mine exploded. We need help for the wounded."

"Stay where you are . . . and stay alert. We will come for you soon." He tossed the handset back at the operator.

"Where is the militia commander?"

"He—he was with the patrol, Comrade Captain."

Loan cursed silently and fumbled with a cigarette. He'd have to trust the cadre commander to keep a lid on things in the camp while he dealt with the threat on the hill. An ambush meant someone was moving on the camp. It could be Laotian bandits looking for loot, it could be a Chinese patrol testing defenses in this sector, or it could be confirmation of the rumor that brought him to this stupid cesspool. Whatever, he'd have to take action before the threat got any closer to Camp 413.

"Find the cadre commander and tell him he is in charge of security here until I return from the ambush site. And tell him he will be held strictly accountable." Captain Loan followed the militiaman out the door and began to assemble his remaining regular troopers for a combat patrol.

Cadre Commander Nguyen Pho Dang stumbled in the dark, barking his shin painfully on a gasoline can some idiot left lying about near the generator shed. His plight drew muted laughter from the internees who were now all awake, squatting, smoking cigarettes, and chattering outside their huts. He shouted for them to extinguish the lights and return to their beds. They were slow to obey but Dang had no time for disciplinary measures.

Reports from the southeast side of the camp were confused but strident. The guards insisted they were being attacked, yet he heard no firing. One of his own cadre met him near the mess hall and led him through the dark toward a section of four sentry posts.

"The militia guards say someone is throwing grenades at them, Comrade, but there are no explosions."

"Then they are not grenades! We don't need Captain Loan to tell us that, Comrade."

At the second sentry post he visited, Dang accepted the invitation to join the nervous man on duty who clutched the cadre commander's arm painfully every time they heard rustling in the low brambles between the position and the near edge of the surrounding rice paddies.

"There, Comrade. Hear that?"

"Quiet!"

"There . . . again. Someone is crawling toward us!"

The uproar on the hill and the rapidly inflating reports of ambushes, fighting, and death to the west of the camp made all the militiamen skittish. Dang thought they were acting like frightened children. He was about to leave and issue stern orders for calm and disciplined behavior when a flurry of missiles sailed into the guardpost.

"Grenade!" The militiaman yelped and sprang from his bunker. Dang and his cadre assistant also flew out of the post and flopped in the dirt with their hands covering their heads. Still no explosions. Snapping his flashlight on, Dang cautiously aimed the beam into the small bunker and swept the dirt floor with light. Nothing but rocks.

"On your feet, Comrades. There is nothing . . ."

His words were cut off by a sharp explosion to the right of the post. "Grenade!"

There was no denying the shout. It was an explosion, very possibly a grenade, but outside the perimeter, as if it had been thrown out of rather than into the camp. The distinction was lost on the guard manning the adjacent sector and he cut loose with his SKS carbine. He fired the magazine dry and was reloading as another explosion split the dark.

By the time Dang and his assistant recovered from the shock, there was an explosion and sporadic shots fired on the north side of the camp. Dang sent his assistant on a mission to restore order and then sprinted for the radio in his hut.

Willy Pud slithered slowly up onto the bank, letting his body sink into the mud and waiting for the sentry to round the corner in his direction. He needed to work swiftly and silently but his luck was already running from good toward phenomenal.

The rock ape ruse had resulted in enough shouting and shooting to cover the noise of his movements and let him work quickly upstream against the current to a position where he could deal with the sentries around Salt's hooch. And when he peeked over the bank to get his bearings, the NVA regulars had been replaced on this critical post by a pair of militiamen who walked like robots and had their attention riveted on the activity elsewhere in camp.

Willy Pud watched the sentry swing around a corner, barely glancing at the river, and then turn his back to head in the opposite direction. He covered the distance to the man in four long strides, wrapped a forearm around his mouth, and braced to haul backward, nearly lifting the sentry off the muddy ground. Willy twisted left, snapping the man's head in that direction and exposing the neck.

Punching downward with the K-Bar, he drove the blade into flesh just behind the man's collarbone and wrenched it back and forth to sever the major arteries flowing past that point. The sentry kicked violently, twitched briefly, and then died silently. Willy lowered him to the ground and pulled back into the shadows on the far side of Salt's hooch.

The second sentry actually tripped over his partner's body and sprawled in the mud. Willy pounced on him, driving a knee into his back and blowing the wind out of his lungs before he could shout an alarm, then punched the thick, keenly honed blade into the man's neck and slashed his windpipe in two swift strokes. He was alone, less than ten feet from Salt's back door.

Captain Loan's radioman died instantly, his chest shredded by shrapnel from the second mine blast. It was unfortunate but Loan was a soldier and he understood the odds every soldier faces in combat: fifty-fifty at best, even less in an ambush or mine situation. It would be Loan lying dead on the trail if he had not been crouched behind his radioman, responding to a frantic call from Comrade Dang when the point-man hit the tripwire.

Now he was crouched in the middle of a slaughterhouse; fifteen or twenty dead, half that many wounded, survivors reluctantly probing the jungle on either side of the trail . . . and that idiot Dang still jabbering on the other end of the line. Loan turned to look toward Camp 413, being careful not to stand or silhouette himself in the light of the bamboo fire on top of the hill. Green tracers lanced from the perimeter, probing the darkness over the rice paddies.

He ignored the chatter from the radio until the ringing in his ears softened to a dry buzz. Captain Loan carefully considered what he knew and what he didn't know and concluded that he'd been outmaneuvered, outsmarted, and outsoldiered. His career was at an ignoble end if he did not make a rapid and complete recovery from this disaster.

"Captain Loan . . ." Dang's voice over the radio was pleading for attention. "Captain Loan, what is your situation?"

"Never mind that!" Loan shouted into the handset in a fit of frustration. "Find the American!"

He was standing by a window, staring at the fireworks display on the camp perimeter when Willy Pud slammed into the hooch and dropped into a kneeling position just inside the door. Balancing the back of the man's skull atop the .45's front-sight blade, Willy ordered him to turn around slowly.

The man's shoulders jumped toward his ears and he automatically raised his hands as if he'd been caught by a cop and told to surrender. Willy repeated the order, watching as the amber glow from an oil lamp slowly illuminated the face he'd come halfway around the world to see.

The man called Salt blinked myopically into the shadows where someone crouched holding him at gunpoint. He smiled weakly. The set of perfect teeth, braced, bonded, and nurtured by expensive American dentists, were yellow stumps dotted with decay. His soft features had sagged, giving him a sad clown countenance. He rubbed idly at the red lump of a goiter beneath his left ear and spoke in Vietnamese.

"English from now on, Emory." Salt's mouth dropped open and he blinked rapidly. His face distorted and he looked like he was struggling to keep himself from crying. Willy rose slowly and stepped into the light.

"I know who you are and I'm here to take you out. Let's get moving." Willy motioned toward the back door of the hooch with the muzzle of his pistol.

"You . . . you're an American?" Salt lowered his hands but stayed rooted near the open window.

"That's right, Emory. I'm a guy you met a long time ago, with your buddy Clay, along a trail in Laos."

Salt took a short step forward, his grin widening, craning his neck toward Willy Pud and blinking rapidly behind his lenses. "Oh, my God . . . shit . . . you . . . are you . . ."

Willy heard the gunfire along the camp perimeter begin to stabilize and then taper off to a few sporadic pops. Time was getting tight. He lunged forward and grabbed Salt at the juncture of his neck and shoulder, pinching hard.

"We can do the introductions later. You wanted out of here and that's where we're goin'. You gonna come along or do we do it the hard way?"

Salt squirmed under his grip but Willy Pud squeezed harder to force a decision. Willy had him halfway to the back door when he heard shouting in Vietnamese and footsteps pounding across the compound. Someone was headed for Salt's hooch in a hurry.

"Who the hell is that?" Willy hissed in Salt's ear.

"It's the cadre commander. He's yelling for me."

Willy Pud shoved Salt toward the front door and then flattened himself out of sight against a nearby wall. "You tell him everything's OK in here . . . and don't pull any shit, Emory. I'll kill you in a fuckin' heartbeat!"

Salt opened the door a crack and shouted something in Vietnamese. Willy didn't understand the words, but the tone sounded relatively calm and reassuring. The running footsteps outside the hooch slowed and then he heard someone climbing a creaky set of bamboo stairs. Salt seemed on the edge of panic, but Willy nailed him with a threatening glance and put the barrel of the .45 against his lips.

Cadre Commander Comrade Nguyen Pho Dang stormed into the hooch behind a rusty revolver that looked too large for his hand. Willy Pud let him take two steps . . . then he grabbed a handful of coarse black hair, screwed the muzzle of the Colt into Dang's left ear, and pulled the trigger.

Dropping the headless corpse to the floor, Willy turned the pistol on Salt. "Your call, Emory. Easy way or the hard way?"

In the dark it was difficult to find the pieces of the puzzle, but Captain Loan kept Camp 413 blacked out and refused to allow his remaining troops to scour the sector with flashlights. He felt certain that the perimeter had been penetrated by no more than five men . . . perhaps another five on the hill . . . manning the painfully effective ambush sites . . . for a total of ten . . . what?

He held the flickering oil lamp close to the bodies of the militia sentries. *Very efficient killers with the knife . . . perhaps H'mong? But why? They stole no weapons, no supplies. Nothing but the American was missing from Camp 413. So the American was the target. The rumor was correct, but certainly not as told to him. No one man, no aging American veteran could stage such an operation. He had help from some source. Chinese? What was the relationship between the Americans and the Chinese these days?*

Loan shifted the light and clinically examined the cadre commander's corpse. *The man's head exploded like an overripe melon: one round in the ear, large caliber, point-blank range. Effective . . . and perfectly safe, given the chaos on the perimeter of the camp. What was that all about?* Loan walked out of the missing American's hut and shouted for his senior NCO.

"Here, Comrade Captain." The man was crouched outside the hut, staring at the dark waters of the Black River.

"Did you finish checking the perimeter?"

"Yes, Comrade Captain. We found no enemy bodies but there were several dead rock apes near the paddies."

"Monkeys?"

"Yes, Comrade Captain. The militia guards reported incoming grenades, but it must have been the apes throwing stones. They do that frequently . . . as you know."

Loan leaned wearily against the wall of the hut feeling a debilitating mixture of shame and anger. The conflicting emotions were clouding his judgment and he fought for control. He would have to do something to rectify this situation, clean up the mess, recapture the American, kill the intruders—difficult work, but it must be done before any report of such a disaster could be made. He shivered briefly despite the muggy air wafting off the water and then forced himself into action.

"Assemble what's left of our unit and the militia."

"There are not many, Comrade Captain. Perhaps we could radio the base at Lai Chau for reinforcements . . ."

"Absolutely not! We will repair this damage by ourselves. The necessary reports will be made when we have the American and the ones who rescued him . . . not before. Do you understand?"

"Of course, Comrade Captain. They must have escaped by water. We will need the boat and flashlights."

"Get them quickly. We will search by boat until dawn and then start with the helicopter."

"Downstream? Toward the swamp?"

"Yes. They must be headed for the border."

"Laos, Comrade Captain?"

"Yes. It makes sense."

Captain Loan stomped off into the dark toward the cadre commander's hut where he could study detailed area maps. There was rugged, inhospitable terrain between Camp 413 and the Laotian border. If he failed in his mission, if the renegade American prisoner and his rescuers managed to escape, Captain Loan was determined to follow them across the border and disappear rather than return to Hanoi.

To his credit, Salt had kept his mouth shut while they clung to the makeshift rubber raft and floated silently down the dark river. There had been some initial chatter—questions, giddy reaction to the successful transmission of his rescue message, pledges of undying gratitude—but Willy Pud put an end to it quickly.

"I ain't yer goddamn pal, Emory, and if you don't keep yer mealy mouth shut, I'll rip yer fuckin' lungs out."

Salt was visibly scared, keeping a death grip on the side of the raft, as they rode low in the water, just enough air in the mattresses to keep Willy's weapons and rucksack relatively dry. They floated serenely for nearly twenty minutes before they smelled the rotting stench that marked the entrance to the mangrove swamp. It was time to turn west.

"Kick for the shore. I'm gonna try to get a line around something."

"That's the swamp over there."

"Yeah, Emory. That's where we're headed."

"Jesus, we can't . . ."

"Listen, you turncoat sonofabitch, you go where I go and you shut the fuck up!"

If Salt sulked, he did so in silence. Willy Pud had no time to investigate and see if Emory was beginning to grasp the concept involved in his rescue. He pulled a full canteen from a pouch on his hip and punched a snap-link through the cap-strap. Then he pulled the 250-foot coil of rope from his ruck and jerked a bowline into the bitter end. Attaching the heavy canteen to the rope with the snap-link, he fashioned an effective heaving line.

On the third toss toward the dark shore, the canteen snagged and held in the tangled roots of a looming banyan tree. Willy began to haul on the line until their raft bumped the riverbank just fifty meters above the entrance to the dismal mangrove swamp.

"OK, out of the water. There's socks and a pair of jungle boots in the ruck. Get 'em and put 'em on."

Salt was clumsy with the laces but Willy was glad to see he'd guessed relatively close in bringing a size 10R in used boots so Emory wouldn't be plagued by blisters. The man stood, grinning and favoring his bad leg, but he seemed stable on the Vibram soles.

"Been a long time since I've had these on my feet."

"Can you hump?"

"What? Oh, yeah . . . little slow on the game leg, but I can walk."

"Let's go." Willy pulled the Steyr from a poncho and shouldered his rucksack. "We got a lot of ground to cover."

"Listen, man, I want out as bad as you do but I don't think we ought to go into that swamp."

"Why not? That's the way I came in . . ."

"Then you know how thick it is in there. We'll get bogged down and they'll be coming with the boat."

"I didn't see any boat."

"They keep it in a kind of shed, near the hut where you found me."

"A powerboat?"

"Yeah. Some kind of Japanese outboard." Salt seemed surprised at Willy Pud's ignorance. "The militia uses it to make supply runs down the river."

"Weapons?" Willy Pud angrily deflated the air mattresses and heaved them into the swamp.

"They got machine guns mounted on each side."

"Shit!" If he'd known about a boat, he'd have taken Salt out a different route. The water he was depending on as an ally, an obstacle to speedy tracking and effective search patterns, had suddenly become a liability.

Troops in a boat could move a lot faster than they could on foot in the swamp. And a search party would figure them to head in that direction. Staying in the river was not an option. It turned southeast at the mouth of the swamp and ran straight for Hanoi.

"Get movin'. That direction." Willy prodded Salt into the gloomy interior with the muzzle of the AUG. He needed to think but he'd have to mull it over on the move. Just two hours until dawn.

Willy Pud crouched and stared up the finger of shallow water that poked into the dense interior of the mangrove swamp from the muddy main artery. The entrance to the inlet was only thirty meters wide, allowing access to shore via a narrow strip of some fifty meters of brackish backwater. A medium-sized craft turning in here would be relatively restricted, like a tank in a narrow alley.

Something even narrower would be better, but the sky was beginning to grey in the east and he didn't have time for further search. He slipped into the swamp and settled as the muddy water rose to a level just under his armpits.

"You sure about the draft?"

"About what?" Salt sat on the bank, ignoring the mosquitoes that swarmed around his head, gobbling one of Willy's sticky riceballs and swilling from a canteen.

"About how much water the boat draws . . . how deep it rides in the water. You said three feet."

"Yeah, I guess that's about right. I don't know . . ."

Willy heaved himself out of the water, slapped the riceball out of Salt's hand, and grabbed him by the jaw, squeezing until the man's lips puckered. Salt's eyes were wide, the eyeballs darting from side to side as Willy Pud leaned in to hiss at him.

"There's a whole hell of a lot you don't know, asshole. And you're gonna start gettin' smart right fuckin' now. I'm gonna stop that boat and you're gonna be the bait that lures it in here."

Willy let go of Salt's face with a painful pinch and pulled a set of handcuffs from his pocket. "When you hear the motor, you're gonna start yellin' in Vietnamese. When they turn in here, you wave and yell like you need to be rescued. Got it?"

"They might shoot me."

"They ain't gonna shoot you. If they were gonna do that, they'd have done it a long time ago."

"What are you gonna do?"

"Let me worry about that." He snapped a cuff tightly around Salt's right hand and clicked the other one around a nearby stalk of bamboo. "You just do what I say if you want to get out of here alive."

"I want out . . . you don't have to handcuff me."

"Yeah, I do, Emory." Willy checked the end of the rope anchored to a large teak tree, picked up the remaining length, and slipped into the water. "There's never no tellin' whose fuckin' side you're on, is there?"

He waded across the water to the opposite bank and climbed into the low branches of a thick banyan. When he was satisfied with his seat some twelve feet above the surface of the swamp, he examined the angle and wrapped the rope around the trunk of the tree, leaving enough slack for the wet line to rest three or four feet under water.

Emptying a canteen, Willy Pud reached into his ruck for a block of C-4 plastic explosive. He molded, prodded, and packed the doughy stuff until his plastic canteen was full of it; screwed the lid back on and then used his K-Bar to neatly slice the top off the lid giving him access to the explosive filler. He unscrewed the fuse from a grenade, poked a hole in the C-4, and punched the blasting cap and striker assembly into the throat of the canteen. Then he taped the whole thing for security, carefully straightened the pin, and tied monofilament to it. Finally, he used a snap-link to attach the finished product to the rope running across the water. All up, he had himself a two-pound aerial bomb that, properly deployed, was quite adequate to knock a whole bunch of North Vietnamese dicks stiff.

Willy was scoping Salt through the night-sight when he heard the roar and gurgle of the patrol boat's outboard motor. Emory had his arms wrapped around his knees, rocking back and forth, but he straightened when he caught the sound echoing across the inlet. Willy saw him glance across the water before he lurched to his feet and began to shout.

Powerful flashlight beams preceded the boat as it nosed into the inlet. The light played on the water briefly, then darted and focused on Salt. Willy heard the coxswain throttle back and a shouted conversation taking place between boat and shore. If Salt betrayed him, if the boat stopped before cruising into the trap, he'd be stuck up a tree, an inviting target for the machine guns and the brace of AKs bristling over the boat's gunwales.

Salt waved his free hand, motioning for the boat to approach. His shouts were convincing enough for the coxswain to add juice and turn his bow across the sunken rope. Willy waited until the broad beam crossed over and then began to tighten the rope. When the stern was nearly across, he jerked hard and braced himself.

The outboard motor canted forward sharply and screamed in protest as the rope snagged the driveshaft and fouled the prop. The boat slewed and stopped, tossing eight soldiers into a tangled heap near the bow. They were struggling for balance when Willy let go of the canteen, holding on to the monofilament and watching as the jury-rigged bomb slid smoothly down the rope toward the boat. When it thunked into the plastic engine cover, he jerked neatly on the line and pulled the pin.

The explosion was spectacular. Willy had to claw at branches to keep himself from being blown from his perch. Debris was still splashing into the roiled water of the inlet when he began to snipe at floating bodies. He expended fifteen rounds before he was satisfied that no one would survive and climbed down from the banyan tree.

It was dawn when he uncuffed Salt and began to push through the swamp headed due west for the mountains along the Laotian border. They had eight kilometers to cover, a helicopter to dodge, and one day to survive before the scheduled rendezvous with Vinh.

Captain Loan pointed at a spot on the pilot's map and keyed his headset. "Here. We know they were in the swamp, they should emerge here. We can spot them in the open before they start up into the hills."

The pilot lowered his visor against the sun streaming in through the cockpit windscreen and glanced down at his kneeboard. "Fine, Comrade Captain." He pulled the Mi-8 into a left turn. It staggered and strained in the air and he saw the needle of the turbine temperature indicator begin to climb. Precision flying was a joke. The aircraft was old, poorly maintained, and balky in responding to the flight controls. Both engines were wheezy and due for an overhaul that the Air Force mechanics in Hanoi were incapable of performing.

"Tell your troops in the back to keep a sharp eye on the ground. We have limited loiter time."

Loan moved back into the troop compartment to add his eyes

to the ten other pairs scanning the jungle below, but he did not disconnect himself from the intercom. The pilot winced as the angry voice drilled through his earphones.

"Comrade pilot, you will loiter, fly, and do whatever else I tell you to do without further comment."

Willy Pud sat next to Cleveland Herbert Emory, Junior, on the edge of the swamp and considered the odds. They were not good. The helicopter continued to sweep their escape corridor, cruising low over an open stretch of one hundred meters or so between the end of the mangrove swamp and the beginning of the heavy foliage at the base of the foothills.

"Couldn't have come at a worse goddamn time."

"It's my leg. I couldn't move any faster."

Willy Pud glanced at Salt and shook his head. "It was the boat . . . cost us two hours of dark. We should have been across here already and into them hills."

"Can't we just wait until he runs out of gas?"

"He'll sit down out there and block the route before that happens. He's got troops aboard that can box us in and I ain't goin' back in that swamp. We got an appointment to keep in Laos."

"What do we do?"

"I guess we run for it, Emory, take our chances."

"I can't make it with this leg."

"Well, I'm flat out of fuckin' ideas right now."

Salt stared up through the thick foliage, watching the helicopter cut figure eights across their lifeline to the border. The pilot made slow, lazy turns at the end of each circuit. He counted silently . . . eight, nine, ten . . . nearly twelve seconds to reverse directions. He got to his feet.

"Let me have your knife."

"Yeah, right, Emory. Sit down and shut up."

"We could make turtles . . ."

"What?"

"Turtles. The, ah, the People's Army . . . when I was, ah, when I was with them . . . when they captured me . . ."

"Emory, don't piss me off. I told you, I know who you are and I know you're a goddamn traitor. You defected to the fuckin' gooks and fought on their side. Now if you got somethin' productive to say, do it and can the bullshit."

Emory dropped into a squat and scratched idly at the welter of bites on his skinny shin. "We used to make a wicker sort of

thing . . . it looked like a big basket . . . a turtle shell sort of . . .
that hid us from airplanes. Very effective. You weave leaves and
vines in it from the surrounding jungle. Every time the airplane
passes overhead, you just scrunch down under the turtle and from
the air, you look like a bush."

It came back to Willy Pud in a rush. He'd spent hours watching
large NVA formations trooping down the Ho Chi Minh Trail with
the wicker arrangements covering their packs and equipment. He
reached for his K-Bar and slid the knife from its sheath.

"Get hot . . . and make it fast. I'll collect the camouflage."

•

It was practically impossible to hear above the laboring whine
of the engines and the bellow of the wind blowing through the
troop compartment. Loan pulled the headset from his ear and
leaned toward the soldier pulling frantically on his elbow.

"Comrade Captain, are we still flying over the same area?"

Loan fought the urge to push the man out the open door. "Yes,
you fool! Are you blind?"

The man pulled on Loan's elbow again and pointed at something on the ground.

"Those two bushes down there, Comrade Captain, I didn't see
them there when we flew over in the other direction."

Loan leaned out of the helicopter and stared at the green
splotches in the waving yellow morass of tall grass covering
the ground. There were clumps of similar bushes in three or four
other places. He rubbed his sore eyes and tried to remember if
he'd seen the bushes on a previous pass. Impossible. From the
ground perhaps, from an infantryman's perspective, but from up
here everything looked the same.

Loan was about to dismiss the man but there was a determined
set to his jaw. He was convinced . . . and prudence was always
wise. He keyed his headset and alerted the pilot, then told the
man to fire on the bushes during the next pass . . . just in case.

As he'd been doing for the past hour, Willy Pud froze when
he heard the whop and clatter of helicopter blades. He scrunched
under the wicker shield, closed his eyes, bit his lip, and puckered
his asshole. There was nothing else to do until the sound of the
Mi-8 faded right or left and he could afford to inch forward.
He'd been trying to keep track of their progress, estimate distance
covered, but it was impossible. The rotor-wash rattled the leaves
of his camouflage and he had no idea how much longer the agony
would continue.

Through the palms of his hands, he felt something thudding into the ground. He heard a rattling counterpoint to the blade noise and suddenly realized they were under fire from the helicopter.

"Emory! Run! They spotted us!"

Willy tripped scrambling to his feet. His turtle shield tangled between his knees and he fell hard, wincing as the aluminum frame of his rucksack jabbed painfully into the base of his skull. He saw the shadow of the helicopter flicker across the ground in front of his nose and caught a blur as Salt ran by, eating up ground in a sort of ungainly, stiff-legged skip.

Bastard can motivate when he has to . . . Willy was on his hands and knees trying to get under the weight of his ruck when the round tore through his left buttock. It felt like he'd been slugged with a sledgehammer, then skewered with a hot poker. The familiar, screaming jolt of adrenaline that boomed through his body right behind the slug kept him from sprawling. He got his right leg under himself and lunged forward. There were thirty long meters to cover before he reached the trees.

Something slammed into his back before he could stagger much more than four or five steps. Three 7.62mm rounds ripped through the ruck and he fell, feeling the Steyr magazine dig painfully into his solar plexus. He vomited and gasped for breath as AK rounds chewed their way toward him.

Suddenly he was jerked halfway to his feet. Emory was dragging him toward the trees, limping on his game leg but hauling hard on his rucksack. Willy Pud got an arm around Salt's skinny shoulders and did what he could to help forward progress with his right leg. They blundered into the forest at the base of the foothills like a pair of reeling drunks finishing last in a one-legged race.

"They made it into the trees, Comrade Captain!"

Loan disregarded the unnecessary update and punished the tree line with the last ten rounds in the magazine of his AK-47. When the rattling at his shoulder stopped, he tossed the weapon behind him, drew his Makarov, and added seven more rounds to the hailstorm of lead pummeling the ground below the helicopter.

"Comrade Captain! Do you wish me to land?"

"No! Not yet. Fire rockets into the trees. Keep them from going up the hill."

They were still locked to each other, arms over shoulders like bosom pals, heading uphill into triple canopy; Willy's wounded left hip pressed against Emory's bad right leg when the first fan of sixteen 57mm rockets burst into the trees. Stung by a hail of

wood splinters, they clung to each other and tumbled back half
the distance they'd managed to climb. When he pulled himself
out from under Salt, Willy saw they were only twenty meters
from the clearing.

Salt was groggy. Willy propped him up near a stout tree and
began to lay out rifle magazines. There was a single frag grenade
left and a couple of spare magazines for the .45. He bounced the
grenade in his hand, listening for the return of the helicopter and
watching Emory regain his senses.

"They don't nail me with the fuckin' rockets, I'm gonna fight
it out right here." Salt eyed the grenade and pistol as though he'd
never seen such objects. Willy Pud shook the weapons under his
nose. "If you want to change sides again, Emory, now's your
chance."

"I don't even know your name."

"Wilhelm Pudarski. I come a long way to see your ass hang,
man, but you earned a shot at—"

The pilot fired short on his second pass, establishing a bracket,
trapping his quarry in a high-explosive box. Two rockets in
the ripple slammed into the base of an eighteen-foot teak tree,
snapping the twenty-four-inch base and tipping it onto a taller
neighbor where it settled, canted and pointing at the sky like a
gnarled javelin.

Willy Pud ducked out of cover, wiped the blood from his nose
where concussion had ruptured several capillaries, and looked at
the leaning tree. It was caught in the stout branches of the tree
to its left, pointing out over the clearing at a shallow angle.
*Maybe . . . but the helicopter would have to come close . . . be in
the right position . . .*

If the pilot kept to his pattern, the next rockets would impact
upslope. That gave him a little time to work below. Willy Pud
explained the plan to Emory and then dragged his ruck toward
the leaning tree.

"Cease fire, pilot! One of them is coming out of the trees."

Loan craned out the door of the Mi-8 and watched the American
emerge, limping and waving. It was the prisoner. Likely the others
were dead, wounded, or fleeing for their lives toward the border.
Maybe his men could run them to ground. That would be the
best of possible results. He could salvage something from this
embarrassing disaster, perhaps even drape the entire mess like a
stinking shroud over the grave of the dead cadre commander.

"Pilot, land and pick him up."

The pilot lowered the collective to lose altitude and executed a pedal turn to point the nose of the Mi-8 at the man staggering around on the edge of the trees. As he watched, the American reeled and then collapsed in a heap. His earphones crackled.

"Quickly, pilot! Can't you see he is wounded?"

"Yes, Comrade Captain. It's just very close to those tall trees."

"If you are unable to fly as directed, Comrade, land anywhere and I will personally carry the prisoner to your aircraft. I will also note your attitude in my report."

Angrily dialing pitch to his rotor blades and goosing the throttles, the pilot dipped the nose of the helicopter and drove his aircraft straight at the foothills separating his country from Laos. When he pulled abruptly into a hover, taking out his frustrations on the balky flight controls, his five main rotor blades were whirling directly over the edge of the tree line.

When the helicopter was fifty feet above the ground, descending gently into his trajectory, Willy Pud lit the short fuse and clambered away uphill. He had about ten seconds to distance himself from the shot, but it was well tamped and the force would be directed straight up . . . if he was lucky.

He was. The one-pound block of C-4 plastic explosive, jammed under the splintered end of the leaning teak tree, detonated and, seeking a path of least resistance to release the violent energy of expanding gases, shot the tree like a huge arrow directly into the rotor-fan of the helicopter. The first blade to strike the dense wood shattered into a thousand slivers. The tree was still ascending when the rest of the helicopter's rotors hit it, tore from their mountings, and tumbled into the jungle.

The Mi-8 whirled madly for a moment in an agony of frustrated torque, flinging Captain Loan and six of his troopers out the doors to their deaths. Salt was nearly crushed by one of the bodies as he scrambled to get out from under a rain of debris. When the helicopter careened into the hillside and exploded, a wave of blast and heat drove him into a tree, gashing his head and knocking him unconscious.

When he came to some time later, the forest all around him was dense with smoke. He rolled painfully into a sitting position and saw flames shooting from the crash site. He was a hundred meters or more from the pile of molten metal but the heat was still intense. He wanted to move. He wanted water. He wanted out of the nightmare. Cleveland Herbert Emory, Junior, closed his eyes and tried not to die.

"You're gonna live."

Emory looked up at Willy Pud. He was someplace else; someplace cooler. The trees weren't on fire.

"Where are we?"

"About four klicks from the Laotian border. We hump until dark, cross the line . . . then pick up our taxi to Thailand at dawn tomorrow."

While Cleve Emory packed sulfa powder into the wound channel in Willy's left buttock and applied a fresh battle dressing, Willy Pud finished the map work. Rechecking the math for the two back-azimuths used to determine their position, he decided it was a nice piece of work for a pair of shot-out gimps suffering from a near-terminal case of kicked ass.

Two fine pencil lines, representing direction from nearby hill masses back to the observer, crossed on Willy's map sheet at a point approximately five hundred meters inside Laos. Relative to what they had just come through, they were home free. Willy allowed himself a grunt of satisfaction.

Emory finished his first-aid chores and began to fiddle with the rucksack shoulder straps. The blisters on his collarbone had appeared less than a kilometer after Pudarski handed him the pack and told him to hump it.

"Know where we are?"

"Uh-huh."

"OK if I ask where?"

"In Laos, Emory. You ought to start recognizing the neighborhood."

Rubbing one of the blisters, Emory felt water begin to dribble down his chest. There were a million questions he wanted to ask, but the man who brought him safely out of Vietnam was not acting like a friendly font of information.

"I guess we're safe."

Pudarski shot him a disgusted look and climbed to his feet. "That's right, *Mister* Emory, worry about your own ass." He kicked at the ruck and motioned for Emory to get it on his back. "If we don't get nailed by a goddamn Pathet Lao patrol or jumped by some warlord's private army . . . and if our ride shows on time . . . and if he can get us back to Thailand in one piece . . . then you'll be safe. But I don't think you're gonna enjoy it much."

"What's that mean?" Salt eased into the rucksack and followed Willy Pud toward a low hill in the near distance.

"Just walk, Emory. We're gonna hole up on the side of that hill and wait for daybreak."

They sat in silence, nestled in the lumbar region of a rocky spine overlooking the clearing where Vinh Sanchahorn's Huey was due to land at dawn. Willy Pud found some tasty scallions to spice the last riceball and they chewed slowly, stretching the food, taking tiny sips from the open canteen between them. The western horizon sizzled into a hot orange slash of final light.

"Mind if I talk?" Willy Pud kept his eyes on the dazzling spectacle of the Southeast Asian sunset and simply shrugged.

"God . . . it's been so long since I spoke English, you know? It feels like a second language."

"You'll get plenty of practice. You got a lot of talkin' to do."

"Yeah, there's a lot I want to say . . . to a lot of people."

Willy Pud arched an eyebrow at Salt, shook his head, and then turned back to the stare at the darkening jungle. "Did the words 'thank you' ever come to mind, Emory?"

"Oh, hey, listen, I'm sorry. Thanks, really. I thought I was gonna be in that camp forever. I really appreciate what you did for me."

"I didn't do it for you, Emory. Don't kid yourself. What I did out here, I did for about fifty-eight thousand dead men and I don't even know how many more guys who served honorably in Vietnam. They may not have liked it, but they kept their mouths shut and did what the country asked them to do."

"And I did what my conscience told me to do."

"You are so full of shit, Emory. Don't give me that conscience crap, alright? You had a major conscience attack, you coulda gone to Canada with the rest of the self-righteous, chickenshit assholes. You didn't just bug out on the war, Emory . . . you came over here, defected to the goddamn gooks, and fought on their side!"

"Look, I don't expect you to understand, but the original idea was to take a stand, you know? To do something beyond just going to Canada or protesting against the war, or holding rallies. I wanted to speak against the war from a credible position. I wanted to . . ."

"You wanted to what, Emory? You wanted to be somebody out of the ordinary, right? You wanted to kick the system in the nuts harder than anybody else was doin' it, right? You wanted to be a big-time counterculture revolutionary? Well, you missed that fuckin' boat."

"I took a minority stand . . ."

"No you didn't! You just put a little different spin on the ball, Emory. The minority was guys like me over here fightin' the war."

"There are people who believe in taking an active role when their country is acting like an oppressor."

"Last time I heard shit like that was from your buddy Clay."

"He was a very angry man . . . and for a lot of good reasons."

Willy glanced over his shoulder. It was impossible to read Emory's expression in the dark. The man was mouthing platitudes, but it sounded to Willy Pud more like rationalization than conviction. A man on the brink of facing the music, whistling in the dark to keep his courage kindled.

"Well, Clay ain't comin' back. You're gonna have to face it alone, Emory."

"And that's why you came to get me, isn't it? You risked everything to get me out so I could face a trial. You think I'm going to be convicted as a traitor by the country that lost the war."

"Emory, let's get clear on the concept here. I decided to have your ass one way or the other the day I saw you operatin' with the gooks back in 1970. I was gonna kill you then, but we blew the chance. Since that day, a lot has happened—to me and to the country—but I never could get the bad taste out of my mouth. You and Clay haunted me like a pair of goddamn demons.

"One day I couldn't take it anymore. I got hold of a friend of mine who was with me when we saw you guys in the bush. We started tryin' to find out who you were. We had no idea you might be alive, see? We just wanted to get the story out about two traitors . . . so you wouldn't get away with something like that while the families of the dead and the ones who made it had to suffer. We wanted to even the score a little bit.

"Then things started to get complicated. My buddy was murdered by someone who doesn't want the story to get out. You know why, Emory? Because this guy and *your own fuckin' father* cooked up a story sayin' you was killed in action. Your old man couldn't deal with having a traitor for a son, so he had you declared a war hero and covered the whole thing up."

"I know about that. They showed me newspaper clippings. That's when I decided to try and get home."

"And you know your father is the kind of sonofabitch that will kill good men to avoid bein' embarrassed?"

"It doesn't surprise me."

"Well, it sure as hell surprises me, and it pisses me off. I'm gonna see you get what you deserve and so does he."

There was a long silence between them, filled sporadically by jungle sounds. Willy Pud heard Cleve Emory breathing deeply, heavily through his nose. There was nothing to see in the velvet black of the Laotian sky, but Emory stared wide-eyed over the jungle canopy. Some unpleasant images were coming slowly into focus.

"You know, I—I don't think I ever really killed anyone . . . not any Americans . . ." His voice was quiet, contemplative, as if he was whispering secret thoughts.

"That ain't what it looked like to me when I saw you on that trail, Emory."

"They kept shifting me from pillar to post. First the VC, then the NVA, political officers, senior commanders. I kept telling them I would be a good propaganda weapon. I wanted to make speeches, write essays, that kind of thing, but they had something else in mind."

"I guess they did."

"They kept pushing us forward where we'd be seen—just for a moment—by the units they were fighting. Shock effect . . ."

"Picture's worth a thousand words, ain't it?"

"It wasn't what I wanted or expected, but there was no way out. Clay dug it all the way, though. He started sneaking up on American units with that M-79 he carried, popping rounds right into their perimeter and yelling at them in English."

"Well, I'll be goddamn . . ."

"What?"

"You just made a major contribution to the history of the Vietnam war, Emory. We now know who the Phantom Blooper was."

The revelation was lost on Emory. He rambled on, talking softly to the dark.

"Then I got wounded in an air strike. They told me Clay was killed in the same raid. All that time in the hospital—no special treatment or anything—and then the war ended. The North Vietnamese won. I thought sure I'd be a hero, you know? At least they could have made something out of it . . . the only American who made the right choice, the guy who had the courage of his convictions. I thought they'd send me out into the Third World . . . excitement, revolution, a whole new life . . ."

"You and Che Guevara, right?"

"Yeah, I guess so."

"They blew his ass away in Bolivia, and they locked yours up because they didn't want any round-eye hornin' in on the great

Vietnamese victory. Has the bubble burst yet, Emory?"

"Long time ago . . . when they put me in the camps with the victorious Viet Cong. I thought they'd understand what a war in the jungle does to you. I thought they'd understand if anybody did . . . but they didn't. I didn't fit into the post-war plans."

"I been there, man."

"What's that?"

"Ain't no way you could know about it, but the vets who came home didn't get much of a break either. It was over; an embarrassment, we lost. Good riddance to bad rubbish. We didn't have much of a place in the post-war plans either."

"We wasted a lot of years, Pudarski."

"Yeah, we did . . ."

They were silent for fifteen minutes or so and then Willy Pud reached for a poncho. He draped it over their heads like a blackout curtain, pulled a cigarette from a plastic case, lit it, and passed the smoke to Cleveland Herbert Emory, Junior.

"Tell me about yourself, Emory. Who the fuck are you?"

Some seventy-five kilometers northwest of the spot where Willy Pud and Cleve Emory sat smoking in the dark, Justin Bates Halley sat up in his sleeping bag and reached for the pistol hanging in its holster on a branch near his head. The sentries were probably asleep again and there was no telling who was thrashing through the bush in his direction.

"Halt! Who's there?"

"Jesus Christ, Colonel, you gonna ask me for the password?"

Carver and Toliver were back from the border recon. Sweaty and stinking from a solid week in the bush, the men bulled their way over to Halley, stacking the rifles and bulky night-vision scopes against a tree.

"Maybe we ought to move again, Colonel."

"We've moved twice, Freddy. I don't want to get any farther from the border."

Breed Toliver rinsed his mouth with canteen water and spit dangerously close to Halley's sleeping bag. "Well, we got a whole shit-pot of company on the Thai side."

"That doesn't tell me anything useful, Toliver."

"Colonel, something's going on on the Thai side of the border. We scoped 'em for four hours and they've put a full company of Special Forces around the landing zone."

"Not unusual. They've probably got some kind of intelligence about smugglers."

"Or they know Pudarski is due out through that sector."

"I've told you before, Freddy. That's impossible."

"You know what I think, Colonel? I think your insurance plan got fucked up somehow. I think maybe Pudarski busted his man out in spite of the alert you passed to the gooks. I think them Thai SF troopers are waiting around just like we are to see if he makes it out."

"How would they get any idea that Pudarski was even inside?"

"Beats me, Colonel. You're supposed to be handling the intelligence side of this fucking mission, remember?"

"You men are just tired."

"Fuckin' right we are, Colonel." Toliver dropped on his ass and lit a cigarette in spite of Halley's strict orders about light discipline. "And I don't mind tellin' you that the rest of the men ain't lookin' forward to tryin' to exfiltrate through all them Thai troopers. They're good. We trained 'em."

"They don't have to look forward to anything but payday, Toliver, and that comes at end of mission—not before."

"Colonel, what about this airstrip business." Freddy Carver opened his map and hit it with a penlight. "We know from your informants that Pudarski got picked up by a helicopter. Maybe he's got himself a ride out also."

Halley took his time and studied the map. He was more worried about the buildup on the Thai side of the border than he was willing to reveal. So many variables; so many unknown factors.

What if the story was leaked somehow? What if Cleve Emory was under pressure already and pointing the finger at him? How would he explain his presence in Thailand? In the goddamn jungle? What if Pudarski actually accomplished what he set out to do, if the North Vietnamese never acted on his tip, or if they acted on it but Pudarski pulled it off anyway?

"If Pudarski's in an aircraft, he simply becomes a bigger target." Halley jabbed at the map with his finger. "This high ground commands the approach corridor. An aircraft has to come in low to avoid Thai radar at Phong Saly and that means it flies on one side of the hill or the other—but not over it—if it's on approach to that airstrip."

"Yeah, so?"

"So tomorrow at first light, Toliver and one other man position themselves on either side of the hill with LAWs. If a helicopter appears from the east, we shoot it down."

"That's gonna cost you extra, Colonel."

"Bag a helicopter and you get a thousand-dollar bonus, Toliver."

"Even if the target ain't aboard?"

"I'll consider it an insurance premium. Now you men had better get some sleep."

"Yeah. We may have ourselves a busy day tomorrow."

"Or we may not. Good night, gentlemen."

Vinh was getting better at landing . . . not good, but better. He kicked the tail-boom toward the east, dropped the collective, and plopped the ancient Huey into the clearing with less than the normal amount of screeching stress on the skids.

Willy watched from the edge of the tree line as Sarang scrambled out of the troop compartment wiping her tiny hands on a hank of calico rag. She shielded her eyes and scanned the bush, breaking into a broad smile when he stood and waved.

Emory squatted at the base of a nearby tree, staring wide-eyed at the rattling apparition and the mahogany-faced gnome who seemed tentatively in control of it. Willy Pud tapped him on the shoulder.

"Ride's here."

"Who the hell are those people?"

"No sweat. They're on the payroll."

"Is it safe?"

"What? Compared to what we already been through? C'mon, Emory, relax. It's almost over."

Vinh climbed down from the cockpit as Willy and Emory approached. Willy gave Sarang a hug and then tossed his ruck inside the Huey. Emory stood by the door, staring wide-eyed at the jury-rigged repairs and the leaky hydraulic lines.

"That's the one?" Vinh stood with hands on hips, staring through his aviator shades at the skinny scarecrow who barely bent the creases in the faded tiger-stripe fatigues Willy had given him to wear.

"That's the one. Been a while since he's ridden in a helicopter. Glad to see you, Vinh."

"Good to see you, Willy. OK deal, huh? You tell your boys on the other side about Vinh Sanchahorn."

"Absolutely right, Vinh. You are gonna be one popular guy with us round-eyes. Let's get going."

"Some trouble on the border, Willy."

"What?"

"Lots of Thai Army around the airstrip. Can't land there this trip."

"You askin' me for more money, Vinh?"

"Never happen, Willy. Deal is deal, OK? But they got beaucoup troops at the airstrip . . . no shit."

. "Well, what are we gonna do?"

"I land you on Laos side, OK? Maybe one kilometer from border . . . no more. Best I can do."

Willy climbed into the Huey, hauled Emory after him, and spread the map on the greasy deck. "Show me where."

Vinh studied the map carefully, turning it one way and another to get his orientation. "Maybe this hill, OK. You walk down, cross the border . . . home free."

Willy Pud nodded. Light pack and a downhill grade, a walk in the park after the trek through the jungles and swamps. "OK, Vinh. Crank it up."

They shivered and staggered into the air. At altitude, Vinh leaned over the back of his seat and showed him a thumbs-up but Willy Pud couldn't respond. Sarang was holding one hand and Salt was desperately squeezing the other.

Former Staff Sergeant Charlie Maxwell hadn't fired a LAW since basic back at Ft. Jackson. He'd crewed a tank on bridge security near Quang Ngai on his first tour in-country and then reenlisted for cross-training in Quartermaster where he spent three much more productive years in Vietnam.

Toliver opened the goddamn thing and set the trigger for him before taking up his position on the other side of the hilltop, but fucking Toliver was a pain in the ass.

Look through here, line up this, check on that, aim center-mass, put the target on this little line here. What the fuck? Point the fuckin' thing, press the trigger, and shoot, right?

Maxwell shouldered the weapon, swinging the muzzle toward the tops of the trees to the east. He could hear the clatter of rotor blades as he tried to decipher the maze of horizontal and vertical lines painted on the plastic front sight. *Gotta wait 'til he's . . . what? Two hundred yards or closer. Which one of these fuckin' things is lead?*

The ratty Huey staggered closer to Maxwell's perch, filling the front sight like a bug under glass. It was definitely going to pass on his side of the hill. Fucking Toliver could kiss that money good-bye. The thought of a badly needed bonus froze his fingers on the trigger bar. His old lady back in Bangkok was bitching about money all the fucking time these days. Better make sure of the score.

Charlie Maxwell shifted his position slightly and let the Huey get closer. He could barely believe his luck when the nose of the bird reared and it slowed, losing altitude. *The bastard's gonna land! Sitting duck!* He maneuvered the muzzle of the LAW, trying to hold one of the red lines on the sight somewhere near the aircraft and then he figured . . . what the fuck, how hard can it be . . . and pressed the trigger.

They were fifty feet off the ground when the 77mm LAW rocket roared past the cracked Plexiglas of Vinh's windscreen like a flaming arrow. Vinh pulled the collective nearly into his armpit, ramming power to the engine, but it was too much for the old bird. It wheezed and rocked precariously, groaning and shuddering but still dropping toward the small clearing on the hillside.

In the back, Willy Pud saw the flash and the plume of telltale debris as the rocket fired and he grabbed Sarang just before she tumbled out the open door. Scrambling forward, he saw Vinh struggling, fighting to stay airborne and escape the trap. He was shaking his head, screaming curses at the madly blinking instrument lights that were telling him there was no way.

If Vinh and Sarang were going to escape the inevitable second shot from whoever was on the ground below, they'd have to lighten ship. At twenty-five feet above the clearing, Willy shoved Emory out the door and jumped after him.

The Huey began to gain altitude slowly, painfully, all components screaming in protest as Vinh kicked the rudder pedal and nursed the cyclic to generate a banking turn away from the hill. He was gaining airspeed and flight stability when the second LAW rocket off Toliver's more-experienced shoulder impacted between the Huey's skids.

Willy was fighting his way out of a tangle of soft succulents that broke his fall when the Huey exploded in a bright ball of fire, scattering flaming debris all over the jungle. He stared at the empty sky in shock. One second he'd seen the aircraft gain altitude, seen Sarang lean precariously out the door to wave . . . and then the roar of a second rocket launch from somewhere behind him. And the people he'd come to respect for their guts, their enterprise, their survivor's instinct, were gone.

He retrieved his rifle and methodically checked it for damage while the old righteous anger flooded back into his heart and settled in his gut. *Payback,* he told himself as he slammed a fresh round into the chamber of the AUG, *payback is a medevac. Payback is a goddamn body bag for somebody on this fucking hill!*

Salt was in pain, holding a swollen knee about thirty meters down the hill where he'd rolled into a thick stand of elephant grass. He was trembling, near shock when Willy parted the tall grass and found him. He started to scream but Willy clamped a hand over his mouth, hugging him until his breathing regulated.

"Can you walk?"

"I don't know. It's my good leg. What happened?"

"Somebody is trying to make sure we don't reach Thailand."

"Who?"

"I've got a good idea. The same sonofabitch that killed my buddy. He works for your old man."

"Can we make it across the border?"

Willy squeezed his shoulder and handed him a canteen. "We can and we will, but first I've gotta take care of some business." He was turning uphill to begin the hunt when Salt stopped him.

"What should I do?"

Willy Pud cranked a round into the chamber of the .45 and pointed the butt at Emory. "You can take this and run if you want to, Emory, but I'm bettin' you've had enough of that."

Salt took the pistol in both hands, stared at the oily black finish for a moment, and then turned to respond. But Willy Pudarski had disappeared into the bush.

"Freeze, motherfucker!"

Charlie Maxwell skidded to a halt, crouched, searching for the source of the bark. He coiled slightly, bending his knees to spring for cover behind a pile of moss-covered rocks.

"You make that move and it'll be your last. Drop the rifle!"

Maxwell hesitated. Toliver was nowhere in sight and the M-16 was all he had. He cut his eyes at the rocks again and saw a bush-beast carrying some kind of space-age rifle unfold from cover. The guy looked lean, hard, and dangerous as a goddamn snake. He was tricked out like a bandit, cut down to the bare essentials for killing, and there was no doubt in Charlie Maxwell's mind that he would turn out to be very good at that. He dropped his rifle and raised his hands.

The bush-beast moved to kick the weapon aside but his muzzle

never wavered from a point just below Maxwell's trembling chin.
"Who the fuck are you, man?"

"I'm the guy you were hired to kill, dip-shit, but I'm gonna kill
you instead."

"Hey, man, I'm just out here workin' for a guy. I don't know
you from fuckin' Adam."

"And that work involves blowin' helicopters outta the sky?"

"I missed! It was Toliver, the other guy. He hit the helicopter,
man. It wasn't me."

Willy Pud jammed the muzzle of the AUG under Maxwell's
chin. "You got ten seconds to tell me the truth, or I'm gonna blow
the top of your gourd off. Who hired you?"

"Guy in Bangkok. He was lookin' for ex-soldiers."

"Name?"

"He never said. The guy who was with him called him Colonel.
That's all I know, man . . . no shit."

"Where is he now?"

"Down below there . . . with four other guys."

Stomping hard on Maxwell's instep, Willy Pud swung the
stock-heavy weapon and dropped the man with a vertical butt
stroke. Maxwell lay gasping as Willy Pud touched him on the
tip of his nose with the rifle's flash-suppressor.

"You get one shot in this game. You've had yours. If you
come down off this hill or make any kind of noise, I'll kill
you."

Toliver didn't bother to find the colonel and let him know the
helicopter was destroyed. Fuck the bonus. He saw the two spooks
in tiger stripes bail out after that asshole Maxwell missed his shot.
It was time to un-ass this AO.

Two of the old Bangkok hands agreed with his assessment and
gathered their gear to follow him. They planned to run parallel to
the border, away from the SF patrols, find a deserted sector, and
get back into friendly territory. He was panting hard, checking
his compass, when he heard the shot.

The man staring over his shoulder staggered backward and then
dropped like a rock from the slug that slammed into the center
of his chest. Toliver and his remaining partner rolled for cover
as they'd been trained to do and held low, spraying the dense
underbrush with fire.

Willy Pud figured that's what they'd do. Standard counter-
ambush drill. He shifted slightly on his perch in the banyan tree
and drilled two rounds into the back of the man on the near side of

the trail. Then he swung the sighting circle of the AUG onto Breed
Toliver and put two more rounds through the top of his head.

"We confirm the helicopter down by ground fire, sir." The U.S.
Army adviser to the Thai Special Forces unit on the border keyed
his handset and squinted to spot the Air Force CH-53 Jolly Green
Giant helicopter orbiting to the west of his position. "And the little
people up forward are reporting small-arms fire very close on the
other side, over."

"Roger . . . wait out." The Air Force colonel flying copilot in the
Jolly Green reached above his head to switch radio frequencies.

"Tarmac, this is Bonfire on station at X-Ray. We have reports
of small-arms fire across the border. Opinion here is that your
boy is on the ground over there . . . probably in trouble."

"Bonfire, Tarmac, how close to the border, over?

"People on the ground say very close, Tarmac."

"Roger, Bonfire, wait one."

In the secure communications room of the U.S. Embassy in
Bangkok, the Defense attaché turned to the ambassador who was
conferring with the President's special envoy and a very senior
gentleman from the Pentagon's Office of POW and MIA Affairs.
They nodded simultaneously.

"Send them in, Colonel. Make it quick and slick."

The ambassador waited until his message was passed and then
turned to the special envoy. "Better alert the press, Paul. Tell
them they can expect an announcement shortly. I'll go speak to
the old man."

The rotor-wash of the huge helicopter nearly blew Freddy
Carver off his feet. He rolled to cover and stared up at the
sky-blue belly of the aircraft. Halley was across the trail staring
at the same sight. His face was flushed beet-red and he looked
like he was actually considering firing at the aircraft.

"Jesus Christ, you asshole! That's an American helicopter. It's
over, Halley. I'm getting the fuck out of here!"

Halley screamed something that was lost in the roar of five
blades and three huge engines. The aircraft was looking for a
landing spot, trying to cut off their route to the border. A burst
ripped into the vines near his head but Carver saw no wink of
muzzle flash from the helicopter. *That was Halley! He's trying
to kill me!*

He shifted directions, sprinting left as the colonel winged more
shots at his back. *Crazy! The bastard is crazy!* Carver turned in the

opposite direction but something snagged at his boot and he fell
sprawling into a tangle of vines. He started to crawl but got less
than a yard before he ran into the muzzle of Willy Pud's rifle.

"Don't shoot, Pudarski! I quit, man!"

Willy Pud uncoiled slowly from prone to a kneeling position,
keeping the muzzle of his weapon pressed into Carver's neck.
"Roll over, asshole."

Carver rolled and Willy quickly stripped his rifle and pistol.
"Who killed Spike Benjamin? One answer. If I don't believe it,
you're dead."

"Halley killed him, man. I didn't have nothin' to do with
that."

"Where is he?"

"Back there somewhere." Carver pointed toward the bush at
his feet. "We took off runnin' when the Air Force showed up."

Willy Pud heard the aircraft thump into a landing. It would
be a while before the troops aboard found them in the thick
bush. He had time. Shifting the muzzle of his weapon, he started
to rise.

Freddy Carver jacked his leg in a quick, practiced movement
and grabbed the knife from the top of his boot. He swung round-
house for Pudarski's belly but Willy was already moving and the
blade sank into his thigh. He swung around, ignoring the pain,
and fired four rounds into Carver's face.

Justin Bates Halley heard the shots and began to move in the
direction of the sound, stalking as he'd been taught so many years
ago; before everything got complicated, when he was a simple
soldier. His mind was a jumble. In fact, he believed he'd lost
his mind. Thoughts would not come coherently to him as they
always had in the past.

One moment he was wailing with despair, the next he was
boiling with anger and frustration, and then he was ticking off
options, trying to build a credible alibi for everything. Only one
thing seemed clear. The stinking war, in this stinking part of the
stinking world, was bound to kill him. And faced with that sort of
thing, the good soldier strikes first. The good soldier survives.

Colonel Halley found Pudarski sitting next to Carver's dead
body, pulling a knife out of his thigh. Through the peep sight
of the M-16, he could see the same chiseled features, the same
square jaw, the same dumb Polack expression on his face. An easy
shot . . . and a long-overdue one. He exhaled calmly and took the
slack out of the trigger.

• • •

Willy Pud heard the shot and whirled for cover. He shouldered his rifle and scanned the bush. There was nothing to see but green. And then Cleveland Herbert Emory pushed his way through a tangle of vines, Willy's pistol dangling from his good hand. He stood staring around at the jungle as if he was lost; searching for some bearing, some familiar landmark.

Willy Pud rose slowly, leaning on his rifle, and limped painfully forward on two bad legs. Salt saw him and parted the bush to reveal Halley's dead body. He was sprawled across his rifle, a neat hole in the back of the skull and the entire forehead missing. Brain tissue leaked like Jell-O onto the jungle floor.

Emory seemed calm but distracted, unsure of what to do or how to act in the presence of a fresh corpse. He looked at his hands, seemed to notice the pistol for the first time, and handed it back to Willy Pud.

"I guess I *have* killed an American . . ."

"Not the way I look at it. That's the asshole that killed my buddy. He's the guy who engineered this whole deal."

"He was trying to kill you."

"Well, you put an end to that, man." Willy heard thrashing in the bush nearby. He flipped the pistol around and offered it to Emory. "Thanks. If you wanna split, go ahead."

"No. You were right. I've had enough of that." Salt nodded toward something at Willy's back. "The prisons are probably nicer in America."

Willy Pud turned to see an Army officer wearing a green beret and flanked by two camouflage-painted Thai troopers break into the clearing. The officer stopped, smiled, and pushed the troopers' muzzles toward the ground.

"Wilhelm Pudarski? Major John Stankowski . . . fancy meeting another Polack out this way."

The helicopter wafted down onto the apron at Bangkok's airport and was immediately mobbed by reporters. A detachment of Marine guards kept them at a distance while the ambassador and his official companions climbed aboard. Willy sat bleeding and exhausted next to Cleveland Herbert Emory, Junior, wondering what had turned the world as he knew it into such a zoo.

Bypassing Emory, the ambassador offered Willy Pud his hand and made the introductions. "My apologies for the circus outside, Mr. Pudarski. Obviously, this is a major news story."

"How did you find out?"

"Your dad is quite a guy, Mr. Pudarski. He managed to get through to the White House. Spoke to the President personally, I'm told. There was a picture and all the information on your, uh, mission."

"My old man?"

"Yes, he's waiting for you at the embassy with Mr. Eddie Miller, the policeman from St. Louis. Now, if you want to talk to the press later, we'll arrange it. Meanwhile, we need to get you to a doctor."

Willy Pud turned to look at Emory. "What happens to him?" Salt was resigned, stone-faced, and staring at the clamoring crowd outside the helicopter.

"Like any other American, he gets his day in court." The ambassador motioned to the Special Forces major who took Salt by the elbow and lifted him to his feet. Salt stuck out his withered right hand.

"There's a lot to account for, Pudarski. Maybe I made up for some of it out there. I hope so."

"I'll tell 'em what happened." Willy Pud shook his hand and watched Salt escorted off the helicopter and into the hands of the law he'd rejected so many years ago.

WASHINGTON, D.C.

Willy Pud found Fowler's name on the black wall and touched it. There was a spark at his fingertips as though this tiny part of the great granite monolith was charged with static electricity.

"Sorry, man. I'm really sorry."

Stosh Pudarski put a hand on his son's shoulder and squeezed. "Ain't nothin' to be sorry for, Vilhelm. Not then and not now."

"I wouldn't let him go on mess duty, Pop. He was short but I took him with me up on that hill."

"You had a duty, son. He knows that. If he was your buddy, he knows that . . . and he don't blame you."

"They oughtta put Emory's name up here too."

"Not no goddamn way is that ever gonna happen."

"He was a casualty of the war, Pop."

"He killed himself, Vilhelm. Took all them pills and died rather than face a trial. Went out the same way as his father did."

"Then they're both casualties from Vietnam."

"No, son. All the good men who died in that war are right here on this wall."

Willy Pud put his arm around his father and led him up out of the shadow of the monument and into the cold, clear sunlight of another day.

"There ain't no wall in the world big enough to hold the names of all the casualties of that war, Pop. In some ways these guys here are the lucky ones. Let's go home and leave them to rest."

TRUE ACCOUNTS OF VIETNAM
from those who returned to tell it all . . .